JUSTICE FOR EMERSON

A MURDER MYSTERY

KAREN E. OSBORNE

Black Rose Writing | Texas

The author grants the final approval for this literary material.

First printing

This is a work of fiction. Names, characters, businesses, places, events, and incidents are either the products of the author's imagination or used in a fictitious manner. Any resemblance to actual persons, living or dead, or actual events is purely coincidental.

ISBN: 978-1-68513-572-0
PUBLISHED BY BLACK ROSE WRITING
www.blackrosewriting.com

Printed in the United States of America
Suggested Retail Price (SRP) $22.95

Justice for Emerson is printed in Garamond Premier Pro

*As a planet-friendly publisher, Black Rose Writing does its best to eliminate unnecessary waste to reduce paper usage and energy costs, while never compromising the reading experience. As a result, the final word count vs. page count may not meet common expectations.

To my husband, Robert. Friends from thirteen and fourteen.
Married at twenty and twenty-one. Fifty-six years later,
he's still my everything.

PRAISE FOR
JUSTICE FOR
EMERSON

"Osborne delivers a heart-pounding, whodunnit murder mystery! Emerson's Vietnam-era dual timeline will resonate with readers familiar with characters Harry Bosch or Walt Longmire."
–Cam Torrens, award-winning author of the *Tyler Zahn* **mystery suspense series**

"Part crime thriller, part romance, and part historical fiction, *Justice for Emerson* is a fast-paced page turner. Osborne paints a complex character in Aria, one who can be decisive and indecisive, confident and full of self-doubt, reticent and strong, simultaneously—these complex women characters are Osborne's forte."
–Eva Silverfine, award-winning author of *Ephemeral Wings*

"Once again, author Karen E. Osborne has delivered a taut thriller that combines the pacing and suspense of a crime novel with the complexity and nuance of literary and women's fiction. She skillfully alternates between two timelines revolving around the life and death of the title character, Cal Emerson; and while we know that the two periods in his life are interconnected, the mystery lies in figuring out how. There is also a somewhat unlikely but charming romantic pairing that I thoroughly enjoyed. A satisfying read on many levels!"
–Ruth F. Stevens, award-winning author of *The South Bay Series*

"Alternating between two timelines, Karen E. Osborne's latest thriller, *Justice for Emerson*, takes readers on a suspenseful rollercoaster ride. Readers will devour this well-crafted page-turner all the way to its twisty conclusion."
–Jill Caugherty, award-winning author of *A View from Half Dome*

"*Justice For Emerson* is an intricate, well-thought out novel. It is as realistic as it is compelling. I highly recommend this riveting page-turner!"
–Susan E. Sage, Award-winning author of *Silver Lady*

"Karen E. Osborne's *Justice for Emerson* is a vividly concocted mystery that investigates far more questions than simply who the murderer is. The main characters must rely on their wits and experience to navigate a threatening situation on the verge of collapsing into tragedy. Harder still, they must reconcile the confusing and complex feelings they have towards each other. *Justice for Emerson* is a thrilling reminder that the past isn't dead, it's not even past."
–Philip Reari, author of *Earth Jumped Back*

"*Justice For Emerson's* greatest strength is its depth of characters. Because the chapters flip between perspectives and protagonists, the reader develops a closeness with several of the novel's diverse cast of characters. It's easy to fall in love with the generous Aria, but I found myself strongly rooting for the troubled Emerson and MJ. Osborne portrays the complexity of Emerson and MJ's situations with compassion and without judgment. My personal favorite aspect is that Osborne ties the ends of the story together with a happy-ending ribbon."
–Elaine Griffin, author of upcoming *Shadows in the Pleasure Garden*

"The seemingly senseless murder of an elderly veteran kicks off this absorbing tale of financial corruption and haunting secrets from the Vietnam era. Recently widowed Aria is a reluctant participant in the threatening events that unfold, but soon proves herself to be a dauntless woman of courage. An overlay of romance lightens the serious tone of the story as the point of view shifts smoothly between the dark events of the past and hope for the present."
–Regina Buttner author of *The Revenge Paradox*

JUSTICE FOR EMERSON

CHAPTER ONE
ARIA

Tuesday, March 12, 2024, Fieldcrest, NY

Breathing is often difficult, but today, I struggled more than usual. My heart raced and my breath turned hot. A cold sweat broke across my forehead and nose. Breathe deep, I told myself. A ragged cough interrupted. I tried again. Panic attacks and raggedy lungs ran in the family. A dangerous combination. Grandma Rae, Mom, and her sister Auntie Vern all suffered the same. Auntie died. The death certificate stated COVID as the cause, but we all knew her fragile lungs did her in. My sister Bella and I inherited the sometimes incapacitating affliction. This bout especially annoyed me since I had so much to accomplish and little time.

Sweat-drenched from either a menopausal hot flash or panic attack, I patted my face dry, dug my inhaler from my bag and pumped medication into my lungs. This time, when I inhaled and exhaled, no coughing spasm ensued.

In search of a bit of joy and calm, I examined the two framed photos beside my inbox on the glass top desk. Last night's fitful sleep resulted in morning melancholy. Panic and sadness were unfit companions. One picture showed three grinning faces–my husband Ben, son Zander at sixteen, and me in the middle. The guys towered over me, like everyone did. Five feet, two inches in my bare, sandy feet. We stood on a Jamaican beach, white-capped waves behind us, palm trees framing the photo, and scudding clouds overhead. I worked hard so I could wear a sexy two-piece with my hair a crown of braids. Great vacation. Also, our last one together. Ben died months later, and the two-year anniversary of his death was days away. That might explain my mood and agitation. For a few seconds, I hugged myself, imagining Ben's arms around me.

The other photograph showed Zan, dressed in cap and gown, the hat perched on top of his Afro. His high school graduation–one of several milestones celebrated without his dad. Joyful moments colored by a wash of pain. Yet, the photos often lifted and grounded me. With my thumb, I traced Ben's face. Thoughts of him infused every day, until recently, when other emotions intruded. Yes, I still mourned and yearned for him, but also, I longed for love. And too often when the realization surfaced, one face, one name, penetrated my consciousness–Jax Oats. The rings on my left hand kept me Ben's wife–a tiny diamond engagement ring, and a plain gold band–all Ben could afford back then. Did I want to take them off and love another?

Two sharp raps on my office door startled me.

I arranged my expression, smoothing away the sadness and worry. "Enter."

Ginger Ryan, one of my most trusted confidants, walked in. Thirty years old, with pale skin, curly red hair, and freckles, Ginger served as my administrative assistant for the last eighteen months. The previous admin quit after my appointment as CEO of The Way Station, a $10,000,000-a-year organization serving the poor, hungry, unhoused, and unemployed. I guessed the older woman refused to work for someone of a different race, or age–my fifty to her seventy. Before I arrived, all the managers were White. My natural coils and deep brown skin might have put her off. When Ginger interviewed for the position, I knew. Bright, funny, with a no-nonsense attitude, I hired her the same day.

"Sorry to interrupt, Aria," Ginger said, handing me a skinny vanilla latte. "Emerson is missing in action. What do you want to do?"

I sniffed the tiny opening on the cup cover and grinned. "Thank you," I said, cradling the cup between both hands. Caffeine fueled my day, and even though I drank two cups of coffee before coming to work, the latte was spot on.

She acknowledged my appreciation with a nod. "The line for men's showers is lengthy already. Security is keeping folks orderly, but we don't have anyone ensuring the stalls are safe. I've checked with every replacement. They're all slammed."

The Way Station's programs started at 7:00 a.m. When the doors slid open, women with their school-aged children rushed in for showers and breakfast. They lived in cars, or worse. Many worked but didn't make enough to house and feed their families. Their circumstances triggered something deep inside me.

Emerson manned the facilities during the second and third shifts–8:00 and 9:00 a.m., when unhoused men drifted by. A female volunteer monitored showers for women and children, but by 9:00 a.m., most left for work, programs, or school.

"I saw Emerson when I arrived." I scrunched my face in concentration. Thick and square, the man I glimpsed wore a sweatshirt with a hoody under a peacoat. It seemed odd. Why would Emerson hurry through the halls, *away* from the showers? Was he moving toward the basement, a favorite spot for the seventy-seven-year old? Confidence in our security team, a stack of "to-dos," and mounting issues kept me from pursuing. "It isn't like Emerson to duck his assignments."

"Some rowdies caused a kerfuffle on the line. None of our regulars were involved, thank goodness. Security has it under control, but their patrols and line monitoring have them tied up." Ginger glanced at her watch before returning her gaze to me. "That's another reason we need someone at the showers, fast."

A solution popped into my mind. "How about a volunteer from Jax's kitchen crew?"

"Hmm. Possible. I'll call." Ginger turned to leave.

"Wait. I'll ask him," I said, trying to sound casual. "Need to stretch my legs."

Ginger pursed her lips and gave me a look but kept her thoughts to herself.

Of course, Ginger recognized my less than truthful reason. Just thinking about Jax made me giddy, even though he was too young, too tall, too rich, and too White. Plus, too soon. Ben's deadly heart attack, two years ago next week, seemed like yesterday. I stood and moved around my desk. "I'll check the basement on my way to the kitchen."

"You have a lot on your plate." She read from her notebook. "Budget meeting at 10:00. The mayor expects your call at noon. Ten minutes squeezed in between meetings."

Anticipating an in-person visit, I wore a bold red suit to project strength. I needed the mayor's help. Alas, a ten-minute phone call would have to do.

"You have Wally and Lacy at 2:00 and Valentine's coming at 4:00."

Valentine Bannister, a lawyer by trade and chair of The Way Station's board of directors, wanted to discuss his financial concerns. While knowledgeable enough, finance wasn't my strongest suit, so I asked Lacy, my childhood friend and the director of marketing and fund development, and Wally, our chief financial officer, to brief me. Financial anomalies weren't the only issues on my mind. Like Emerson, Zander appeared to be missing in action.

"Finding Emerson shouldn't take more than a few minutes and dropping by the kitchen several more. I'll return in a flash."

Last year, Emerson relapsed after years of sobriety, and became belligerent with staff and fellow volunteers. Nothing physical but angry outbursts and accusations. The behavior was out of character. I got him back into detox, AA, and an anger management class.

I tilted my now empty cup towards Ginger. "Thanks again for watching out for me."

"Of course." She returned to her desk just outside my door.

I hurried down the narrow, brightly lit hallways. My three-inch heels tapped a fast rhythm. From thirteen-years old, I reached my pathetic adult stature. Shoes that hurt by the end of the day made my shortness less of an issue. At least for me.

Peeling paint, scuff marks and dents decorated the walls. Surely, minor cleanups and repairs were affordable. I made a mental note. Yes, money was tight, and the new building sucked most of it up at an alarming rate, but how much could a paint job cost? I picked up my pace.

Everyone knew Emerson, a fixture at The Way Station, where in addition to the hot showers and daily breakfasts, we fed guests lunch seven days a week, gave takeaway meals for their dinners, and offered a variety of services helping people get back on their feet. The computer room on the second floor stayed full, as did the legal aid space, another popular program. In an array of rooms, staff and volunteers navigated school issues, government programs, and filled out job applications with our clients. We offered life skill classes and after-school homework assistance. Once a month, a medical van pulled onto our front lawn and provided free health and dental care. Emerson used it all. Clean-shaven, with still smooth mahogany skin, and a full head of white hair, he ate his meals, showered, shaved, attended AA meetings, and volunteered daily. Once we finished the new building and offered free, accessible apartments, Emerson will sign up for that as well.

I reached the basement. Storage bins, a comfy sitting area, vending machines, and shelves of used books volunteers and staff could borrow filled the space.

Emerson often went there after his morning shift.

The door stood open. I clicked the light switch, but nothing happened. With my index finger, I flicked again. Mental note–remind maintenance to fix. This wasn't the first time we experienced electrical problems. Because of previous issues, a flashlight, large and square, rested on a shelf at the top of the basement stairs. I grabbed it, pressed the on-button, and with the beam guiding me, started down. The stairs creaked, and the air smelled hot, as if an electric heater was on. I slowed. A sound, like a cough, followed by a groan, stopped me. My right foot hovered over the step below.

"Hello? Is someone here?" I listened. "Emerson, is that you?"

I heard another groan, this one louder, then a muffled pop, pop, pop, followed by a heavy thud.

I pressed my back against the wall, turned off the flashlight, slid along the stairwell wall, and backed up the stairs.

"Stop." A commanding voice spoke from the darkness below.

Someone, dressed in a black pea jacket and pants, a knit cap, and a mask covering his face, stood at the bottom of the steps. The only illumination came from a street level window. With care, I stretched behind me and tried the light switch again. This time, it worked, bathing the intruder in a fluorescent glow. In his gloved right hand hung a blood-stained kitchen knife, and in his left, a gun with a long silencer lay against his thigh.

The figure raised the weapon and pointed it at my head.

CHAPTER TWO

Unable to move my feet, I stared at the black-clad man. My breathing became shallow. I noticed his thick build but couldn't tell if he was Black or White, young or old. Dark, shining eyes stared at me from behind the mask. In my head, I prayed. Not for myself, but for Zander. What if I died too?

The lights blinked. Footfalls thundered up the stairs. I sucked in overheated air, flattened myself against the wall, and gripped the flashlight in my right hand. Zander would not be an orphan. The intruder stopped and turned to face me. Without hesitation, I swung up hard, catching him on his chin with the flashlight.

"Fuck." He staggered back against the opposite wall, dropped the knife, but kept a grasp on the gun.

I smelled his sweat, heard his rapid breathing. I'm not going down like this. Not today. With my heart thudding, I opened my mouth wide, screamed in his face, and swung again. The shriek propelled my upward thrust. This time, the flashlight smashed into his left elbow.

"Fuck, fuck, fuck." He grabbed his arm. "You're a dead woman." Spittle dampened his mask. He pivoted and ran the rest of the way up the steps, turned and disappeared.

I fumbled for the cell phone in my pocket, a coughing fit making it hard to think. What was Security Director, Tito Johnson's number? Unable to produce it, I dialed a number I'd memorized.

"Hey," Jax said.

An alarm boomed. The intruder likely opened the emergency door to the alley.

"What's going on?"

Phlegm in my throat choked me. "I'm in the basement," I said in a hoarse whisper.

"Are you okay?"

"In the stairwell. Please come."

The alarm continued to blare. Security would arrive any second. I should wait for Jax or an officer, but someone was hurt. Still hugging the wall, I eased down the steps. My legs and hands trembled.

"Aria?" Jax, huffing as if he ran the entire way, bounded down the steps, a thick bat in his left fist. "Are you injured?"

I pointed.

"What the hell?"

Emerson lay on the concrete floor, his chest slashed, shirt drenched, a hole in his forehead, and a pool of blood oozed from the back of his head. Bits of brain, bone splinters, and blood dotted crates of supplies, an armchair, and scatter rug.

Jax bent over the body and probed for a pulse. He shook his head and stood. Intense green eyes swept over me, as if looking for signs of trauma.

I couldn't speak. When I tried, my body convulsed in spasms. In two steps, he was in front of me, wrapped his arms around my shoulders and pulled me close.

"Did he hurt you?"

One part of my mind loved that my welfare was his first thought. Not, did you see the murderer, or what happened, or anything like that. But the other part left me without words. Shaking racked my body, like storm-fueled crashing waves.

Two security guards hustled down the steps.

"I called the police," Jax said, rubbing my back. With his index finger, he pointed the guards to Emerson's body. Then Jax guided me to the basement steps and eased me down.

I buried my face in my hands and wept.

•   •   •

The Way Station sat on the corner of East Fir Street and Madison in the southeast and poorest part of Fieldcrest, a community of 60,000, forty-five minutes north of New York City. Over the past three years, the town received an infusion of development. New businesses and housing sprang up. A mogul, and crook, people called Spider Booth ended up in jail, but other investors moved plans forward, including a school attached to the local community theater. The refurbished property included two swimming pools, tennis, pickle ball, and basketball courts. But The Way Station's part of town remained depressed. No investments reached our corner. Until now. Standing to the west of our existing building, a new structure was going up. Slowly. Stalled. But I intended to remedy that.

I looked around. Police car strobes colored the tableau. Crime scene tape encircled the entire building. Hungry and cold clients milled about. A toddler wailed above muffled conversations. Staff members and volunteers huddled in small circles. Ginger and Lacy Quarles stood on the other side of the entrance, just outside the tape. A uniformed officer guarded us, preventing Ginger and Lacy from approaching Jax and me.

The scene from the murder looped in my brain. Why was the intruder here? To kill Emerson, or did Emerson catch him in an illegal act? Nothing valuable in the basement. Money from the vending machines might buy drugs. Did Emerson get ensnared in the middle of something sinister and bigger? Poor Emerson. My heart broke for him.

Jax asked the closest police officer, "How much longer?" We were waiting for the homicide detectives to return from searching the building in case the murderer was still inside. Others, the officer explained, covered the alleyway behind the building and the adjacent construction site.

The cop shrugged in response to Jax's question.

A stiff March breeze bit into me. The scent of the killer's breath still filled my nostrils. His body heat a vivid memory. The hate he spewed at me felt physical... and personal.

"You're sure you're okay?" Jax asked.

I nodded, still unable to speak. Uniformed officers moved from person to person, asking questions and writing comments in notebooks. Additional cops canvassed The Way Station's immediate neighbors–the owners and customers of the bodega next door, laundromat two doors down, and staff and patrons of the ancient and poorly stocked library across the street.

Jax said, "They can't keep you here. Go home, rest, and speak to the police tomorrow or the next day. Whenever you're ready."

I turned and looked up at him. At forty, he appeared even younger. His dimpled chin, creased tip of his nose, thin upper lip and full bottom joined his arresting eyes to make him pleasing to look at. Not handsome but...

"I'll drive you. Just say the word."

Yes please, I said in my head.

Voices caused me to shift my gaze. The detectives reappeared.

"All clear." Detective Errol Glover spoke to a man in a camel overcoat.

The person standing next to the camel coat guy wore a navy jacket with the words Medical Examiner stamped on its back in bright yellow. Errol, who I dated before meeting Ben, faced Jax and me.

"This is my partner, Detective Yun." Errol pointed his thumb at an Asian woman about my height and weight. "Shall we go inside?"

Jax said, "How about we take this up tomorrow? The lady experienced a scare."

"Of course, that's up to you," Errol said, facing me and ignoring Jax. "But we'll catch this killer faster if we speak now while your memory is fresh." A deep frown wrinkled his chestnut-brown skin.

Jax's offer to drive me home sounded good, but what if the murderer tracked me down? The thought sent my mind spiraling. Why come for me? Emerson was a sweet man. An addict on the mend. Why kill him? I shook my head, trying to stop the loop of questions, but more came. Should I stay with Lacy instead of going home? Wouldn't she be at risk? I couldn't move in with my parents and put them in danger.

"We'll protect you," Errol said, as if reading my mind. "But we need a description, details."

"You have the knife. Won't there be fingerprints?" Jax asked.

Errol gave Jax a hard glare before returning to me. "It won't take long."

For fifty-years I made sure I was a good girl, woman, wife, mother, and friend. A caring boss. Did the right thing. "Okay." My voice cracked. "We can speak in my office."

Detective Yun said to Jax. "Join us."

Without waiting for Jax's consent, Errol lifted a stretch of crime tape, and I stepped under it. I glanced back, seeking Jax's reassurance. The female detective, and doubled-over Jax, scooted under the tape and walked behind me.

In my office, a large glass-topped desk centered the room. To the right stood a cream-colored couch and two upholstered chairs. Small, round glass-topped tables provided places for drinks, papers, briefcases, or purses. Framed diplomas from Barnard College, where I earned a B.A., and New York University, where I received my master's, hung on the right wall. My hidden door to the ensuite bathroom shared the right wall with the diplomas. Bookshelves filled with professional books on leadership, relationship building, and psychology lined the left.

We all shed our winter coats and jackets. Errol and Yun both wore dark grey suits and white shirts with their detective shields on their lapels. This contrasted with Jax's signature black pants and turtleneck, a techie uniform still, set by Steve Jobs many years ago. My bright red suit seemed out of place.

The detectives took the chairs, and Jax and I sat on the couch.

In a gentle voice, almost soothing, Errol said to me, "What's Emerson's full name and how do we contact his family?"

I searched my memory. Did Emerson have another name? Was Emerson his first or last? Did he have people? Why didn't I know? I swiped my wet eyes and cheeks. My words disappeared again. Jax put his arm around me, and I sagged against him.

CHAPTER THREE

I felt foolish. Crying on Jax's shoulder in front of Errol and Yun made me appear less than competent. I wasn't a helpless victim. Didn't I fight back? And what did Jax think? He spoke sparingly, leaving me clueless about his thoughts.

He and his two brothers owned an in-demand cyber security firm—The Vault. Jax ran the cyber sleuthing, prevention, and resilience departments, plus research and development. Despite his big job, he carved out time to volunteer in the kitchen four mornings a week, for all three early shifts, before driving the twenty minutes to White Plains, his company's headquarters. Like Ben, and unlike me, he found ways to do more. Thanks to Jax, The Vault donated annually, and Jax personally gave $25,000 a year unsolicited. Another reason he wasn't right for me. I imagined the headline in the local paper—CEO Caught Canoodling with Top Contributor. If we dated, might people suspect I only wanted his money? Not that he'd asked me out.

My jumbled thoughts swirled. Emerson murdered, me threatened, and I'm busy obsessing about Jax. Ridiculous. Well, equally pathetic was an overpowering need to see my parents. Yes, to warn them, but also, I craved their comfort and wisdom.

•   •   •

Yvonne and Ramon Upton, Mama and Daddy, lived in the affluent community of Westwood, a northern part of Fieldcrest with a separate zip code, something influential members of the neighborhood lobbied for. Bella and I, two years apart in age, enjoyed terrific childhoods. Our cul-de-sac included six families, and each with at least one child our age. A diverse corner of the mostly White community included three Black owners, including ours, one Latino, one Asian, and one White—making our block a lovely oddity. The parents were all friends, although some were closer than others, who helped each other out, and monitored all seventeen children. Excellent schools, clean streets, no unhoused folks living under bridges.

My passion for serving those in need didn't come from our neighborhood. My parents, grandparents, and pastor inspired my calling and profession. Right until I left for graduate school, we fed and helped homeless folks who lived south of us. Every Friday evening, we packed up enough hot meals for fifty. In addition, we packaged baggies of peanut butter and jelly sandwiches, toiletries like toothbrushes, toothpaste, tampons, shaving cream, and soap, and clothes, sneakers, and blankets. Then we drove to the poorest sections of Fieldcrest and fed as many people as possible. When Bella and I became teenagers, we begged off, but Daddy and Mama weren't having it. Our family helps those without privileges like us, they explained. Period.

Once, a girl my age approached me. I recognized her but couldn't remember from where. She gobbled down the night's offering of chicken, green beans, and rice. After wiping her mouth with the napkins we provided, she looked at, and into me, to a vulnerable place. "One day I'm going to do this for others," she said. "So don't believe you're so special."

Is that what I thought? Better than the hungry girl? Did I help from a place of pity and obligation and my attitude showed on my face? That encounter changed me. She inspired my insistence that we refer to all unhoused, unemployed, and hungry people who came to The Way Station as customers or clients—individuals who deserved dignified service and support.

Exhausted, I pulled into my parent's driveway. The two-story colonial, front porch rocking chairs waiting for impending spring, welcomed me. I'd called ahead and my mom met me at the door, her eyes crinkled in worry. Short like me, and seventy, her smooth skin and clear eyes belied her age. Not to mention the lack of gray hair, thanks to regular trips to Roxy and Carl's Salon. Her straightened hair, dyed auburn, brushed her shoulders.

"Hey Mama." I hugged her.

"Are you hungry, sweetie?"

I realized I'd not eaten since breakfast, followed by the latte Ginger brought me. "I wouldn't turn down a glass of wine and some munchies."

"Well, aren't you fortunate. I have some ready for you."

We sat in the living room. In the fireplace, flames popped, creating spark-showers. They licked around and through the stacked logs. Water crackers, softened brie, raw veggies, dressing, and assorted nuts sat on a tray. All my favorites. I sipped Cabernet from a crystal glass and let the warmth of my childhood home soothe me.

My dad walked in. Unfortunately, I did not inherit his height. Six feet tall and lean, he carried himself like the soldier he was in his youth. On the fortunate side, I looked a lot like my darn cute mother.

"What's happening with the case?" Daddy asked. "Not much info on the television."

"Nothing so far." My face flushed. "I didn't have the strength to answer Errol Glover's questions today." Tears puddled.

"Oh, sweetie." Mama sat and pulled me in. "I'm sure Errol understood."

Daddy, ever the gentleman, handed me a cloth handkerchief. I blew and wiped.

"Does Glover know how the killer got past security?"

My parents remembered Errol as part of our teenaged-crowd, and my brief time dating him as a young woman. When he returned from law school and joined the local police force, we were all happy for him.

"No," I said. Another troubling piece of the puzzle. We don't allow guns or weapons of any kind, and metal detectors and security guard searches were there to stop anyone carrying. And yet...

"Is all this drama hurting The Way Station?" Daddy asked. "I imagine adverse publicity could slow donations for the new building."

My mind swung back to our fiscal state. "Something is financially hurting us, but it's too soon for the murder to be the cause."

"The killing is a dangerous situation. Time enough to worry about money," my mother said.

"That's why I'm here."

"To move in with us until they catch this monster," my father said in his military, make-it-so, voice.

I expected him to take this tone, an attitude that used to infuriate me as a teenager, but also made me feel safe. Despite the sharpness of his words, he was a gentle and loving man, determined to be my protector. "I'm not moving in."

"Yes, you are," he insisted. "Your mother has already prepared your room." Bella and I each had our own and shared a bathroom. They both looked just as we left them when Bella travelled to Brown University, and I headed to grad school.

"I'm 50-years old. With responsibilities. I want to make sure you both are taking precautions, turning on the alarm even when you're home, checking doors and windows, and alerting the neighbors. At least the Madisons." I called the folks who lived to our right Aunt Rachel and Uncle David. They'd moved in the same month we did, and became close friends, like family.

My mother stayed quiet during this conversation. I glanced at her. "If you see anything out of the ordinary—"

"I did."

"Oh."

My father jumped in. "You didn't say anything to me."

Her large brown eyes opened even wider. "Probably nothing."

"Tell us," Daddy said.

"A black car with tinted windows idled in front of the Lopez's place for the longest time." Their house stood on the eastern side of the cul-de-sac. "They're in Puerto Rico until April."

My father peppered her with questions, but my head swam. Could the killer track down my parents? I suppressed my paranoia. The driver of the idling car was taking a break, or someone looking for a quiet spot to eat her lunch before heading back to the highway. "You guys must be careful."

Daddy agreed. "I'll check all the windows and doors. Alert Dave Madison." Daddy turned to me. "Stay with us. I'll drive you home and bring you and your belongings back. Even your snobby cat."

That brought a smile to my face. Princess and my father enjoyed an entertaining love/hate relationship.

He reached for his coat in the hall. "What about Zander? Is he coming home? Have you called Bella?"

I hadn't spoken to Zander in over a week, which was unlike him. The phone rang and went straight to voice mail. I still needed to warn Bella. I'd come seeking comfort, but agitation and worry won out. My parents, Bella, Zander, how do I keep everyone safe? Another question nagged. Why would they be in danger? Emerson had nothing to do with my family. "I'll check on them both as soon as I get back in my car." No sense adding to their worries by sharing Zander's disturbing silence. I rose. "Time to go. Errol and his partner are picking me up in the morning and they've sent two officers to watch the house." I hugged my father and kissed my mom's soft cheek. "If you see the black car again, or anything suspicious, dial 9-1-1. This man is evil."

CHAPTER FOUR

Wednesday, March 13, Fieldcrest, NY

I awoke with a start, my heart pounding and bedclothes wet with sweat as if a high fever had just broken. I lay still, listening, but only heard the soft hum of the central heating system. Everything seemed in its proper place. I sat up and rolled off the bed. Decorative pillows lay stacked on an upholstered bench. The narrow bookcase, tucked in a corner with favorite novels, looked normal. On its shelves stood photographs of my mom and dad on their wedding day, my sister Bella, and her family of four, and a portrait of Ben, Zan, and me, this one taken by a professional photographer several Christmas cards ago.

I eyed Ben's uncrumpled side of the bed–his nightstand empty, except for a lamp and clock. It made me sad. When he was alive, he placed his keys and loose change in an old ashtray left over from his smoking days. The charger for his iWatch, and a pair of reading glasses, occupied assigned spots. He used his iPhone as an alarm, but liked the big, illuminated numbers on the electric clock, which now read 6:00 a.m. I vowed to sleep in the middle of the bed. Spread out. But it didn't seem right. Yet.

The television sat on the bureau facing the bed. I picked up the remote from my nightstand and turned on the local news. Half-listening, I padded to the bathroom.

The murder remained high in the local news cycle, but with no added information. Distracted, I listened while washing my face and brushing my teeth. The Way Station didn't need this type of publicity. We relied on the larges of donors and government grants. And money flowed out faster than it came in. My building project stalled. Each month, we choose which bills to pay, and when. The murder might make donors and government agents less comfortable with us, cripple our financial support even more. I stopped these thoughts. What was wrong with me? Someone murdered Emerson, a kind and generous man living a productive life.

I met Emerson three weeks after becoming CEO. During a walk around, he asked for a moment.

"I monitor the shower line," he explained. "Make sure folks have clean towels, toiletries, and a change of clothes."

"Thank you." I'd noticed he treated our clients with dignity. "We all appreciate your work."

He appeared embarrassed. "That's not why I'm telling you this."

Smooth skin and hooded eyes made me wonder how his younger self looked. Handsome no doubt.

"I listen and watch, but keep my mouth shut."

Seconds passed before he spoke again.

"Don't let anyone make you doubt yourself. You belong here."

It was a strange thing for him to tell me, especially because I was questioning my decision. The dismissive administrative assistant supporting my office unnerved me. Some of the senior team acted standoffish. And my board chair, even though he served on the search team that chose me, seemed less than confident of my abilities. I was the first Black CEO, and first female. Plus, younger than several of the leadership team. If I expected enthusiasm, it had yet to surface.

"I see you," Emerson said.

Now, blood-soaked pictures filled my mind. Shudders swept through me. Did the police find his family? How could I be there for Emerson?

Another memory pushed forward. I'd collapsed in Jax's arms. Humiliating. And I didn't finish my testimony or even start. My crying jag went on for minutes, stopped, and started again. Errol gave up and agreed to come for me at 9:00 a.m., take me to the police station, and try again to unearth my story.

"According to the county police, Aria Wright, the CEO, is not a suspect or person of interest," said the television reporter, sounding grave. "Even though she, alone, discovered the body."

The co-host added, "It's still early in the investigation."

Isn't that comforting? Not a suspect *yet*. Did Errol suspect me, like the reporters implied? I spat out toothpaste and rinsed my mouth. Of course not. No reason to.

Yesterday passed in a blur. After my embarrassing weeping swoon, an officer walked me to my Mini Cooper, still parked in The Way Station's back lot. I drove straight to my parents. A tense goodbye left us all unsettled. Jax wanted to drive me, but the detectives persuaded him to stay and answer questions. He only said yes after Errol promised to park a patrol car in front of my house all night in case the killer came looking for me. Grateful for Jax and the police presence, it still felt intrusive and frightening. Should I ask Errol to post a car in front of my parent's home? For the first time since he left for college, I was glad Zan wasn't here. Distance, prayerfully, kept him safe.

Princess, my three-year-old tabby, mewed and circled my legs, demanding breakfast. I pulled on a warm robe, stepped into my slippers, and scooped her up.

"Good morning," I said to the cat. Her gold eyes looked at me with impatience. I carried her into the kitchen. White cabinets and granite countertops glowed under overhead lights. Too early for sunrise, the gray sky looked dark through the windows, reminding me spring and 6:30 sunrises were weeks away.

The automatic coffeemaker held two cups of Sumatra Bold, waiting for my mug. After emptying a can of cat food in a bowl and re-filling the water dish, I sat on a stool in front of the island, took my first sip of coffee, and scrolled emails, texts, and voicemail. Several messages came from Lacy, Valentine, Errol, and Jax. Rather than respond to the lengthy list, I dialed Zander's cell phone. I wanted to hear his voice and know he wasn't in danger. The killer had no motive to harm Zan, but still...

"Leave a message," Zan's recorded voice said. My heart made a double beat, followed by another. I missed him. Since Ben's death, Zan and I looked out for each other, but not this past week. Of course, at 6:30 a.m. what college freshman was awake?

"Call me," I said after the beep. "As soon as you get this message."

I left several since Sunday, our normal day to chat, and still no response. For the third time, I tugged on one dangling curl of coiled hair and let the spiral spring back in place–a nervous childhood habit. Before this dry spell, we communicated with each other at least three times a week. Sunday Face-Time visit, and then texts, sharing bits of our day. Was I overreacting because of the murder? He'd made friends, no doubt, and had exams to cram for. Did he meet a girl? Or run into trouble?

I understood Zan's struggles. Losing his dad two years ago left a hole I couldn't fill. The first months at Cornell University, after sailing through high school at the top of his class, found him scrambling. Still. You call your mama every week and you always respond to her texts and messages. No matter what.

Would the police allow me to drive to Ithaca? The city, three hours north by car, expected two feet of late winter snow according to the weather station. The idea of searching the snow-blanketed campus, wandering around clueless, seemed ill-advised, but I had to do something.

I thumbed in the Dean of Students' number.

"Our office hours are 8:00 a.m. to 5:00 p.m. Please leave your name and a detailed message and we'll return your call." I hung up. Try to contact an official later.

Princess wound around my leg, purring.

"I've got to burn up this anxiety," I explained to the tabby, who responded by leaving the room, her tail high in the air.

"Well, thanks for the sympathy." I laughed aloud. Some of the tension eased.

Ben built an exercise room in the basement, along with a laundry room and a space filled with a ping-pong and pool table, chess set on a bench with two chairs, recliners, and a humongous flat screen television mounted on a wall. Most mornings, I completed forty-five minutes on the treadmill, followed by reps with free weights. Today, my heart wasn't in it, but I pressed on. Air Pods in and music blasting, I ran at a brisk pace, keeping my troubles at bay.

Ninety minutes later, showered and dressed, I prepared to face my day.

I had an hour before Errol collected me, so I used the time to listen to voicemail and read the texts.

"Morning. Valentine here. The news about the murder devastated me. I suppose you were too upset to notify me. Learned about it from Lacy. Call me when you're up to it."

Big sigh, as our middle schoolers liked to say. I wrote a quick text in response. "GM. The police are questioning me this morning. I will try you this afternoon."

I read the message. Too curt? "Thank you for your concern. I hope you're well," I added.

Bless Lacy, who spent a lot of time coddling board members. I re-read the message and deleted it. Started again. "Thank you for your call and caring. I'm okay, heading to the police station for further questioning, but will call you this afternoon. Please reach out to the rest of the board. I don't want them to worry. With gratitude, Aria."

Errol left a short and to the point message. "Will be at your house at 9:00 a.m. sharp. Thanks for being prompt."

I didn't bother to respond. We'd agreed on the time yesterday. This morning's message reminded me of dentists and doctors who sent multiple messages reminding people of their appointments, as if their patients were all irresponsible. I suspected Errol, old friendship aside, wanted to establish a professional relationship.

I listened to Jax's sweet message. "Hope you're okay. Worried about you."

"Rested and ready," I typed. "See you soon."

"Let's grab lunch or afternoon coffee. Compare notes. I'll alert my office that I won't be in today."

That gave me pause. I still felt his arms around me, stroking my back and whispering comforting words as I wept on his chest. Unprofessional and unacceptable, carrying on like a wounded schoolgirl. Better to have a colleague-to-colleague relationship. CEO to volunteer. "Can't. Too much to do. But thanks for the invitation." An accurate message, but also protective. I read his messages again, and without my consent, my mouth turned up in a grin.

I called Lacy.

"Oh my God," Lacy said without even a hello. "How are you? I've been frantic with worry."

Tears welled. Like yesterday with the detectives, I couldn't stop sobbing. Jax's strong arms wrapped around me then. Now, once again, I was alone.

"Aria?"

I usually controlled my emotions, something I worked on. "Sorry. I'm a mess."

"Understandable. A murder. I'll drive over."

"Errol Glover is picking me up." I mopped my eyes with a tissue. "Thanks, but I'm okay."

"You're not."

"I will be."

"Reporters are stalking the place and making our people uncomfortable. The police let us back into a part of the building, so we're getting folks washed up and fed."

"Thanks for holding down the fort."

"Of course." She paused. "Is it weird having Errol manage the case?"

"Not yet." I hung up after promising to drop by her office when I returned from the police station.

The phone rang again—an unknown number. It could be someone from Zander's school, or the police department. I clicked the answer button. "This is Aria."

"I know where you live, bitch." The angry voice sounded muffled, like the murderer's did through his mask. "Where your parents live, your sister and her boys, and where your kid goes to college. Don't do anything stupid. Say anything and you're a dead woman."

I threw the phone across the room.

CHAPTER FIVE

I fought down surging panic. My deep breathing routine slowed my heart rate but fear still gripped me. The living room rocking chair, and a multi-colored afghan knitted by my mother, did little to comfort me. My mental playlist failed as well. All my life I carried a playlist in my head. I summoned just the right song. Now, no soothing music emerged.

With shaking hands, I clutched the blanket tight around me, oblivious of my rumbled suit. How did the killer find me? My son? Parents? Sister Bella? Would the police protect them all? Why target me? I couldn't pick him out in a lineup. Because I fought back? The ego of a sociopath? Are voice matches possible? Even if they were, his muffled words made it unlikely. And what did he mean by "don't *do* anything stupid"? About what? I possessed no information connected to Emerson's murder. Argh. So crazy.

Rapid bangs on the front door made me jump. Errol called out. "Aria?" More pounding.

I couldn't move or speak. The murderer's threats rang in my ears.

"We're coming in."

Oh, no. They'd crash the door open. "Wait." I forced myself up. "Be there in a sec."

The detectives stepped into the foyer, their heads swiveling right to left, hands on their holstered guns.

Errol said, "Are you alone?"

"Yes. He phoned me. Left a message." I realized my call to the police station must have sounded garbled and frantic, as if the murderer were in the house. "The patrol car out front disappeared, and...." I pulled the afghan tighter.

Detective Yun spoke up. "I'm sorry, Ms. Wright. I told them we were on our way to pick you up and sent them home. We're short-staffed. The flu, COVID, lots of uniforms are out."

I caught the look Errol shot at Yun.

"Too soon, I realize now," Yun said, sounding chastened.

Errol asked, "Are you still up for a conversation?"

Uncertain, but I said yes. "Should I call my parents and sister first?" Zander's lack of communication—was there a connection? "My son, away at college, hasn't called in days, which is unlike him. Could the killer...?" I groaned. Please, God, let Zan be safe.

"One step at a time." Detective Yun took my elbow. "Are you clothed under there?" She smiled. "Let me help you get ready, and we can discuss everything at the station. Make some plans."

I dashed off notes on my mental to-do list. Call the Dean of Students again. Try Zan's cell again. Check on my parents and reach out to Bella. "I'm dressed. Just need my briefcase and purse." I looked around, unsure where I put them. "Give me a minute."

After shedding the afghan, my mind on Zan and the rest of my family, I walked through the house, not remembering why. Ben and I bought the two-story colonial when we moved back to Fieldcrest after living in Connecticut, Upstate New York, and Brooklyn. My parents were aging and being near them made sense. Because Ben's consulting work let him live anywhere provided a nearby airport existed, he'd agreed. We moved six months before I started at The Way Station.

My head ached. What was I looking for? Princess followed me as if also curious. Police. Interview. Safety. A plan. It came back to me in fragments. I spotted the briefcase and purse in my home office, grabbed them both, and returned to the front door.

Wait. "Errol, will my tabby be, okay?" Princess sat watching me as if she understood the conversation. "Don't murderers kill pets?"

He heaved his shoulders and spoke in a tight voice, like someone struggling to sound reasonable. "Can you take her with you in a carry case?"

Errol was not a cat person. "Give me a sec. I'll see if my neighbor can keep her until I return."

I finally got Princess squared away. Like many cats, she possessed a strong, independent streak.

The ride to the police station gave me more time to collect myself. The killer called me on my personal cell. If that's who phoned me. How'd he unearth my number? The Way Station provided a work mobile phone. It appeared in my email signature and on our website, along with the office landline. Was the person who threatened me friends with someone in my inner circle or were cell phone numbers easy to find?

Detectives Yun and Errol stayed quiet, so I did, too. The car stopped at a traffic light. Deep in thought, I looked out the window. The city, draped in its winter coat, gave no hint of spring. Cars filled the parking lot in front of Stop & Shop. People carrying reusable shopping bags struggled onto a bus parked at the corner. The steamed windows of the car waiting next to us needed defrosting.

Bella's birthday was March 23 and mine March 26. We always celebrated with our parents–dinner, presents, and music. Ben and Zander claimed we over did it, made fun of us. "Are you two toddlers?" But Bella and I loved our parties. They made us feel like kids again. So yeah, five and seven, we'd say, laughing at ourselves.

How might we celebrate this year with a murderer stalking us?

· · ·

The Fieldcrest police station, a municipal patrol operation of the Westchester County Department of Public Safety, took up a half a block on Obama Avenue, north and west of The Way Station. The well lit, square brick building looked welcoming rather than ominous. Errol offered his hand, warm and firm, and helped me out of the unmarked car.

Once settled in a windowless and unadorned interview room, they offered me coffee, water, or soda. Already two cups of coffee in, I said, "Water, please."

Detective Yun said, "I'll bring some for all of us."

"We'd like to record this conversation," Errol said. "Okay?"

He sat opposite me across a white table. Two metal chairs were on his side and only one on mine. I looked around for a two-way mirror, but only saw white walls. Facing me, a camera winked from a corner.

Errol's hazel eyes and gentle voice lulled me into submission even though I watched enough crime shows to know I should ask for a lawyer. Maybe the police suspected me. Not Errol. But there were others involved, including his boss. Why tape the interview? I glanced up at the camera again. "Are you recording me already?" I pointed to the blinking instrument near the ceiling.

"Not without permission," he said in his liquid voice and not the curt version. "You're not under arrest."

"Why would I be?"

"You're not. We have no reason to. So, do I have your consent?"

Yun returned with three plastic bottles of chilled water and handed me one. I unscrewed the cap and sipped before saying, "Okay."

He switched on the recording device. "Tell me how your day began yesterday. What time did you get to work?"

I outlined each step and explained why I went to the basement.

Errol asked, "When he spoke to you from the bottom of the stairs, did you recognize his voice?"

Something was familiar. "The mask distorted the timbre, or he disguised it." I shook my head. "Not sure."

"Okay. What happened next?"

I shared how the murderer rushed toward me with the bloody knife and gun. I pantomimed clocking him with the flashlight.

"Wow," Errol said, his eyebrows raised. As if he regretted his amazement, he shifted his tone to chastisement. "A dangerous move."

Detective Yun got us back on track. "When he confronted you, did you see any distinguishing marks?"

His eyes were the only feature visible from behind the black mask. I pictured their strange luminescence. Contact lenses? Something else?

Before I could answer, Errol said, "You told us his eyes were brown. What shade?"

The relationship between the detectives puzzled me. Errol made a point of his role as leader of the team. Showing off for me? I found it quite annoying. So, I turned to Yun first. "I'm sorry. I don't remember any distinguishing marks." Something nagged.

Errol said, "What? You just remembered something?"

"No. I mean, a memory is lurking, but I can't pull it up."

"And the shade?"

"Nondescript brown." I questioned my memory. Terrified, I failed to notice details, or forgot them. "With a glassy appearance. My memory is fuzzy."

"And the phone call... What did he say?"

I repeated the comments.

"Is there something you're not telling us? Keep quiet about what?

"I don't know."

CHAPTER SIX

Over the next two hours, I repeated everything that happened. Again, and again. When the questions shifted to my relationship with Emerson, I explained, "Respectful and professional. We discussed the needs of our clients and volunteers. Observant and savvy, Emerson often shared insights I missed."

"Did he have any run-ins with clients, volunteers, or staff?"

"As I explained earlier, not to my knowledge. He had a good relationship with everyone. We all liked and respected him." When I told Errol about last year's setback, I emphasized Emerson didn't hurt anyone and returned to his rehab program.

"Okay. Let's go over everything once more."

No, no, no. Let's not. "I'm exhausted. Now, it's your turn. What did you learn about the security failure? How did the killer get past the metal detectors?"

"You tell me."

Argh. "You spoke with our head of security, Tito Johnson?"

"Yes. We're looking into the protocols, reviewing footage from your cameras."

Tito was another holdover from the previous CEO. "Do you suspect a member of my security force?"

"The list of possibilities is long."

Detective Yun said, "We start with a wide net and then narrow the list as we investigate. Takes time."

"I see." Of course, it did. But if the murderer is on staff, then what? I shifted gears. "How will you protect my clients, staff, and family? My son? How will you protect me from this maniac, especially since you haven't uncovered how or why he got into the building?"

Yun said, "An empty threat. From all you've told us, he has no reason to go after you. Why bring increased police scrutiny? It makes little sense."

I gave her an incredulous stare. "Sense or not, he's threatened my family and me."

Yun shifted her approach. "Where do your folks live?"

"Here in town. Westwood."

"Hmm," Errol said. His eyes dropped to his folded hands on the table. When he raised them to meet mine, he said, "I can ask the District Attorney to put you up in a motel, someplace in the County, but not in town."

"A motel? For how long?"

"The time being."

"What does that mean? Suppose you don't find him before 'the time being' is up?"

"DA's decision."

Yun pulled out a notebook. "Give me everyone's information, and we'll contact the local authorities. Ask them to make wellness checks." She handed me a pen and notepaper. "And the college. We'll call them, too."

Glad for a concrete step, I pulled out my iPhone and looked up each address and phone number. Adrenaline pumped through me during the interrogation, but now my system crashed. After providing Yun with the information, I covered my face and steadied my breathing before lifting my head and facing the detectives. "I'm calling an Uber and leaving now." Jax jumped into my head, which happened too often. "Or someone. But I'm done." I rose. "People depend on me, so I'm not moving into a motel."

"Not wise," Errol said. He stood as well. "We can't protect you unless you're in a safe place and staying put."

"I thought you don't believe I'm in danger."

Yun said, "To be cautious."

This made sense, but... "Thank you for the patrol car in front of my house. Can it continue for 'the time being?'" I regretted the sarcasm. "Sorry. I realize you're doing your best."

"We are," Errol said. "You need to let us do our job." A deep vee between his eyes underscored his words.

"I can't let this... this murderer intimidate me. He's a coward and a bully. I hurt his feelings when I hit him. Twice." How would I find Zander if I lived under guard in a motel? Plus, The Way Station faced a financial cliff and required my full attention. I turned toward the door and pointed. "Is it locked? Am I free to go?"

Errol said, "Patrol cars stationed in front of your house cost money, too." He rubbed his chin. "But I'll send the request up the chain and see what comes back."

His tone, while professional, belied the look in his eyes. I realized, in a flash of recognition, Errol was on my side, and I needed his help. To get him to continue assisting me and pressing the higher ups for protection, my response required warmth and gratitude. "Thank you. I appreciate you looking out for me."

He bit his lip. Nodded. "Can't promise anything, but I'll do my best."

I gave him a broad, encouraging smile, but my mind drifted. What if his best wasn't good enough and the higher ups denied protection? Could Jax help me with security? Provide a recommendation?

"I'll walk you out," Errol said.

The police station hummed with activity. Phones rang, men and women in uniforms and suits sat at computers, typing, reading, and scrolling. Others stood in tight circles, drinking coffee, and talking. No one looked up as Errol and I passed.

We stepped outside, facing the parking lot. The sun from the morning disappeared. Snow flurries swirled. A chill engulfed me. I pulled on my gloves, slipped a scarf from my soft-sided briefcase, and wrapped the fabric around my head, covering my hair, ears, and neck.

"I can drive you home," Errol said. His breath condensed in the frigid air, making misty clouds when he spoke.

His offer seemed genuine and personal. We were old friends. An easy yes sat on the tip of my tongue.

Yun leaned out the door. "Glover, the chief is looking for us."

"Be there in a sec." He turned to me. "Sorry, I gotta go."

"No worries." I texted Jax.

Errol didn't leave. "I'm not supposed to say this until we officially rule you out, but I don't believe you killed Emerson. I mean, there's no reason. You were never a suspect."

I sensed Errol's eyes on the top of my head. Being short was so annoying.

Jax texted back. "Ten to fifteen minutes."

"Yesterday was terrifying," I said, looking up at Errol. "And this morning compounded it. How did you rule me out?"

"Forensics, motive, and alibi."

"The murderer wore gloves, so that leaves motive. I called the police. Is that how you eliminated me?"

"You didn't. Call the police, I mean."

One minute, Errol acted like he suspected me, then he turned on the charm. And now?

"Jax Oats called us." Errol looked at his watch and then at the road beyond the parking lot. "How long did your Uber driver say he'd be?"

"A friend is coming for me." I followed Errol's gaze. "He'll be here."

"Oh."

I ignored whatever colored his "oh." An awkward situation. Former lovers in the middle of a murder. He frequently shifted persona and attitude. "You believe me? You're not just saying that?"

"Truth."

A lot of time had passed since we were friends. I'd only returned to Fieldcrest two years ago. I shifted my head so I could see his face. "I'm trusting you, Errol, to keep us safe and find the killer."

"Doing my best."

I smiled in response. Handsome men in power operated at an advantage. People wanted to please them. And Errol was good looking. Time added depth to his eyes and a sprinkle of grey to his wavy hair.

Yun called again, "Glover, the boss is waiting." The door slammed behind her.

"Contact me if you learn or remember anything else," Errol said.

"And you tell *me* how the wellness checks go in Connecticut and Ithaca."

"Promise." He seemed torn between heading to his meeting and not wanting to leave me in the parking lot alone. Once again, he scanned the road.

"He'll be here. You don't have to wait. I'll be fine."

He looked at me. A hard quizzical study of my face. "Oats?" Suspicion or something else I couldn't name tinged his question.

"Bye, Errol." I tipped my head toward the door Yun closed. "I don't want you to get in trouble because of me."

He continued to stand next to me, hands in his pockets. The cold turned his dark nose red. "Okay. Be careful. This guy sounds serious. And dangerous."

"Always." Not really. I refused a hotel room and still planned to work every day.

Errol strode away.

I tried Zander again. Voice mail. I texted him. "Call me. Now." Crap.

CHAPTER SEVEN
EMERSON

April 4, 1968, somewhere over the Pacific Ocean

Cal Emerson and Maurice "Mo" Alexander sat next to each other on the 727-charter flying them and a plane full of airmen to Cam Ranh Bay, a stopover before reaching their various deployments in Vietnam. Some were stationed to the north in Da Nang and others south in Tan Son Nhut, close to Saigon. Emerson and Mo's destination was an air base in Tuy Hoa, a medium-sized, central coastal city on the South China Sea.

"You saw the babe from last night," Mo said. His six-foot frame looked squashed in the seat. Shifting, he thrust his long legs into the aisle. His combat boots lay on their sides under the seat before him. Mo wiggled his sock-covered toes. "She was hot."

Emerson met Mo during basic training at Lackland AFB in Texas and, by good fortune, they stayed together for tech school, Turner Air Force Base in Georgia, and their last deployment before Nam, Forbes Air Force Base in Topeka, Kansas. Now, three years since they first met, their tour of duty almost up, they headed to war. "What did Kiki say about the 'babe?'" Emerson asked, referring to Mo's stateside pregnant wife.

"Don't be like that, man." Mo elbowed Emerson. "Anyways, marriage and a baby were not part of my plan."

"Uh huh." Emerson didn't understand why Mo married Kiki, a woman he'd known for less than six months. Since the first wars, men felt compelled to solidify relationships before being shipped out. Something to do with mortality and having a child to continue their line. Mo's mind didn't work like that.

He and Kiki met in a club in Kansas, just outside of the base. Mo and Emerson came with some guys in search of party-loving ladies. Kiki and her girlfriend sat at a table close to the dance floor. Without a word, just an extended hand, Mo walked Kiki into the crowd of dancers. She rocked her hips to the beat. Small feet executed the Boogaloo with flair. Perspiration glowing on her Afro-framed face, Emerson watched with hungry eyes. After three dances, Mo invited both women to the table he shared with Emerson.

Kiki possessed everything Emerson wanted in a woman—smart, pretty, petite, with nice breasts and rear. For him, it was love at first sight. Lots of people don't believe you can fall for someone in an instant, but Emerson did. Kiki didn't reciprocate. Mo's smooth moves, talk, and looks took her in. Emerson understood the temptations when the one you loved still lived in Kansas. But he doubted Mo loved Kiki—the forever kind—the way Emerson would love her given the chance.

"I counted on this stupid war winding down by now." Mo slid lower in his seat, crossed his long legs at the ankles and closed his eyes. "We got less than a year to go." Eyes still closed, he grinned. "At least we'll be in the air, running recon, and not in the mud, getting blown up."

The Vietnam War began in 1955, and by 1968, it still slogged with no end in sight. The war took a sharp turn in January when the Tet Offensive began, a Viet Cong push-to-win. After Tet, support for the war at home took a decisive dive. Until then, the government claimed the US was winning. Over 250 men died that month and the mood at home soured.

Mo asked, "Remember the bar brawl in Topeka?"

Emerson cringed. "Not something I'm proud of."

"Wadda, you talking about? We scared those dudes shitless."

An argument started over a woman. Mo didn't discriminate against any race or size. If she was pretty, Mo flirted. A White woman said yes to a dance. Her guy didn't like it. Pool shooting friends helped her boyfriend out. Black airmen, unknown to Mo and Emerson, jumped in. In the service, the brothers stuck together against common enemies.

"We kicked butts and, once again, you backed me up, my friend."

Emerson didn't enjoy fighting. As a kid, he used to beat up his younger brother, but Emerson outgrew that behavior. Mo never met a brawl he didn't want to be in. Reluctance to rumble aside, Emerson believed friends helped each other out, especially in the racially tense service. People enlisted from all parts of the country. A lot of southern White guys served, drank, and slept next to poor Black men. Differences and biases led to far too many conflicts. So, the brothers stuck together. No matter where you were, a brother sees you, he says hello. If you're new, he shows you the ropes. Get in trouble, he's got your back. The only criterion was being Black in a White man's world.

Mo said, "You and I should start a business."

Emerson eyed Mo but made no comment.

"A high-end men's clothing store with beautiful women serving champagne and strawberries while the customers get their fittings."

"What do we know about—?"

"Okay, okay. But something cool. Anyways, ponder it." He shut his eyes again and in seconds was snoring.

Emerson turned eighteen on August 10, 1965, one year after the US began conscripting men for the war effort. The letter from the government declared him 1A. No way he'd end up in the Army for two deadly years, so before his enrollment date, he enlisted in the Air Force. He didn't mind. Being on a flight crew excited him. He'd travel on the government's dime. When he signed the papers, he imagined himself a pilot. But without a college degree, he didn't have a shot. Since graduating from high school, he attended college at night, and worked for a bank by day. No deferment for poor Black guys. And no officer or pilot school. When his dad was drafted in World War II, he made it to officer's candidate school on his smarts even though he only possessed a high school diploma. Those days were over.

Until now, all Emerson's assignments were in the States, but today, Mo and he flew towards the fray. They were both aerial photographers assigned to the 1370th Photomapping Wing, responsible for charting the terrain for intelligence officers. On a flight crew. Almost as good as being a pilot.

Emerson closed his eyes too, listened to his friend's breathing. Mo either reminisced or imagined cushy opportunities when his four years were up. Kiki and the baby never seemed to fit into Mo's dreams.

Unlike Mo, Emerson focused on the here and now. Thirty-thousand feet in the air, a sergeant's chevrons on his uniform, soaring over the largest ocean on Earth, to an unknown fate. It felt good. Even though Kiki remained off limits, he'd find the right woman.

The crackle of the intercom woke Mo. "What's up?" He scrubbed his eyes.

"Listen." A foreboding moved through Emerson.

The pilot announced, "We just learned that an assassin killed Dr. Martin Luther King, Jr. in Memphis, Tennessee. Shot while standing on a balcony outside his second-floor room at the Lorraine Motel. He died today at 1905 hours central time."

What the fuck? It sounded like the pilot was reporting turbulence or time for chow. Emerson stood. Heat pumped through his body. There were groans and some inappropriate laughter. Emerson scrutinized everyone he could see from his spot. Most of the airmen were White. Only eight brothers were on the flight, sitting together in two rows.

Mo jumped up and stood next to Emerson. "This is fucked up."

Another Black man rose. "What the hell are we doing here?" he yelled at the White faces staring at him. "Who are we fighting for?"

Black men asked this question since World War I and even earlier. At least during the Civil War, they knew. Before, during, and since then, people treated Black folks like crap, discriminated against, lynched, stopped for no reason, and shoved into jail. They signed up for WWI, hoping for change that didn't come. They answered the call in WWII, like Emerson's dad, trusting things would improve. The G.I. Bill helped some earn college degrees, and there were housing programs, but memories were short and bigotry flinty. Life returned to discrimination and slammed doors. When the Vietnam War started, the government drafted and shipped men to South-East Asia while anti-war protestors called the service men names, and the privileged received deferments. Some fled to Canada.

Dr. King envisioned something different—a way forward. Well, so much for that dream.

One of the White airmen shouted down Mo and the other Black men. "You're fighting for your country. The good ole US of A. Shut the fuck up."

Mo remained standing, expression tight as a fist, and his long arms clasped on the back of his head.

Emerson flopped into his seat, looked away, and let the angry voices swirl around him. His breath turned hot. Fighting for whose country? Blown up in the mud. Die in cages after being captured and tortured. Last year, brothers made up twenty-five percent of combat units despite being only twelve percent of the military. But things were supposed to be better. Dr. King pushed for change—the end of racial disparity in combat units and the lack of Black officers. A glimmer of hope Emerson embraced. Hours before, he looked forward to an adventure, believed the war was central to America's interests like President Johnson said, and racial inequities were being addressed. He was protecting democracy from communism while getting to see the world. Fly secret missions. Win-win.

But they murdered Dr. King—a man preaching peace, non-violent change, and hope. Now it all tasted like ashes of stupidity. Fury surged through him. Like a boxer toughening up his hands, he punched his right fist into his left palm again and again, until the physical pain became unbearable.

CHAPTER EIGHT

April 8, 1968, Tuy Hoa, Vietnam

In the late afternoon, Mo and Emerson's plane landed on the Tuy Hoa Air Base. A wall of sweltering heat slammed Emerson the minute he stepped out of the plane. Perspiration dried as fast as his body produced it. He clambered down the aircraft steps. The stunning news of Dr. King's assassination cloaked him in despair.

A corporal gave them a quick tour, pointing out the mess hall and noncom club next to the officer's spot. Grunts hung out some place else. An infirmary and barber shop stood close to the clubs. Smells of diesel fuel, the funk of sweat, cigarettes, and unfamiliar food assailed Emerson's nostrils. Tiny Vietnamese women, dressed in flowing tunics and pants, swept past them on their way to work assignments on the base. Their guide pointed out soldiers from South Korea, Thailand, and the Philippines, all allies in the war.

The first night, Emerson couldn't sleep. Their Quonset hut, a semicircular structure made from corrugated metal, which served as living quarters on the base, housed twenty men. Single cots lined up with footlockers at the end of each. The latrines, wood structures standing next to each other, were a quick walk from the hooch, the name used for sleeping quarters.

Every time a bomb exploded, which seemed never-ending, Emerson jolted. Death seemed imminent. Terror gripped his gut. He looked around and saw no one else quaking with fear. Men snored in the surrounding beds, oblivious to the noise and earth shaking. Someone played music on a record player–a song begging a young girl to get out of his life.

Most of the men arrived weeks and months earlier. They warned Emerson about the constant explosions and told him he'd get used to it. The Americans, their allies, and South Vietnamese army used the bombs and shellings to keep the Viet Cong at bay, retaliate for an attack or to destroy their supply lines. The enemy fired back. Tuy Hoa's proximity to the sea made it a strategic staging area. This knowledge did not make Emerson feel safer.

Two days later, the bombings kept him up, but the terror subsided. Okay, perhaps this was it, the place and hour he'd die. He couldn't let fear rob him of his remaining time. Live in the moment, he reminded himself.

A crumbled gum wrapper hit Emerson in the head.

"You awake?" Mo asked from his cot an arm's length away.

"I am *now*." He opened his eyes. Mo sat on his bed; his long, slender frame hunched forward.

"Can't sleep? Me either."

The blasts were only part of the reason for Emerson's sleeplessness. Dr. King's murder consumed Emerson. Like the sweat oozing from every one of his pores, a rage-tinged sadness festered just below the surface. Street riots and protests broke out all over the US. In Nam, the anger simmered.

The clock read 0200 and eight-five degrees Fahrenheit. Although they were on the coast, the beach within walking distance, no ocean breezes cooled them. Inside the hooch, the air smelled like stale beer, dried sweat, and the ever present acrid scent of cigarette smoke.

Like Emerson, Mo wore briefs and a T-shirt. Sweat stains yellowed the cotton under each armpit and perspiration coated his face. "This place is crazy. The base is crawling with Vietnamese women."

"You gonna clean the latrine, wash sheets, scrub pots?"

"Okay, but how do we know some of them ain't the VC?"

A distant bomb shook the ground. "I donno. They check IDs?" Security posts ringed the base. Several check points stopped visitors at regular intervals. "But I get your point. They're all the same people." He grabbed his smokes, shook one out of the pack, placed a Winston between his lips, and tried to light it, but another bomb's reverberations sent it flying.

"I gotcha," Mo said. He retrieved Emerson's cigarette, lit it, and then helped himself from Emerson's pack.

Emerson sucked the smoke into his lungs and blew it out and away from Mo's face. "It will be good to get into the air tomorrow." Except he'd yet to sleep. He took another drag.

Vince Quick strode over. "Can't sleep, either?" Unlike Emerson and Mo, the older man wore fatigues, dark green with his last name stenciled in white on a blue patch over the right pocket, and U.S. Air Force stenciled over the left. Five chevrons on his sleeves denoted his rank as Tech Sergeant, above Mo and Emerson's positions of Staff Sergeant.

"Thought you long-timers were used to the bombs," Emerson said, offering his pack of cigarettes.

Quicksilver, the name other guys called Vince, shook his head. "That stuff is lethal."

"Nah," Mo said. "According to who?"

"What's got you up?" Emerson asked. He didn't want a discussion about smoking. Chances were, he'd die in Nam, so why worry about cigarettes? They kept him calm, helped pass the time. He wasn't about to give them up.

"Dr. King." Quicksilver's words sounded bitter. Emerson guessed Quick's age was late twenties compared to Emerson's soon to be twenty-one.

"Yeah," Emerson said. "Makes ya wonder." Over chow earlier, and during drills, the brothers muttered about Dr. King's murder, the lack of civil rights for Black folks, and the blatant racism of most of the White guys on base. Or it seemed that way. A look interpreted as a dig rather than curiosity. But there was enough overt stuff to keep you on your toes and disgruntled.

"Makes me mad," Quicksilver said. "Nothing to wonder about. White folks gunned him down, just like they always do."

"Heard anything else? What the Feds doing about it?" Emerson asked.

"FBI dogged King for years. Feds won't do jack shit," Mo said.

Quicksilver eyed Mo as if deciding something. "Folks are rioting all over. Chicago, DC, and Baltimore."

"Not according to the *Stars and Stripes*," Emerson said, referring to the only newspaper available. "Two new guys filled us in."

"Keep your head on a swivel," Quicksilver said. "White folks be jumpy, wondering what we're thinking, what we gonna do. Stay cool."

Emerson hit his fist against his chest in acknowledgement. He'd run into racism in Texas and Georgia, a lot less in Kansas. But once the news hit about Dr. King, he reassessed every encounter.

Quicksilver walked over to the next bunk where the brothers were sleeping and stopped. Emerson couldn't hear what he said. Looked like Quicksilver woke them up.

After several minutes of silence, Mo said, "When I get out, I'm gonna open a club."

Emerson's eyebrows rose. "That's what you're thinking about?" Once again, Mo left today for the future. That was okay. Focusing on King, the Viet Cong, race riots. Too much.

"My own place," Mo continued. "It'll be hopping, playing Motown and jazz. Not this Okefenokee stuff." He tilted his head toward the music's source.

The singer wailed again, 'you're much too young girl.' The guy must have played the same song a half dozen times. Guilty conscience?

"My place will have gorgeous women working the bar and gambling in the back room." He grinned. "Legal stuff only."

"So, not a men's clothing store." Emerson ground out his cigarette. He'd hang with Mo in his daydream. If Emerson didn't get some shut eye, his brain would be mush in the morning. Pleasant thoughts about Mo's club might make sleep possible. Except images of Kiki often intruded, making him feel guilty and disloyal.

Mo laughed at himself. "Anyways, what are you gonna do when you're back in the world?" The world was home.

"First, I gotta stay alive tomorrow. Then the next day."

"A man needs plans. Hopes."

Emerson's dad used to say that. "Find your purpose and direction, son. Can't drift through life without a compass and a map."

Once again, Emerson noted Mo's omission of Kiki and the baby. Maybe she'd be free by the time they left the service. Mo hooked up with another woman. He nodded to his friend, hoping his face didn't betray his thoughts. "I'll try to keep your advice in mind."

Mo lay back on his bed.

Emerson closed his eyes and tried not to think.

CHAPTER NINE
JAX

Wednesday, March 13, Fieldcrest, NY

Jax Oats couldn't stay still. He rose up and down on his toes, as if exercising his calf muscles, shoved his hands in his pockets, pulled them out, and then repeated the action for the sixth time. Starbucks, packed with people like Jax and Stephen, waiting to order or milling about until their drinks were ready, exuded busy comfort.

"You're wired," Stephen said. "Better skip the caffeine."

Few people believed Jax and Stephen were brothers. And no one believed Charlie was. Jax's eyes were deep green, his hair curly and chestnut brown, and his feet, arms, and fingers were long and lean. In contrast, Stephen, Jax's older sibling by a year, was a sandy brunette, blue-eyed, four inches shorter. A scruff covered his cheeks and chin. Jax looked like their biological father, and Stephen, their mother. If one examined them, they'd see the same wide-set eyes and curly lashes their mother bequeathed them, and their father's prominent nose with a crease at the tip, like the dimple on his chin. Diplomates, their mother liked to say. Even distribution from both sides.

Charlie entered the cafe. "Order me coffee black. Vente." The largest size Starbucks offered. "I'll grab a table."

The third sibling was not a blood relative. Brothers by choice. Charlie's tawny brown complexion, shaved smooth, contrasted with opaque violet eyes. Broad shoulders made up for his shorter stature.

Jax and Stephen advanced in line.

Stephen asked again, "What's going on?"

"It's Aria."

"You got the courage to ask her out," Stephen said, chuckling. "And she turned you down?"

"A guy got killed in Fieldcrest."

"I heard."

"Aria found the body." Jax tapped his fingertips together. "She clocked the murderer, twice. He threatened her. I mean, in her face. Said he'd kill her."

"Whoa. That was *your* Aria?"

"She isn't mine." Jax's only long-term relationship ended in heartbreak. He wanted marriage and children. Maria did too, but not with him. "Aria and I are friends."

The barista, a pretty woman with a pouty mouth and blue streaks in her black hair, asked, "What can I get started for you?"

The Oats brothers ordered drinks, plus three slices of pumpkin bread. Pop music played in the background. Servers with headphones took orders from drive-through customers. Stephen and Jax joined the small group of people who expected their name to be called as soon as their drinks were ready.

"Jax," a barista called. Stephen and Jax grabbed their beverages.

Charlie stood and waved his brothers over.

"We might have a problem," Charlie said the minute Stephen and Jax sat down. He passed his phone to Jax. Stephen leaned in to read the text message as well. "*Watch your back. Someone clever and dangerous has pierced your defenses.*"

"What does that mean?" Stephen asked, his voice tinged with scorn. "Who the hell sent it?"

"Unknown number."

Jax stared at the message. "It could be a crank. Why not identify themselves?" The technical side of their cyber security business was his responsibility. Stephen ran sales and customer service. Administration, HR, legal, and finances fell under Charlie's authority. "I'll check everything out and report."

"It's nothing," Stephen said. "Someone is messing with us."

"Yeah, well," Jax said. "Just in case."

The table fell quiet as the men ate and drank.

Stephen broke the silence. His eyes on Charlie, he asked, "You hear about the murder in Fieldcrest?"

"Yeah. Isn't that your girl's operation?" Charlie asked Jax.

"She's *not* my girl," Jax said again, sounding annoyed. Except both of his brothers knew Jax fell in love with Aria during the early months they worked together–he as a volunteer and donor, and she as the boss.

"And won't be at this rate," Stephen said. "You gotta make a move, big guy."

His brothers, both married with young children, teased him all the time. "When's the last time you got laid?" "Who are you bringing to the holiday party? Better not be cousin, Faye." In his twenties, Jax didn't miss having a steady relationship. They were building a company, innovating, scrambling to stay ahead. Then, he met Maria and fell hard. Women always perplexed him and with Maria, he had no clue.

"I can't stay," Jax said, changing the subject, but not. "Need to head to The Way Station."

"What are the police saying?" Charlie mumbled, his hand covering his pumpkin bread filled mouth. "Any leads yet?"

"Nope."

That was the problem. No clues. At least none they were sharing. Only Aria saw the killer. No one stood out on security footage. Nor did anyone trip the metal detector alarm. The killer escaped through a back door. Instead of the cameras on the exterior walls photographing him, a blind spot let him slip through the alley undetected and the next door Bodega's camera failed to pick him up when he left the alley. As if he knew where the cameras focused, the guy disappeared in broad daylight.

In an exasperated voice, Stephen said, "Details, please."

His brothers often got frustrated with Jax's reticence. He tried to do better. After explaining the camera situation, he said, "Two neighborhood kids, looking in a nearby dumpster for an errant soccer ball, spied a discarded black mask near The Way Station."

"Okay," said Stephen. "Progress."

"Nope again."

"Why not?"

"According to the police, the kids, excited by a murder happening so close to home, ran to The Way Station and told an officer parked in front."

Before Jax finished the story, Charlie asked in a skeptical tone. "For real? They took it to the cops?"

"We have a strong neighborhood police program."

"We?" Charlie asked.

"The Way Station."

"Cool," Stephen said, but Charlie still looked doubtful. "So, what happened?"

"No fingerprints or other identifying markers. All the trash in the dumpster compromised DNA from the mask."

"Whose keeping you informed?" Stephen said.

"Aria, who received a personal briefing from the lead detective." That was another problem—Glover, spending time with Aria. Good-looking guys like him enjoyed more women than they could bed. Jax knew because of Stephen. Women threw themselves at him. From as early as their teenaged years, Stephen got invited to parties and exclusive gatherings. Charlie and Jax were tagalongs. "I gotta jet. Meeting Aria, then heading to the office. Meanwhile, I'll call E-Man, and get his crew started on the possible fissure in our cyber walls." E-Man led the security team under Jax.

Charlie said to Stephen, "Be prepared to soothe our clients in case the breach is real."

"Yeah, already thought of that."

Jax stood. "I'll be there by one."

"Why so late?"

"Personal matter." Jax planned to take Aria to lunch. Of course, he'd not asked her, and yesterday she turned him down. The text message nagged him, but he put it aside. If the breach was serious, E-Man would track Jax down.

CHAPTER TEN

Jax sat across from Aria in the small diner on Gov Ave, the main street that ran north to south and marked the east and west sides of Fieldcrest.

The narrow diner held red booths on both sides of the center aisle. The kitchen in the back spanned the width of the trolley-car-like structure. Red and black vinyl covered the seats, and white table tops gleamed from recent polishing.

"One club sandwich?" the server asked, holding two plates.

"Here," Jax said. "Thanks."

She placed the Cobb salad in front of Aria. "Can I get you anything else?"

"I'm good," Aria said.

"Me too."

They both tucked into their meals and didn't speak for several minutes.

"How's Zander?" Jax began, hoping for a safe start. Aria's lips disappeared, pulled in with a grimace. "What? Is he okay?"

"I don't know." She pulled a tissue from her purse and patted her eyes. "He's not called or texted me. I'm thinking of driving to Ithaca tomorrow." She blew her nose. "Sorry."

"No. Don't be."

"This crying has to stop."

"You experienced a terrible shock." Her distress sent ripples of emotion through him.

"The police want me to stay in town. But he's my son and his first time on his own. He never even attended summer camp. Enjoyed hanging with my husband and me."

"What does the university say?"

"He missed all his classes this week. Detective Yun asked the local police to make a wellness call, but he wasn't in his room." Aria's eyes filled up again, and tears rolled down her cheeks. "Poor Emerson. And now Zan. I…" She didn't finish her sentence.

Jax wanted to slide next to her and pull her close. "I can go with you."

Aria looked up. He loved her face. Rose brown skin as smooth as someone twenty years younger. Big brown eyes. A mouth he'd wanted to kiss.

"To Ithaca?"

"Sure."

"I couldn't ask you, but thanks."

"You're not asking. I'm offering. Don't go by yourself."

"I can take care of myself," she said, her tone offended, but her eyes were still teary.

Jax recognized the chip she sometimes carried on her shoulder. It appeared when people doubted her. "For sure. But I drive a Jeep, which is good in the snow, unlike your Mini Cooper."

"My car is just fine." She stared at him, as if daring him to disagree.

Damn. The last time Jax felt like this was ten years and a heartbreak ago. There'd been other women, but casual. And those were nothing like this.

"Don't you have work?"

The whistle-blower's text popped into his head. "I have to check into a potential problem this afternoon, but I can clear my calendar for tomorrow."

She chewed her lower lip. "I have so many meetings."

He watched her figure things out. He could look at her all day. What a sap I am, he thought.

"Yes. Thank you. I will make tomorrow work." She dabbed at her eyes and cheeks. "Where do we begin?"

Jax struggled to keep his tone serious. He didn't want to scare her away by letting her see his joy. Dating rules eluded him. When are you supposed to show your feelings, how often to call, how do you know it's not working out? Maria complained all the time that he was insensitive. A computer nerd and serious introvert, sharing his feelings came hard. "Not to worry. Sleuthing is my business. We'll figure it out."

She smiled at him. A bright, beautiful smile.

They finished their food and coffee, slid out of the booth, and grabbed their coats hanging on hooks next to them.

Jax asked, "How are you getting to the office?"

"Driving." She gave him a look.

"Okay, but are you taking precautions? What did Glover say?"

She frowned at Jax. "Nothing." She pulled on her gloves and wrapped her head in a bright blue scarf. "Like what?"

"Not being predictable in your routes and stops. Stuff like that."

The frown deepened.

Jax couldn't believe Glover didn't give her tips and warnings. Were they taking the murderer's threats seriously? "Stay on Gov Ave. Lots of traffic this time a day. Be aware of your surroundings. Lock your doors. Check your mirrors."

They moved toward the diner's front door. The woman who brought them their lunches sidled by them, both hands holding plates of food above their heads.

Aria gave a little laugh. "That's what I told my parents."

"See. Good advice. And don't park in the lot behind The Way Station," he added. "Ask one of your security guards to park for you."

She looked up at him. "That's not their responsibility."

"It is." He used the tone he heard Charlie project when he wanted to end a debate. His this-is-my-final word voice. "Call security now and tell them you're coming. Ask them to meet you at the front and to please park your car." He waited. Charlie was much better at it. Quiet like Jax, his collaborative and accomplished team gave Jax no reason to cajole. "Please, Aria. This is important. Someone murdered Emerson, and the killer is still out there."

Aria's annoyed expression disappeared. "You're right. I'll call from the car."

"I'll pick you up tomorrow morning."

And there it was again. Her bright, beautiful smile.

CHAPTER ELEVEN
ARIA

I pulled my Cooper in front of The Way Station and waited for security. Jax's offer to go with me to Ithaca lifted my spirits. Scared me too. We'd need to keep the trip on-the-down-low. Valentine would frown on a personal relationship, even a platonic one, with a top donor. Of course, this was a friend helping. And how come Errol and Yun didn't warn me about being predictable? Once again, I felt grateful for Jax.

I ran through my mental action list. Ask Ginger to move Thursday's and Friday's meetings to Monday just in case Jax and I ran into roadblocks finding Zander and had to stay over. The snowstorm might cause problems as well. I pursed my lips and puffed out air. Everyone will understand I need a break–a long weekend to get my equilibrium back.

I returned to my to-do list. Best to tell Ginger where I'm going. Lacy too. Funeral arrangements for Emerson–what to do? On his volunteer application, he listed Kiki Alexander as next of kin. I called her. The conversation left me sad for Emerson. She gasped when I told her how he died, but other than that, no real emotion.

The mayor, although sympathetic, rescheduled our ten minutes to later in the month. I required her help to secure a state grant, but that was the least of my problems now. Ginger squeezed the budget meeting and time with Valentine, Wally, and Lacy into this afternoon. Just thinking about all the meetings made me tired.

A young woman in a security uniform walked toward me and pulled the car door open. I clambered out. She stood a few inches taller than me in my heels, a solid build buffed up by the bulk of the uniform and gear.

"Afternoon, Ms. Wright."

We approached the building, and she pulled open the lobby door. I stepped inside and waved to the receptionist, Gladys, behind the glass. She buzzed us in, and the officer held the second door open for me as well.

"Thank you." Her name escaped me. "How is your day going?" I glanced at the left breast pocket of her shirt. "Anything suspicious to report, Officer Applegate?" When I became CEO, I insisted we refer to our security team as officers. That designation increased both the respect given by the staff and the public and enhanced the team's feelings of self-worth and, therefore, their effectiveness.

"All's quiet."

I handed her my keys. "Thanks for parking it for me, even though valet service is not in your job description."

"No worries. Happy to do it."

Her voice held a note of caution. She appeared ready to say more. "But...?"

She hesitated for a few more beats. "Folks are still on edge. There's a worry-vibe zipping through. Your call kinda added to it."

"Indeed. That's an excellent description. Prayerfully, things will return to normal soon." I glanced around. "Are you on duty by yourself?"

"Officer Samson is taking a quick bio break."

"Okay. Stay vigilant."

"Not sure what I'm looking for. The killer returning to murder again? Why The Way Station?"

Good point, with no rational response. "Precaution. I lack answers."

"Okay," Officer Applegate said, her tone tinged with worry.

"May I ask you a question?"

"Sure."

"How did the shooter get past security? Any theories?"

We instituted a strict check-in system. Because of the neighborhood and mass shootings in the papers with increased frequency, visitors entered the building into a lobby. A receptionist behind a reinforced-glass partition greeted them, scrutinized their ID, and asked whom they were meeting with. Then checked with the staff member or volunteer and alerted them.

Clients entered through the west lobby and walked through a metal detector. How did the killer get by? Do we need to add more security guards? I made a mental note to bring the issue up with Tito Johnson and Wally, the CFO.

Officer Applegate said, "The police interrogated us. Took the camera recordings. No clues."

I wrung my gloved hands. "That's what the detectives said."

"Perhaps through the front door as a staff member or volunteer's guest."

"Do we need metal detectors in the front lobby too?"

"Mr. Johnson is on top of things. I think he is." She shrugged. "I'll put your car in your usual spot."

"Please wait for your partner to return."

"Gotcha."

As I walked to my office, instead of thinking about how the killer got inside with two weapons, a song tried to push through. A most inappropriate one. "Walking on Sunshine. And Don't It Feel Good?" What was that about? I laughed at myself. Of course, I understood. Amid worry and danger, Jax dominated my thoughts. Yikes.

Refocusing, I glanced at my watch. Valentine agreed to come at 4:00. Although the entire board of twenty-one members served as my boss, the chair held power. I needed him on my side, a partner, helping me solve the organization's problems. To prepare for the meeting, I re-set time with Wally and Lacy, so I could have a strong understanding of our financial exposure, the reasons behind our crummy balance sheet, and why our building project stalled. I'd have to miss the budget discussion.

•   •   •

Wally Wallace possessed an unfortunate face. The forehead typically occupied a third of the face. In Wally's case, it covered one half, like a shiny movie screen above his eyes. The rest of his features looked diminutive.

Eyebrows, eyes, nose, mouth, and chin cramped together on the bottom half. I'd often thought a beard might help him look more balanced. But his bright white skin held no shadow of hair. Anywhere.

"Isn't Lacy joining us?" Wally asked. He plopped into an armchair in the sitting area.

Lacy Quarles, rich brown, five-foot-nine inches of tight muscles, director of fund development and marketing, befriended me in high school. Shy and lacking confidence, I often walked to school, ate lunch, and returned home alone. Lacy rescued me. Outgoing and confident, she introduced me to her friends, invited me to all the parties, and defended me when bullies made fun of my diminutive stature.

I rose from behind my desk, laptop in hand, carried it over to the couch and pulled up the charts Wally sent earlier.

Lacy dashed in. Shrugged out of her fitted long coat, brick red that matched the tam on her head. She tugged off her matching red gloves, pulled the hat down, and stuffed all three items into her coat pockets. "It's so cold out. What happened to global warming?" She laughed. "Just joking." She smoothed her hair. "I'm ready."

Lacy and I faced Wally. I called the meeting to order with a question. "We expect Valentine in..." I glanced at my watch. "Ninety minutes. I need to give him an honest, fact-based assessment and a plan for moving forward concerning our diminished balance sheet and stalled building project."

My vision, a reaction to a stubborn and dehumanizing problem, was to build an accessible apartment complex of temporary housing units for unhoused families, and adults, who enrolled in our career and school programs. On the first floor, we planned daycare and a second after-school center for residents, both services free as long as the parents gained skills and applied for permanent jobs. School-aged children had to attend classes, and their parents stayed involved. The plan called for twenty apartments with one year leases.

"What do you have for us, Wally?"

Wally appeared and sounded uncomfortable. "You receive the same reports I do."

This was a poor response. "Pretend I'm Valentine Bannister."

Wally squirmed. "You missed the budget meeting."

I gave him a withering look.

"Okay... I've scrubbed the budget. Got it down to bare bones." He cleared his throat. "Cut back on one of the food shifts. Or stop the dinner takeaway cartons. I've seen people take three or four."

"Feeding people nutritious food is a staple of our core mission." I suspected Wally lacked compassion for the people we served. When I became CEO, he'd been on board for many years. Valentine suggested I keep Wally and with time decide for myself. I agreed since I had a slew of other changes to implement. "They're welcome to extra portions." I mentally shook my head. "Besides, those meager cuts will not close the gap."

Wally shifted his eyes away from mine. "Lacy needs to close larger gifts."

"Oh my. News to me," Lacy said.

I jumped in. "Okay guys, neither sarcasm nor finger-pointing is going to solve our financial woes or save me this afternoon." I remembered the security situation. "Plus, we might need to hire more guards and strengthen our protocols."

"Don't put them on payroll." Wally sounded emphatic. "Sub-contract, so we don't have to pay benefits."

That made sense. Despite a large contingent of volunteers, payroll made up our biggest expense, second only to the under-construction apartment building. Jax might know a good firm. I could also check with my fellow CEOs of other charities and ask for referrals, starting with Joe Dawes, who ran The People's Theater. He knew everyone and finished an expansive building project. I added this item to my mental to-do list.

"The officers are just one minor issue in a sea of them," I said.

"Look," Wally said, "inflation is killing us, supply chains are broken, and investing in this part of the city unappealing. We need deep cuts. Period."

Lacy leaned forward, "We're waiting for a yes from the Laura Garrison Foundation. That, plus an increase from Valentine, might smooth things out. The apartment building is a different issue. Every time I check, the cost-estimates go up." She sat back. "We're not the only organization in this fix. At a recent meeting with my peers, several mentioned similar problems."

Wally almost growled. "That's what I'm saying. Inflation. But we can't slow down or abandon the housing project, since we've already sunk a lot of money into it."

"One thing at a time. Lacy, doesn't Laura invest in the arts? We can't count on her foundation coming through."

"Valentine knows her from the People's Theater board. Yes, she supports the arts but cares about Fieldcrest. The Boys and Girls Club receives annual gifts from her foundation. I'm sure others do as well. She prefers anonymity."

The local community theater, after struggling for years, enjoyed a rebirth, thanks to Laura. I scheduled lunch or drinks with CEO Joe Dawes at least once a quarter. He shared how Laura saved the theater a few years back. "I can pick Joe's brain." He may have ideas for approaching the foundation for Hope House, the name I dubbed our future building.

Lacy said, "Perfect conversation with Valentine. Explain, we've slashed the budget, are making solicitation calls and visits, and we need you to increase your gift and secure a substantial one from your dear friend Laura." Lacy grinned. "Give him work to do while we make moves over the next few weeks."

"Okay." Something still bothered me. "Wally, I'd like to see a comparison of expenses for the last two years, to this year. Also, the original bids from the contractors, how much they've spent to date, and how their first projections compare to what they are charging now."

He groaned.

"Is that a problem?"

"No," he said, sounding the opposite. "It'll take me some time."

That didn't sound right either, but I let it go. "Let's shoot for Monday."

CHAPTER TWELVE

Valentine Bannister wheeled into my office. His muscled arms handled the chair with ease. To get around, he drove a modified Tahoe van which didn't require the use of his feet. Instead, he accessed the gas pedal and brake from hand gears. He kept his collapsable wheelchair behind the driver's seat and swung it outside via the automatic sliding side door. Next, he leaned from the front seat, opened his chair, and lowered himself into it. Bulging biceps spoke to his ability to take care of himself.

"Good afternoon," I said, approaching Valentine with my right hand outstretched. "Let me hang your jacket." I took his outer garment. As always, he wore a suit and tie. But he liked to shed the jacket and roll up his sleeves when meeting with clients, fellow board members, and me.

"Any news from the police?" he asked, rolling himself closer to my desk.

"No, unfortunately."

I pulled a chair over, so we were eye to eye. Valentine was a good-looking man. His gray hair streaked with the remaining black complemented gray eyes. Square-jaw and a muscled chest gave off an air of vigor that his wheelchair didn't diminish.

"I checked in with the chief of detectives," he said. "We're old friends. His assessment of Glover and Yun is positive. They're the ones you've been dealing with, correct?"

Fieldcrest's power brokers and wealthy homeowners were few. Most knew each other.

"It's good to hear the chief respects them," I said. Not the topic I wanted to discuss.

He eyed me with a penetrating stare that expected a truthful answer to whatever question was coming. "How are you holding up?"

"I'm fine."

"In what way?"

That was a strange query. "As expected, given the circumstances."

He nodded as if agreeing with my assessment.

I pivoted to the chief topic. I didn't want Valentine or any board members to question my ability to carry on. "Wally is available to review the financials. Did you receive the reports via email earlier today?"

"Not edifying."

True. I unclenched my hands. "Wally will be here until 6:00. Before meeting with him, I was hoping we might discuss gap-closing gifts."

He opened his mouth as if to speak, but I plunged ahead. "How are you doing with securing the $500,000 from Laura Garrison's foundation?"

Laura Garrison was a lovely woman. She no longer lived in Fieldcrest. When she married her now deceased, wealthy husband, she moved into a mansion in a neighboring city. But her hometown remained important to her, especially art programs in our schools, a small museum she helped build and curate, and the community theater.

"I've yet to follow up. Wanted to see our numbers first." Valentine slid out a slim briefcase that rested between his hip and the right side of the wheelchair. "Things look bleak to me."

So much for my pivot.

"I will meet with Wallace, but I'm asking you. What the hell is going on?"

Crap. "No clue," I said, abandoning my strategy to focus on him. "Lacy, Wally, and I just met. I've asked Wally for a two-year expense comparison against this year and construction costs compared to original bids. Something is amiss."

Valentine dipped his head forward. "I agree. And I expect a better answer than 'no clue' when next we meet."

Ouch. I braced my shoulders. "I'll ferret it out," I said. "We'll make things right." Lacy's voice came to me. "Meanwhile, I was hoping to discuss your gift."

. . .

I stayed at my desk, unsure of Valentine's preference after speaking with Wally. There was always work to do—requests from human resources, programs, security, volunteer management, finance, marketing, or fundraising. The stack of waiting thank you calls sat on the corner of my desk.

"Can I come in?" Lacy asked, standing in the open doorway, a shopping bag in her hand.

"Of course." A friendly face who brought good news or solutions rather than trouble.

Lacy flopped on the couch, kicked off her heels, and put her feet up on one of the facing chairs. The bag rested on the floor under her legs. "How'd things go with Valentine?"

"Tough conversation. He's with Wally. I'm waiting to hear." I paced around the room, nervous energy surging.

"Saw Valentine drive off."

"Oh." That was odd.

"Did he say yes to increasing his contribution?"

I stopped moving. Embarrassed, I said, "I asked, but failed to get an answer."

Lacy shook her head. "No worries," she said, letting me off the hook. "Any discussion of Laura Garrison?"

"Promised to follow up after he felt more confident of our financials."

Lacy said, "Cop a squat."

I sat next to her, my shoeless feet up as well. "I need a glass of wine."

"Lacy to the rescue." She tugged open the shopping bag and pulled out a bottle of Chianti and two wine glasses stuffed with paper towels to protect them in transport. The screw cap twisted off, and she poured.

I took a long gulp. "Ahh." Took another swallow, sipping this time rather than swigging. "I have a favor to ask."

"Anything."

"We'll need to bury Emerson. Can you pull something together?"

"Sure. Do we know what his family wants?"

"In our HR records, Emerson entered his full name–Calvin Ross Emerson, and listed Kiki Alexander as his next of kin with no reference to their relationship. He scrawled a phone number for her, but no address."

"What happened when you called her?"

"Took the news in a matter-of-fact manner, except when I explained how he died, and by the end of the conversation, confirmed she and her son plan to attend the funeral. So, I responded."

Now Lacy looked concerned. "You told her...what?"

"I'm sorry. Hoping we can hold his service on Saturday."

"We?"

I laughed. "The royal we."

"Kiki Alexander and her son are not interested?"

"Only as guests."

"How are *we* paying for it?"

I lifted my shoulders and hands palms up. Tilted my head.

"Okay. I got the message. Ginger and I will figure it out."

"Pastor Joy might have ideas. It's her wheelhouse." Like Lacy, Joy was a childhood friend.

"I'll call her." Lacy patted my knee. "How are you?"

Her tone mirrored Valentine's, demanding a truthful response. But it was a hard question to answer. A murderer lurked. Money woes dogged us. Zan might be in trouble. My face must have shown all I was thinking.

"As bad as that?"

"Hmm."

"What's the latest?" Lacy took a ladylike sip of Chianti.

"Jax and I are driving to Cornell tomorrow." I filled her in on the missing Zander and Jax's offer.

"Sure you're making the right move?"

"No." My confidence plummeted every few minutes.

"I thought Jax was wrong for you–too rich, too White, too young, and, if I remember correctly, too tall."

"How do basketball players make love with average height women?"

"What?" Her mouth twitched like she was suppressing laughter.

"I've been trying to imagine it."

"Girl. Are you and Jax planning on shacking-up in Ithaca?"

I twisted my head toward her. "No. Of course not." My cheeks flushed. "Just wondering."

"I'm sure the mythical basketball player and his petite lady will figure it out. Is that why you keep running from Jax? You're afraid you won't be able to have sex because he's so tall?" This time, she laughed aloud.

"Don't make fun of me."

"And since when is rich a negative? Pu-lease." She topped off both of our glasses.

"He's a donor and a volunteer. Conflict of interest." I put my glass down since I still had to drive home.

"Ben's been gone two years."

"Never dated a White man."

"First time for everything. Jax is good people."

I was about to add he was single at forty. According to his bio, Jax never married. Why not? Instead, I smiled at my friend. Saying my objections aloud made them seem small and silly. Except that it *was* too soon. And Zan. What would he think? "We'll see."

CHAPTER THIRTEEN
EMERSON

April 19, 1968, Tuy Hoa, Vietnam

Life on the base felt schizophrenic. The airmen flew recon for a day and then rested for two. The Army guys patrolled the dense jungles, slogging through muck every day. Charlie, the Viet Cong, or Victor Charlie shortened to just Charlie, waited for them, hid, struck, ran, and darted back. Soldiers returned to the base, eyes vacant, with mud stains up to their necks. Some didn't return. Huey helicopters flew to the nearest hospital base, those too mortally wounded for the infirmary to treat. The phat-phat-phat of Huey's blades always spelled trouble.

Army guys rarely spoke to airmen. Plus, the Army was taking over the Airbase. Emerson saw the signs as more Army brass arrived and a group of Vietnamese men built an officers' club.

Meanwhile, crew members like Mo and Emerson lazed around. When they were flying and working, Charlie shot at their C-130. Emerson carried a loaded revolver, even though regulations called for it to be empty. What did the brass expect him to do if Emerson's plane got shot down? Load his gun while parachuting into enemy hands? The chances of the plane being hit by a mortar were low. The plane flew 30,000 feet in the air. It was more unnerving than dangerous.

The schizophrenia also applied to the officers, noncoms, like Mo and Emerson, and the privates and corporals–the grunts. Plus, the Black and White issues. Vietnam and the war were a unique experience depending on one's race, gender, rank, and branch of service.

After flying all day on Thursday, Mo and Emerson sat on the sandy beach that edged the base, a good distance from the firepit, where Kobe steaks sizzled. Insects buzzed, thriving in the dense, humid air. Airmen, some in fatigues, others in T-shirts and shorts, dotted the shore. Frothy waves rolled in and receded, tinging the air with a salty scent spiced with the aroma of grilling meat. A captain and his crew, off for two days, flew to Japan and brought back the prized meat. Although it was only two in the afternoon, they'd all been drinking since eleven that morning watching the F4s bomb the VC in the surrounding mountains, cheering every time one hit.

The brothers sat in their own circle. It was a good day. One of the best since Emerson landed in Nam. The sun, for a change, wasn't furnace hot. The ocean breezes soothed their sunburnt skin. Lots of people, including Black folks, don't think Black skin can burn. Wrong. The sun turns dark skin into a wrinkled, ashy mess. Emerson pulled his jungle hat low over his brow.

"You gonna grab some?" Mo asked, tilting his chin toward the makeshift grill.

Emerson wasn't hungry. A nice hum filled his head. Sweat dripped from his scalp into his eyes. "You want some?" He swatted an insect droning near his ear.

"Yeah, but don't think I can get up." Mo pondered his circumstances. "Crawling's an option." Laughing, he got on all fours. "Whatcha think?"

"Nah." Emerson would have laughed too, but he was trying to navigate. "I'll get you some." Emerson swayed on his feet and then steadied. He stumbled toward the firepit, tripped on a piece of driftwood, and banged into a big dude carrying a tin plate of meat.

"Watch where you're going, boy." With one hand still holding his meal, the man shoved Emerson, who staggered backwards and landed on his butt.

Out of the corner of his eye, Emerson saw Mo scramble up. But he knew Mo was too high to help, so Emerson pushed up from the sand. He lurched toward the man and knocked his plate away. Meat flew in the air and landed with a thump. "You better watch where *you're* going."

To Emerson's surprise, Mo stood next to him, ready to brawl.

"Gotcha, bro."

Emerson's legs failed to cooperate. His knees buckled. The man dressed in fatigues Emerson now saw was a Captain. "Mo. No. It's okay." But Mo didn't hear him.

The captain was about Mo's height but twice as broad. Thick arms and barrel chest. A right landed in Mo's gut. He doubled over. Two fists, fingers entwined, came down on Mo's head and sent him crumpled to the ground. "You and your boy better get outta here," the captain said. "I'll have your asses locked up." Striking an officer was a serious crime.

With surprising strength, Mo sprang up and pushed into the captain, grabbing him around his middle. The momentum caused the captain to stagger backwards.

Emerson swayed and fell again.

Three brothers came and stood next to Emerson. One moved forward and separated Mo and the captain.

"No problem," the Black man said to the captain. "We all been drinking. You too."

Emerson recognized Quicksilver's voice.

"Come on, captain. We're all fucked up," Q said, sounding sober.

The captain glared at the men. "Cause it's you Quick. Only reason I'm letting this go." He turned and walked back toward the pit.

Quicksilver offered his hand to Mo and pulled him up. Did the same for Emerson. "You two need to sober up. He might change his mind."

"That motherfucker called Emerson boy." Mo spit out his words. "Shoved him. These crackers think they can push us around."

Quicksilver placed a hand on Mo's chest. "He ain't worth time in the brig."

One of the other brothers steadied Emerson on his feet.

"Let's go," Q said.

The men walked back to their spots. Quicksilver patted Emerson on the back. "You okay?"

Emerson wasn't. Shame washed over him but he nodded. "Thanks."

"You did fine, if that's what got you worried."

It was, but Emerson stayed quiet.

"Give yourself a break," Quicksilver said. "Everyone is drunk." He left as quietly as he'd appeared.

Mo grabbed another warm beer and gulped. There was no ice around, nothing to keep the beers cold. "What happened to you? I'm fighting and you're on your ass."

"Sorry." Bile roiled in Emerson's gut, despite what Q said.

"Soo-kay." Mo finished his beer. "Feel like crap." He flopped down, face first.

Emerson grabbed his friend by his armpits and hauled him up. "I gotcha."

But he didn't. Not when it counted, and it wasn't okay.

CHAPTER FOURTEEN

May 4, 1968, Bangkok, Thailand

Bangkok was a city on the move. Traditional Thai culture merged with a modernizing urban landscape. Three-wheeled vehicles called Tuk-tuks, bicycles, rickshaws, wooden carts, buses, US military Jeeps, and vintage cars crammed the streets. The sharp scent of diesel mingled with spices from street vendors.

Mo and Emerson arrived at 0900 on a Hercules, the C-130. A captain, with a series of hush-hush strategy meetings in Bangkok, commandeered the plane. Grateful Mo brushed aside the beach fiasco, Emerson invited Mo to join them, after clearing the invitation with command.

Three glorious days in this crazy place, thought Emerson. Mo grew up in a small Pennsylvania town. Although Emerson lived in New York State, it was a rural and impoverished community and the family rarely ventured south into The City, which was what New Yorkers called Manhattan.

They hopped out of the rickshaw, paid the driver in US dollars, and stared at the spectacle before them. Service men, tourists, and locals, moving shoulder to shoulder, packed New Petchburi Road. Neon signs, crowded together on the famous thoroughfare, announced establishments in Thai. The evening air, thick with humidity, cooled to a comfortable seventy-eight degrees–twenty-five Celsius.

The two friends scanned the road for the infamous Jack's American Star Bar–a reported haven for Black servicemen. Back home, protests against the war, and for civil rights, brimmed over into student rallies on college campuses, marches, riots, and police actions. News from the US created tension on the Tuy Hoa base. White servicemen kept to themselves, and brothers did the same, but sometimes they crossed paths and clashed like they did on the beach. Emerson's crew included four White members and Emerson. During flights, they worked well together, everyone doing his job. Wherever they landed, they split up along color lines. Just the way things were.

Emerson said, "The joint is supposed to be along here." He searched the traffic for an opening to cross.

Mo glanced left and stepped into the street. A Jeep barreled toward him.

Emerson grabbed Mo by his shirt collar and yanked. The Jeep swerved, missing a rickshaw by inches. Yelling ensued.

"They drive on the opposite side. You gotta look right, my man."

"Shit," Mo said. "Thanks."

They made their way down the strip. Mo said, "I need to get laid tonight. That's my goal. A beautiful Thai woman who digs brothers."

Before he thought better of it, Emerson said, "What about Kiki and your baby?"

Mo stopped. "You keep fixating on what isn't your business."

This wasn't the first time Emerson stuck up for Mo's stateside family. "I'm sorry. I can tell Kiki's special, is all."

"Yeah well. Is she here?"

They continued to the end of the strip. There it was. Neon lights, a painted American flag, and red star on a poster announced they'd found it.

The door swung open, and a brown-skinned man stumbled out. "Watch yourselves," he said, his words slurred.

"Copy that." Emerson intended to heed the warning.

With caution, Mo and Emerson stepped inside. A cloud of cigarette smoke enveloped them. Dim lights created a haze. A cacophony of voices, laughter, and soul music playing from a jukebox greeted them. On the dance floor, Thai women and girls sporting Afro wigs moved to the music, some with men and others alone, looking for someone to buy them drinks. Just as the service men segregated themselves, so did the Thai women. Some only worked the bars where country music played, and White men frequented. Others hung with the brothers.

Mo said, "Now we're talking."

Emerson, the inebriated man's words still echoing, took it all in.

Mo pushed forward. "Let's grab a stool."

They muscled their way through the throng to the bar. A thin Thai man with tattoos on both arms took their orders. Emerson asked for a beer and Mo chose whiskey. The music changed, and a sweaty song by James Brown came on.

Mo pushed away from the bar. "I'm gonna rock with one of those ladies."

James Brown moaned, "Try me, try me, darlin, tell me, I need you."

Emerson hadn't held a woman in a long time. The song spoke to him. Kiki's pretty face flashed in his mind. Did Mo even think about her? Emerson swung around to face the dance floor. A petite girl no older than sixteen smiled at him.

She swayed over. "Want to dance with me?"

He did, but the song from the base popped into his mind. Young girls were trouble. He shook his head.

She cocked her head to the side. Small hands with painted nails skimmed her body. "You don't like me?"

"Like you fine," he said. "But I'm just watching tonight."

Her smile disappeared and revealed a hard face. She turned and moved along the bar to the next guy.

Mo held a young woman close. His hand slipped to her butt and squeezed. The music changed and Mo returned to the bar.

"You see her?"

"Yeah."

"Damn pretty, right?"

"Young." Again, Emerson wasn't sure why he was dogging Mo today. Lonely? Jealous?

"You're getting on my nerves."

"And you're married." He sounded peevish.

"Now you're my mother and father. Later for you. I'm gonna get some action. Don't wait up." He headed for the heavy red drapes with the armed bouncer standing guard.

For a minute, Emerson thought about accompanying Mo. Whatever was behind the red curtains was probably bad news. Mo was sure to get into trouble. Fuck him. Mo could take care of himself. Emerson downed his drink.

A live band set up on a corner of the dance floor. Black and White musicians played soul music, the drummer thumping the beat. A pretty light-skinned woman, with red lips, dressed in a mini-skirt that barely covered her privates, sang the lyrics. The dance floor thrummed from dozens of feet hitting wood and the volume in the bar reached ear splitting decibels. The singer sang Aretha Franklin's "Respect." Emerson, ready to party, searched the floor for a lady who was at least eighteen. He paused. Where was Mo? Emerson walked to the red curtains. The burly guard, his gun bulging under his jacket, was still at his post.

"I'm looking for a friend," Emerson said to the frowning bouncer.

"What's it to me?"

"Can I check?" Trouble never looked for Mo because he found it first. Emerson palmed a five-dollar bill and held his hand out to the guard. "Just a quick look around."

The guy eyed the bill, took it, pulled the curtain, and let Emerson enter.

Craps and poker tables crowded with players and watchers lined up in rows. Mo was a poker man. A young girl sat on his lap. He sucked on a cigar and blew the smoke toward the yellowed ceiling. The pile of chips in front of him wasn't high. Emerson walked over.

"How's it going?"

"I'm down," Mo said. "But not out."

Although Emerson still wanted to party, it was time to go. "Let's head back. Don't wanna enrage the Captain."

"Let me re-coup. This next hand is mine."

The girl slid off Mo's lap.

"Where you going, baby?"

"Find a winner," she said.

"Big mistake." He handed her a few chips. "For your company."

She took them and moved on. Now Mo's pile was loser low.

Emerson watched Mo fold on the next hand. The dealer dealt again. Short with a barrel chest, the winning man pushed a stack of chips forward.

Mo said to Emerson. "Loan me a few bucks." He nudged Emerson under the table.

Emerson glanced down at Mo's hand. A straight flush. Damn. He dug into his pocket and pulled out a wad of bills, money he planned to use to purchase clothes from one of Bangkok's exceptional and inexpensive tailors. He knew his role. "I can't watch you lose everything," he said, shaking his head. The ploy set to fool the others, making them believe Mo held a losing hand. Emerson gave Mo the money. "I'll wait for you at the bar."

"Don't do me like that."

"Thirty minutes. Then I'm leaving."

From the time he met Mo during basic training at Lackland, women, gambling, and perceived offenses dogged him and too often dragged Emerson into one Mo quagmire after another. But they also laughed a lot, shared powerful experiences, and a straight flush was hard to walk away from. He hoped Mo won and left the table ahead. The other player, with the pile of chips, worried Emerson. Something about his eyes sent a chill. Emerson turned and walked back toward the heavy red drapes.

CHAPTER FIFTEEN

Emerson gulped the last of his beer. A woman screeched, followed by grunts and thuds. He jumped and swung his head left and right. What?

Mo and two men spilled onto the dance floor. Dancers scattered. Fists landed punches as the three men grappled. People backed up, giving the rumble room. Emerson pushed his way to the front of the circle where customers watched. For a minute, it looked like Mo was holding his own. Emerson wanted to even the odds. He reached for the butterfly knife he kept for protection.

The three men continued throwing punches. Mo scrambled up. A switchblade glistened in his right hand.

Emerson stepped forward. An arm swung in front of his chest and put a vise-like hold on his left arm. "Don't do that," the bouncer said. "Not in here."

"He's my buddy."

"We don't tolerate liars and cheats."

What did Mo do? It sounded like he screwed up.

The burly guy gave Emerson a pointed look. "You and I understand each other?" The grip on Emerson's bicep tightened.

"I gotta help him."

One thug twisted Mo's arm behind his back while the other attacker landed two punches into Mo's gut.

"Nah, you don't." The bouncer twisted his grip.

Pain shot up Emerson's arm. The guy twisted harder.

The enforcer dropped his arm. Emerson wiped his mouth with the back of his hand.

Mo pulled away and his knife flashed through the air, slicing one of the attacker's cheek. The cut brawler howled, his hand over the wound. The other attacker knocked Mo on his ass. Mo backed up, shimming away still on his butt. The cut man grabbed both of Mo's legs and dragged him back. Fists smashed into his face.

"You cheated the wrong person," the man yelled as he kicked the downed Mo in the ribs. Another kick elicited a low cry of pain.

With a quick look at the burly guy, hand on the handle of his knife, Emerson charged forward.

The enforcer grabbed him and threw him back. Sent a punch to Emerson's belly. He doubled over; the knife clattered to the floor. He raised his head. Mo lay curled up, his arms and hands cupped around his head.

People in the crowd were taking bets. Money passed hands. Yells, whoops, and laughter from the watchers confused Emerson. Waves of anger and helplessness washed over him. He looked around, his eyes sweeping the crowd, searching for an empathetic Black face. None of the other military guys, Black or White, stepped in. Was it an unspoken law of the club? Brothers always backed each other. What the hell?

The manager, a pocked-face Black man holding a bat, stomped toward the three brawlers. "Break it up." His voice boomed.

The slashed guy kicked Mo in the ribs. The man swung the bat. "This is my place. Get the fuck out." He swung it again, whizzing by the slashed man's face. "Take your beef outside."

The slashed guy didn't move. Blood oozed from the jagged wound. He stared down the bat holder.

The crowd grew quiet.

Like a ballplayer, the owner raised the bat. "You not hear me, nigga?"

With a slow backward step, the slashed-cheek thug moved, leaving Mo on the ground.

Emerson scooped up his knife, rushed forward, grabbed Mo by his armpits, and hoisted him up. "Gonna get you out of here."

Mo groaned. His legs, useless, skidded under him as Emerson pulled and dragged Mo to the door. That's when Emerson saw the gun pointing at Mo's head.

Bang. Bang. Blood, bone fragments, and brain tissue flew into the air and sprayed Emerson's face and clothes. People screamed. Several brushed against him as they ran for the exit.

Emerson kept his eyes on the shooter, who still held the gun. His lip was bloody and swollen, and one eye bruised and closed. The two men locked eyes.

"Iggy, let's boogie," the second assailant said. "Police be here any second."

Iggy blinked and lowered his gun. "You lucked out *this time*," he said to Emerson.

Emerson, still holding Mo, watched them back out the door, their eyes sweeping the crowd, and then returning to Mo. The door swung closed.

People brushed past Emerson and the now dead Mo, getting out before the authorities arrived, but Emerson stayed. You never left a brother behind. Like the Marines. He squatted, cradling what remained of Mo's head on his lap.

CHAPTER SIXTEEN
ARIA

Thursday, March 14, On the Road to Ithaca, NY

Jax and I started our trip early Thursday morning. Once again, I dropped off Princess with my lovely cat-people neighbors. Princess complained for a few minutes and acted standoffish, but she liked the company and this way I didn't have to worry about a murderer hurting her or worse. The thought of the killer in my house made me shudder.

Dressed in jeans, boots, and a purple sweater under a wool coat, I was ready for Ithaca's cold and snow. March weather was unpredictable. Last week it reached sixty degrees, followed by a terrible snowstorm. Jax's jacket was on the Jeep's backseat, but I was too cold to shed my garment.

Jax said, "Our ETA is noon if all goes well."

I packed water, fruit, and nuts for the trip. If we found Zander quickly, which was my fervent prayer, we could lunch in a nice local restaurant. But if not, we might require my snacks. I rested my feet on the small cooler and buckled up. "Thank you again for doing this."

"No problem." He fiddled with the radio dial. "Music?"

On long trips, I enjoyed music. I blasted songs from the eighties or current hits from Beyonce, Mary K Blige, rap, and R&B singers. Or I listened to an audio book–a passionate romance, or an edge-of-the-seat thriller. But today, I wanted company to distract me from worrying about Zander, and what might happen next. Zan had to be okay with a simple explanation for being MIA. Or, if not simple, at least benign. I gripped my hands together to keep them still. Zan is fine, I told myself again.

Although I researched The Vault, Jax's business, I thought that was a safe place to start our conversation. Not too personal, but interesting. "Later. Tell me about your company. You're in it with your brothers, right?"

"Yeah."

I shoved my hands under my legs and took a calming breath. Worrying was useless. "How did it get started?"

Jax peered at me for a second. "You okay?"

My facial expressions are often loud. "Anxious. Please tell me about The Vault's beginnings."

"Sure." He paused, as if gathering his thoughts. "Charlie is an idea guy. We all attended college in Boston and during Charlie and Stephen's senior year and my junior, Charlie shared a vision."

"You graduated from MIT. So, they did too?" I asked.

"Nope. Charlie attended Harvard and Stephen attended Boston College. We're six months apart."

"Okay, wait. How does that happen?"

Jax laughed. "Stranger than that, Charlie's Black."

Warm air pumped from the car's vents, taking the chill off. Traffic on Route 9 was light. Stands of leafless trees and evergreens gave way to the majestic Hudson River. The winter sun, pale in the sky, added warmth through the windshield. I took off my coat and tossed it on the back seat alongside Jax's jacket. "Before you tell me about Charlie's idea, please explain how the three of you are brothers."

"By choice. We met in elementary school. Stephen was a grade ahead of Charlie and me. Became fast friends. Every day after school, we'd go to Charlie's house. His mom was a schoolteacher and arrived home the same time we did."

"Why didn't you go to your house sometimes?"

"Our parents traveled for work. Their idea of parenting was making sure the nanny, when we were little, and later the maid and personal secretary, liked us well enough to watch us while Babs and Peter worked."

Nanny, maid, personal secretary. Whoa. I had a grandma, grandpa, and aunties. "You call your folks by their first names?"

"Yup."

No more information, but so far Jax didn't seem as annoyed by my questions as his taciturn manner might have suggested. I did a quick check-in. "Are my queries okay?"

He shot a glance my way and smiled. "Yeah."

I laughed to myself. Yup and yeah were not answers, but I pressed on. Distraction wasn't my only motive. Although I didn't want to admit it to myself, I was hungry to learn more about him. Every time I was in his presence, as corny as it sounded, goose bumps popped. And guilt, too. As if I were betraying Ben. "I gather you and Stephen came from money."

"Babs and Peter both inherited from my grandparents, and my folks worked hard, made a lot more."

"And Charlie didn't?"

"They weren't poor, just broke, as Dad, Charlie's father, explained."

"You called him Dad."

"Yep, Mom and Dad."

Jax had a pleasant voice. Deep and smooth. Not liquid like Detective Errol's, but warm. I judged men by things like that. Voice, walk, the way they carried themselves. "How'd they become your parents?" His smile was also great. Nice even teeth. If Lacy were listening to my thoughts, she'd roll her eyes.

"Over the years, from third grade on, we spent more time at Charlie's. Our place was lonely. Sometimes the latest personal assistant cared enough to get to know us but didn't stay longer than a year. Maids and cooks were kind, but that wasn't what we needed. Mom fed, hugged, and taught us board and card games, helped with homework that she insisted we finish, and after a while, even went to the parent-teacher meetings for us."

"And Charlie's father?"

"He's a lawyer in his own single-man firm, doing well enough now. But that took years. Back then, they didn't have discretionary dollars."

Another long Jax-pause. I watched loaded barges chugging along the Hudson River while I waited.

"Dad was about work. Unlike Babs and Peter, Dad didn't let it stop him from being an engaged father." There was a touch of anger in Jax's tone.

That made me sad. I thought about Ben with Zander. All in. Then I thought about how many times I got home late, after Zan and Ben already ate. "How so? You said your adopted dad was about work. What does that mean?"

"He believed you earned a living rather than inherited one. 'Find your passion, purpose, and talent sweet spot,' he told us more than once. 'God gave you gifts. Discover and use them for good.' He shared lots of sayings all with the same theme."

"They sound like great people. I'm blessed with parents like them." My recent conversation with my father came to mind. "Stubborn, but wonderful."

"Did they impart lots of wisdom?"

"Yes, about boys. And honesty. Faith. Forgiveness. No drama and lots of love and encouragement." My parents' warnings and teachings stayed with me, and I passed them onto Zander, but I wasn't sure how well they took root. Zan. My heart clutched again. I glanced at the clock. Still hours to go. Where was he?

CHAPTER SEVENTEEN

We turned off Route 9 and traveled to a traffic circle, which took us onto Route 6. From there, we crossed the Hudson via the Bear Mountain Bridge, a short narrow passage toward Route 17 North. I'd driven this way before when Zan and I first visited Cornell during his sophomore year in high school. During the fall, the foliage dazzled. Even now, with naked trees, the vista was grand.

Jax said, "I didn't say no drama. We're an odd family and raising and feeding three growing boys wasn't easy."

"How come?"

"We wrestled, argued, goaded each other to do stupid stuff. But Mom and Dad never dumped us, not even on the weekends. If we wanted to stay, we could."

"For a little while, two cousins with family problems lived with us. Bella and I shared our rooms. We're still like sisters today."

"Family is what you make it, at least for me."

"Did your bio parents ever complain?"

"At first, they didn't seem to notice. They called and spoke with us most weekends. We'd go to the house when they told us they'd return."

"And?"

"If I remember correctly, one of the personal assistants told them we were never home."

"This is super strange."

"Yeah."

"So, what happened after your parents figured it out? Did they visit Charlie's parents and sort things out?"

"Babs said, 'If they make you happy, it's fine with us.' We split Thanksgiving, Christmas, and birthdays between both households. But we vacationed with Mom, Dad, and Charlie." Jax's voice became low. "It's not that they don't love us, although Stephen disagrees." He stayed quiet for several beats. "I guess they were relieved." He switched lanes and glanced at the GPS map on the dashboard.

"Were Charlie's parents annoyed? Want compensation?"

"They never mentioned it to us. They loved and accepted us."

In my nonprofit work, I met many people for whom children weren't a priority. The kids suffered because their parents didn't want them, or love them enough, or couldn't afford them. "Why does Stephen believe they didn't love you? It's fine if you don't want to answer."

"That's okay. I don't talk about this stuff, but with you, it's easy." He sounded embarrassed. "Their crime was neglect, not lack of love." Now he sounded sad and resigned. "Stephen and I both wanted more. So, we found more with the French family—Trudy and Mel, Mom and Dad. Best people ever." He rubbed his nose and drummed his thumbs on the steering wheel. "But Stephen dreamed they'd come for us, change."

I waited for him to say more, but he stayed quiet. We turned onto Route 17 toward Binghamton.

Jax shifted the conversation. "Have you told your folks what's happening?"

"Yes." The question brought me back to the current situation and my increased anxiety. "They took it in stride, but I'm scared for them. Do you know how I can get security for their home?"

"What does Glover say?"

"He asked two uniform officers to make wellness checks, which doesn't sound like protection to me."

Several cars passed us. Then another three vehicles whizzed by. The road was sometimes two lanes and at other points, four. The posted speed limit was sixty-five mph. Those guys had to be doing seventy-five at least. Jax checked his rearview mirror and then turned his head, looking into the side-view mirror. His eyes narrowed.

"What's the matter?" I twisted around. A black SUV with a tinted windshield drove behind us. A Nissan Rogue according to the front bumper.

"Probably nothing." He eased his foot off the gas and let the car slow down.

The Rogue slowed too. My heart rate ticked up. I remembered the car my mother saw. "My mother said the plate started with QRT, but she couldn't read the four numbers that followed." It was a Rogue too. I tried to read this one's license plate.

"Did you tell the police?"

"No. I told my mom and dad to report it if they saw the car again, but when I checked, they said everything was fine." I twisted around again, trying to read the plate's letters and numbers. "This one starts with LVC. It's not the same."

"Stolen and plates switched up?"

"People do that in the real world?"

"Yeah."

I faced front again, my anxiety building with each passing second.

"Make sure your phone is handy. I'm going to pull over right before the next exit. See what he does."

I tugged my phone out of my bag. Ahead was an exit sign, and the shoulder was blacktop and gravel. Jax signaled and maneuvered to a stop. The Rogue rolled by.

"That was scary," I said.

"Right." He sounded more thoughtful than agreeing.

"How much further?"

"About an hour. Binghamton is just ahead. From there we hit Route 79, which takes us to Cornell."

Was it the same car my mom saw with switched plates? I stared out the window, peering into the side-view mirror, watching. My mind raced along various storylines. "If the murderer is following us," I said. "Then he knows we're looking for Zan."

"Whoa. Big leap."

Perhaps.

Jax said, "Can your folks stay with you for a while? Until we catch the guy?"

I noticed the "we." "Do you believe the police aren't doing a good job?"

"Everyone can use a hand."

My career preparation did not include investigating murder. Nor did Jax's, from what I knew.

"Safest strategy is everyone together and the police checking on you."

"My sister lives in Connecticut. She has a guest room where my parents sleep when they visit, plus a sofa bed in the finished basement."

"That sounds good."

"For Zan and my parents. I'm not going anywhere."

Jax shook his head but didn't speak.

I tried to imagine insisting my parents move in with Bella. Zander too. Not simple conversations.

Jax changed the subject. "I have a close friend who does private security."

"To protect us and The Way Station?" I could cash in some of my retirement savings. I made too much for Zan to receive a full scholarship. The $69,000 a year was almost half my salary, so I refinanced the house. Money was tight. "How much would it cost?"

Again, he didn't respond right away.

Oh. What if he thought I was angling for financial support? "I'm sure I can manage it, whatever the expense. And my parents have savings. We'll be fine."

He turned his head toward me for the briefest of seconds. "I'll make some calls after we find Zander."

Embarrassed, but not sure why, I glanced at the side-view mirror. The Rogue was back, a car's length behind.

CHAPTER EIGHTEEN

The Rogue stayed with us. "The black car is back."

"I see him."

Jax's calm tone did little to settle my stomach or slow my heart rate. "I'm calling 9-1-1."

"Tell them we're being followed and describe the car."

I punched in the number. The Binghamton police dispatch answered. "What's your emergency?"

I explained and told them where we were.

"What makes you think the car is following you?" asked the dispatcher.

I told her about the murder.

"A State Highway Patrol car is on its way. There's a filling station about a quarter of a mile ahead. Pull in there."

Within minutes of us reaching the gas station, a patrol car drove up, and another blew by the exit. The Rogue was nowhere in sight. We both clambered out. The air smelled like pending snow. Clouds obscured the sun. I pulled my scarf tight around my neck.

A man and woman approached us, both White, each wearing a grey uniform, purple tie, and a patch on their right sleeve. He was clean shaven, and she wore her hair tucked under a wide-brimmed hat. His matching hat pulled down low, hid his eyes.

"Morning," the man said. "Heard you're having some trouble." He looked my age or younger, his mouth set in a fake, friendly smile.

The woman peered into the Jeep, clearly making a visual check. Both wore guns on their hips.

Jax said, "As Ms. Wright told dispatch, we believe we're being followed and are in danger." He shared the make, model, color, and partial plate number.

The female officer walked around the car and joined her partner on the driver's side. "Where are you coming from?" she asked. Her serious expression conveyed confidence and professionalism. Much better than a fake smile.

"Westchester County," I said. Most upstate folks never heard of Fieldcrest. "We're on our way to Ithaca." Time was slipping by. Suppose the murderer... Another thought interrupted. There were two people in the SUV. I was positive. Did they keep driving toward Cornell? Was Zan in real danger?

The male officer spoke into a device. "Anything?" He listened to the reply and then faced us. "No black Nissan Rogue. We'll check the cameras, but it either pulled off or—"

"It was real. We both saw it," I said in a huff.

"I'm sure you did." His fake smile returned. "There's nothing we can do. We'll check in with the Westchester County police and alert ours."

They took our contact information.

"Stay safe," the female officer said.

They both climbed into their cruiser and left us.

• • •

Nestled against the Cayuga Lake, Cornell's campus was beautiful. Snow covered rolling hills and a mix of old and modern architecture. It was as different from my college experience as possible. Both my schools were in New York City. Ben and I encouraged Zander to consider my Alma Mater, NYU, close enough to us but still too far to live at home. Competition to get into an Ivy League university was intense. Ben didn't live long enough to learn Zan beat the odds with top grades, packed social and educational clubs, including leadership positions, dedicated volunteer work, which was in the blood, and a terrific essay. With Ben's insurance payout, I hired a college entrance tutor for the essay and another to help with the interview. When I think about our clients, all the young people whose parents don't have the means to give their high school seniors any of the opportunities Zan received, I feel sad, angry, and committed to helping each high schooler who walks through our doors.

Right after Ben died, I often spoke to him. I waited until Zan retired to his room, poured a glass of wine, and sat on the couch facing Ben's favorite chair. Images of him watching me filled my head. I told him about my day, funny stories about my parents or Bella's kids, and of course, my latest proud mama moment or worry. I stopped. Why? When I searched my memory, I realized it was last year when I noticed Jax's interest in me.

"Where do you want to start?" Jax asked.

We hurried across the campus. Stately red brick buildings with grey towers and slanted roofs lined the broad road. The clouds cleared, uncovering a pale blue sky. Students and faculty members moved with purpose while others stood in small groups chatting and laughing despite the biting cold.

"Let's go to his dorm first," I suggested. "Most logical."

"Finding friends of his will help us a lot."

A biting wind kicked up. I covered my nose and mouth with my scarf. Zan lived on campus for less than three months. He never mentioned close friends. When I asked him how he was, he complained about tough classes, but I sensed loneliness. A conversation we had in October broke my heart. "I wish Dad were here. He'd just get me and bring me home."

Using the security code Zan gave me when he first moved into the dorm, we found Zan's room and knocked.

"He's not here," a voice said from behind us.

I spun around.

"Hasn't been around for a while." She was petite, with shiny dark hair tied in a ponytail.

"You know my son, Zan?"

"Sure. I live across the hall and down one room." She used her thumb to point over her left shoulder.

"He hasn't called and I'm worried."

The girl shrugged. "Could be with Darcy at her place. Did you try there?"

Darcy? Did Zan have a girlfriend? "My name is Aria Wright, and I'm Zander's mother. My friend and I drove here from downstate because I'm super concerned."

Jax held out his hand. "Jax Oats. What's your name?"

She shook Jax's hand. "Glynis."

"Glynis, please tell me how I can find my son?"

"Darcy lives in town. She runs Climate Action, an activist-type organization on Commercial Avenue. It's like a pop-up store in a vacant clothing shop." She smiled up at Jax. "Lives in the back of the store."

Relief washed over me. Until now, no one shared any useful information. I'd spoken with the student advisory office, the campus police, and I knew Errol said the town police were called with no results to report. "Thank you, so much."

On the drive into town, we both watched for the Rogue. We passed several, but none with tinted windows.

Commercial Avenue was easy to find. A major thoroughfare lined with shopper-filled stores on each side. Decorative banners hung from the telephone poles and adorned shop windows announcing an upcoming book fair. A cafe called me. I required coffee and a lady's room. Plus, I needed a Darcy strategy. If she was the reason for Zan's silence, she might not give me information. After a check to see if anyone was watching, we entered the cafe and found a table.

Jax said, "Let me go in first. Say I'm interested in the organization's work. Ask some questions like an inquiring volunteer or, even better, a potential benefactor."

A quick stop in the washroom eased some of my stress. Now, with both hands wrapped around my mug and several sips down, I felt better. Less afraid. I could see the front entrance to Climate Action across the street. "I'll wait for you here."

He finished his coffee and ate the last bite of his croissant. "Be back in a few."

I watched him walk across the street. I popped up and dashed to reach him. My son. My responsibility. Jax stopped and waited.

"We'll go in as a couple." I slipped my arm through his. An unlikely pair, as he towered over me, and his long strides were hard to keep up with. He must have realized because he slowed his gait.

The shop offered a ragtag appearance. Stacks of posters and newspapers rested on a metal desk. Graphic photos of fires, floods, mudslides, denuded forests, and cratered land covered the walls. Different colored pushpins dotted a map of New York State.

The young man who approached us looked scruffy. Jeans, mud stained boots, checkered shirt hanging to his side pockets, went with the thick long beard, an unattractive, trendy style. I must be getting old.

"Can I help you?" he asked in a polite and curious tone.

"We're looking for Darcy," I said with a big smile. "We're interested in learning more and perhaps helping."

The kid nodded. "I'll get her." He turned. "What's your names?"

Jax jumped in. "Oats."

"Okay." He knocked on a door. "Darcy, there's a couple out here interested in helping." He glanced at us as if assessing our importance and then faced the closed door. "You're gonna want to speak with them, if you get my meaning."

The door swung open. A medium height woman with long locks stepped out. People stopped calling them dreadlocks because the name was offensive. She too wore jeans and a loose fitting white shirt. And she looked older than Zan. In her mid-twenties, at least. Zander came up behind her.

"Mom? What the heck?"

Darcy gave me a cool once over.

Relief flooding my system, I rushed forward, passed Darcy, threw my arms around Zander, and pulled his stiff body close.

CHAPTER NINETEEN
JAX

Jax watched with trepidation. Darcy Phillips, Zander, Aria, and Jax sat in the cafe across the street from Climate Action. Tension zipped between and around them.

When Aria demanded to speak with Zander in private, Darcy said no. Aria ignored her and pulled Zander aside. That's how they ended up in the cafe. A compromise.

The coffee and pastry shop was half-full. Round tables, each with four wire-mesh chairs, stood crowded together, maximizing the small space. The server assigned to their table wore a white shirt, black trousers, and a short apron tied around her waist. A tattoo peaked out from the unbuttoned shirt collar.

"Can I get you all anything else?" the server asked.

Aria, lips pressed together, shook her head, declining for all of us. The second the server left, Aria jumped in. "Ms. Phillips, are you aware Zander is 18 years old and attending college on the Wright Family Scholarship? I'm paying all his expenses."

"So you mentioned earlier." Darcy appeared unruffled.

Zander shrank in his seat. His entire body folded in and down. A good-looking kid who must resemble his father, because Jax saw little of Aria in Zander's coloring, features, or stature. Light brown, tall, and with a wide, turned-down mouth.

Darcy flung her locks over her shoulder. "He's with me and he's fine."

Jax wondered about statutory rape. Was Zander at the age of consent in New York? He pulled out his phone, and holding it under the table, did a quick search.

"Is that true, Zan?" Aria asked. "You're dropping out of school? Throwing your education and future away for..." Aria shook her head. "What?"

Under seventeen. Zan was eighteen, so rape wasn't a viable threat. Jax put his phone away.

Zan finally spoke up. "People are destroying Earth, draining ground water, leveling forests, polluting the air we breathe. If we don't do something now, my education will be meaningless."

To Jax's ears, Zander sounded like an over-prepped speaker, sharing the company line. It wasn't Jax's place to step in, but he saw tears glimmering in Aria's eyes, so he spoke. "With a degree in environmental studies or business, you can have a bigger impact. Do more for the cause."

Zander looked at him. "Who are you?" He straightened up and turned to Aria. "Who's this dude and why's he here?"

"I introduced you. Jax drove me."

"He's your chauffeur?" The sarcasm was obvious.

"Don't be rude. Check the attitude."

Zan's tone downshifted. "I'm sorry I stressed you." He pushed back from the table and stood. "I shoulda called and explained, but I knew you'd freak, fail to understand. And I was right."

"I'm trying," Aria said.

"Darcy and I are together doing essential work."

"You've known each other for a few months, but you're together?" Aria rose as well. "You are going back to school." Each word came out sharp.

"I'm not. I'll pay you back for—"

"What? Zander Wright, we are leaving. Now. You're coming home with me."

Darcy eased up. A smirk played around her mouth. She took Zander's hand again. "Nice meeting you." Another snarky smile. "Not."

The woman sounded like a privileged teenager rather than a grownup running an organization. Aria trembled with rage or fear. Her mouth opened and closed.

Jax stood, towering over all of them. "Hey," he said, taking a different approach. Everyone turned to look at him. "You're both in danger. That's why we're here."

"What are you talking about?" Darcy asked with mild interest. "Danger? From you?" She laughed at her own joke. No one else did.

Jax ignored the woman and focused his eyes on Zander. "Your mom witnessed a murder, and the killer threatened her and her family. He knows you're here. In fact, we believe he followed us."

Darcy's eyes went wide. Zander sucked in a breath. Everyone sat back down. Jax nodded to Aria. It was her story to tell.

She started at the beginning, leaving nothing out. Even Darcy paid attention without comment. Jax listened but also scanned the street, looking for the Rogue. The black SUV wasn't in view. But a man, standing in front of Climate Action's office, arms crossed, appeared to be watching them. Was he someone connected to Darcy? From Jax's point of view, this was not the stocky, hooded man Aria described to the police. This guy was as tall as Jax. A baseball cap pulled low obscured his eyes.

Jax said, "Someone is watching us now." He lifted his chin toward the window. "Do either of you recognize him? One of your volunteers?"

Darcy peered out the window. "No." Her bombast notched down several rungs.

Zan looked worried. "Geez, Mom. What are the police doing to protect you? Did you tell them—"

"I'm fine. It's you I'm worried about."

Zander looked at Darcy, then back at his mother. "We're all right too." He glanced out the window at the staring man. "We'll keep our eyes opened, right D?"

Darcy's smirk and snark returned. "We take care of each other. The sooner you leave, the safer Z and I will be. No one's been following us and lurking around until you got here." She paused, as if waiting for Aria or Jax to object. "Besides, I'm an excellent shot."

Aria groaned. "You carry a gun?"

"Second amendment. I have a license."

This gave Jax pause. If Darcy were levelheaded, having a gun could prove useful. If not, it was dangerous. Dad taught all three of the brothers to shoot. Charlie gave his gun up when he married, and Stephen kept his, but locked it away. Jax held onto to his weapon too, and now it lay in the Jeep's secure glove compartment. Jax said, "These guys are no joke. Do you practice?"

"Since I was twelve."

Aria said, sounding alarmed, "We've alerted the Ithaca and campus police. I don't see any reason for you two toting a pistol." She gave Jax a withering look. "Zan, you'll be safer on campus or at home with me." She sounded both desperate and angry. "Let's visit the local police and get their advice, without mentioning your gun." She stood up. "We can go right now."

Jax decided not to tell Aria about his Glock. It was so easy to upset her, which was not his intention. Not his lady, not his kid.

Zander shook his head. "I'm not leaving Darcy."

Jax searched Aria's grief-stricken face. He'd not seen her like this. Afraid, mourning a loss he'd never experienced. A mother's love for her child she was losing. Did Babs ever feel like Aria looked?

"Okay, Zan," Aria said. "Let's take a step back." Her voice was steady but edged with emotion. "I'll book a room and stay over. We can all sleep on this. It's a lot to take in. Tomorrow, we can speak with the local authorities. Get their perspective and recommendations." She folded her hands in her lap and glanced at her watch. "I'll come by in the morning. Is 9:00 a.m. okay with you?"

Jax noticed Aria left him out of the arrangement. Did she expect him to leave her, go back alone? When he was with Maria, he always felt on edge, afraid he'd say something to upset her. He felt like he understood Aria better because he listened more, studied her, but maybe not.

Zander looked at Darcy as if waiting for her to decide.

She huffed, pursed her lips, and then nodded. "Okay. We will reconvene tomorrow. But so you know, we're a team taking care of each other."

Aria stepped forward and put her arms out to Zander. He stepped in and hugged her. "It's going to be okay, Mom. For real."

She let him go with a trembling, no teeth smile. "I know it will be."

Together, Aria and Jax watched the two leave.

Jax felt out of his depth. He and Aria were friends at best, colleagues at worst. He'd been taking things slowly over the last year. This was the most intimate time he'd spent with her. Stay the course, he told himself. Be a friend and help her through this crisis. Then what?

CHAPTER TWENTY

Jax pondered. If Zander were his kid, what would he do? Teenagers always think they're grown, not realizing how much there is to learn. Their brains are still developing until age twenty-five, and maturing through their late twenties, something he didn't figure out until he was thirty.

Jax remembered confronting Babs and Peter when he was sixteen, two years younger than Zander, standing up to them the way Zander stood up to Aria, thinking he was a man and not a child dependent on his mother's support.

Harvard accepted Charlie. Tuition, room, and board came to $36,000 a year. He received a small scholarship but had to take out a substantial loan. Mom and Dad didn't make enough to expense his education. Jax tracked down his bio parents. He'd not seen them for at least two months and the regular calls dried up. They appeared content with the arrangement. Or they accepted the French family raising their sons but didn't like it.

Jax lucked out and found them both at home. "I'm on my way," he said, and hung up before they could ask questions.

The three sat on cushioned chairs on the upper deck. The air was April warm, and the oaks and maples shimmered with new leaves. Babs, dressed in silk slacks, a matching blouse, and blue blazer, sipped a glass of red wine. Peter's unknotted tie hung from his collar.

Peter asked, "What's this about, son? You sounded urgent on the phone. Is Stephen okay?"

"Charlie got into Harvard. You need to pay for his tuition, room, and board for all four years. Plus, graduate school."

Jax was always a quiet kid. Stephen did the talking. When Babs and Peter demanded they attend a family or business function, because they didn't want others to know a Black family was raising their sons, it was Stephen who argued against it. "We have a game." "We're going to a party." "It's Mom's birthday, Mrs. French's, I mean." Which was odd, because Stephen wanted them to care, but avoided opportunities to let them. In all cases, Jax stood by his brother.

Peter scowled. "Watch your tone. You're in no position to demand anything."

"I am. You cover all of us. The Frenches fed us, took us on family vacations, equipped us for the sports we played, and attended most games. Did you know I played on our varsity basketball team or Stephen sang and danced in the senior high school play?" Jax didn't realize how much pent up disappointment and anger lingered. "Just say yes. It's the right thing to do."

Babs looked stricken. "We thought that's what you wanted. To be with them and not us."

Jax couldn't look at his mother. He focused on Peter's jutted chin. "Come by the house and announce it. A thank you for raising your kids."

Peter blanched. "I'll say no such thing."

Babs made a strangled sound.

Jax steeled himself. Too little, too late. "Yeah, you will. Tomorrow. After church."

To this day, Jax remained conflicted about the conversation. He never told Mom, Dad, Stephen, or Charlie. He was proud of his successful negotiation, but also ashamed he bullied Babs, and his parents didn't think of it themselves. It worked out for the brothers. Graduate school too, for Charlie and Jax. Stephen was done, but stayed in Boston until Jax got his masters.

Now he faced Aria. "What do you want to do?"

"Weep."

"Okay, after that?"

"What can I?" She sagged back into the chair. Their coffee was cold and pastry untouched.

The cheery server approached them. "You still working on that?" She pointed to the blueberry muffin. "Want a refill?" She lifted the coffee pot in her hand.

"It's time to switch to wine," Aria said with a little laugh.

Jax paid the bill. "We need to find a hotel."

Her 'you've overstepped look' glared at him, but Jax ignored it. "We'll get two rooms, find someplace for dinner, and figure out what's next."

Jax dreamed about spending the night with Aria, but never like this.

•   •   •

Jax and Aria checked into adjoining rooms in the Ithaca Marriott on the Commons. The hotel, in the popular, pedestrian only, four-block commons, included a restaurant and full bar, but they passed on both. Instead, they walked, stopped in an open pharmacy, souvenir store, and a local eatery for dinner. Once again, Jax was happy. It felt like a date. Then he noted the sadness etched along her mouth and in her eyes. His joy seeped away. Not a date. Not a special moment.

They agreed on an Italian place with an appealing menu, ordered glasses of Chianti and fettucine with clams. Aria picked at her food.

Jax couldn't blame her. Zander hurt her, choosing Darcy instead of the life Aria offered and planned. Cornell wasn't cheap, Zander skipped school, and might be in danger.

A new thought hit Jax. Or were they following me? Jax assumed a connection between the guys in the Rogue and Emerson's murder. Might two distinct problems be in play. Most cyber-assaults came from foreign players–Russian, Chinese, Iranian, or Nigerian. Hackers didn't follow targets to remote Ithaca. Still, a big coincidence.

He twirled fettucine on his fork and put it into his mouth. Damn, that was tasty. Warm Italian bread with seasoned olive oil added deliciousness to the meal. He dipped a piece into the sauce. "Try to eat." He pointed to her still full plate. "Five star good."

"No appetite. Tired."

"I get it," he said, putting his fork down. "What will you do if you can't persuade Zander?"

She looked at him with sad eyes. "Is that what you think will happen?"

"I don't know him." Jax sipped his wine. "But teenaged boys often think they're men. I did."

"Even when mom is paying the bills?

"Yep."

"I'm afraid for Zan." She nibbled on a piece of bread. "I googled Darcy Phillips."

Jax did too, but he waited for Aria to share.

"Not much comes up. Photos of climate disasters, like the pictures on the office walls, fill her LinkedIn page and not much more. Facebook and Instagram are the same. She's popular on TikTok. Lots of views and followers."

"How about the organization?"

"They don't even have a website. No list of board members or staff. How's she paying rent?"

"Patron? Donors?"

"Hmm." Aria sipped her wine.

He didn't want to add to her misery but felt compelled to remind her about the man watching them. "It might have been a coincidence. Perhaps Darcy was his focus." He paused. "Or me."

"You?"

"It's possible. A cyber-attack struck The Vault."

"Oh no."

"The connection is unlikely. Two men following us instead of one. Different heights and builds from the murderer." He watched her mouth tremble. "I didn't mean to frighten you."

"Well, you have." She blinked several times. "What if Darcy is a target?"

"A possibility we need to investigate."

"When? How? We both must return to Fieldcrest." She swallowed the last of her wine. "I won't leave him here."

"You can't force him."

"Who's following and spying on us?"

That was the question nagging Jax all afternoon. Who were the two guys? Who was the watcher? And why?

CHAPTER TWENTY-ONE
ARIA AND JAX

Jax and I walked back to the hotel. Too wired to sleep, I glanced at my watch. 9:00 p.m. Maybe Netflix. Something happy and predictable. The idea of popcorn and a movie felt quite appealing. Lacy and I enjoyed regular sleepover dates since Ben's death. A bottle of wine, warm popcorn with real butter, and a rom-com. Ben liked action movies and thrillers–the hero rescuing the US president from disaster. Tom Clancy or a Grisham story starring Tom Cruise. I enjoyed them too, but Lacy and I stuck with "love blossomed, disaster hit, and love found its way back." Were rom-coms fueling my risqué dreams?

"Do you like films?" I asked.

"Sure."

"Want to watch one this evening?" This felt dangerous. I didn't want him to get the wrong impression. I wasn't inviting him to my bed but being alone this evening seemed unbearable.

"Did you see a movie theater?" He glanced at his watch. "Kinda late."

"Netflix. I noticed the hotel offered it and I have an account." I couldn't read Jax's expression. Shocked? Embarrassed? What? "That's okay. I'm sure you have—"

"No. I mean yes. I'd like that."

"Fair warning. I need…" I decided it was too inappropriate to watch a romance. "A comedy."

"Okay."

He still sounded weird. This was a bad idea. "Each room has two chairs." No sitting next to each other on the bed.

"Okay," he said again.

We walked the rest of the way in silence.

Once we reached the hotel, I went to the little market area near the front desk. Sure enough, I found bottles of water and microwave popcorn. Red and white wine splits with screw on caps lined one shelf. I remembered the check-in clerk telling us every room included a small refrigerator, coffee maker, and microwave. We already drank enough wine. At least I had. Plus, buying wine sets a different mood and expectation. I grabbed two waters and a package of popcorn and brought them to the desk clerk. "May I charge—"

"I got it." Jax pushed over his credit card.

"No," I said. This wasn't a date. And even if it were, I'd still pay my way. We encountered the same problem at the restaurant. Over his objections, I insisted on splitting the check.

Jax looked crestfallen or embarrassed. I didn't know him well enough to discern his moods or expressions. I smiled to put him at ease.

In silence, we rode the elevator to the third floor. My heartbeat did its double beat thing. "Give me five," I said, trying to remember how I left the room.

This time he didn't speak, just nodded his head.

Once inside, I scurried around, hanging my coat, putting my packages away and checking the bathroom for cleanliness. Then I called my neighbor to check on Princess. Everything was fine.

Jax knocked, and I opened the door. Oh my. Those bright green eyes did me in. I loved his full bottom lip and dimpled chin. I stood there looking up at him, wanting him to lift me in his arms and kiss me.

"American Fiction is available. I missed it." I heard myself babbling. "Supposed to be excellent with a powerful message wrapped in laughter. Unless you've already watched it. Is there something else you'd rather see?" I walked toward the television and grabbed the remote. "You can pick."

In two strides, he was next to me. He bent way down and kissed me. Soft and tentative. I leaned in. His lips felt just like I'd imagined them. Better. I blinked. "I can't," I said.

For several seconds, he stared at me. Hurt and confusion filled his eyes. "Sorry. It won't happen again."

And then he was gone.

• • •

Jax went to his room. Oh, man. His heart was thumping. I blew it. What was I thinking? She looked like she wanted me to kiss her. Didn't she? I read it all wrong. I've screwed everything up. How do I recover from this? He plopped down on the bed, sat for seconds, and then jumped up. Paced in the small corridor between the bed and television. This was bad. Should I call her, apologize again? Tomorrow will be awkward. Better to clear the air now.

He picked up his cell and called her. It rang several times and then voicemail came on. He clicked off. She didn't even want to speak with him.

That's when he noticed four missed calls and text messages. Two were from E-Man, The Vault's lead cyber sleuth. "I found something. Call me." Jax glanced at his watch. It was too late to disturb E-Man. First thing in the morning. The other two messages were from Charlie. "We've got trouble. Are you back? Call me."

Jax punched in his brother's number.

"Hey. Where you been?" Charlie said the second the call connected.

"In Ithaca with Aria." He stared out the window into blackness with dots of lights from cars and homes. He felt heavy, like sacks of remorse and disappointment weighed down every part of his body. Charlie met Dot in college and married her right after graduation. Stephen and Stephanie connected online in Boston. They married two years later. What was wrong with him?

"With Aria, like—"

"Not with. I told you I was driving her to Cornell."

"Didn't mention spending the night."

"You said we have trouble," Jax said, annoyed with Charlie and himself. "What's up?"

In the background, television voices and music hummed. The sound became fainter as if Charlie walked into another room.

"E-Man called this afternoon. Said he tried to reach you." Charlie paused.

"Lots going on. Two guys followed us here."

"What?"

"Yeah. We called the police. Long story."

"We're breached for sure. Two of our clients as well."

It was inevitable. That's why they developed Resilience Protocols—ways to survive when it happened. "Which ones?"

"Do you think it's connected? The guys following you and the cyber-attack?"

"Don't know yet. Maybe."

"Bad Ass Tunes," Charlie said, answering Jax's earlier question. "And Clover Quarters, the office space rental folks."

"I'm guessing your urgent call means there's more to this story." At least this was a problem Jax could solve. In his wheelhouse. Aria was not. Nor was murder.

"They want $1,000,000 to back away, release our clients' data, and not smear us. Said if we didn't pay, we'll put other things at risk."

"Any idea what they meant?" The Resilience Protocol included encrypted backups, so when a breach happened, neither The Vault nor the clients had to meet ransom demands.

"The anonymous text that warned us...the one I showed you in Starbucks."

"Yeah?"

"Sent me another. Said the blackmailers have names of employees. Know where they live. I called the police, and they notified the FBI."

"Whoa." Jax's mind spun. The murderer told Aria he knew where she and her family lived. Now this cyber crook is making a similar threat. "This is crazy."

"I know. Feels dangerous and personal."

"What's the end game? Just the money? Tearing down the company?"

"Don't know."

Charlie and Jax stayed quiet for several beats. Jax asked, "What does Stephen and E-Man say?"

"We need a confab. When do you get back?"

"In the morning." Aria might stay through the weekend. If she did, he'd stay too. Just because she didn't feel about him the way Jax felt about her, didn't change his need to protect her. "If not, then Monday for sure. But I'm available 24/7. I'll check my phone. What does E-Man think?" Jax asked again.

"He and his sleuths are on it."

"The police and FBI?"

"Nothing yet."

"Okay, let's talk in the morning."

The phone clicked off. The bed had six pillows. Four to sleep on, covered with white pillowcases, and two decorative ones. Jax flung all but one onto the chair next to the bed and, still clothed, lay down. The company he and his brothers built from nothing into a fine business that supported them and over one hundred employees was in danger. His responsibility was to figure out how to safeguard everyone. The Way Station too. And most of all, Aria.

Jax remained uncertain about being with Aria. Sometimes, he sensed she liked him, not just as a friend. And then...

Tomorrow, Jax planned to tackle everything within his grasp. Aria was not. He groaned aloud, pressed the remote, found a sports station and watched a west coast basketball game.

CHAPTER TWENTY-TWO
EMERSON

May 7, 1968, Tuy Hoa

Sleep eluded Emerson. Not just because of the nighttime bombings, or the guys' snoring, or the guilt and memories of Mo's death, his head blown away, the remains splattered across Emerson's face, arms, hands, and chest. It was the man called Iggy. His opaque eyes, blood oozing from where Mo slashed Iggy's face, his cold, congealed voice. Every time Emerson closed his eyes, the smell of death and Iggy's face and voice hovered.

Quicksilver approached Emerson's bunk. Like each night the sergeant made his nocturnal rounds, Quicksilver dressed in full uniform.

"How's it hanging?" Q sat on the edge of Emerson's bunk. "Seems like you never sleep."

"Can't." He sat up and swung his legs over the edge. "You either. How come?"

Quicksilver took his time answering. "Nighttime is friends with the devil. Nasty shit can happen to a brother sleeping in his bunk. I keep watch."

Three White Army men jumped a Black airman the other night. All stumbling drunk, and no one knew what provoked the attack. Since then, the brothers stayed extra vigilant.

"Appreciate you," Emerson said.

"Worried about the investigation?"

"How you know about it?" Dumb question. Q had complete knowledge of the base.

"Saw the Security Police bring you home."

"I did nothing wrong." I failed Mo, left him alone, and didn't have his back. Iggy killed Mo, and I let him.

As if reading Emerson's mind, Q said, "Not your fault. You know that, right?"

Once again, Quicksilver reassured Emerson. His mom used to do that, but his father said, "Take responsibility, son. Own your shit."

Emerson tried to tell the local police what happened. But an ambulance took Mo away and two Thai police officers hauled Emerson to his feet. Others questioned the one who swung the bat. From Emerson's vantage point, it looked like a friendly conversation. The manager pointed to Emerson and the officers stuffed him into a police car. Did they believe Emerson cheated and lied too? Not just Mo?

Five uniformed officers dressed in khaki shirts and belted pantaloon pants tucked into calf-high boots crowded into an interrogation room at the police station. Emerson couldn't read the insignias or decipher the ribbons over their hearts worn by various officers, but he understood who was in charge. A dude with slicked back hair, and clean shaven—the only person asking questions. The others stood ringed around the room, while the man questioning Emerson sat across from where they'd placed him.

"Why am I here?" Everyone in the club saw the fight and Iggy.

"You and your dead friend came to make trouble." The man's accented English came out menacing.

"No. I sat at the bar minding my business." Did they question the witnesses? Who else did they haul in? "What happened to the guys who killed my friend?" Emerson made a gun symbol with his index finger and thumb, held it to his forehead, and pantomimed a shot. Then another.

The questioner's voice rose, and he pointed his finger in Emerson's face. "You caused trouble." What did he suspect Emerson did? Killed Mo and then sat around waiting for the police with Mo's splattered head in Emerson's lap?

As if receiving a signal, the questioning police officer stood, turned, and exited the room. The rest followed him. No explanation. Did they even understand English? They left Emerson in the interrogation room for hours. The bar scene kept flashing in his mind. Mo's beating. The enforcer's iron grip on Emerson's bicep. His rage and helplessness. Flashbacks of the fight on the beach. The stink of blood, urine, feces, of death filled his nostrils. For a few seconds, he thought he'd faint and topple off the metal chair.

Then the cavalry arrived—two uniformed security police officers. One spoke Thai. They collected Emerson and escorted him to the airfield. No one asked him questions on the return trip to the base, but they explained the murder would be a joint investigation between the Thai and American authorities. Emerson returned to Vietnam. Lieutenant Colonel grounded him. No flight time until cleared of wrongdoing. That would never be. Emerson was guilty of letting thugs murder Mo.

Quicksilver said, "Shit happens out here. More bad crap will come. You gotta hold your head up. Do your job. Don't let them see you sweat."

"Them who?"

"The brass, White boys, whoever. Give no quarter. Right now, you're feeling sorry for yourself. That won't do."

Q spoke the truth. Instead of sympathy for Mo and Kiki, fear, guilt, and self-pity saturated Emerson.

"Not sure how to change."

"Hum the tune 'til you know the words."

Emerson lifted his bloodshot eyes, turned, and looked at Quicksilver. "I'll try."

"Trying is for losers, for folks who get themselves killed, or court-martialed, or demoted. Don't try. Do." He patted Emerson's knee. "I'll check on you in a few days. Get your shit together or this will be a never-ending war for you."

After Q left, Emerson pulled out his smokes and lit up. What could he have done differently? And what would he tell Kiki when he tracked her down? How could he face Mo's child? Hum the tune, Quicksilver said. Don't try.

•   •   •

June 7, 1968

They cleared Emerson for flight status the last week of May. It felt good working again, contributing. Sleep still eluded him, but he found a few beers before bedtime helped. At least in falling asleep. He frequently awoke after a few hours, haunted by horrors. He squirreled away some beers in his footlocker for bad nights. When the beer stopped working, he switched to whisky.

Friday morning, he woke up hung over. He needed to clear his mind before a 0900 recon flight. After gulping several glasses of water, he pulled on his blue flight suit, grabbed his headset, aviator sunglasses, and strapped his loaded 357 revolver onto his hip.

The day was furnace hot. Emerson trotted out to the airstrip, perspiration coating his face and drying the next second. He'd missed chow. No appetite, and when he ate, he got nauseous. Weight loss made his clothes bag. He knew flying sleep deprived put everyone in danger, but he could power through. Hum the tune.

Their mission would lead them to the outskirts of Hanoi, the trip's riskiest leg. Emerson climbed aboard, swung into his seat in the center of the plane and fired up his console.

"Thanks for making time for us," the pilot said in Emerson's ear–his sarcasm clear.

"Sorry." He focused on his electronics. The lack of sleep and whisky hangover left him groggy. His vision blurred. He blinked hard, generating moisture to help clear his sight.

Gus, one of the few White guys Emerson sometimes hung with, walked past steel and netting, the uncomfortable seating that lined each side of the C-130, known as the Vietnam workhorse. It hauled supplies, troops, vehicles, and, on Christmas Eve, presents for South Vietnamese children. But Emerson's plane existed to take recon photos. People counted on him, and soldiers' lives depended on his accuracy and thoroughness. Although big enough for forty to sixty airmen, Emerson flew with the same four men and no passengers.

"You up for this?" Gus asked. He was lean with sharp blue eyes. Blonde curls that got him teased crowned his head.

"Yeah. Coming down with something, but I'll be okay."

Gus eyed him. "Been watching you," he said in his funny Brooklyn accent.

"I'm good."

Gus gripped Emerson's shoulder. "You say you're fine, then you are." But he sounded skeptical.

Since Dr. King's murder, the entire months of April and May remained tense. No brother ate or walked alone. White folks steered clear. Emotions quieted down on the base in June. Emerson noticed the brothers getting along better with their White counterparts. Not hanging out, but friendlier. Everyone returned to hating Charlie instead of each other. Tensions eased enough for Emerson to feel comfortable during the day.

They lifted off on time. The cloudless blue sky made takeoff easy. Instructions from the tower and flight plan kept them on course and out of harm's way.

The pilot spoke in Emerson's electronic ear again. "Did you hear about Bobby Kennedy?"

Emerson's heart clutched. "What?"

"Arab guy smoked him yesterday in LA. Died this morning. Ain't that something? First King and now Kennedy."

Emerson closed his eyes. Someone gunned down Bobby. What the fuck? Before King's murder, and then Mo's, Emerson looked forward to finishing his tour. Now, he didn't want to go home. Bobby Kennedy pledged to create laws that helped poor and Black people. Shit. Why go on? Quicksilver's voice echoed in Emerson's ears. "Do your job. One step at a time." He turned his attention to his cameras and imagined the drink he'd have when they landed.

CHAPTER TWENTY-THREE
ARIA

Friday, March 15, Ithaca, NY

Another panic attack tried to take over my body. The situation with Zander and Darcy required self-control, positivity, and firmness. My relationship with Jax baffled me. I sent tons of mixed messages. Please kiss me. Don't you dare. I want you. Stop. I behaved like this with Ben as well.

We dated for eight years before marrying. My mother's frustration spilled out during most visits home. "Your chances of having a baby are running out. What are you two waiting for? I want to live to see my grandchildren." My father took a different tack. "If Ben isn't the one for you, stop stringing him along. Let him go. Find the right guy." Ben tired of waiting too, but I wanted to have a career, my own income and bank account–independence markers taught by both of my impatient parents.

Ben worked for a major consulting firm. No big salary, but ambitious plans. I intended to bring value to the marriage. At first, when I explained this to him, he supported me, and said he liked my independence. After year five of still dating and refusing to set a wedding date, he accused me of making excuses. Not true. We lived together. Why couldn't that be enough until I reached my career and financial goals? My parents hated us living as a couple, with only an engagement ring on my finger. "How can we face Pastor?"

Now here I was again.

Cleaned up and dressed in my hand washed and hairdryer-dried underwear and smoothed out clothes from yesterday, I completed several repetitions of my breathing exercise until my heart quieted. I searched my mental playlist. It landed on Mariah Carey singing "Hero," reminding me to dig deep and recognize the hero within me.

• • •

At 8:30, we met in the lobby. I eyed Jax. He looked shaven, combed, and unrumpled–his expression unreadable.

"Morning," I said in my cheery voice.

He nodded, pushed out the hotel door, and held it for me. In silence, we walked to the Jeep. The air chilled my face and hands. I tugged on gloves. "I apologize for not answering the phone last night."

"No problem." He opened the passenger side door and helped me climb in. Once again, I wore snow-boots for the weather, taking away three inches of height I enjoyed in my heels.

"Thank you." Geez. So awkward. Jax climbed in on the other side and started the car. "I'm sorry for being so mixed up and sending you jumbled signals."

He turned and looked at me. "I didn't mean to..." His voice trailed off.

"My fault." Why was I so conflicted and indecisive? At work, I made dozens of decisions a day. Studied the issue, examined the data, listened to the manager in charge, considered, and decided. Boom. With my non-existent love life, decisive Aria disappeared.

Jax stayed quiet, so I did too. We hit the first red traffic light.

"How will you handle Zander and Darcy?"

I admitted I had no clue. "I'm hoping they'll discuss protection with the local police. Get some reinforcement. They might suggest he go home." I heaved my shoulders. "Perhaps a compromise. Take a leave of absence from Cornell rather than drop out. Stay in touch with me."

"Sounds good," Jax said.

"You could help me kidnap him."

Jax laughed.

"Last night I dug deeper into Climate Action, but found nothing, not in the local newspapers, or television stories posted online."

"Other than they're three years old, I found nothing," Jax said.

"My point. Surely, they've achieved something worth posting or reporting." I paused. "Zan is smart. If he's so wrapped up in the cause, she must have offered him proof of successes."

"Or..."

"Or what?"

Jax gave me a look like the one Lacy gives me when she thinks I'm being dense. Then it hit me. "Oh." At eighteen, Zander reached the peak of his sexual drive. Something I didn't want to acknowledge but saw it in the moony looks and handholding. I'm so dense.

We arrived and disembarked. Icy tire-tread streaks marked the streets and edged the sidewalks with frozen snow. We crunched our way to the same cafe where we met yesterday. Although Jax and I arrived ten minutes early, we found Darcy and Zander already seated, heads together in deep conversation. Groups of seniors and young moms with infants and toddlers packed the cafe. We navigated around tables and strollers and startled the couple with my "Hello."

Zander jumped in his seat, looked up, his eyes wide. He stood, came around and hugged me–quick and lean-in rather than my preferred sink-in and linger.

"Morning, Mom."

Winter-dry skin and chapped lips touched a mom nerve, but I resisted mentioning either or offering to get him products at the pharmacy. Nor did I whip out my extra Chapstick. With a returned nod to Darcy, we all sat down.

It took some time for the busy server to take our order. The awkwardness of our polite, and off-point conversation, got me tugging on a curl and letting it spring back several times until I caught myself and forced my hands onto my lap.

Once we ordered breakfast, the normally quiet Jax started the conversation. "Your mom had a smart idea. She mentioned it yesterday. Let's all meet with the local police and campus security. Get their thoughts and at least alert them to the men who followed us and the man lurking by your office yesterday."

"*Thank you*, Jax." He made it sound so reasonable. "Yes. We can go when we finish eating."

Darcy said, "I've been wondering about that man. We have detractors. But no one ever threatened us, and we've been fighting for years. Ithaca is safe."

"You could be in danger. Even the safest places have criminals."

Her eyes darted in my direction and then away. "We're not seeing any reason to go to the police. It will call unwanted attention to our upcoming actions."

"What are you planning?" My voice rose in alarm. What activities required secrecy from the police?

The server with the tattoo interrupted us. "Who has the All American Breakfast?"

Jax's phone vibrated on the table. He pointed to his place in response to the question, glanced at his screen, and stood. "I have to take this." He hustled outside without his jacket.

Once the server sorted everyone's meal and left, I said, "Darcy, I asked about the actions you mentioned."

"We don't discuss them with outsiders. The elements of surprise and anonymity are essential."

What the hell? "I'm his mother, not an outsider."

"Mom. Come on, back up." He sounded embarrassed.

"Can you get arrested? Is it dangerous? Illegal?" I was not having this.

"Thanks for breakfast," Darcy said in her snarky tone from yesterday. "We have to go." Her meal remained untouched.

"No." I stood up and blocked their way. "Are your plans illegal?"

Silence.

"Zander Wright, you answer me. Can you get arrested?"

He shot a look at Darcy and then faced me. "No. It's nothing like that. The element of surprise helps us get publicity."

Jax reappeared, his face covered with worry. He appeared startled to see us all standing and glaring at each other.

"Everything okay?" he asked.

"No. They're involved in a criminal—"

"Mom, stop." Zander spoke with force. "We're fine." He looked just the opposite.

"Are we going to the police?" Jax asked.

"No," Darcy said. She faced Zan. "Right Z?"

"Right." He'd dropped his eyes and wouldn't look at me.

They turned toward the door, leaving full plates of food. Wasn't wasting food bad for the environment? What might bring him back to his senses? Nothing. All the anger swept out of me. "Call me." I pleaded to his retreating back.

Zan twisted toward me and nodded.

"Promise?"

He nodded again. Darcy took his hand, and they walked out.

I felt helpless and inadequate only once before, during Zander's bike accident. He'd been racing his friends on a twisty path along the Hudson River. Five boys, their bikes crowded together, dodged dog walkers and joggers. Zan loved his ten-speed English racer. Flying along, leaning right, and left as the path twisted through tree stands and brush, they came to a blind curve. A deer jumped right into Zander's path. The animal went down and Zan tumbled over his handlebars. Another kid, unable to brake in time, slammed into him.

The deer stumbled up and ran off. Dazed, banged up, and in fierce pain, Zander lay on the concrete, moaning. Fortunately, a physician and fellow rider who came upon him stopped and took charge. He piled the two crumpled bikes and hurt boys into his van and drove them to the hospital. Zan's concussion, broken arm, bruised ribs, and damaged lung kept him in the hospital for three weeks. Terror and helplessness gripped me as I sat in the emergency room, waiting for news.

Jax touched my arm. "What do you want to do?" We checked out of the hotel. Hanging around would accomplish nothing. "I'd still like to meet with the police and campus security, stop by the Dean of Students' office as well. See if they can prevent me losing $40,000 for the semester." To my ears, my voice signaled defeat.

Jax looked concerned. "Yeah. Let's go now."

We hadn't eaten our delicious-smelling breakfast, but I sensed his desire to hurry. "Something bad on that phone call?"

"Work."

He'd been so helpful. I couldn't ask for another day. "Okay. I'll call from the car."

"You sure?"

The various people I wanted to speak with might have appointments and tracking them down could take all day. "Yes. We'll hit the road, and I'll call as we go."

We both checked for lurking men or the Rogue, but nothing appeared suspicious. My entire body thrummed with uneasiness, plus a heavy layer of sadness, but Jax pointed the Jeep toward Binghamton, and we headed home.

CHAPTER TWENTY-FOUR
JAX

Skilled at compartmentalization, Jax's current state left him confused. Thoughts of Aria intruded no matter what task he tackled. More unwelcome news from E-Man. The cyber thieves hit three additional clients. The Resilience Protocols held up, but rumors were spreading. No word from the anonymous texter. The FBI tried to trace the messages, but he or she used a burner. So far, a dead end. Jax's phone buzzed. Plugged into a USB port, the call appeared on the Jeep's dashboard. Charlie.

"Hey, brother," Jax said.

"You alone?"

"No. Aria and I are in the Jeep." Jax glanced at Aria. She appeared deep in thought, and not paying attention to his call. "What's up?"

"The whistler-blower reached out again."

"Another text?"

"Yeah. And a second warning about families being in danger."

Aria sucked in a breath.

"Our guys, clients, or both?"

"Both."

Jax eyed Aria again. She looked at him. He didn't want to send her stress levels higher. She was doing her nervous hair thing. Now she twisted a curl around her finger. This Jax found distracting. Last night, breathing in her scent when he kissed her, he'd sunk his fingers into her hair, held her face, found her mouth, and tasted her for the first time.

Charlie's voice brought Jax back. "You still there?"

"Sorry. I missed the last thing you said."

"You, Steven, and I need to confab the second you get here. What's your ETA?"

"Why not include my team? This is a sleuthing and technical problem. My guys can produce answers."

"We'll have to pull our remote workers in. People have families. Weekend plans." Charlie, a dad of three ages five and under, managed human relations among other things, so he worried about the impact on the staffs' family lives.

"I get it." Not actually, since Jax didn't have children. A situation that made him sad. Ready for a family, he wondered if Aria desired another child? They could adopt an older kid. Whoa. Inside, he laughed at himself.

"So, just us?" Charlie asked. "Jax, are you listening?"

"Sorry. Yeah. This is an emergency. We need the team."

"Okay," Charlie said, his tone resigned. "What time?"

Jax glanced at the bottom of the display screen. "ETA 12:45. But I have to drop off Aria, make sure she's safe, so let's make it 2:00."

"See you then." Charlie hung up.

They sped down the highway doing seventy, Binghamton twenty minutes out. Light traffic and no snow flurries made the drive smooth. The weak winter sun gave a warm glow to the frigid outside air. Jax turned off his seat warmer. "Temperature, okay?"

"Fine. What's happening at your office?"

"Cyber-attack."

"Oh, no. Isn't your job to prevent them?"

Exactly. How did this happen? And why? Extortion, but also threats. "We prevent, stop, help clients survive them, investigate and sometimes bring the perpetrators to justice."

"And one got through?"

"Hit clients and us."

"What will you do?"

Jax scanned his mirrors, still watchful for the Rogue. "We're meeting this afternoon to come up with a plan." The key was uncovering the identity of the whistleblower. E-Man, a master sleuth, managed a talented squad. They'd discover the truth and give us a leg up in stopping the crime spree.

The city of Binghamton's skyline rose on the horizon. A city of 48,000 people, known as the Carousel Capital of the World, owned six antique carousels. The city also suffered from one of the highest crime rates in the country for a municipality its size. Jax stayed vigilant.

The highway skirted the city, but the traffic both increased and slowed. A dump truck trundled in front of them. Behind, another Jeep inched forward in tandem with Jax's. He glanced in his side-view mirror. Nothing out of the ordinary.

Aria said, "Seems like a lot of coincidences. Emerson's murder, the killer threatening me, two guys following us, the man lurking in front of Darcy's place, and a cyber-attack."

"There's no common link between each situation," he said. "Yes, a lot of coincidences, but I'm having a hard time seeing how they're connected."

"When you're cyber-sleuthing, how does it work?"

"First, we protect ourselves and clients from further damage and then gather data. Facts."

She turned on the radio but only heard static, so she shut it off. "Once you have more information and the police dig deeper, we'll find a common denominator."

"Could be," Jax said. But his brain was having difficulty making that leap.

"If it won't bother you, I have to make those phone calls."

With half an ear, Jax listened to Aria negotiate with the university's bursar office, and the head of campus security. A sergeant from the Ithaca police listened to her summary, took their information, and promised to get back to her. The other half of his brain ran through scenarios. Once again, he ruminated on the coincidences that crisscrossed between his troubles, Aria's, and the murder. Pieces were missing, but what?

Aria hung up from her last call and put her phone in her tote.

"Got things squared away?" Jax asked.

"Sorta." She tugged on her curls again.

"Try not to worry." Good advice for Jax to take as well.

•   •   •

The team filled every seat in the large conference room. A coffee urn and electric teapot stood next to pastries and fruit, cups, and condiments. Multicolored notes filled the whiteboard. Charlie rolled his shoulders, put the marker down and grabbed his seat at the head of the table. Open computers, pads, pens, empty and filled coffee cups, and crumbled paper dotted the oval conference table. Stephen sat at the foot. He tilted his chair back and rubbed his eyes. They were two hours into the meeting, but no concrete solutions emerged.

Jax rose. "We're going in circles. Stephen, you focus on customer service and the media. Manage the angst. E-Man and I will check the dark web again, retracing our steps. Charlie, this is going to cost us real money. Give us three scenarios. Worst case, best case, and likely."

Everyone shuffled out.

Stephen grabbed Jax before he could leave. "What's happening with the murder and your lady?"

"She's not my—"

"Whatever." He waved his hands in a dismissive gesture. "Anything new?"

"Two guys followed us to Ithaca." Jax recapped the trip. "It's a lot of stuff happening at once."

"Connected?"

"That's what I'm wondering."

"Let me investigate that angle. I've got contacts in the FBI and State Police." Stephen, the rainmaker and connector, knew all the local politicians, CEOs, philanthropists, police chiefs, and savvy reporters. "I'll get my folks on client handholding and jump into what's going on at The Way Station and in Ithaca."

"Thanks, brother." Jax rubbed his chin. "It's been a lot to process."

"I've got ya."

Stephen took being the big brother of the three seriously. When they were kids, Stephen kept his brothers safe from bullies and hooked them up with girls and parties. Charlie and Jax, serious nerds, needed all the help they could get. Stephen was the opposite.

"And you and Aria? How's that going?"

Jax licked his lips remembering how much he enjoyed kissing her. "I've got it bad." He laughed. "But she doesn't."

CHAPTER TWENTY-FIVE
ARIA

Saturday, March 16, Fieldcrest, NY

I hated funerals. For me, holding a celebration-of-life several months after the person's death is better. That's what I wanted. Being with people still numb from the loss, sobbing relatives, and open caskets held no appeal. In Emerson's case, however, there were few mourners.

Once Jax dropped me off on Friday afternoon, I called Lacy to inquire about the funeral arrangements. Hiring Lacy was one of the best moves I ever made. She and Ginger made the arrangements, including paying for the cremation and service. I left a message for Kiki Alexander with the time and location.

Lacy and Ginger started a collection at The Way Station, and staff members and volunteers chipped in. The money paid for the funeral home, including the simple repast that would follow—crackers, cheese, fruit, and cookies. Coffee and tea as well. Lacy called a few of her most generous donors, including Valentine, who paid for the cremation and covered the cost for the niche in the columbarium, where the funeral director would place Emerson's ashes. It seemed like a lot for someone no one might visit, but Valentine insisted. My dear friend Joy agreed to officiate and refused compensation. Generous people surrounded me, and I was grateful for each one.

Marshall's Funeral Home sat on the corner of Ocean and Fifth. In the spring and summer, tall maples and oaks shaded the grassy plot. Today, an icy coat covered the bare tree branches. Winter held on stubbornly.

Inside, several private rooms, some with mourners and others empty, made it clear where we were. A black-suited man with a protruding belly escorted us past a large room filled with seventy people. They sat at round tables covered with white and gold tablecloths. An enlarged photo of the deceased, surrounded by stands of flowers, stood next to the casket. Soft music played in the background.

Emerson's funeral was the exact opposite. The urn holding his ashes sat on a podium in the smallest of the rooms. No flower arrangements, thirty mostly empty chairs lined up theater-style.

Except for a woman and man in the front row, everyone in the room either volunteered or worked for The Way Station or the police department.

Errol stepped next to me. His aftershave, a pleasant scent, flavored the air. "Good afternoon," I said. "I didn't expect to see you."

"You look nice," Errol said, surprising me.

I stammered, "Oh, well, thanks." The royal blue dress always worked for me. Fitted, short, with a scoop neckline, flattered my stature, curves, and coloring. Jax came to mind when I put it on, and I blushed at the thought. This was a somber occasion.

As if correcting a lapse, Errol's voice changed to his all business one. "Sometimes, killers show up for the funeral or burial, so stay alert. Tell me if you recognize anyone."

I couldn't imagine the murderer coming to a service of twenty people. How would he blend in? "Sure," I said, rather than explain my skepticism. Errol wore a tailored, three-piece, pinstripe suit, white shirt, and paisley tie. Once again, I noted his movie star looks. "Is Detective Yun joining you?"

"She's keeping tabs on who enters and leaves." He smiled down at me. "How are you holding up?"

Good question. Today marked the fourth day since the murder, and so far, no leads. "I'm fine. Thank you for asking." Except my shot nerves and morning panic attacks continued to plague me. Not to mention how much Errol and Jax unnerved me. Was I attracted to Errol too? "Anything new?"

A tall skinny White man in a flimsy raincoat walked up to me. "People call me Twitch," he said, holding out his hand. "You're Miss Aria?"

I shook his hand. "Yes. And your relation to Cal Emerson...?"

"His sponsor." He put his hand toward Errol. "I'd like the answer to Miss Aria's question as well. Any closer to solving the murder?"

Errol squinted. "Let's talk after the service. I need a fuller picture of Emerson. You must have known him well."

"Confidential. Can't tell you anything. Guess you're not sharing either."

I sensed Jax rather than saw him join us. With a silent count of four, I breathed, turned, and smiled up at him.

Errol introduced Twitch to Jax.

"Mr. Twitch," I said. "I don't think you're under any moral obligation of confidentiality once your charge is dead. Don't you want to help us find Emerson's killer?"

Twitch twitched. "Sorry. Can't help. I'm honor bound." He tipped his head toward me. "He liked you a lot. Respect."

"Oh." My eyes filled up, which was ridiculous. During our many conversations, Emerson never spoke about anything personal, including his sponsor. I searched my memory, but the name Twitch didn't exist. Last year, Emerson and I spoke about his illness, the horrible disease of addiction. I urged him to return to AA, and he agreed, but we didn't discuss his progress or struggles. I only learned his full name after the murder. Shame warmed my face.

"Good man," Twitch said. "This shouldn't have happened."

"I agree," I said, still teary. "I cared for him. Who would kill him?" Was there someone in AA who held a grudge? "Do you have any thoughts?"

"I can't stay. Just wanted to offer my condolences." He nodded to Jax, Errol, and me, turned and left.

That was a non-answer. I glanced at Errol. He looked concerned, perhaps feeling the same way I was about Twitch.

Jax asked me, "Are you okay?"

I tilted my head so I could look up at him. Those mesmerizing eyes smiled at me. I loved their bright green under thick black brows. I found my voice. "Yes." But I wasn't.

Pastor Joy Johns bounded in, interrupting my thoughts and questions. On his volunteer application, Emerson listed his religion as Baptist. We inquired at every Baptist church in Fieldcrest, but no one recognized him, so I asked Pastor Joy to officiate. We met in high school where Joy, Lacy, and I became close friends. Joy moved away when offered a minister's position, one of five, at a large church in Connecticut. When our pastor of thirty years left The Lighthouse Church, Joy was the first person I called.

"Sorry I'm late." She leaned down and kissed my cheek. Her eyes swept the room and returned to me. "Is this it? Are you expecting more?"

I shook my head. Errol eased away. Was he following Twitch? "The lady and gentleman in the front row might be his family. I was just going to introduce myself."

"Let's do it together." She shrugged out of her coat.

Jax took it from her, pointed to where he'd hang it, and introduced himself.

"Oh, so you're Jax Oats. Nice to meet you."

His eyebrows rose and my heart clutched. Pastor Joy never divulged confidences. What had I told her about Jax? Could she tell how enamored I was?

"I understand you're a valued volunteer."

Ahh. Whew. Jax went to hang her coat and Pastor Joy, and I walked to the front.

The woman, who I guessed was sixty or seventy, aged well. Creamy fair skin showed only tiny lines around lively eyes. The man sitting next to her looked my age.

"Mrs. Alexander?" I asked.

"Yes." She smiled. A missing molar left a noticeable gap. "Please call me Kiki."

"I'm Aria Wright. We spoke." I sat down next to her. "This is Pastor Joy."

Joy squatted until the three of us were at eye level. "I'm so sorry for your loss." She lifted her chin toward the man. "How are you connected to Mr. Emerson?"

The man's eyes were the same color as Kiki's.

"Mo, my husband..." Kiki paused and glanced at the man beside her. "Maurice Jr.'s father died... in Vietnam."

The man said, "I go by M.J." He darted an annoyed look at his mother. "No one calls me Maurice, Jr."

Kiki pursed her glossed lips. "As I was saying, Mo and Emerson met the day they signed up as airmen and stayed friends until Mo's murder."

Murder. The word hung in the air. Cold. Bloody. I must have made a sound because Kiki said, "It's ironic. Both killed. Such a strange coincidence."

There was that word again.

"That's not irony, Mom," M.J. said in the patient tone a parent might use with a child.

She shrugged. "M.J. is a lawyer and constantly corrects my English."

"Sorry." He sounded contrite.

"That's okay," Kiki said. She faced me again. "He stayed in touch over the years. M.J. saw him last Christmas." She turned to her son as if seeking confirmation.

M.J. made a sound I couldn't interpret.

"At one point we were a family," Kiki said. "Didn't end well."

M.J. scowled.

Kiki shrugged. "For me, our parting doesn't negate the good. That's why we're here."

Silent M.J.'s frown grew tighter. I tried not to stare, but Errol's comments rang in my head. "Killers sometimes turn up at the funeral or burial." Were this man's expressions conveying anger, hatred, enough to kill Emerson? I studied M.J.'s face, looking for signs of recognition. Even though I'd only seen the murderer's eyes once, I would remember M.J.'s distinctive sepia color if they belonged to the killer. Then I recalled the strange luminescence. Contact lenses can change eye color.

"Please forgive my son. He came because I asked him. Couldn't face the trip alone." She patted M.J.'s leg. "Couldn't survive without him. Aging alone is not fun."

Pastor Joy asked, "Kiki, when did you last see Mr. Emerson?"

"Hmm. Decades ago. M.J. saw him, but not me. The booze and crack took him away."

M.J.'s responding growl laced with... what? Sadness? Pain? "He took himself away. Drugs don't possess a mind. They can't decide."

Kiki turned toward her son. "When did you see him before last Christmas?"

"Don't remember."

She gave him a quizzical look, shrugged, and faced me again. "It's been a minute, but for a while, we were close."

Pastor Joy reached her hands across Kiki and grasped M.J.'s. "I hear your pain. It is difficult to love an addicted family member, but—"

"Loving isn't hard, it's living with one that's tough," M.J. said.

"Forgiving others... and ourselves, isn't easy either."

I felt M.J. and Joy were having a different conversation than Kiki and me.

Joy said to both mother and son, "I pray something said or sung today will bring you insight, and perhaps peace." She stood. "We should get started. Mrs. Alexander, did you want to say anything?"

Kiki declined.

"M.J.?"

He appeared to consider. Hesitated. Then shook his head.

My mind swam with names and images–the killer, the two men following us, the lurking man in Ithaca, and now M.J. And Emerson's friend Mo, also murdered. Too much. Errol's face filled my mind. He confused and flustered me. And what was I to do about Wally Wallace and the suspicious funding reports sitting on my desk? How was I going to get Hope House completed?

"Hey." Jax reappeared at my side.

Even though we were in a public space peopled with staff and volunteers, I leaned against him.

He put his arm around me and squeezed.

Of all the voices I needed to hear, including my wonderful pastor's, Jax's voice and touch were what I needed most.

CHAPTER TWENTY-SIX
EMERSON

April 1970, New York

Two years later, Emerson still found sleeping difficult. The boarding house on Lenox and Fifth in Harlem housed over twenty men who lived without women or children, although many had families. Some recently arrived, hoping for jobs and enough money to pay for bringing wives and kids to New York. Many came from the South and Midwest. Others, like Emerson, returned from the war adrift with nowhere else to go.

Leaving the Air Force was both easy and difficult. Emerson couldn't wait to get back to the world and see his family. Re-connect with his life before the service. The discharging-sergeant asked him if he wanted to re-up. No way.

The difficulty hit the minute he got home. His family, not his parents, but the extended relatives, acted aloof. They looked at him with hardened eyes. A cousin asked how many children he murdered. Most of his high school friends, guys he grew up with, attended elementary and junior high school together, were still in the service, or stayed in the place of their last deployment. Kenny and Lavar, his closest buddies, were in Nam and not due out for another six months. Guys he remembered but barely knew hung out on corners, talking basketball or who got laid the night before. They expressed no interest in Emerson's time in the Air Force. Asked no questions. They, and the rest of America, were not glad he and his fellow vets were back. Emerson was lucky. He flew over the war. So many guys' bodies and minds were destroyed with no one to help them. People didn't understand. Nor did they want to. Happy in their ignorance or anti-war anger.

The job market was rough. His parents made room for him and paid for whatever he needed, but it was hard on them. They had little. So, he headed for the city.

When he left for Manhattan on a Greyhound bus, his mother cried. His father, a square-built man, like himself, who could never deny Emerson since they looked so much alike, shook Emerson's hand. "Find some peace, son." He patted Emerson's back. "Ease up on the booze. Figure out why you need it." He pressed a fifty-dollar bill into his son's hand. "Call your mother regular."

The bus pulled away. His mother sagged against his dad, who gave a brief wave. Emerson twisted in his seat and watched them until they disappeared from his view.

The alarm clock shone in bright red numbers 2:00 a.m. Emerson groaned and almost expected Quicksilver to come by. "Can't sleep?" His deep voice, concern, and empathy grounded Emerson. Quicksilver always had an encouraging and practical word. Like Emerson's father–old school wisdom.

Bleary-eyed, Emerson shifted his aching head with care and looked around. The rented room held a narrow bed with a questionable mattress, a dresser, and a small table for his illegal hot plate and half-full bottle of Johnny Walker. Smoky air yellowed the walls. His bladder spoke to him. The bathroom in the hall accommodated the five other men on his floor. Although Emerson was used to sharing and living with men, the odors, roaches, rats, and noise inside and out depressed him.

He got up, but instead of making his way to the head, the common military term for the bathroom, he grabbed a plastic cup and poured two inches of whiskey. His father's warning words whispered in his ear, but he downed the drink anyway, reached for his smokes, and lit up. The housing situation and no decent job were only part of his gloom. When his dad returned from World War II, there were parades, jobs, housing, medical support, and opportunities for college. The vets were heroes. Not so much now. Anti-war protests and social unrest dominated the news he watched on his bar-of-choice's television. Some vilified President Nixon. Others were angry too, but not at the president. They hated the long-haired protestors, draft dodgers, and college students. Where was Nixon's silent majority when Uncle Sam shipped men, women, and a disproportionate number of brothers to war? How did so many White folks who made up Nixon's supporters skip the draft? What were they all doing while Emerson flew over the tropics being fired upon by the Viet Cong?

He slumped back into bed, his ashtray resting on his chest, and finished his cigarette. In a minute, he'd get up and pee. He closed his eyes. Mo's murder still haunted him. The images and sounds stayed with him–raw meat stink of Mo's blood, the crazy dark eyes of the guy called Iggy, and the guilt for not being there when Mo needed him the most.

His mind drifted from the murder to Kiki's smile. After all this time, he still remembered her scent. Tomorrow, he'd visit her. Re-introduce himself and make amends for letting her husband get murdered in Bangkok. Not that Emerson had any hope for redemption.

• • •

The April day smelled ripe with budding trees, trimmed hedges around small front yards, and daffodils waving in the breeze. Kiki lived in an apartment in a two-story house in the Bronx on Fish Avenue with her sister, brother-in-law, two nieces, and Maurice Jr. The number five elevated train left him off at Eastchester Road. From there, he walked to her block. The Bronx was new to him. Children rode their bikes in the street, jumped rope, and hopped off the concrete steps that led to the front doors of each house.

Emerson climbed his way to Kiki's foyer. There was a spring in his step that was missing yesterday. Getting out of the dense city to a safer and less crowded neighborhood added to his mood. It wasn't country like his upstate home, but he liked the vibe.

A woman huffed behind him. She was overweight with swollen feet, her arms filled with paper bags of groceries.

"Let me help," Emerson said. "I can carry them both."

She paused and eyed him. "Who are you?" Her accent was southern rather than New York.

"I'm a friend of Mrs. Alexander. Came by to say hello."

"What kind of friend?" She placed her groceries on the step above her and continued giving Emerson the hairy eye.

"Her husband and I served together in the Air Force." Emerson kept his annoyance from his voice. What business was this of hers? "Came by to pay my respects." He hoped his breath was fresh enough, with no trace of his morning cup of Johnny Walker and coffee.

"You in the war?" she asked in an accusatory tone.

"Yeah." What the hell? He started lying about Nam because people made assumptions. Pity clouded their eyes or disgust. Hate too. He felt good, so he told the truth. The woman surprised him.

"Okay. You can help me."

That made Emerson smile. Did she expect a thank you for carrying *her* bags?

The woman finished climbing the steps and walked past him with her key in her hand. "Well, if you're gonna help me, grab those groceries. I got ice cream melting in one of them." She unlocked the aluminum front door.

"She expecting you?"

"Yes." He called yesterday and set up the morning visit for today.

"Come on then." She held the door open and Emerson, both bags in his arms, walked in.

"Push that second bell. She'll come down and get you." The woman unlocked her door and shoved her keys back into her jacket pocket. "Just put the bags down. I don't invite strange men into my home."

Lucky me, Emerson thought. "No ma'am. Best be safe."

The door to the second-floor apartment swung open.

"Cal, how wonderful to see you." Kiki threw her arms around his neck and kissed his cheek. "Come in. Come in."

The greeting surprised and pleased him.

Not so for Kiki's landlady. The older woman made a disapproving noise. "Howdy do, Miz Alexander."

Kiki leaned around Emerson and waved. "Lovely day." She pulled back and suppressed a laugh only Emerson witnessed.

Kiki looked good. Different from his memory. Even better. She was sweet and sexy. Her full Afro framed her face and made it seem smaller and narrower than he remembered. Wide-set eyes, the color of sepia photos from years ago, smiled up at him. Large hoop earrings swung from her earlobes. The African print dress hugged her narrow form. Emerson followed her up the steep steps to a wooden door with glass inlays. The same old pull remained.

CHAPTER TWENTY-SEVEN

They entered a dining area adjacent to the kitchen. A vase of daffodils sat in the center of a colorful Formica table. Kiki veered right into the living room and Emerson followed.

"Have a seat. Can I get you anything? Water, juice?"

A toddler's cry rang out. "Mama."

"Oh, that's Maurice Jr., waking from his nap. Way too early. I'll give him a bottle so we can talk."

Emerson watched her walk back the way they came, through the dining area, to a bedroom. When she returned, all was quiet.

"He usually sleeps for another hour, but..." She shrugged.

They sat on a sofa covered in plastic. A glass-topped coffee table stood in front. Emerson looked but didn't see an ashtray. Nor did the house have the telltale scent of cigarette smoke. He left his pack in his pocket.

"So, how are you making out?" Kiki asked. "You've come home to crazy times."

"I'm okay. How are you and the boy doing..." He paused for the briefest second. "...without Mo?"

A wedding photo of Kiki and Mo, with Emerson grinning behind them, rested on an end table. It was the same picture Emerson carried in his wallet. His heart rate quickened.

Across from the sofa and coffee table, a television stood on another. Family photos ringed the TV. A framed picture of Dr. King hung on one wall, next to a Black Jesus and a poster of a Black man in a beret, his fist raised in defiance. King, Jesus, and a Black Panther, the activist group that didn't believe in nonviolence. A strange mix. Kiki was speaking, but Emerson missed the first few words.

"...VA benefits plus Social Security, but it still makes living in New York tough. I'm attending evening classes at Bronx Community College, hoping to get a decent job once I finish my AA degree. I'm going to put Maurice in daycare so I can graduate quicker." A sigh accompanied the last bit of news.

"You can't stay with him longer?"

She shook her head. "It'll be fine."

"As soon as I get on my feet, I'll help."

"Oh, no. You take care of *yourself.* My sister and brother-in-law are assisting me." Her upbeat protest sounded forced, as if she were convincing both Emerson and herself.

"I promised Mo." Which wasn't the full truth. He'd promised himself while he was cradling Mo's shot-up head, his blood oozing between Emerson's fingers. Once again, he smelled the raw meat stench. A chill moved through him.

"You sent me money from Nam. There's no need to do more." She shifted in her seat, so she was looking at him more squarely. "Are *you* okay?"

The way she asked made Emerson worry about his breath again. A prostitute told him, in a pitying tone, the booze leaking from his pores stunk. "Adjusting to the hate spewed at vets," he offered to explain his situation, but didn't share all. The cheap booze on the base made it easy to get drunk, to let the whisky blur the images of Mo's murder. A buddy introduced him to heroin, but he only tried it once. Walked away. But memories of the mindless high stayed with him.

Kiki made an odd expression. Did he miss something else she said? "Do the anti-war radicals bother you?" Emerson asked.

She shrugged.

"So, what? You agree with them?"

Kiki stayed quiet for several beats. "It's a dumb-ass war."

Yeah. All that killing for what? His last conversation with Quicksilver came back to him. They were saying goodbye–Emerson heading home and Quicksilver to his new deployment.

"This war ain't right," Q said.

"Not right how?"

"They're lying to us."

Emerson didn't understand what Quicksilver was talking about then. Not exactly. Guys complained, hinted at things neither they nor Emerson knew for sure.

"We're losing this fucking war," Q said. "How can you tell the enemy from a friend? VC and South Vietnamese, they're the same people. Not cousins. Brothers and sisters." He shook his head. "Put this shit-show behind you. Get Sober and make a new life."

Kiki's voice brought Emerson back. "I didn't mean to upset you."

His expression must have reflected his thoughts. "After they murdered King, I found it hard to justify Black folks fighting. Then they murdered Bobby."

"Exactly."

He waited.

"I volunteer in a veterans' organization."

Emerson still stayed quiet. She was trying to tell him something.

"Black vets against the war and for our civil rights."

"Oh, wow." That wasn't what he expected.

Her face lit up. "The war needs to end. Look at the money and lives wasted. We're murdering people and losing. It will not end well."

"Protesters disrespect our service. Is that what you're doing?" Emerson remained conflicted. He knew the war was a huge mistake, but he was also proud of his fellow service men.

Kiki's cheeks flushed. "Brothers by the thousands come home addicted, torn up, disabled, and to what? Spit on for their service. Layer on discrimination, poor or nonexistent health care, and no jobs because they're Black."

It still confused him. White hippies who didn't serve yelled at those forced to go. "You're out there protesting. Waving signs?" His hands twitched, so he shoved them into his pockets. "What would Mo think?"

A shade came down over her eyes. "Sorry I brought it up." She rose. "You drop by any time. For a meal. Or visit. Reminisce."

"I didn't mean to upset you. Just trying to understand."

Her sepia eyes turned darker gold. "With each passing month, my memories of Mo fade." Her tone hinted at sadness. "We weren't together long."

Emerson stood, too. "I'm not judging." He couldn't explain his conflicting emotions—separate rivers comingling.

"Of course not." A phony smile spread across her face, forced, and a bit trembling.

He tried to recover. "I'd like that. A meal and conversation, I mean. I'm a good cook and I'd be happy to serve you dinner."

Now her smile looked genuine. "What kinda meals can you prepare?" She sounded amused and incredulous.

"Fried chicken, steak, sweet potatoes. I make a mean macaroni and cheese."

"Well, well, well."

"And you call me if you need anything," Emerson added. "Someone to make a store run, babysit, or whatever." He bit into his lower lip, trying to decide if he should make the offer sitting on his tongue, waiting for permission. "If you want someone safe, who won't take advantage, to squire you to a party or the movies, I'm your guy." He hadn't intended to make an offer that represented a date. She smelled so good, like delicate flowers he couldn't name. Small, round breasts, and long legs poking out from her miniskirt, got his heart rocking. "You can reach me at the number I gave you. A fellow roomer will give me the message in case I'm not there." Nervous, he wondered if he'd gone too far.

He was only two inches taller than Kiki. She leaned in and kissed his cheek. "Thank you. I will keep that in mind."

She had a sweet smile. Not broad. Kinda halfway, showing tiny white teeth.

As if the entire conversation about anti-war protesting never happened, she said, "Next time you come, we can take Maurice Jr. to the park. I don't want him to forget the father he never met. Share stories."

"Excellent." Emerson turned to go. He needed a smoke, a job, and... a drink.

The baby let out a wail.

Kiki hurried to him. Over her shoulder, she said, "Wait one more minute."

Emerson did as he was told.

"Come on in," she said. "I have to change him."

The powerful stench of urine hit Emerson. The narrow room held a twin sized bed and a crib. Large bags of Pampers, stacked on top of each other, filled a corner. More family photos decorated the windowsill. Loose jewelry, jars and pots of creams and makeup, covered the dresser. Sunlight streamed in between the venetian blind slats.

She made cooing noises as she changed the boy. His fat legs kicked with what looked like joy. Diaper-change complete, Kiki lifted and bounced him in her arms. "Meet Uncle Cal. Say hi."

The boy eyed Emerson. "Hello. I'm Maurice."

"He talks," Emerson said, surprised.

"Of course he can. And count. He knows his letters and colors." Kiki sounded proud.

The baby looked just like Mo, except for Kiki's sepia-brown eyes. Carbon copy. Did he want to be an uncle? Somehow, it sounded wrong in his ears. He harbored other thoughts about Kiki, and being an uncle didn't fit. He shoved the anti-war crap away from the future taking shape in his mind. "I'll be back," he said with conviction.

CHAPTER TWENTY-EIGHT

May 15, 1970, New York City

The news exploded on the streets, in the bars and shops. On May 5, Kent State shootings screamed from the headlines and news stations. During a demonstration, the Ohio National Guard gunned down anti-war protesters who were upset by President Nixon's extension of the war into Cambodia. Four died and nine others taken by ambulance to the hospital. Emerson shook his head. It was hard for him to care. Hippies and privileged White kids angry about a war they didn't have to fight and no one they knew did either. He watched guys returning in body bags, or others with brains scrambled. Junkies and alcoholics. Mama and daddy paid for a fancy education, and these college kids rioted on campuses. He didn't get it.

The shootings at the HBCU, Jackson State, eleven days later was a different matter. It was 6:00 p.m. The space was dark and cool. Faux mahogany rimmed the bar while Gladys Knight and The Pips sang, "If I Were Your Woman" on the jukebox in the corner. Johnny Walker kept Emerson company.

"You hear about those kids killed at Jackson State?" the wiry Black bartender asked. He had a bald head and scruffy beard. Tattoos ran up both arms.

"Yeah."

The joint was filling up. Folks on their way from work stopped in, meeting up with friends. Burgers, fries, and chicken wings were available at the bar. More at the tables. Emerson stayed put. He rubbed his chin and took another swallow.

"When those Kent State White kids got ripped, the outcry was everywhere. White cops gun down ours and you find the story buried on a back page."

Once again, Emerson wondered why he served. King, Bobby, the kids in Mississippi, all killed for being Black or standing up for their rights. And no one cared. He took another pull on his drink. No job. When he put Vietnam Vet on his application at a photography shop, and added his experience taking aerial photos, the woman behind the desk made a sour expression. "Sorry," she said in a tone that was everything but.

The bartender wiped the space in front of Emerson. "Another?"

"Thanks." Why the fuck not? What was the point? He'd hoped to help Kiki and Mo's boy. Now, he couldn't even help himself. He finished his drink and started on the fresh one.

"Ask me, we got no cause killing gooks," the bartender said.

Emerson hated slurs. The South Vietnamese men and women he met on the base were kind and generous. A genial man cut Emerson's hair and provided a scalp, neck, and back massage. When Emerson offered a tip, the guy always refused, but Emerson left it on the counter. Folks from the local town were poor.

"Fools went to kill and be killed. Now we're in Cambodia. Who even knows where the fuck that is?"

Emerson nodded as if he agreed. He didn't want a fight, but the bartender disrespected Emerson. He served his country. Bad enough hippies called him a killer, even though he shot no one. But hearing it from a brother was too much. Emerson took a long swallow. An empty stomach reacts to alcohol differently than one full of burgers, fries, and chicken wings. When did he last eat? Breakfast? Coffee and Johnny Walker with a muffin? Was that today or yesterday?

The song on the jukebox switched to "Stoned Love" by the Supremes. The warm buzz of the alcohol comforted him. He imagined slow dancing with Kiki. Her flower scent washed over him. What would Mo think if he knew about Emerson's carnal thoughts? How might Kiki take it? Back in Nam, when Mo stepped out on Kiki, Emerson felt sorry for her. If he were her man, he'd be faithful. Love her and treat her right. He always wanted the love his father and mother had. They danced in the living room, joked, and laughed. That's what Emerson craved. Maurice Jr.'s chubby face came to mind. He looked like Mo. Would that matter? He was young. Emerson could become his dad, with thoughts of the father he never knew gone.

Several new customers came and sat down. One man seemed familiar. Emerson stared at the reflection in the mirror behind the bar. From where did he know this man? The buzz in Emerson's head also clouded his eyes. His lids drooped. He sensed someone watching him. His eyes flew open, caught malevolent dark eyes, and scarred left cheek. Nah. No way. Emerson closed his eyes and shook his head to clear it. Looked again, but the guy was gone. Was the man Mo's murderer? The guy called Iggy? He's in Bangkok. Why would he be in Harlem? Emerson ordered another drink.

By 8:00 p.m., Emerson stumbled out of the bar, swaying on unsteady feet. That last drink was a mistake, left him dizzy, his mind clouded. One too many. A couple brushed past him, almost knocking him over. Swaying on his feet in front of the bar's entrance, he tried to clear his head. Which way to the boarding house?

"Need some help?"

As if looking through the lens of his aerial camera back in Nam, Emerson squinted one eye, trying to focus on the young man speaking. He looked like a teenager. As if liquid, his features ran together. Maybe the guy was older. "I'm fine." Emerson used a shooing sign with his right hand.

The man stepped closer. "Looks to me like you need help." He looped his arm through Emerson's. "Let's step out of folks' way."

The hair rose on Emerson's neck. Danger alarms rang in his ears. Shove the guy away. Pull your butterfly knife. But the man had a vise-like hold on Emerson's arm, not unlike the bouncer in Bangkok, holding Emerson back from helping Mo. Emerson's feet didn't work like they were supposed to. "Leave me."

"We're almost there," the man said. "Few more steps."

"No. Not right."

The guy shoved Emerson against a brick wall. Patted him down. Pulled his wallet out of his pocket. "What do we have here?"

Emerson only had forty dollars. His father sent him money the first of each month, "until you get on your feet." It had to last another sixteen days. "Gimme that." Emerson pointed. "Mine."

A fist hit his gut and doubled him over. Then another, followed by an uppercut to his chin and a right to his left cheek. Pain exploded. Emerson crumbled to the ground. A sneakered foot slammed into his ribs.

"Nigger. Baby killer." The guy dropped Emerson's wallet and spat into his bloodied cheek.

Then everything went black.

Emerson woke up in the emergency room of Harlem Hospital. He lay on a bed in a space with three others. Nurses and physicians rushed by. No one stopped to check on him. Disinfectant that failed to mask other unpleasant odors infused the air.

Everything hurt–face, ribs, stomach, and back all screamed. Something lay next to him on the bed. He patted down his side until his fingers found a plastic zippered bag. A tug got it onto his chest. He probed and found his watch and wallet. What had the guy taken? Emerson eased out the wallet and searched. All his money was gone. How much? He couldn't remember. His driver's license, Social Security Card, and birth certificate were still in their assigned places. He found his Air Force ID ripped into four pieces and stuffed back in its slot. The thief left the most precious item-Mo and Kiki's wedding photo, with Emerson smiling in the background. The same one he saw in her living room.

He returned his documents and slid on his watch.

"Oh. Oh. Help me." A male voice moaned from the bed next to Emerson's.

With care, he turned his head toward the groaning man. His bloodied face, one eye shut, twisted side to side.

"Oh. Help me. Help me."

A woman's voice yelled in the hall. "Gunshot victim. Two bullets to his stomach and groin." The voice trailed off down the hall.

What was Emerson doing here, among beat up and gunned down people? Should he call Kiki to come and collect him? What would she see or think? Emerson moaned under his breath. What would his father think? Or Quicksilver?

He drifted off. When he awoke some minutes later, his mind quieted, and he had an epiphany, laying on the hospital bed in awful pain, next to a bloodied man Emerson didn't know. Drinking was going to kill him. Johnny Walker wasn't his friend, and Kiki would never take up with a drunk.

He vowed to get sober.

CHAPTER TWENTY-NINE
ARIA

Monday, March 17, Fieldcrest, NY

I awoke with a song in my head. Wisps. I couldn't recall it, yet it stuck, unwilling to either reveal itself or go away. The elusive music stayed with me throughout my treadmill workout, shower, getting dressed, feeding Princess, and alerting the police officer parked in front that I was going to the office. What was it?

The bounce in my step came from a wonderful, restful Sunday. I slept in. Attended the second church service rather than my usual time at 9:00 a.m. On my way home, Zander called. I saw his number and, for a second, froze. With my left hand, I covered my mouth and clicked on the answer button with my right.

"Zan?"

"Hey Mom."

I forced my tone into warmth and unruffled. "Hey yourself. How are you?" A jumble of scenarios swept through my mind. Was he coming home? Did the watcher outside the cafe approach him? "Are you in danger?"

"Danger?"

I caught myself too late. "Sorry. The murder is coloring everything and..." My words trailed off.

"That's right. I forgot." He sounded apologetic.

Silence. I waited.

"Thanks for coming up. I'm sorry I worried you."

To concentrate, I pulled the car over. "It's okay. I love you." My eyes filled up.

Silence again. We always said, "love you and love you more," to each other.

"Love you more. Everything is going to be fine. Just wanted to tell you I was sorry I scared you."

Should I ask about Darcy and the demonstration or action they planned? "Thanks for calling me. You've lifted my spirits."

"Try not to worry."

Fat chance of that. "I will."

"Gotta go. Love you, Mom."

"Love you more."

The phone clicked off. Be happy, I told myself. This is a good sign. A step. An opening. Worry took over. The conversation didn't answer any of my questions or quell my fears. I looked in the car's mirror on the back of the visor, smiled and spoke aloud to my reflection. "My boy is back... Kinda." After wiping my eyes and blowing my nose, I pulled out of the parking space into the slow-moving traffic.

Princess and I spent the rest of the day on the couch. We watched Julia Roberts rom-coms, ones we'd seen dozens of times. I ate popcorn and ice cream for dinner and went to bed at 9:00, two hours earlier than my normal bedtime.

Now, refreshed, I said good morning to the receptionist behind the glass partition. Gladys was on duty this morning. A woman I didn't recognize, dressed in a too-big-for-her coat, approached me.

Gladys called from her station, "Ms. Iris Bussing is waiting to see you. I didn't let her in because Ginger wasn't expecting her." Gladys sounded apologetic.

Ms. Bussing, hands clasped, tried to smile, but her mouth didn't succeed.

"I'm Aria Wright, the CEO here. How can I help you?"

Skinny and drawn, Iris introduced herself. "Every day, my kids and I come here." She pressed her lips together again. A flush colored her beige skin.

Sadness swept over me. How old was Iris? She looked middle-aged, but I suspected she was a lot younger. "How many children do you have?"

"Three." She held up three fingers.

Bloody cuticles and bitten nails sent another stab to my heart.

"But it's my oldest I'm worried about."

Iris stayed quiet, as if unsure what to say next, how to explain her immediate need when there was so much she required.

"Let's walk to my office and you can tell me about your oldest. Girl or boy?"

Together, we made our way through the halls. I waved to the people I passed. For the past week, Emerson absorbed all my time, when my attention should have been on Iris, her family, and all the people who stumbled through our doors.

"Morning," Ginger said. Her expression, always serious but unruffled, looked wary.

"Mrs. Bussing needs some help. Won't you join us?" I extended my right arm, inviting both women in. The three of us settled in seats in the living room section. I introduced Ginger and explained her role. I asked Iris, "Tell me what's happening."

She clutched her hands together. "We're living in...our car. Move around when the police roust us." Her face flushed again. "I'm working and so is my man. Our oldest girl, Vonnie, works after school. The littlest ones..."

I offered Iris a bottle of water. "Take your time."

"Leaving the babies alone is wrong." Wet hazel-brown eyes looked up at me. "Please don't call child services. I'm begging—"

I cut her off. "We're here to help, not hurt you or your family."

Ginger pulled a box of tissues from off my desk and handed it to Iris.

"Even though we all work, we can't afford a place."

I nodded. This was why The Way Station existed and why we needed Hope House. Now.

"I have a friend; she lives in a nearby shelter and checks on the young ones. Takes them to the bathroom. Vonnie brings them home from school and then goes to work." Iris lowered her eyes. "She's turning thirteen in a few weeks."

A twelve-year-old working after school to help pay bills. Little ones living in a car untended. I swallowed and tried not to show my emotions.

"Kids make fun of her. Her clothes don't fit right. I do the best I can from the thrift shops. She owns a torn-up backpack, and all the kids outgrow their shoes so fast."

My heart stuttered. "We can help you with better fitting clothes and a new backpack–consider it done. Can Vonnie bring the little ones here after school?"

"She'd have to ride the public bus and would be late for work." Her hands flopped down into her lap.

"I see." My mind whirred. Florence, our social worker, would figure something out. "We'll get this sorted for you. Please don't worry."

"Thank you. But that's not why I came."

There was more? I pressed my fingers against my mouth to keep my feelings from spilling out. Not that Iris' story was unique. So much unmet need and Fieldcrest was one small city. What about those suffering in other towns? "Tell me."

"She got her period. Tampons, and other girl stuff, are expensive. She's not the only one. I promised to speak with you."

I reached over and hugged her. "Oh, Iris." I turned toward Ginger.

"I've got it," she said.

Questions swirled in my mind. Why didn't Iris approach the head of children's programs? Didn't anyone on my team notice this was a problem? "Let's get you some clothes, a backpack, and feminine products right now. Then we'll work on the rest." I stood. Why can't two adults house and care for their family despite having jobs? I had to solve the problems that stalled Hope House.

Ginger walked Iris out. I used the time to settle my rocketing heart. Practiced my breathing. Sipped water. Said a silent prayer.

When Ginger returned, I asked, "Everything okay?"

Stupid question. Of course it wasn't. As heartbreaking as her story was, helping Iris Bussing was easy. Saving everyone who needed us was daunting. Add dealing with police patrolling outside, extra security guards walking the halls, and an unsolved murder hanging over our heads left us in a sea of anxiety.

"Fine." Ginger's frown belied her answer. "You have a lot going on today." She studied her clipboard. "Wally's report is on your desk. You'll see him at 1:00. Lacy needs 30 minutes…" Ginger glanced at her watch. "Fifteen minutes from now." She looked up. "Then you meet with Valentine."

I flopped into my executive chair. My head hit its high back. "I'd like to absorb Wally's report before I see Valentine."

She shook her head. "Tried. Wally is out and doesn't return until 12:30. Valentine can only meet at 10:00. You have fourteen minutes to read the report before Lacy arrives." Ginger turned. "Don't let me keep you." She pivoted. "Oh, and a man named Twitch called. Said you knew him." Her voice rose like she was asking a question.

"Did he say why?"

"His exact words were, 'Tell her it's in her best interest to return my call.' Sounded threatening to me."

I groaned inside but responded in a reassuring tone. "I'm sure it's nothing."

"His number is on your desk with the report." Ginger held my gaze for a few awkward moments. She left, closing the door behind her.

I shoved the phone message aside, flipped open the first page of Wally's report, and read. Ten minutes later, my head swam. If Wally's numbers were correct, we paid three times more for supplies than we did in previous years. And construction overruns were off the chain. None lined up with the contractors' bids. Wally's written explanation in an overlong, dense cover letter came down to inflation and supply chain issues, his same answer to his earlier reports.

A sharp rap on the door.

"Enter."

Lacy's royal blue suit looked stunning. Her hair, swept up in a French twist, and minimalist makeup, reminded me I needed a trim and a manicure.

"Thanks for squeezing me in." She pulled up a chair. "I come bearing good news. In fact, great news. And from your expression, it appears you can use it."

I managed a smile. "Please shower me with positives."

"Laura Garrison and I are having lunch today."

The triumph in Lacy's voice told me she'd worked hard for this appointment. Laura, a generous philanthropist, could disappear our money woes. "That is indeed terrific news. How can I help?"

"Come with me."

"What? I can't. I've been out so much."

"Laura's used to dealing with presidents and CEOs. Little-ole director me won't be enough."

"But she agreed to see you."

"Thanks to Valentine." Lacy leaned forward. "You must do this."

The illusive song from this morning popped into my mind. "The Velvet Glove" by The Red Hot Chili Peppers. A song about devastating addiction. Did Emerson's plight push this song to the top of my internal playlist? Was Emerson trying to tell me something?

"Aria." Lacy waved her hands in front of my eyes. "You with me?"

"Sorry."

"You'll come?"

Although I started the day with lots of energy, weariness came over me in a crash. Constant worry caused my adrenalin to pump nonstop. A week on a Caribbean beach would restore me. Ha. Like that was going to happen. I forced an upbeat tone. "Of course. I'll push Wally's meeting back and join you. Please alert Ginger on your way out."

"I'm optimistic about Laura. I'll swing by to get you at 12:30. We're going to that new restaurant near The People's Theater. Brambles. Excellent reviews." Lacy squeezed my hand. "Ask Ginger to get you a latte. You'll feel better."

Would I?

CHAPTER THIRTY

One thing I liked most about Valentine Bannister was his attitude. When he was a new teenaged driver, he suffered a devastating injury in a three car pileup. He'd been in a wheelchair ever since. Foolishly, I'd asked him if he worried as a parent about his children driving when they were teenagers. He had a daughter and a son. Both were adults in their twenties now. "Did your accident make you an overprotective parent when they began driving?" His answer both humbled and instructed me. "There are many possibilities that concerned me about my children," he said. "And several remain. But since everything good in my life happened after the accident, meeting and marrying my wife, having my children, starting my business, I didn't worry about what happened to me, happening to them."

Today, he wheeled into my office as dapper as ever. "I spoke with the police chief. So far, no headway in solving the murder."

"I have the same understanding." Which was super frustrating. I read if a murder wasn't solved within the first forty-eight hours, the chances of finding the killer dropped to twenty percent, or something like that.

Valentine's expression turned grim. "We must still carry on."

"Of course." I anticipated his next remarks.

"You've taken a lot of time off." He put his hand up to stop me from defending myself. "Understandable, but still a problem."

I waited him out.

"Wally sent me his less than edifying report and moronic conclusion."

"I read it this morning, and—"

His hand rose again. "Let me finish. We need to hire a forensic financial consultant to help us get answers and solutions. I've discussed this with Barry and Liv, and we're agreed."

Barry served as board vice chair and Liv led the finance committee. All three were wise and supportive counselors.

"I concur." What choice did I have? A smart move, but another big, unplanned expense and time suck. "Do you have any recommendations?"

"Yes." He handed me a sheet of paper with two companies, contact names and phone numbers printed in block letters. "Let's dig out the truth."

I waited.

"I recognize how much Hope House means to you, and how important it is for the people we serve, but one solution might be postponing construction." This time, he didn't dissuade me from speaking. Instead, with his head cocked to one side, he waited for my response.

All the reasons for moving ahead almost spilled out. Iris' story, one of many who needed a decent place to live as soon as possible, was on the tip of my tongue. With one year leases each, thirty-six families could turn their lives around. I would let no one derail the project. Although Valentine said postpone, too often that means stop. In addition, construction prices will rise and by the time we try to re-start, building costs might be beyond our reach. "Thanks for connecting us to Laura Garrison," I said instead of arguing with him.

"Lacy is quite persuasive. But make no mistake. Laura's a savvy woman. She'll want assurances concerning our finances." His expression softened. "I'm on your side, Aria. I respect all you've accomplished in a brief time. Let's hire the consultant and see where we are."

Dread descended. "I'll let you know how it goes," I said in my fake, optimistic voice. "Both with Laura and the forensic consultant."

• • •

I returned Twitch's call as soon as Valentine left.

"I have information," Twitch said after I identified myself.

His voice caused the hairs on my nape to rise. Alarms rang in my head. There was something off about him. Under my desk, my feet swung back and forth. "May I put you on speaker so I can take notes?"

Without waiting for his permission, I did so. My freed left hand tugged on a coiled curl.

"You won't need them," he growled. "Iggy Smalls, an old friend of Emerson's, is who you're looking for. He's a mean bastard, and he's your killer."

A jolt straightened my back. My questions tumbled out, one on top of the other. "Why would an old friend kill him?" Only breathing came over the phone. "How did you come by this information? Who told you? Were you there? Hello...?" I waited a beat. "Have you contacted the police?"

The phone clicked off.

·   ·   ·

My instinct was to let Errol and Jax know about Twitch's call, but I had to prepare for the lunch meeting with Laura, read Lacy's notes on the shared donor drive, and get my head in the right space.

The new building surpassed mere dreams. People like Iris deserve safe places to live, to raise their children, get on their feet. Besides the apartments, the plans called for a community vegetable garden. Jax offered cooking classes once the building and garden were up and running. And our talks with Habitat for Humanity should bear fruit. Permanent homes built by volunteers on vacant land donated by the city. The plan will work. It had to.

Brambles, several doors down from The People's Theater, looked lovely from the outside. Tiny white lights wrapped around the tree-trunks gave a festive and welcoming air. Lacy and I walked in.

The hostess greeted us in a velvety voice. "Good afternoon."

Lacy said, "We're meeting Ms. Garrison."

"Yes, she's expecting you. Follow me."

We walked past square tables covered in crisp, white tablecloths. Soft music played in the background, and delicious aromas perfumed the air. Fresh bread, olive oil, spices. I realized I was hungry.

The host led us to a quiet spot in the back, no doubt to afford us privacy at either Lacy's or Laura's request.

I'd run into Laura twice since coming to The Way Station. Both times at fundraisers—one for the wonderful community theater where she chaired the board of directors, and once at a Boys and Girls Club gala. Everything about her spoke to quiet wealth and elegance. Today, she wore a creamy pearl-white jacket and slacks. The mauve blouse enhanced her eyes and complexion.

"Thank you for meeting with us," Lacy said, settling in her seat. "You remember Aria Wright."

"Of course," Laura said. She extended a soft hand. Clipped fingernails, painted in a lighter shade of mauve than her blouse, looked perfect. After a brief handshake, I folded my hands on my lap, wishing I'd taken time for a manicure.

We chitchatted about the weather, the upcoming primaries, the wonderful new play being staged next week. Roxy, a hair stylist by day, was one of Fieldcrest's own writers and this new play, her second, was getting buzz. Even the *New York Times* arts section, the Westchester edition, listed it as something good to do, along with six other artistic happenings.

Once the server brought our beverages, bread, and salads, Lacy turned the conversation to our purpose. "I asked Aria to join us so she can share her vision for our unhoused and poor. I think you will see how compelling it is. Then we'd love to hear your thoughts and questions."

I launched into the project, the much needed new building filled with studio, one, and two-bedroom apartments free for a year to those taking part in our programs. I emphasized their accessibility, so handicaps were not an obstacle. A true way station, providing a lift on the road to permanent housing and employment. The garden, cooking classes, and partnership with Habitat for Humanity rounded out my case.

Laura appeared engaged, nodded, and smiled as I spoke. A small notebook lay next to her plate. Periodically, she made notes. I viewed these as excellent signs. I wrapped up my pitch with Iris Bussing's story. Telling it thickened my voice with emotion. There was moisture in Laura's eyes, as though she was close to tears. I paused.

Lacy said, "We'd love your reactions and questions."

To my dismay, instead of responding to the vision and to Iris' story, Laura's expression of empathy turned into a deep frown. "I heard about the murder. A terrible thing."

"Yes." I hoped my face didn't convey my feelings. I wanted to inspire her. I failed to do that.

"Where does the investigation stand?"

"The police are following every clue," I said, forcing optimism into my tone.

Laura leaned forward. Her eyes locked onto mine. "How are you keeping yourself and your people safe?"

"Patrol cars in front of my home, extra security officers. Being vigilant." I rallied. "We're taking every precaution. I'm confident the police will find the killer."

Laura folded her hands on the table, her eyes never leaving mine. "Do you suspect someone on your security team? I mean, how did the knife and gun get inside?"

How did she know this? "Tito Johnson, our head of security, will uncover the answer and report."

Laura gave me a hesitant smile. "I ask because this appears to be an unwise time for fundraising."

My heart sank. "Iris Bussing, her family, and so many just like her—"

Laura cut me off. "I'm sympathetic and intrigued. Love the promise of your project. I think you must work on safety before moving ahead." She placed her pen on top of the notebook. "It's a noble endeavor and much needed. I see that."

She sounded like Valentine. Did they compare notes?

"However, investing at a time of grave uncertainty seems foolish." She put her hands back in her lap. "I rarely meet to say no. A phone call will do."

It was as if she read my mind. Why lunch?

"Once you sort everything, call me and we can discuss the project in greater detail."

"By 'sort,' do you mean once the police catch the killer?" My parents told me my facial expressions had loud subtitles. I hoped I'd arranged my features in an unruffled manner.

"Yes. And security restored."

In a way, Laura's words were what I needed to hear. Emerson's killer had to be caught. Financial problems solved and security at The Way Station impenetrable. And the sooner I arrived at solutions for all three, the faster we'd build Hope House.

CHAPTER THIRTY-ONE
EMERSON

May 1970, Upstate New York

The taxi pulled along the sidewalk in front of Emerson's childhood home. An ancient elm tree shaded the cut lawn. Stone pavers, swept clean every day by his mother, reflected the afternoon sunlight. A house wren, its distinctive brown and gold plumage identifying it, pecked at seeds his parents placed in the bird feeder. Calls and songs filled the spring air. Everything about home was inviting, and yet Emerson hesitated. This was a hard first step.

The cab driver, a man about Emerson's age, twisted around in his seat. "Fifteen dollars, like I said. Is there a problem?"

"No. Sorry." Emerson dug into his wallet and paid the fare. "Thanks." He grabbed his duffle bag from the seat next to him, pushed open the car door, and stood facing the walkway and front door.

Sobriety without help was too hard. He tried, but within hours, he took another drink. The longest stretch without one was twelve hours. He rang the bell. The house key lay loose in his pocket, but he hadn't called ahead and didn't want to barge in unannounced.

His mom came to the door, pulled him into a hug, and called for his dad.

Once Emerson decided to get sober, even though he failed too many times, his resolve stayed strong. After two weeks of stumbling around, he sought help. Safety, trust, and wisdom all wrapped up in one man.

The two men sat in the backyard. Emerson took a sip of his Coke. "Dad, I'm in trouble."

"What kind?" Emerson and his father looked so much alike people often mistook them for brothers. Same dark skin, thick tight hair, and square build.

"The drinking."

"Police involved? Were you in the drunk tank?"

"No. Nothing like that."

Emerson weighed his next words. Lavar, his childhood buddy, just returned from Nam. They met at a bar near where Emerson lived in a rooming house in Harlem. Emerson ordered coffee instead of the whiskey he craved. When Lavar asked, 'What's up?' Emerson confessed his desire to sober up for a girl. A woman and her kid. Lavar shook his head in a knowing way. "Can't do it for anyone but you. Won't work. Or stick. Been there."

What should Emerson tell his father? "I hate feeling this way every day. Need to get well." He didn't add for who.

"What does getting well look like?"

"Stay sober, work, get married and have a family." The breeze stiffened. Emerson zipped his jacket. He craved a cigarette. Something to ease his gut cramping.

"Got someone in mind?"

"Yeah."

"Son, is this about a woman?"

Now his dad sounded like Lavar. What difference did it make? "I'm determined to get sober."

His father nodded his head. "Okay. Of course, your mom and I will help you." Sadness and worry colored his words. "This is gonna be a hard road. Short-term fixes never work. You gotta be in it for the long haul."

"I get it." But did he? 'The long haul.' 'Can't do it for someone else, gotta be for you.' The words echoed but faded. He didn't understand, but he was ready.

•   •   •

June 1970, an Alcohol Treatment Center in Upstate, NY

For the first two weeks, Emerson lay on his cot, trembling. The vomit bucket next to the bed remained full, but he was in too much agony to care. Explosions of pain wracked his head, and his mouth stayed cotton dry. An aide gave him a shot, promising he'd be better soon. Yeah, well, soon was a relative term. Death would be better than this.

Detox was hell. Twenty minutes from his parents' home, they came to see him every Sunday, the only time inmates, and that's what it felt like, the worst jail ever, could receive visitors.

By week three, the vomiting stopped. His hands trembled less. He got out of bed without experiencing excruciating pain. The cravings were still strong but dulled, less sharp, and nightmares plagued him, but he visualized the end. Sober and pain free. Nine days to go.

Now he sat in a circle of twelve other men–all addicts trying to kick their habits.

"Anyone want to share today? How are you doing?" the counselor asked. He used to be one of them and now worked to get others to follow his path to sobriety.

Men shifted in their seats, looked down, or sideways. Someone coughed.

"How about you, Emerson? It's been twenty-one days."

"Okay," Emerson said. His eyes swept the circle and landed on the leader. "Things are better. Not so bleak, anymore."

"Good. I'm glad to hear that. Any strategies to keep sober once you're out?"

They wanted him to stay beyond thirty days, get psych therapy, hit the gym, and join another group, one with men who made it to day thirty and were still in the facility getting additional care and support. "I have someone waiting for me," he said every time someone, including his parents, asked the same questions.

He'd called Kiki and told her he had a thirty day out-of-town job. For weeks he lay on his cot in agony and alone with his demons. Remorse and shame choked him. Mo haunted him. Until he didn't. That was another difference day twenty-one brought. Some of the Mo-guilt faded. Thoughts of Kiki, imagining holding her, making love, cooking together, replaced the nightmares. Mo cheated on her. Didn't love her. It was okay for Emerson to be with her.

By day twenty-nine, the headaches and tremors subsided. On day thirty, fifteen pounds lighter, sober, and against the advice of the program aide assigned to him, he walked out.

His father, dressed in jeans, a polo shirt, and work boots, waved Emerson over. "You look healthy, son." The two men hugged.

"Thanks. Feel good. Strong." Emerson nodded, agreeing with his own assessment. He looked up at the sun. Everyday sounds–traffic, birds, and a dog's bark all added to the crispness that moved through his body. Sharp. On point.

"Wondering...," his dad began.

Emerson faced his father. "Wondering what?"

"If this is the right move. The best thing to do right now."

Not wanting to disrespect his father, Emerson stayed quiet, but he wasn't going back to rehab jail.

"The administrator called your mom and me—"

Emerson cut him off. "I'm cured. I promise."

His dad was wise but didn't understand alcoholism. The most he drank was a couple of beers on the weekend. His mom sometimes sipped sweet wine. One glass got her giggling. "I better quit before I say or do something foolish," she said. Emerson was ready to rejoin the world. And seeing Kiki was the highest priority on his list.

CHAPTER THIRTY-TWO

With each step, the pressure in his chest increased. He'd lied to her. Should he confess all? Living with toxic secrets added to stress and the need for a drink. That's what the counselor preached at the rehab center. Step five of The Twelve Steps of Sobriety called for unburdening oneself and admitting the exact nature of your sins. Steps eight and nine called for making amends to the people you wronged.

He rang the bell.

The door swung open. Damn, she looked good. She wore bright lipstick, purplish, and black mascara outlined her lids. A Kinta cloth bandana with lots of gold that complimented her sepia eyes held her Afro back from her forehead. Big hoop earrings swung as she spoke.

"Hey stranger. Welcome back." She made room for him to enter. "Come on in."

Emerson followed her up the steps. He failed at averting his eyes from her round, perfect butt.

"Tell me about your trip. Want something cold? I have lemonade, or do you want a beer?"

There it was. His chance to come clean. "Lemonade sounds good." He craved a cigarette. "Lots of ice, please, if that's not too much trouble."

Her voice sounded like music. "No trouble at all."

They sat down on the plastic covered couch. It made a crackling noise as they shifted their weight to get comfortable. "Where's your sister and her family? And Maurice Jr.?"

"My brother-in-law is working. My sister, God bless her, took all three children to the park. They'll return in an hour. Then it's my turn to feed and play with the crew so she can meet her husband for a romantic dinner. They call it date night."

"Sounds like things are working out."

"Pretty much. I need my own place, but for now..." She scooted back into the corner where the seat met the armrest, kicked off her sandals, and wrapped her arms around her folded legs.

Emerson wanted to kiss her. Right then. He took a deep breath. "I've been in rehab." He took a sip of the sweet drink. "Recovering from alcoholism. Drying out, as they say."

Her eyes went wide. "Oh."

"I wasn't sure how to tell you. Nam..." He was about to blame the war. The free and plentiful booze everyone drank all the time. But the steps called for owning your shit. Should he tell her about the guilt that gave him nightmares? "Anyway, I came back from the service addicted. That's where I've been and I'm sorry I lied."

Kiki cocked her head to one side, reached out, and touched his thigh. "I'm glad you told me. And I'm proud of you."

Emerson's grin spread across his face. "Me too." No need to tell her anything else. Not yet.

●   ●   ●

August 1970, Bronx NY

Emerson wasn't sure about participating, even though he joined the dozens of people packed into Kiki's living room. They sat on the couch, armchairs and armrests, folding chairs, on the floor, leaned against the wall or stood in tiny circles of two or three. *Black Vets Against the War and For Civil Rights* signs and posters covered the coffee table. Each poster included a raised Black fist followed by the words *The Time Is Now*. Music played, sometimes drowned out by voices talking and other times drowning out the voices. Edwin's Starr's song, "War. What is it Good For? Absolutely Nothing" blasted from a turntable.

Men sporting long sideburns and colorful dashiki shirts filled the room. A surprising number of women attended. Emerson admired their big Afros, bright dresses, bellbottom pants, and tucked in tops.

Kiki, dressed in white capri pants and an African print top with swirls of gold and purple, wove between people clusters, offering cups of water.

Emerson hoped he hadn't made a mistake. When Kiki invited him, his instinct was to say no thanks. His experiences with anti-war people were all bad. They viewed him with hate, as if he caused the lost American and Vietnamese lives. Horror stories found their way into the televised news and national papers. Atrocities, napalmed villages, seared women and children, painted a grim picture of the war. The US was losing, people dying, noncombatant Vietnamese women and children destroyed.

Kiki reassured him. "We're new and still small. More vets will find us. Your perspective will help us better understand and, therefore, be more effective."

In truth, he said yes to please her. Simple as that.

Even with the Venetian blinds pulled up and the windows wide open, it was hot. A tabletop fan did little to cool the crowd. For Emerson, the heat was nothing. Nam was searing. New York? Not so much.

A plump, older woman who still processed her hair straight yelled above the conversations. "May I have your attention, please?" She waited, but everyone continued to chatter. "Attention please," she said again.

"Shhh," a younger woman said. "Blossom's trying to start the meeting."

Like a wave rippling out from an epicenter, quiet settled on the membership.

Blossom cleared her throat. "Thank you for coming. I'm Blossom Atwood, president of this esteemed organization."

A smattering of handclaps put a smile on her broad face.

How did a woman lead a vet's organization? Emerson's wariness increased.

"Thank you," she said and tipped her head forward. "First item on the agenda. Are there any new folks?" She looked around.

Several hands went up. Emerson kept his in his pockets.

Kiki urged, "Introduce yourself."

He shook his head.

"Welcome," Blossom said to the newcomers. Each shared their names, a brief bio, and how they heard about the group.

So far, no other veterans. They all looked like the White protesting college students, housewives, and hangers on except the people here were varying shades of black, brown, and tan.

The need for a cigarette pulled. Proud of his sixty days sober, nicotine helped keep his addiction at bay. It was hard. A daily fight. So far, he was winning.

Kiki stood next to him and offered a cup of water. In a faint voice, she asked, "You doing okay? You look shaky."

"I'm fine," he whispered back with a reassuring smile. "Quite the crowd."

"I hope you like them and get involved. We need more vets like you."

Blossom's voice boomed again. "Our next action is August 28, commemorating the 7th anniversary of the March on Washington." In 1963, 250,000 people from all over the country, traveled by plane, bus, train, and car, descended on the National Mall in the shadow of the Lincoln Memorial. It was there Dr. King gave his famous, 'I Have a Dream' speech. "It's fitting that we make our stand on the anniversary."

Emerson hadn't intended to speak, but he raised his hand.

"And you are?" Blossom asked.

"Emerson. Former Air Force Staff Sergeant. Finished a tour in Nam." He sensed Kiki's eyes on him. "I'm wondering about the connection between marching for civil rights and an anti-war protest."

"Of course, they're linked," Kiki said, a frown dissolving her smile. "Dr. King was *against* the war and *for* Black folks' freedom."

"Will people get confused?"

Voices rose. Eyes bore into him as if he were an enemy poisoning their group.

"Brothers are dying in the White man's war." A tall, slender man with coal black skin pushed through the crowd and came into Emerson's space. "Who did you murder?"

Heat filled Emerson. "Did *you* fight? Are *you* wounded?" He swung his head left and right. "Any other vets in here?" What the hell?

Kiki surprised him.

"Step back, Roger," Kiki said. "Emerson and my husband served together. You will not disrespect him or Mo's memory."

Another man raised his hand. "Army," he said. "Got out in January."

A petite woman pushed forward. "Army, too," she said. "Combat nurse."

Roger closed his mouth, his lips compressed into a straight line.

"My boy is over there now." The speaker's eyes were dark with sadness. "Helicopter hit. Crashed. No word from him in a month."

"Where?" Emerson asked. Over 300,000 troops were in Nam with hundreds shot down and captured.

"Saigon, last he wrote. No one telling me anything useful."

"I'm sorry."

Blossom said, "I have two sons. One in Vietnam and one in jail for defending himself against a police officer. We're here for both causes."

"Me too," Kiki said before standing on a folding chair. "I'm raising a Black boy in a world that thinks he's less than. And I'm doing it without his father, who died in Nam." Kiki's voice filled the small room. "We're *for* Black folks and *against* this war. Right? Are we for Black vets or not? Anti-war and not anti-soldiers? Which is it?"

The crowd murmured. A few voices called out and then clapping began. "Anti-war. Pro Black vets." Others picked up the chant. Roger raised his fist and joined the chorus.

Emerson's heart rate sped up, this time not from anger, or fear, or cravings. He loved Kiki ever since they met in Kansas. Sobriety was for her and the boy. For Mo. But now, watching her chanting and leading the crowd, he realized he loved her in a way he'd never imagined possible. He wanted to be with Kiki forever.

CHAPTER THIRTY-THREE
JAX AND ARIA

Monday, March 18

Jax's eyes swept the room. Present was his top crew, the smartest folks he knew. Four women and eight men sat at the oval conference table at The Vault. Sunlight shone through the large windows overlooking the city center. "What are the facts so far?"

E-Man spoke first. A natural leader, he was average height and a bit porky. A thatched beard hung below his collar bone, and a knit cap covered his balding pate. He was proof there's someone for everyone because he'd been married for ten years to the gorgeous Rachel, and they had four children under eight years old.

"Not much. The breach hasn't spread beyond the three companies. Nor has an additional note arrived from the whistleblower. All protocols are active and containing the situation." They'd been able to restore the data for all three customers. Stephen's team reassured clients about future cyber-safety.

Phyllis raised her hand. Tiny, like Aria, she chose not to wear shoes that elevated her. Gold converse sneakers covered her petite feet, swinging in the air from her chair. "I've added several more layers of protection. We've got the breach contained."

This was the best news so far. Cyber security was Jax's responsibility, and it sounded like they'd dodged a bullet. He looked at each face watching him. "Does anyone have anything to add?"

Coleman jumped in. He'd been with the company since its founding, and Jax trusted him. "I'm nervous. Yeah, we're good, but something doesn't smell right. Still digging."

Stephen said, "I've been checking with my police contacts, and so far, our breach has no connection to anything else going on."

Jax understood Stephen's reference. The Way Station and The Vault were two different problems as far as Stephen could tell. Yet, he too, remained uneasy. "Thanks people. Let's stay vigilant."

The meeting broke up. Murmurs, nervous laughter, and groans floated past Jax as the team left.

E-Man approached. "Got a minute?"

"Yeah. Sure."

"Like Coleman, I'm not sure we're out of the woods. Can I show you something?"

The open floor plan ensured no one had a private space. Round and square desks dotted the old warehouse footprint. If you needed to make a confidential call, you'd go into one of the old-fashioned red phone booths that lined the far wall next to the table of packaged snacks, soda, and water. There were several exercise phone booths where staff pedaled or worked out on an elliptical machine while speaking with clients or vendors. Even Jax didn't have a private office.

The two men walked to E-Man's desk and bent their heads over his computer.

"What am I looking at?" Jax asked.

"A scary backdoor that I can't close."

Little ruffled Jax. He was an unemotional man. Except with Aria. He shoved thoughts of her aside and squinted at the screen. His mouth went dry. "Where did the breach come from? The dark web?"

"Inside."

"What?" He pulled up. "Who?"

"Don't know yet. Lots of bouncing around the globe from one IP address to another, but I'm certain it originated from one of our cloud-servers."

Jax felt gut punched. They took care of their people. Daycare. A gym. Flexible hours. Work from home options. Top pay and stock options. Liberal vacation. Who would betray them? And why?

. . .

Lacy and I left the luncheon in silence. A stiff breeze made spring seem distant, despite being just a week away. We walked to the parking lot, which was now packed with cars.

"Two setbacks today," I said, my voice muffled by the purple scarf I pulled up to my nose.

"Two?"

I explained about Valentine's visit and the financial forensic consultant I had to hire. "And now Laura demanding the police catch the murderer before she'll back Hope House." On the one hand, I understood Laura's caution. Suppose the killing scared off more donors. Why should she invest now? Waiting might be best. But her investment would send a powerful message to others. Inspire more grants and gifts. "What else could we have said to help her understand the urgency?"

"I have a different question," Lacy said. "Who are the two moles she suggested we have in our ranks?"

They reached Lacy's BMW and climbed in.

"Moles?" I pulled off my gloves and unwound my scarf.

"Laura knew a lot. She suspects an inside job. Didn't you get that vibe?"

"Yeah. I did." My head hurt. Too many spinning plates and juggled balls crashing to the floor. "I've been wondering the same thing. Is Tito involved? I'm going to discuss this with Errol."

"With Errol?" Lacy's tone was as arched as her eyebrows.

"There's no need for that tone. Nothing to see."

With a laugh, Lacy said, "Like you'd notice. You're oblivious."

"Are we discussing my non-existent love life? Because if we are, stop it."

"You broke it off if I remember correctly. Is Errol still interested?"

"No. It was a lifetime and marriage ago."

"What difference does that make?"

Forget Errol, what about Jax? I pushed him away so many times, I was afraid he'd stop trying, which is what I wanted. Right? "You said two moles."

"Laura's source for her inside information."

"I assumed Valentine." I heard the hollowness of my assumption. Valentine wanted The Way Station to succeed. He wouldn't sabotage our chances by speaking negatively to Laura. "But he's on our side, and getting Laura focused on a potential traitor..." The word hung in the air. "Makes no sense," I added. But then who? And why? The list of unanswered questions and lines of inquiry were long. But I needed to get back to the office and tackle our financial problems. The police had to solve the murder. Right? I answered my question. I owed Emerson to find his murderer. Plus, getting this chapter closed was essential to our mission, vision, and work. Being on the sidelines was not an option.

Lacy drove us back to the office. Traffic was heavy and slow. I reached for the radio dial and clicked on Sirius. Found Hip Hop tunes that brought me back to our teen years when Lacy, Joy and I were in school together. "Hey Mr. D. J., keep playing that song. Everybody move your body," the two of us sang. The music got us bouncing in our seats and laughing.

I didn't see the truck.

It slammed into Lacy's car from behind. Spun us into the next lane of traffic. A Camry clipped our front bumper, jarring me forward in my seat and then knocked me back. Lacy fought the wheel, trying to stop the car's spin. Too late, I saw the concrete pillar ahead. When the BMW smashed into it, the airbag deployed, crushing my chest. I heard myself screaming in pain, out-of-control terror, fighting to breathe. But I couldn't stop.

• • •

Jax sat at his desk with his head slumped forward. Too much was going on. The word coincidence popped into his head. Again. There were so many threads to untangle. Were any of them connected? All of them? He pulled out a notepad, grabbed a pen, and made a list.

Who killed Emerson and why? The killer's target? If not the intended victim, who was? Why bring a gun and knife if you don't intend to use them? Protection or malice?

The murderer threatened Aria. Is she a target, or was he just reacting to her counterattack?

How did the killer sneak in the weapons? Did an insider help him?

Why were the cameras off? Coincidence or deliberate?

Is Glover focused on the investigation? Why no progress?

Who followed us to Cornell?

Is Darcy's organization connected to the murder? Why follow us to Ithaca?

Are the cyber breaches at The Vault and the murder connected?

Who inside The Vault would betray them and why?

Can I keep Aria safe?

He paused and read his list. Missing were the biggest questions. Do I stand a chance with Aria? Is Glover after her? Does she like him? Jax laughed at himself. Huge weighty issues covered the paper and yet his pathetic love questions dominated his mind. And why was he afraid to ask Aria about Glover? They appeared comfortable with each other, like old friends. She called him Errol.

His phone vibrated. He saw the number but didn't recognize it. Spam? "Hello?"

"Jax, this is Lacy Quarles."

Something in her voice shouted trouble. "Is Aria okay?"

"We've been in an accident."

A sharp stab of pain hit Jax's chest. "How serious?"

"She's hurt. The ambulance is taking her to Fieldcrest Hospital."

Jax grabbed his jacket, checked for his keys, and jogged to the door. "Tell me." He realized he didn't ask about Lacy. "Are you okay?"

"I'm fine. Not a scratch, but I think..." A sob. "She has some broken bones. But she's alive..." Another sob. "She asked me to call you."

"I'm on my way." He clicked off. A scary thought jumped into his mind. Was this deliberate? Another coincidence? Phone in hand, he ran down the stairs rather than waiting for the elevator. When he reached the lobby, he searched for Detective Glover's cellphone number and thumbed it in.

"Yeah?"

"This is Jax Oats." He pushed through the doors. An icy wind hit him in the face. "Aria's been in a car accident. I don't have details." He huffed his way to his car. "But—"

"Where is she?"

"Fieldcrest emergency room."

"Meet you there."

Jax climbed into his Jeep. Did the same thought hit Glover? No accident? Or was his response more about his feelings for Aria?

CHAPTER THIRTY-FOUR
JAX

Jax reached the Fieldcrest Hospital Emergency Room in twenty minutes. On the drive over, he called Lacy and hit her with a barrage of questions. "Any news?" "Have you seen her?" "What are the doctors saying?" "Are they admitting her?" Lacy had no added information.

People filled every chair in the waiting room. A thin man, his foot in a cast, leaned against a wall. No one gave up their seat for him. A small boy whimpered, his head on his mother's shoulder. Another child played with dinosaurs and dragons on the floor. The hum of conversation rose and fell. Four intake staff members sat behind low desks with a queue of patients in front. Jax searched for Lacy.

She waved her arms from where she sat on a deep windowsill.

With care, trying to avoid stepping on or bumping into anyone, he wove his way to her.

Lacy said, "Aria's parents arrived a few minutes ago. I called them right before phoning you. They're with her." Lacy's voice cracked with emotion. She dabbed her eyes and blew her nose. "Her father promised to call me the minute they had information."

Jax sat on the windowsill next to Lacy. "Are you able to tell me what happened?"

She nodded her head but didn't speak for several beats.

"I'll get you some water." He hurried toward the vending machine.

When he returned, Lacy sipped. "The truck came straight at us. He loomed in my rear-view mirror. Closer than tailgating." She took another swig. "I honked. Cars on both sides made swerving to avoid the truck impossible." Lacy covered her mouth as if trying to hold something in that might escape.

"It's okay, take your time." The noise of the waiting room disappeared. Jax's focus was so intent, he only heard Lacy.

"The truck sped up and crashed into us. Hard. He must have been speeding because we spun around and hit another car." She looked at him with tear-filled eyes. "Aria screamed with so much pain and terror, but there was nothing I could do."

The stabbing in Jax's chest came back.

Her eyes wide, Lacy said, "What if someone got hurt in the car we hit?"

"It's not your fault." He searched her face to see if she believed him.

"I drove. We were singing and rocking to the music."

Jax said, "The guy who hit you and put Aria in the hospital, *that's* where blame lies." He gave her back a quick rub. "Did the police arrest him?"

"Not yet." She bit into her lower lip. "I've never been in an accident."

"Maybe this wasn't one."

"What?"

"An accident."

Before Jax explained, he sensed a presence and looked up. Errol Glover stood in front of them.

"How is she? Any news?" He unbuttoned his tan raincoat. A gold shield hooked to his suit jacket collar gleamed under the fluorescent light.

Jax said. "Waiting for an update."

The detective eyed Lacy. "I understand it's your car that was hit. You up for some questions?"

"I guess." In a stronger, less terrified tone, Lacy went over the accident again.

Jax listened for added details.

"What make, model, color?" Glover asked.

"Red." She closed her eyes. "Ram?"

"Good. That's good." He tugged a notebook and pen from his coat pocket. "Did you see the driver?"

"Baseball cap. Yankees. And aviator sunglasses."

Glover scribbled on the paper. "White, Black, short, tall?"

She shook her head. "He wore a surgical mask."

"License plate?"

"No."

Glover turned to Jax. "Were you with them?"

"Lacy called me from the hospital." Irrationally, he felt bad about not being there to help Aria. "So, the guy hit and ran?"

"Appears so." Refocused on Lacy, Glover asked, "Did it seem deliberate?"

Glover articulated the thought nagging Jax.

"Who'd want to hurt..." Her voice trailed off. "Oh. Of course. The murder."

Another coincidence? Jax doubted it.

•   •   •

One hour later, Lacy, Aria's mother Yvonne, father Ramon, and Jax stood in the corridor outside Aria's second-floor hospital room. Errol Glover was inside, quizzing Aria.

Ramon, a Styrofoam cup of coffee in his hand, looked weary. Tired eyes, mouth drawn down, he spoke in hushed tones. "Broken sternum and wrist, but thank God, nothing worse. Banged up, but she'll be fine," Ramon said with the confidence of a man used to being right.

"The attending physician explained they'd watch our girl for twenty-four hours before sending her home," Yvonne said. "It turns out sternums self-heal, but the wrist requires a soft cast."

This was the first time Jax met Aria's parents. Yet they recognized Jax, which seemed like a good thing. Both of his brothers understood who Aria was and what Jax hoped would happen.

"She asked if you were out here." Ramon's tone held accusation or annoyance. So, not a good thing.

Choosing to ignore the edge in Ramon's voice, Jax asked, "How did she seem?"

Ramon was as tall as Jax. And Aria looked just like her mom—pretty, with coifed hair and subtle makeup.

"She's worried about Lacy," Ramon said.

"I hope you told her I'm fine."

"Of course," Yvonne said. She put her arm around Lacy's waist.

Jax remembered that Lacy and Aria were childhood friends. Joy too. And, as it turned out, Glover also. Lacy let it slip.

"We tried to reach Zander," Yvonne said.

Ramon said, "She's concerned this was no accident." He finished his coffee with one long swallow.

"Me too," Jax said.

"Me too what?"

"Hit and run. Smashed into her hard in a forty-five mile per hour zone. The rear window shimmied into sand, without a shard of glass remaining. Had to be doing at least sixty when he hit her."

"You sound like Errol." Ramon cleared his throat. "I told her to stay with us." He lifted his shoulders and eased them down. "Stubborn woman."

That made Jax smile. "Determined more than stubborn." At least that was his observation. He sensed Ramon's eyes on him and realized too late that he'd made a mistake.

"I *know my* daughter."

"Of course. Sorry." So much for a good first impression.

Ramon stared for another second before looking away.

Why such an unfriendly attitude? What did Aria tell her father? Jax pushed this aside. More critical issues to concentrate on.

Lacy said, "When can we see her?"

"I'll check." Ramon poked his head into the room. "Almost done? We have folks waiting."

Jax wanted to see Aria but decided to corner Glover first.

CHAPTER THIRTY-FIVE
ARIA

My room, in Fieldcrest Hospital, was neat and clean. I had the space to myself in the Orthopedic Unit–the place where they mended broken bones. An IV drip sent fluids into my bloodstream while a machine monitored my blood pressure and heart rate. Another drip provided pain meds. Light streamed in from the large window behind and disinfectant scented the air.

From my bed, propped up with pillows, I looked at Lacy and Jax. "I'm fine." Their sorrowful expressions were almost funny except I recognized they came from a place of caring. "Sore." My chest–black and blue–looked like someone beat the crap out of me. I ached everywhere, but especially around my neck and breasts. "We could have died—"

My comments elicited groans from both.

"But we didn't. And the head nurse told me I can go home tomorrow."

Lacy sat on the edge of the bed. "I'm so sorry."

"Stop it. There was nothing you could do." I squeezed her hand.

Jax said, "I tried to pry information from Glover, but he brushed me off. Did he share anything with you?" Those intense green eyes studied me.

"He's coordinating with the local police. Examining street footage, speaking to witnesses. He offered nothing helpful to me, either." I searched their faces again. "Do you have opinions?"

Their silence told me a lot.

Jax said in a grave voice, "It was deliberate. Did it seem that way to you?"

"I spooled out the accident reel dozens of times in my head." I tried to remember what the truck looked like. From Jax and my road trip to see Zander, I learned to check license plates, but all I recalled was being sure death was imminent. The awful pain and my screams–like a wild animal caught in a trap. "Yes. I suspect he intentionally hit us."

Lacy said, "Jax and I agree. People are after you."

"And this time," Jax added. "Instead of following you, they've leveled up the threat."

As ominous as Jax's words sounded, I didn't feel alarmed. I guessed the pain meds were keeping me calm. "Errol said to report threatening phone calls. As if we shared a secret that I don't remember. If connected to the murder, I'll hear from... them. Whoever they are."

As those words came out of my mouth, my personal cell phone vibrated. I glanced down and saw an unknown caller with a local number.

"Put it on speaker," Jax said.

I did. "Hello?"

"Second warning. There won't be a third. The next time will be for real unless you cease talking to the police and stop digging."

The phone went dead.

I opened my mouth in reaction, but my cell buzzed again.

"Mom?"

I clicked the phone off speaker. My breath caught and hands shook. So much for the meds keeping me mellow.

"Mom, are you there?"

Panting, I said, "Yes. Sorry about that." I breathed through my mouth, sucking in as much air as possible.

"Grandma said you were in an accident."

My chest ached inside and out. Often, when emotions swamped my systems, breathing and, therefore, speaking became difficult. I gulped for air. Lacy grabbed the phone and tossed my purse onto the bed. She pantomimed me using my inhaler.

"Hey Zan, Auntie Lacy here."

With trembling hands, I dug for the device while I listened to Lacy's end of the conversation. I pumped medication into my damaged lungs.

"Banged up. Broke her sternum and wrist, but all patched up now. They'll release her tomorrow."

Still shaky, I pulled out my ear pods from my bag, waved my one good hand at Lacy, asking for the phone, and slipped the devices into my ears. "I'm here, son. Having a mild attack." Zander knew about my condition. When he was much younger, pneumonia and bronchitis dogged him every winter. He was asthmatic, too. The Upton family curse. "What's happening with you?"

"Do you need me to come home and take care of you?"

Aww. There was my sweet boy. Not the Darcy-captured kid we left in Ithaca.

"I could stay for a few days."

Yes, yes, yes. "No, that's okay. Grandma, Granddad, and Auntie Lacy, they're all here. And Auntie Joy is coming by tomorrow." I glanced at Lacy for confirmation. She nodded. "So, how's the climate work going?" Please, tell me you've left her. Gone back to school.

"I wanted to run something by you, but if you're too—"

"Fire away. I'm not *too* anything."

"Darcy and I... and the group... we're shifting our focus."

I waited. Concentrated on taking in even breaths.

"Are you aware of The Jungle in Ithaca?" His voice took on an excited bounce.

"No. What is it?" Alarm bells rang in my head.

"You can Google it."

I clicked on Safari and typed in The Jungle in Ithaca, New York. Photos of an enormous dump filled the screen. Shopping carts, car parts, old sofas torn and filthy, broken-to-bits bicycles, junk piled upon twisted debris as if a category five tornado spiraled through–a *New York Times'* article from the previous year appeared. "The Jungle is an off-the-grid community, homeless encampment, and drug den."

"I'm looking at a story now," I said, forcing down the telltale panic. "What are you and Darcy planning?"

"You see the environmental disaster it is. The county ordered Ithaca to clean it up, but only a portion. We, Darcy, me, and our fellow activists, think the entire encampment needs cleaning and shelters built to house the folks who live there. Apartments like you're doing."

Part of me was super proud. But my mom-radar pinged louder and louder. "How will you accomplish that?"

"A sit-in. Old school, with locking arms and staying put until the authorities meet our demands." Zan was speaking fast, his excitement clear. "I'm head of recruitment and Darcy is head of the details. People are meeting here, at our store front, in about an hour. It's going to be epic."

"And dangerous? Suppose the police try to remove you by force?" My lungs tightened. I heard my choppy breathing and unhealthy wheeze. "I don't want you to get kicked out of school."

"Mom. I'm doing what you and Grandma and Granddad taught me. Help others. Fight for what you think is right."

This was too dangerous. I had to stop him. "My accident was deliberate." I gasped these words out. "People are... after... me and it's not... safe for you." I sank back against the pillows and handed the phone to Lacy.

"Zan, listen to your mom. I'll call you back."

"What's wrong with her? Sounds like an asthma attack."

"Don't worry. We've got her. Meanwhile, don't do anything stupid."

Jax sat next to me. "Tell me what you need? How can I help?"

Lacy rushed out of the room.

My lungs shut down.

CHAPTER THIRTY-SIX
EMERSON

August 28, 1970

Gun Hill Road in the Bronx was a major crosstown thoroughfare. The Anti War-Anti Racism Walk began at the intersection of Gun Hill and White Plains Road–a popular avenue lined with establishments selling clothing and groceries, along with tax preparers and realtor offices. A storefront church invited all faiths to join them for Sunday service. The El Train rattled overhead.

Summer heat, the air clogged with humidity, made walking tough. The protestors carried signs that bobbed as they trekked and chanted, "Stop the War." "Stop Killing Black men."

Blossom shouted through a bullhorn, "What do we want?"

"Peace and justice," the small group of marchers responded.

"When do we want it?" she boomed again.

The protestors called back, "Now."

From Emerson's point of view, it seemed dumb and useless. People protested all over the country, mostly students in large cities. Tomorrow, the National Chicano Moratorium Against the Vietnam War planned a huge 20,000 person protest in California. Even planning the march made news. No one cared about a ragtag effort in the north Bronx.

Pedestrians eyed the group as they walked around them. A woman hefting two shopping bags wagged her finger at him, but he didn't understand what the gesture meant. You're in my way? Shame on you? America turned its back on the vets, racism continued to hold back Black folks, police still hassled Black men, and the war raged on. Emerson believed all these ills needed to stop, but the protests wouldn't be effective. Despite his skepticism, he wore his fatigues and combat boots anyway, and carried a sign–Black Vets Against the War. Among the walkers, several other vets showed up. Roger from the meeting at Kiki's apartment wore a baseball hat with message-pins covering most of it. "Make Love Not War." "What Are We Fighting For?" One of the larger pins displayed the international peace symbol.

Kiki walked next to Emerson. They passed a bar already open for business. The image of a cold beer swelled in his mind. Why not stop, grab a cold one, talk and laugh, rather than pound down the street, feet aching, body sweating? His drenched shirt clung to his torso.

"Where's the reporter and photographer Blossom promised?" Kiki asked, her head swiveling. "Blossom said a few agreed to cover us."

Emerson didn't respond. At least a story in the newspaper, or on television, would reach more people and make the protest worthwhile. But with only fifteen marchers, why would a reporter come or stay?

The cold beer grew bigger in his mind. He closed his eyes and licked his lips, tasting the brew. His nostrils flared as the earthy aroma of the imagined beer filled his nose.

Kiki said, "Are you okay?"

Emerson opened his eyes and blinked hard several times, trying to banish the images of a drink. That's when he saw him, Iggy Smalls, Mo's murderer, only steps away. A keloid-raised scar traveled down the side of his face. Round sunglasses hid his eye, and a jean jacket hung on his frame. Thin. Wiry. What was he doing in the Bronx? Didn't Emerson see him in Harlem, too? Emerson blinked again to clear his vision.

"Did you hear me?"

He missed what Kiki said. "Sorry."

His mouth felt dry and his eyes stung. They stopped at an intersection. Where did Iggy go? Emerson swung his head around, searching. The abrupt movements made him dizzy.

"What's wrong with you?" Kiki asked.

"What did you say?"

She tugged on his arm. "Let's get out of this sun. You don't look well."

Emerson's eyes swam around. If he didn't sit down, in another second, he'd topple over. "Need a beer," he said, before sliding onto the sidewalk.

•   •   •

A breeze from a fan dried the sweat from Emerson's face. He opened his eyes to pale blue walls decorated with a rainbow arched over frolicking animals on stuck-on decals.

"Welcome back," Kiki said, smiling at him.

Was he dreaming? "Where am I?"

"You're resting in my room. Sorry the bed is so narrow."

She wore a different outfit from the protest. How long had he been laying there? "It's fine." His mouth felt cottony. "What time is it?"

She glanced at the large-faced watch on her wrist. "Six. Are you hungry? I made a pot of stew."

"Thirsty."

She frowned. He guessed she was thinking about the beer he'd asked for and disapproved. Wondering if he'd fallen off the wagon.

"For a glass of water, please." Did an imaginary drink count? "What happened to me?"

"You collapsed."

He remembered the march and heat, his craving, and the dizziness. "How did you get me... here?" Not wanting to make a misstep, he caught himself before saying "home." There was something intimate about lying in her bed.

"Roger helped me get you into his Volkswagen Bug. We tried not to hurt you, but that car is so little." She chuckled. "Squashing us in made me laugh, despite being terrified for you."

"Thank you." Something else came into view. Iggy Smalls. Did he conjure him like he did the cold glass of beer? "Where's your family?"

"Daryl, my brother-in-law, helped Roger and me get you up the steps and into bed." That made Emerson laugh at himself. He spent months yearning to bed her, and this was how he got there. Fainting. Embarrassing himself.

"Can you sit?" She put her arm around his neck, her hand resting against the back of his head. "I'll help you."

He eased up and sat. "Iggy?" Did she see him too?

"What?"

"Nothing. I'm sorry." What's the matter with me? Kiki didn't know Iggy existed. "Still wobbly."

Kiki helped Emerson into the bathroom and gave him a washcloth, towel, toothbrush, and paste. He washed up. The face in the mirror looked rough. Tired eyes.

"Dinner's ready." Kiki called from outside the bathroom door.

They all sat around the kitchen table only big enough for four–Kiki, Emerson, Daryl, and Yolanda, Kiki's sister, who could be her twin. Kiki's nieces had a children's table low to the floor, painted pink with two kid-sized chairs. Maurice Jr. napped.

"Thank you," Emerson said to everyone. "Feeling much better."

"We can make you a bed on the floor in my room. Just to be safe," Kiki said.

In her room. Emerson felt his heart rate kick up. "Don't want to trouble you."

Daryl said, "Not a problem." He spooned a big helping of stew into a bowl and passed it to Emerson. Kiki offered a roll from a basket covered with a cloth napkin.

Emerson tucked into his meal. "Wow. This is excellent." He guessed they served juice and water because of him. He saw beer in the refrigerator. Put it out of your mind, he told himself. Be grateful. Stay focused. But beer, booze, and Iggy Smalls intruded.

• • •

Emerson had trouble sleeping. The bedding was comfortable enough, but his mind churned. Should he make a move? She could have made him sleep on the couch in the living room, right? Instead, Kiki made up the bed in her room. Neither Daryl nor Yolanda made any comment about the arrangement. Why not? Kiki's done this before with other guys? Emerson let his imagination take him to unsubstantiated places. He rolled over.

"Emerson, are you still awake?"

"Yeah." He tried to stay calm and not anticipate.

"Can I join you?"

"Sure." His johnson swelled.

She slipped off her bed and scooted under the covers with him. "I'm lonely."

Was that enough for him? He pulled her on top and wrapped his arms around her. "Me too."

She pressed her lips against his, eased her tongue into his mouth, and rubbed her body against his swollen joint.

They kissed for a long time. He wanted to please her. Not rush. Her moans and pleasure registered on her face told him all he needed to know.

CHAPTER THIRTY-SEVEN
IGGY

1970, New York

Iggy Smalls watched the guy they called Emerson, the friend of big-mouth-no-longer-breathing cheat, stumble out of the bar and onto the street. Iggy learned their identity from a Thai cop on the club payroll. A grifter followed the drunk, gave him a beat-down and robbed him. Of-all-the-gin-joints kind of moment. Meet a guy in Bangkok and run into him in Harlem. Or not surprising. Vets returned from Nam hooked on heroin and booze, smoking joints, and shooting up. Why wouldn't Iggy run into someone he met over there?

SoSo shrugged when Iggy told him. SoSo experienced no highs or lows. "How's it hanging?" received a grunt and, "So, so." "Wada, you think of your meal?" Same answer. Even when hookers came over, he gave the same "okay" assessment. Crazy. Sex was always great, including bad sex.

Iggy didn't mind since SoSo's lack of emotions was his only negative. A standup guy, business partner, and a loyal friend. Iggy moved on impulse. SoSo deliberated first.

They met in juvie, Iggy in for a smash-and-grab and SoSo for knifing a bully. You needed a buddy in jail. Gangs, crazies, thugs, and mean-ass guards were against you. SoSo didn't flinch. Big for twelve with rock-hard fists. When trouble came at him, he threw down. Iggy was tall, but spaghetti thin, so opponents underestimated him. From age six, he studied Martial Arts and boxing. His Aunt Marie dragged his cousin and Iggy to classes every week until someone shot Marie in a drive-by. The lessons stuck. With SoSo by Iggy's side, the other baby-felons left the pair alone.

When they aged out of juvie, neither had a home to return to. Aunt Marie died from her gunshot wounds and her son went into foster care. SoSo ran away from home at ten years old and joined a gang. No relative welcomed them. Just as well. They needed to earn, find their old crews, and get back into the game. But everyone they knew from twelve died or landed in jail. Sleeping under a bridge, begging for food, lifting wallets in the park, was not the future they envisioned. Commodore rescued them. A gang captain with a house in Queens, and an apartment in Harlem, he offered Iggy and SoSo each a bed, three meals, all the weed and booze they wanted, free sex with hookers, plus a purpose. Protect his assets and he'd take care of them. Iggy and SoSo signed up.

After working in New York for several years, Commodore offered an amazing opportunity–Bangkok. He needed muscle while he pushed dope in bars frequented by the military. The operation started on the ground floor of the soldiers' fall into the heroin haze–the cloud nine the Temptations sang about. It remained a sweet gig until Mo cheated Commodore at the blackjack table. And then bragged about it–pasted the winning card on his forehead and laughed. Yeah, the guy was drunk, but Commodore never accepted booze as an excuse.

Killing Mo was a first for Iggy. They beat up folks, broke bones, made sure the offenders understood the seriousness of their missteps and never did it again. But Mo had a knife and slashed Iggy. Him or me, the way Iggy saw it.

The Bangkok police and the owner of Jack's American Star Bar were pissed. Commodore shipped Iggy and SoSo back to New York. Still on the payroll, they once again protected Commodore's interests. They appreciated the money, but they no longer liked being "owned" by Commodore. They needed their own cash-flow. So, on their off hours, they cruised joints where vets hung out–bars, clubs, protests, and AA meetings. Failures were far more common than success stories and therefore a fruitful spot to help a guy out. They sold product on the side–cocaine, heroin, and weed. Dangerous, because Commodore forbade side hustles, but the gigs charted a path to a better future. Worth the risk.

Something about seeing Emerson at the bar and again at a pathetic anti-war protest in the Bronx disturbed Iggy. He'd not killed anyone since the evening in Bangkok. Didn't think about himself that way. Sometimes Mo's bloody face disturbed Iggy's dreams. Back in juvie, a seventeen year old talked about signs from the universe. "Watch for them. Take heed," he warned. They called him Mystic. Iggy never believed before, but now, seeing Emerson after a couple of nights of Mo's jacked up face hovering, got Iggy jittery. A message from the universe? What did it mean? "Remember how things turned out in Bangkok? Back up. Play it safe." Or did it mean "Strike out on your own, even if people must die?" Iggy liked *that* version. Would Commodore let them go without paying a price?

When Iggy discussed the Emerson-omen with SoSo, he said, "It could mean anything or nothing."

By nature, Iggy was an optimist. "You're a force, an earner, an opportunist," he reminded himself. They agreed to make their own way. No matter the risk or cost.

CHAPTER THIRTY-EIGHT
ARIA

Tuesday Morning, March 19, 2024

When I woke up in the hospital, a song by DeJ Loaf spun in my head–*No Fear*. The lyrics told a tale about not being afraid to take a chance. The refrain stayed with me while I washed up, the duty nurse checked my vitals, and I ate breakfast from a tray. My right arm, wrapped in a soft cast, made eating challenging. Scrambled eggs, toast with jam, and a chicken-sausage patty. Coffee and orange juice rounded out the meal. The medicine and disinfectant smells affected the taste of the food, but not so much that I didn't enjoy breakfast.

I decided not to analyze why the song stayed with me all morning. Just let the lyrics and Jax be. No fear. Today was also the second anniversary of Ben's death. Too much assaulting my system.

With care, I pulled on the robe Lacy brought me the night before. My chest and neck still ached even though the nurse gave me pain killers. The white board on my wall noted the doctor's anticipated arrival at 1:00 to check on me and the head nurse said she'd sign me out right after the doctor's visit. The clock in the room read 10:00 a.m.

"Hey, you." Pastor Joy rapped on the open door and stepped into the room. "You gave everyone a fright yesterday."

The song in my head stopped. "Sorry." I pushed the movable tray aside and downed the last of the coffee. Joy looked good. An orange band of cloth framed her face. Locks hung down her back.

"I spoke with Zander," she said.

"What did he say? What did you ask? How is he?"

"Whoa." Joy flopped into the recliner that stood next to the bed and crossed her raised legs at her ankles. "He's worried about you." She gave me an encouraging smile. "He's also sad. Understandable."

"Ben."

"Yes." She climbed out of the chair and sat next to me on the bed.

"Who called? Did he phone you?" To Zander, Joy was Auntie, long before she became the family's pastor.

"I called to both check on him and give him an update." She pulled a thermos from her enormous bag and sipped. "Your accident shook him up. I'm sure the thought of losing you both has him swimming in concern."

Poor Zander. For some, being eighteen meant grown because of circumstances or upbringing, not true for Zan. Ben and I pampered him. Cocooned until time to let him go.

Joy said, "We prayed for you. And Ben."

That made me smile.

Lacy arrived. "Who prayed?" She waved to Joy, leaned down, and kissed my forehead. Lacy, Joy, and me-forever friends. "How are you? You scared us."

"I'm fine. We're talking about Zan."

Joy said, "He promised to call this afternoon and tell you all about how their protest at The Jungle will stay safe and peaceful."

"He told you about it, or did you bring it up?" I shared with both Joy and Lacy, Zan's new mission. "Did his plans sound responsible to you?"

"He's yours and Ben's child. *Not* dumb," Joy said.

I swung my legs over the edge of the bed. "That woman has him twisted up."

"Possibly."

As teenagers, Lacy charged ahead. I worried and dithered. But Joy reasoned. Her confidence came from a deep well of beliefs. Even at fourteen, she knew her calling.

Lacy said, "Errol told me he'd drop by this morning." She waggled her eyebrows in a silly gesture.

Ignoring her foolishness, I said, "Jax informed me."

Jax called late last night. I was awake and breathing easier, medications opening my squeezed lungs and pain killers numbing the aches. We talked for over an hour about the murder, threatening phone calls, cars following us, The Vault breach, and car crash. Then the conversation turned personal.

"If you could get away, where would you go?" he asked.

"Either to a deserted beach in Hawaii, or to the Amalfi Coast in Italy," I said, selecting places Ben and I never visited but discussed. "How about you?"

A long silence on the line. "Wherever you wanted to go."

Oh my.

To my best friends, I said, "I spoke with the detective in depth yesterday. Why is he returning? Is there new information?" Emerson died a week ago, and still no progress. Instead, someone crashed into Lacy and me.

"No explanation offered," Lacy said.

Joy asked, changing the subject, "How's that going? You and Jax."

"Too much serious stuff happening. No time for romance." To my ears, I sounded defensive. "Ben's death still raw."

"I understand," Joy said. "But perhaps it's time..." She let the unspoken thought hang in the air.

When you have friends who've known you since childhood, it is hard to hide things. "Okay. Yes. I like him." My mouth twisted right and left. "Is it too soon?"

"Only you can answer that," Joy said, in her pastoral rather than girlfriend voice. "What's your heart telling you?"

"He's too tall... and too young."

Lacy said, "Not that again. You've got to get over this."

"I agree with Lacy." Joy reached over and took my hand. "I'm *not* entertaining your list of 'too this and that.' What are you afraid of?"

"My top priorities are keeping my family safe, solving the murder, and whatever else is afoot." In my medication haze, I realized fraud was a real possibility. But who? Wally? Someone on his team? "I must get us on solid financial footing. Then I'll have time to unwind my list of 'too this and that.'"

"You're what list?" Errol asked. With his trench coat draped over his arm, he walked into my room.

For the first time, I noticed Errol's eyebrows didn't match. One, thicker than the other, had a feathered appearance. They added interest to his movie-star good looks. A random thought whizzed through my head. Errol wasn't too anything–medium height, civil servant salary, a little older than I am, and Black. Plus, he didn't volunteer or give to The Way Station. Why not him? I answered my question. Electricity didn't zip through me just hearing his name.

"Have you found the hit-and-run culprit?" I asked.

"We know who he is," Errol said. He placed his coat at the end of the bed. "But we haven't located him yet."

I huffed in disappointment.

"We will."

I stood up and pulled my robe tighter around me. "Who is he?"

"A thug for hire with a long jacket."

"Jacket?"

"List of crimes and convictions."

"Did he murder Emerson?"

"I'll ask him when I arrest him." He didn't sound sarcastic, stating a fact.

Joy said, "Come on, Lacy, let's leave our two crime fighters alone." She leaned in and kissed my cheek. "When Zander calls, please remember you and Ben raised him right."

I hugged her, forgetting my bruised body. "Ouch."

She pulled back. "Sorry. You okay?

"Fine. And you're right. Zander has a strong moral compass."

Joy's twins and Zander were close friends all their lives. One year apart, they knew each other from family parties and outings, school, and church. Lacy's marriage ended in divorce with no children, but she too was part of the extended family, helping Joy, her husband Francois, Ben, and me raise our children together.

"Lacy," I said, "Please attend the meeting with Wally and the consultants." I gave her a pointed look that I hoped she understood. With Errol within earshot, I didn't want to mention the fraud I suspected. "Call me after the meeting." The forensic finance firm the board hired started their work.

"Will do."

Errol watched both women leave before telling me, "We have the hit-and-run guy on street cameras. It won't be long before we grab him."

I sat back down. "Is he our only lead in the murder? Are they connected?"

"We're tracking down every clue, call, theory of the crime."

"So, that's a, yes?"

"I came by to check on you." The professional confidence in his tone disappeared.

Nice dodge. "Thanks. I'm fine." Drugged, in pain, confused, sad, but other than that, just dandy.

"When are they releasing you?"

"This afternoon."

"Want a ride home? I have some time. Happy to pick you up."

The offer sounded...what? "I'm covered, but thanks."

"Jax?" he asked in an arched tone.

"What's this about–your apparent animosity towards Jax?"

His eyes darted away, and his professional voice returned. "You're misreading me." He paused for a few beats. "Are you two together?"

"That's a super personal question." I needed to end his speculation. "But I will answer. No, we are not." The song 'No Fear' started playing in my head again.

Errol's phone rang. "Glover." He fished out his notebook and a pen. "When? Okay. On my way." He turned to me. "We got the scum who t-boned Lacy's car."

Relief washed over me.

"A police officer is outside your door." Errol jutted his thumb in the hall's direction. "She'll be there until Jax comes for you." His voice dropped an octave. "Be careful."

"I will." The warning sounded genuine. Not a polite throwaway phrase.

Errol pivoted, grabbed his coat, and exited the room.

My phone buzzed. Distracted by Errol's news and warning, I clicked on the green accept button without checking caller ID.

"You don't want those jerks going over your books. Trust me on this."

My breath caught in my throat. "Who is this?"

"You won't like what they learn. All the moves are in *your* name. *You'll* get arrested. Lose *your* job. What'll happen to Zander while you're rotting in jail?"

Sweat bathed my face. "Why are you doing this? Who are you?"

"I'm the guy who can save you. Stop the investigation. Tell no one, especially the police, and you and your kid will be safe. Cross us, and what happens next is on you."

The phone went dead. I glanced down at the unknown number. If I called Errol, he could trace the call. Should I? Ignoring the pain, I threw on my clothes, grabbed my purse, ran past the female officer guarding me, and flew down the hall.

"Ms. Wright. Wait." She thundered behind me.

I spun around. "Can you drive me to my office?"

"After I call in." She pulled out her phone.

No time. I sprinted for the exit.

CHAPTER THIRTY-NINE

I stopped, both to catch my breath and dial Uber, since my Cooper sat in The Way Station parking lot. The police officer caught up with me.

"I have the go-ahead," she said, sounding breathless. "I'll drive you."

We clambered into her Fieldcrest Police white and black vehicle and sped east on Madison Street. She hit the siren. Cars pulled over, some turned onto side streets. We flew by.

"Want to tell me what's happening?" The young officer had light brown skin, a trim figure, and dark hair pulled into a tight bun.

"Emergency at work."

"Don't shine me." She rolled her eyes in my direction before facing the traffic in front of her. "What's got you leaving the hospital before they discharge you? We can't help you without info."

I couldn't think. Could the officer trace the number without telling Errol? Would that count as "no police?" I pulled out the notepad I kept in my purse and wrote the number down, tore off the sheet, and handed the note to the police officer. "Someone threatened me just now. Can you find out who?"

She glanced at the paper before stuffing it into her pocket. "Tell me why."

"I can't... Please help me."

We arrived at The Way Station in fifteen minutes. I reached across my body for the door handle. Locked. Pain shot through my chest. "Please, let me out."

"I'm going in with you. Give me a minute."

She called in our location, slid out the driver's side, and came around. Her head swiveled from side to side, scanning the surrounding street, before she pulled the passenger door open.

Gladys buzzed us in, and I dashed to the second floor in search of Lacy. The officer, taking two steps at a time, hurried behind me.

When I reached Lacy's office, I turned to the police officer. "Can you wait here?"

She looked annoyed. "Sure."

I mom-knocked, simultaneously rapping, and opening Lacy's shut door.

Like many of the offices on the second floor, it was cramped. Whenever visitors came, Lacy met them in the shared conference room at the end of the hall. Two computers, one a desktop and the other a laptop, sat on her steel-gray metal desk with an ergonomic executive chair behind it. Several file cabinets lined one side of the room, and framed affirmations decorated the opposite wall. "Create the highest, grandest vision possible for your life because you become what you believe." From Oprah Winfrey. Another quoted Maya Angelou. "I have found that, among its other benefits, giving liberates the soul of the giver."

I spun around. No Lacy.

Was Wally complicit or in trouble? Did I trust him enough to ask? No. I glanced at my watch. Noon. Lacy might be at lunch. Or volunteering. Lots of the staff pitched in during mealtimes to help serve. Jax would have left for his office. He planned to pick me up when I called. Dizzy, I sat. Tried to think. Between the meds and the pain, my mind felt slow.

"Hey." Lacy walked in. "Why aren't you in the hospital?" She pulled up a folding chair next to me. "You don't look well."

I lowered my face into my hands and sucked in air. The meds dulled my pain but also left me depleted.

Lacy put her arm around me. "Let's go to the infirmary."

We staffed a small space for minor cuts and bruises, cramps, and headaches. Two nurses shared shifts. The room included a cot and lying down sounded appealing.

"No." I lifted my head and gathered myself. "Have the forensic finance people arrived yet?"

"They called and said they'd be here tomorrow. At least, that's what Wally said."

"Why? Did they give a reason?"

"To Wally maybe, but he didn't share it."

Lacy handed me a bottle of room temperature water. I drank. "Why do you say it like that, as if you doubt Wally?" I suspected him, but why did Lacy?

"The books aren't adding up, from what I can tell, and his reports read like camouflage covering for what's happening."

The man on the phone said, "we." Two men followed us to Ithaca. Was Wally part of the "we"?

The officer leaned into the room. "No luck with the phone number you gave me."

Blood pounded through me.

"It's a burner–cheap pre-paid phones criminals buy with cash, so no money trail can help us find them."

"Is there anything you can do?"

The officer shook her head. "Only if it's tied to an ongoing investigation."

"Doesn't murder qualify?" I asked.

Lacy said, "What the heck? Has there been a recent development?"

The officer stepped into the office, notebook in her hand. "How's it connected?"

"I can't say. The caller threatened me."

Lacy asked, "Who? The same guy who called you before?"

"Thank you, officer," I said, ignoring Lacy's alarm and questions. "Probably nothing." I turned to Lacy. "Heading to my office to check in with Ginger, then I'll drop by Wally's office." And call Jax. He'd help me think things through. "Sorry for all the histrionics."

"I'll come with you," Lacy said.

"No. I'm good. Alone is better right now."

"My job is to protect you," the officer said. "So, no, ma'am. You're not going anywhere without me."

Great. Now what?

CHAPTER FORTY
WALLY

Sweat poured down Wally's forehead, stinging his eyes and blurring his vision. His armpits stank. If he smelled them without sniffing, so did others. He mopped his face with a shredding tissue.

Minutes before, a rough male voice gave Wally instructions to come to the Hope House construction site. "Now." Two months behind in payments to a greedy shark, left Wally with few options.

He hurried through the corridors, waved to security, and bolted out the side door. The scent of turned earth and new foliage quieted his nerves. He'd explain. Buy time.

When Wally arrived, a rough voice called and waved Wally over. Moving his arm revealed a gun in a shoulder holster under his jacket. No accident. He intended to scare Wally.

They approached the trailer/office, empty for weeks. Construction ground to a halt because of the impossible overruns Wally caused. A security guard usually walked the perimeter. Three guards, each with an eight-hour shift, but Wally saw no sign of surveillance. Did the crooks payoff a guard? Another ominous sign.

They entered.

Three men stood in the narrow space. Architectural drawings, pencils, a scale ruler, dusting brush, and a site map covered a small metal desk. The rough-voice guy pushed Wally into a chair. It creaked and rocked. Wally steadied it. His brain told him to calm down, but his gut growled with fear.

Two men, both armed, leaned against the walls. One of them held a crowbar in his left hand. It hung at his side. A third thug stood off to the side.

The rough-voice man questioning Wally wasn't the leader. The loner with his arms crossed against his chest gave the orders. Not because he spoke the most. The other three darted their eyes in his direction, as if gauging his reaction. Nothing about him stood out. Average height and weight, bald, no facial hair or distinguishing marks or tattoos. Wally prided himself on his ability to notice details, the bedrock of good fiscal management.

"May I have some water, please?" Drowning in his stink and sweat, he swept his eyes around the trailer looking for... what? Something to protect himself? Four against one. Besides, Wally wasn't a fighter. Kids beat him up in school and he never fought back. "I'm thirsty." His voice cracked.

"When we're finished." Barrel chest, thick neck, and hands. He'd taken off his jacket, his gun in plain sight. "We want your assurance that you comprehend the gravity of your situation."

"I do." His gut made another embarrassing noise. He needed to shit. It became harder to concentrate. "I have to use the john—"

"Like I said, when we're done."

Wally closed his eyes, sucked in his gut, and squeezed his anus shut, begging his body not to betray him. It was an anxiety thing. Plagued him all his life. Kids teased him about his forehead. Bullies did worse. Please, please, please.

"Look at me," the big man said in a booming voice. "You keep the money flowing, or you're a dead man. Dead. Buried where no one can find you. After we chop off your fingers, dig out your lying eyes, and send them to your wife. Claudia, right?"

Oh no. Claudia. Would they hurt her too? That did it. Wally shat his pants. Tears mingled with sweat on his face.

One man at the door covered his mouth and nose. The other sniggered.

The bully, the one doing all the talking, said, "This ain't a movie or a TV show. Fix it."

All four turned to leave. The rough-voice man said, "Next time, it will be your blood running down your leg."

Wally stayed frozen in his chair. Excrement, the loose kind, slid down his pants leg, and filled his shoes. How did he end up in this mess? How could he get the project back on track and keep Aria and the consultants from uncovering the truth before he paid his debt? Looking down at his soiled clothes, the stench filling his nostrils, he snorted. And how would he get from the trailer to his car with no one seeing him? Flashbacks from school left him unable to move. Jocks leaving him in the locker room, swimming in his shit. His father's fury. He expected his son to fight back.

Wally fished in his pocket, pulled out his phone, and called Claudia.

CHAPTER FORTY-ONE
KIKI AND EMERSON

Christmas Eve 1985, Fieldcrest, NY

Realtors claimed the wood frame house on Washington Street was a two story, three-bedroom, one bath. The third bedroom was the size of a narrow walk-in closet, but Kiki, Emerson, and M.J. didn't mind. The house was theirs. Thanks to the G.I. Bill, Emerson made a $5,000 down-payment. Kitchen, dining and living rooms filled the first floor. The bedrooms and one bath were on the second. And a basement gave them space for storage. Number 14 stood alongside a row of identical houses, each with a shared walkway to the backyards–postage stamp patches of grass.

The best part was the block faced a park with basketball hoops, a softball field, and an outdoor gym. Sixteen-year-old Maurice Jr.'s high school, who they now called M.J., was on the other side of the park, something they didn't have when they lived in the Bronx. Every day, Kiki sat on the porch and watched M.J. play basketball or baseball with his friends. Buffing up his arms on the chinning bars and rings was a source of pride. During the week, she kept track of him walking to and from school.

In 1972, thirteen years ago, Emerson and Kiki moved in together. Picked a place close to Kiki's sister. Yolanda and Daryl covered the first months' rent until Emerson landed a job at the post office. On the side, he worked as an off-the-books photographer. Graduations, anniversaries, birthday parties, and an occasional wedding brought in extra money and allowed Kiki to stay home with the baby.

The war ended in 1975. So did the protests, now ten years behind them. Emerson's uneven struggle with alcohol was also in the rearview mirror. He reached his five-year clean milestone a few months ago. It took a while for Kiki to trust him again, but now, in their new home, she felt safe.

Emerson still went to his AA meetings. Holidays like Christmas, New Year's Eve, and the Fourth of July were especially challenging. Even though he wasn't Irish, the flow of booze on St. Patrick's Day was another time to stay home and hide from alcohol.

This was their first Christmas on Washington Street. Kiki refused all of Emerson's marriage proposals. The relapses during their early years, the lies, sneaking around, caused her to turn him down each time he asked. She'd left him several times. Moved back in with her sister until he got sober. Sometimes that took a while. Did she love him? Must be. Not how she desired to love a man. All in. Crazy. Wonderful. She didn't love Mo that way either. It was more a teenaged crush that resulted in pregnancy. But yes, she loved Emerson. He was great with M.J. and a good provider. She'd always wanted a house, and now they had one. He wanted to have a baby together, but Kiki needed a sober man she could count on. No more babies. Not yet.

•　　•　　•

Emerson parked their blue Oldsmobile Cutlass in front of the house. He'd filled the trunk with unwrapped gifts, rolls of wrapping paper, Scotch Tape, bows, and ribbons. Even though M.J. was a moody teenager and acted uninterested in Christmas, Emerson loved to surprise both M.J. and Kiki with unexpected gifts. So, he hid everything in the family car.

Kiki's present was in his pocket. A gold and diamond engagement ring. This proposal was going to end right. Yes, she'd say to him when he showed her the ring. In the past, he failed at romance. "Let's walk down the aisle." "We're married already, common law. Why not make it official?" "M.J. and the new baby we'll make will need us to be legal." This proposal would be about love.

Colored blinking lights Kiki strung along the porch railing greeted him. Before hopping out of the car, he grabbed his Binaca breath spray and squirted. Then he locked the car and rushed up the steps. Kiki turned down an invitation to the party a co-worker hosted. The food, music, and company made him miss her, so he left early. The four glasses of wine he drank were a mistake. He knew it the minute the host placed the glass in Emerson's hand. "Let's toast the team." It was impolite to refuse a toast. Of course, he could raise his glass without taking a sip. But this time, confidence emboldened him. Life was good. The photography business was taking off, and he'd just received a promotion and an increase in pay, so he took a gulp of wine. It soothed him like an old friend. Tasted great. Another sip wouldn't hurt. He'd go to a meeting once New Year's Eve was over. Holidays were dangerous. He'd go right after Christmas. He forced himself to stop at four glasses. In control. No sweat.

Kiki always looked happy to see him. Her smile brought him to his knees. Beautiful, smart, with a great body, and the world's best mom. Once they married, they'd produce a little girl who looked just like Kiki. They weren't too old. Kiki kept herself fit. She loved to laugh and dance. Friends helped push the living room furniture to the side, while Emerson spun records, and they danced. Next door, a fun couple they befriended invited them to play Bid Whist. The card game became a regular Friday evening activity while the kids slept upstairs. On those nights, they let M.J. stay over at a friend's house. Saturdays found the three of them at the movies. So far this year, their favorite was "Back to The Future."

Emerson unlocked the door and popped a breath mint for added camouflage. If asked, he'd say to hide the garlic and onions he ate at the party.

He entered his beautiful new home. Christmas carols greeted him first. "Oh, Come All Thee Faithful" played from their turntable. The spruce, its scent filling the air, stood in a corner of the living room. Multi-colored bulbs, wound around the tree, and decorations M.J. made when he was a kid, that now embarrassed him, reflected their life as a family. They bought and decorated the tree last week.

Emerson's parents were coming for Christmas dinner tomorrow, something else they'd each contribute to. M.J. still enjoyed baking apple and pumpkin pies with Kiki. And Emerson made a mean roast turkey, gravy, and cornbread stuffing. Kiki liked vegetables, especially spinach, broccoli, carrots, and squash. His mother would bring her famous sweet potatoes and presents would fill his dad's arms as if M.J. was still a little boy.

Kiki hurried to him, her face glowing. Emerson fingered the jewelry box in his pocket.

"Hey, babe."

.   .   .

Kiki's disappointment and grief washed over her. It tugged her mouth down and shoulders into a slump. Tears filled her eyes. Not again. Not after five years. "You've been drinking." She saw it in his eyes, the shiny–stoned glaze. Heard it in his voice, the extra gaiety-bounce.

"Nah." Emerson shook his head. "One glass to be polite."

Now the sadness flared into anger. "Don't lie to me."

"I walked away. Had a drink and that was it. I'm in control." He grinned and spread his arms, inviting her for a welcome home hug and kiss.

Kiki stepped back instead. How many times had he said those exact words to her? M.J. angry, sad, confused. "Why are we leaving?" "I don't want to go."

Emerson's tone turned belligerent. Sometimes he'd weep and beg her forgiveness, but other times it wasn't his fault. "You should have come. I stay sober when you're with me."

She understood alcoholism was an illness. And she also knew it wasn't her responsibility to keep him sober. They'd been down this road too many times. If only Kiki stayed with him, he'd have the strength not to drink. Each time she walked out, he begged her to stay, to return, to help him fight his demons. Well, not this time.

"We're leaving." Where would they go? Back to her sister?

M.J. bounded down the stairs. Kiki swung around. "Stay in your room." He was as tall as Emerson. The fuzz on his cheeks and upper lip and his deep voice were a source of pride.

"What's wrong?" M.J. approached his parents. Lately, he began calling Emerson Dad.

"Your mother's upset. Let us talk." Emerson's words slurred.

"He's drinking again," she said to M.J. in a quiet voice, the anger gone as quickly as it arrived.

"But it's Christmas Eve." M.J.'s anguish ripped at Kiki's heart. "You're sorry, right, Dad?" M.J.'s voice choked with tears.

"I am. I screwed up, but I'm back on track. Going to a meeting right after Christmas."

His tone begged for understanding and he looked so dejected. Why not give him another chance? The issue wasn't how he treated his family. He wasn't a mean drunk. He never raised his hand to M.J. or Kiki. Her resolve weakened. But he lost jobs. Got stopped by the police and hauled to jail. Lost his license. Could have killed someone while driving drunk. Kiki bit into her lower lip. No more. "M.J., you and I are going to Auntie's."

"To live? I'd have to change schools. What about football? And the school play? This isn't right." He shook his head. "He's sorry."

"We can stay here until after Christmas," Kiki said. "But then we have to go. No argument."

"I'm not leaving. Things are good here. I'll live with Freddie or Denise." M.J. pushed past Kiki and Emerson. "I'm not leaving." He bolted out the door.

Kiki dashed behind him. "Maurice, you come back here." He didn't have his coat, hat, or gloves. Frosty December air smacked her face. She ran down the steps to the sidewalk and yelled after him. He sprinted away without looking back. Kiki wrapped her arms around her slim frame and trudged up the stairs. Christmas Eve. A joyous time. But not today.

Emerson stood at the top of the steps.

"I'm sorry. Don't do this. We're a family."

She believed him, but his apology wasn't enough. "I'm going to Freddie's and if M.J. isn't there, I'll drive to Denise's house." She mounted the stairs and walked into the house with Emerson behind her. "I'm taking the car."

Kiki grabbed her coat and warm scarf, tugged her gloves out of her pocket and slid them on. "We'll be back. Stay for Christmas and leave right after that." Steeling herself, she didn't look at Emerson. "Sober up before we return."

CHAPTER FORTY-TWO
ARIA

Tuesday, March 19

The police officer held her phone close to her ear. I only heard snatches of the agitated conversation. "Babysitting someone who doesn't want..." Silence. "Nothing. Quiet." The officer paced, glanced up at me, and then resumed her mini-walk, back and forth in front of Lacy's office door. "Okay. I'll tell her." The uniformed officer clicked off and gave me a once- over. "Detective Glover would like you to call at your convenience." The last two words came out snarky. "I'm heading back to the station."

Good. "Thank you for your trouble. I'm fine."

She shrugged and left.

Lacy said, "You're not ditching me too."

That made me laugh. Not a ha-ha sound, more relief than amused. "Thanks, pal." I recounted the threatening phone call. "They told me to stop the financial investigation or else."

"Tell your buddy Errol."

"Not yet. No police. That's what he said. But Jax isn't a cop."

"And he's going to help how?"

This time, I laughed for real. "Make me happier?"

Lacy grinned. "Call. I'll bring Ginger up-to-date and meet you in Wally's office in five."

I fished out my mobile phone and punched in Jax's number but got his voice mail. "Hi. It's me. I left the hospital early and I'm at The Way Station.

Can you come by? I'm sure you're busy..." What was I doing blathering on? "When you can." I hung up. Geez.

●   ●   ●

Tucked away in a corner on the first floor, I found Wally's door locked. I slipped out my key ring from my pants pocket and located the master. As always, Wally's space was neat and organized. A clean desk, labeled files, and a window facing the construction site. Where to start? And what was I looking for? Malfeasance in plain sight? Lacy opened some drawers and rifled through. I examined the books on the shelf lining one wall. This was a waste of time. Frustrated, I glanced out the window.

"Lacy, come here, quick."

She peered out the window next to me.

"Who are those men leaving the trailer? Do you recognize anyone?" I asked.

"No."

Neither did I. What were they doing there? And where was the guard? I grabbed the desk phone and punched the red-labeled number 2.

"Security. Officer Applegate."

"This is Aria Wright."

"Oh, hi. How can I help you?"

"Who's on duty at the construction site?" My voice rose higher with each alarmed word. "I'm looking at it now. Four strange men left the trailer and there's no guard in sight."

"I'm on it."

"Lacy, let's check it out."

"Wait for the armed guards."

"The men are gone. Come on." I grabbed Lacy's arm and pulled her through the doorway.

My phone vibrated. I glanced down at the ID. "Hey, Jax."

"Hey yourself."

I heard ambient traffic noises. He was driving.

"Why aren't you in the hospital?"

"Well, Dr. Oats, I checked myself out. Lacy and I are heading for the trailer on the construction site. Can you meet us there?"

"In five. What's happening?"

I filled him in, but hung up with a breezy 'See ya,' before he told me to wait.

•   •   •

The smell hit me first. Foul like an overflowing toilet filled with urine and poop. I knocked. The door swung open.

I screeched. Lacy made a similar sound behind me. My instinct was to leave. No one should see their employee in this state. The tears that filled my eyes surprised me. Poor Wally.

"Go away," Wally yelled. "Leave."

I tried empathy. "Tell me how I can help you." I wanted to cover my nose and mouth. "Is your wife on her way?"

The man sobbed. Head down, his entire body shook.

I heard heavy footsteps and swung around. Two guards were at the door. Shielding a view of Wally, I walked with my hands raised in a stop gesture. "There's been an accident and I'm taking care of it. Could you guard the door from the outside and wait for Ms. Claudia Wallace? You can let her in."

Lacy said, "I'll be outside too. Warn Claudia before she enters."

I turned back to Wally. Looked around for something to help him clean up, but I spotted nothing obvious. Bottles of water still wrapped in plastic were under a metal desk. I grabbed two, unscrewed the caps, and handed them to him.

With trembling hands, he wrapped his fists around them both, used the first to wash his hands, and downed the second one.

"Did Claudia call your doctor?"

Wally wiped his mouth with the back of his hand. "They threatened to kill me," he said. "And hurt Claudia."

"They who?"

"Crooks." His terror was clear.

Lacy called from outside. "Claudia is here."

I wanted to ask her to wait until Wally told me more, but how could I interrogate him sitting in a pile of runny excrement? "Once you're home and better, I'll come by."

His voice rose to a screech. "I can't stay home. They track me."

"What difference does that make? Tell me what's going on."

Claudia Wallace was a formidable woman. Like everyone, she towered over me, but I suspected she was several inches taller than Wally as well. Although we'd spoken on the phone several times and Wally shared bits and pieces of their lives, I'd never met her in person. Hair cut in a severe bob, she wore denim coveralls over a plaid shirt. Tiny gold studs decorated each earlobe. In her arms were clean clothes, washcloths, and soap all in a bucket.

"I've got this," she said to me. "Leave us."

Her matter-of-factness made me suspect they'd dealt with his situation before. Was Claudia aware of the four men who caused Wally's... I had no words to describe his condition.

"He says crooks threatened him."

Her face registered surprise. "Please let me take care of my husband."

With reluctance, I left the trailer. What did Wally's predicament have to do with Emerson's murder? There had to be a connection. Probably. The amount I didn't know could fill an empty bathtub.

Outside, two guards and the head of security–Tito Johnson–stood in a tight circle. Jax and Lacy were in a deep conversation. I assumed she was bringing Jax up to speed.

I smiled hello at Jax but turned my attention to Tito. He'd worked for The Way Station forever. I was his fourth CEO. Hair and mustache dyed jet black made him look older and a little macabre. "Four men were in there." I pointed to the trailer. "They left Mr. Wallace in a state. Who are they?"

As he should, Tito looked embarrassed. "No idea, ma'am, but I'll find out."

"Who was supposed to be on duty?"

He almost shuffled. "There was a mix-up."

Jax came over and stood next to me. "What kind? Because this looks damning."

Under normal circumstances, this would bother me. A man taking over when I was doing fine by myself. But I found it endearing. Silly me, right? Jax was so imposing. All six-feet-two of him, confident, and worried about his lady... Stop it, I told myself. You haven't even dated.

Tito knew Jax, of course. "They both called in sick, and I expected my number two to assign replacements, but..." His voice trailed off, letting us fill in the blanks. Jax wasn't having it.

"But what?"

"I dropped the ball."

"We've had a murder. Unknown evil-doers threatened Ms. Wright. And you didn't find it odd both officers called in sick?"

Tito moved to offense. "I don't answer to volunteers or rich donors throwing their weight around."

"That's right, you answer to me. Please respond to Mr. Oat's question."

Behind us, there was movement. I swung around. Claudia had Wally wrapped in a blanket. Wet towels and dirty clothes filled the bucket. The stink was less intense, but still noticeable as the couple pushed past us.

"I'll come this afternoon," I said to their retreating backs.

"No need," Claudia said.

"Around five."

Wally raised his head. "I have to be in the office." His voice trembled. "I'll be back in an hour."

Claudia ignored him. "No need for you to come. As soon as he's better—"

"No." He straightened up. "Once I've changed... recovered, I'll return to work."

Claudia made a clucking noise. Wally eased into the passenger seat.

I poked my head in. "Do you need security at your house?"

Wally started crying again.

"Leave us," Claudia screamed, and hurried to the driver's side. They roared away.

Jax said, "Let's go to your office and figure out what comes next. I have news."

I nodded and then turned to Tito. "Hunt down your missing guards and get explanations, send maintenance over to clean up the trailer, and meet in my office in one hour with answers."

Tito looked unhappy. "Okay."

"Thank you," I said, but I didn't mean it.

CHAPTER FORTY-THREE
M.J.

Christmas Eve, 1985

M.J. sat on the edge of Denise's bed, his head out the back window, smoking a joint. She sucked on one also and exhaled the smoke into the frigid air. He'd hoped for snow, but the sky was clear.

"What time will your folks be home?"

"Couple of hours," Denise said with a shrug. "They're distributing toys to children in need."

Denise was his lady. They'd met during tryouts for last year's school play. She had a gazillion earrings going up the side of each ear. A purple streak in jet black hair and a serpent tattoo wriggling up her left arm defined her as a hardcore fan. Or punk. Her whiter-than-white skin added to the label. In the eighties, you hung with people who jammed to the music you liked. Little crossover.

"I can't believe they're making me move. Again."

"Don't go." Denise sent another cloud of marijuana smoke into the crisp air.

"And do what?" Both his mom and Emerson drummed into him the importance of education. Graduate from high school. Go to college. His grandparents, Emerson's mom and dad, concurred. "You earn a diploma, certifications, whatever you need to take care of yourself and your family, the one you're going to have. That's what a man does." M.J. believed them. "I'm not dropping out of high school."

"Of course not. Stay with Freddie."

Denise, Freddie, and M.J. hung together from sophomore to junior year.

Freddie's parents were leftover hippies. They smoked joints, played old school music, preached free love and peace on earth. To each their own. Stoned, M.J. crashed often. "Can I stay with Freddie tonight? We're cramming for an exam." That was always a winning argument. "Wouldn't work."

"Why not? White people's angst and self-righteousness. You'd be doing them a favor. Saving you or something."

M.J. pulled his head back into the room. "I'm so mad at them. Not sure who's worse. They're thinking of themselves. What they want. Not caring how their decisions land on me."

Denise joined him. "That's how they do." She made a groaning noise. "Selfish parentals."

They stayed quiet for several seconds. Denise asked, "What was the fight about?"

"My dad came home from a party. He drank."

"And that's bad, why?" She leaned across him and grabbed two bottles of beer from an open cooler she kept in her room under her bed. She opened both and passed one to M.J.

"He has a problem." M.J. understood Emerson's drinking wasn't healthy. When M.J. was seven, Emerson stumbled through the door and passed out. M.J.'s mom screamed and cried. That was the same year Emerson lost his job, and they moved to a smaller place. But Emerson did nothing bad. Television reporters talked about fathers beating their wives or doing terrible things to their children. Emerson was always kind and sorry. They moved a few times without him. Once, they even lived with Emerson's parents. Life had been great in recent years. The bad old days, as his mom called them, were over until now.

Denise leaned over again and kissed M.J. She slipped her beery, marijuana-tasting tongue in his mouth and pressed her round breasts against his chest. She pulled back. "You should call Freddie now. Move in with him. At least finish the school year."

M.J. pulled her back into his arms. Yes, but not right now.

•   •   •

At first, they kissed on the floor, then moved to her narrow bed. His swollen penis throbbed against his constraining pants. Denise let him climb on top, lift her sweater and bra, and kiss and suck her nipples. He came in his pants.

The bell shrilled. M.J. jumped off Denise. It rang again–a loud, insistent noise. "It's my mom." He looked down at his damp pants. Can't go home like this. "I'll sneak out the back and walk to Freddie's."

Denise didn't appear to notice his humiliation. "Stay here for now. She'll go there next."

But she might have tried Freddie first. "I'll take my chances." Dejection and shame weighed him down.

"Borrow one of my dad's jackets." She rolled off the bed and ran out of the room. When she returned, she had a washcloth, towel, briefs, slacks, a knit hat, and a down ski-jacket. "He won't miss them."

Now M.J.'s mortification was overwhelming. He took the offerings and slouched down the hall to the bathroom. This was one of the worst nights of his life.

CHAPTER FORTY-FOUR
JAX

Lacy, Aria, and Jax trooped across the construction site. Aria held her arm, still in a soft cast, against her chest. There were so many ways the crash could have gone bad. But here she was, striding along in her three-inch heels, as if nothing happened. Aria was fearless. Focused. He loved that about her... He loved *everything* about her. Jax licked his lips–an involuntary reaction to thinking about Aria. It seemed like months, but was only days since he kissed her in Ithaca. He still tasted her. Did she think about the kiss? About him?

His phone buzzed. Jax checked. E-Man. "Gotta take this," he said, slowing his gait until he was several feet behind the women. "What's up?"

"I found him."

It took Jax a second to process. Found Emerson's killer? The hit-and-run driver? The characters who cornered Wally in the trailer? His mind cleared. "Our hacker?"

"Yeah."

Jax stopped. Aria turned around and questioned him with her eyes. He put up one finger. "Who is it?"

"Barker from billing."

An alarm rang in Jax's head. "You've proof?" The Vault team took different actions based on the level of certainty. Concrete and damning evidence, proof, was the platinum standard.

"Yeah. Ninety-eight percent certain."

"Have you approached him?"

"Nah. Wanted to check with you."

Jax forced himself to pause. Under normal circumstances, they'd go to the FBI, report their findings, and share the evidence. Let the law take it from there. But Barker worked in the finance department that invoiced clients and took in payments. Aria suspected Wally of financial fraud. The hacker launched his cyber-attack days after Emerson's murder, or at least that's when E-Man detected the breach. Could the three events be coincidences or were they attached to an illegal maze?

"I'm going into a meeting at The Way Station. I'll be back in a few hours. Can you keep Barker there? Give him an urgent assignment?"

"I'll tell Charlie. Ask him to help."

That made sense since Barker's department reported to Jax's brother Charlie.

"As you get closer, send me your ETA."

"Will do." Another thought. "Let's pull in Stephen too, so both my brothers are aware. We'll meet in the conference room. I'm guessing I'll be there by 2:00." Jax hung up, broke into a trot, and caught up with the two women as they entered Aria's office.

•   •   •

Ginger greeted Lacy, Aria, and Jax with a curt nod. Her face expressed curiosity, but she only asked what everyone wanted to drink. They all passed.

The second the door closed behind her, Jax said, "Lacy filled me in about Wally and the four vanishing men. What do you suspect is going on?"

Aria launched into the construction overruns and the drained bank account set up for Hope House. "Wally is stealing from the project at the behest of crooks, is my estimation."

Jax asked, "Was this why someone killed Emerson? He stumbled onto the scheme?"

"Maybe," Aria said.

"We kept all donations designated for the project in that account," Lacy said.

Aria groaned. "If it's true, if Wally syphoned off funds, we have a bigger problem than no new building. Wally deposited donors' money and government grants into the Hope House account."

Jax pushed all the puzzle pieces around in his head.

"Someone threatened me again," Aria said.

"What?"

"In the hospital. The male voice demanded I stop the fraud investigation, or I'd be the one in jail. My name is on the paperwork. Forgeries." Most times, Aria was fierce, but now she appeared shaken. "I'd go to prison and Zander would be alone." Her voice snagged on the last few words.

Without thinking, Jax pulled her close. She didn't resist. A surge moved through him. "I will let nothing happen to you or Zander." She relaxed against his chest.

After a few seconds, she eased back. "They figured out how to frighten me. Well, enough of that." She rolled back her shoulders. "We need to go on the offensive."

Aria baffled Jax all the time. The embrace and pushback symbolized their relationship. Yes. No. Maybe. Her conclusion, however, was spot on. They had to get ahead of the bad guys and stop playing catch-up. And, as much as he didn't want to admit it, they needed professional help. "Glover needs to know about the fraud."

"The caller said no police." Aria tapped her fingers on her chin. "When I asked the officer who was protecting me to trace the number, she explained it wasn't possible because burner phones were difficult and expensive to trace. But she said they had technology available if I tied the burner to an important case."

"Murder ought to make the list," Lacy said.

Aria stepped out of her heels and paced her office. "Are they watching us? Will they figure out we've pulled the detectives into Wally's mess?"

Jax said, "We'll tell him to assist on the down low."

"To be safe, it's time for Zander to come home."

Lacy said, "Stay with Pastor Joy. She's not connected, and Zan loves her."

"Good idea," Aria said. "What else? I call Errol, get Zan to Joy, and we quiz Wally the second he's back in the office. He sounded panicked, so I'm sure he'll return today."

"Don't forget Tito," Lacy added.

Jax forced himself not to worry about Glover's interest in Aria. He couldn't hang around to watch the two of them while failing to investigate the threat and tie to his company. "I'm going to follow a thread at The Vault," he said. "We need to cover every base." He brought both up to date. "Seems tied."

Aria looked at her watch. "It's noon. Wally and Tito are due at 1:00."

"Who's interrogating them?" Lacy asked.

"My responsibility."

"Talk it over with Glover." He hated saying those words.

Aria frowned at Jax. He saw the chip back on her shoulder. "We agreed we need professional help."

She stared Jax down. The memory of leaning against his chest forgotten.

"Call and talk it over with Glover. I'll be back."

"*Okay.*" Which sounded just the opposite.

Jax turned to go.

"Wait," Aria said. "Let's meet at your office. Ask Errol to come around the back. Away from where those hoodlums watched."

"Good."

"What do you need me to do?" Lacy asked.

"Hold down the fort," Aria said. She hugged her friend. "And call me the minute Wally returns and Tito shows up. Ask Gladys and whoever is at security at the side door to alert you."

"You'll have to keep them here. Timing is tight," Jax said.

"I'm on it."

"Let's roll." Jax reached for Aria's hand, and she took his, which made him smile.

CHAPTER FORTY-FIVE
ZANDER

Tuesday, March 19, Ithaca, New York

Today was the second anniversary of his father's fatal heart attack. The scariest, saddest day of Zander's life. He let the sadness settle around him. Honored it. Today was also the day for moving forward on Climate Action's next protest. He didn't tell Darcy about the anniversary. It was important that she saw him as strong, confident, and dependable.

Darcy and Zan drove around The Jungle for several minutes, scoping out possibilities for their protest. They searched for a spot large enough for thirty to fifty activists to stand and shout slogans and close enough to a road where drivers could see and hear them. Zan suspected a lot fewer people would show, but he didn't want Darcy to think he doubted her. Tears, screams, and tugging out her hair taught him to stay positive. She interpreted questions as disloyalty. Plus, she'd kick him out of her bed. The sex was so good. He'd never been with a woman before. Darcy had experience. And, well, damn. It was better than anything he'd imagined.

They chose South Meadow Street, a major thoroughfare that ran adjacent to an accessible section of the massive dump and home to many unhoused folks.

Darcy pulled over and parked. "I saw a clearing under a tree behind us."

Zander swung his door open. The stench hit full force–damp earth, decaying garbage, and the faint, acrid scent of smoke from makeshift fires. He swung his head right and left.

"Over there." She pointed to an ancient oak standing guard. A ragged path ran alongside it and meandered deeper into the brush. Three men with dirty blankets wrapped around them huddled close to the thick trunk. A stiff March wind swayed the leafless branches.

"Looks promising." Zander popped the trunk open.

Inside, take-away covered trays filled with hot food stood stacked in a large bin. Stuffed around the bin were paper bags packed with peanut butter and jam sandwiches, fruit cups, and water. Zander approached the men under the oak. "Are you hungry? We have hot spaghetti and rolls, plus sandwiches."

One man looked up and glanced at his neighbor. "Yeah. Sure." He struggled up before offering a hand to the person beside him, a woman with buzzed hair and a dagger tattoo over her left eye. The other man didn't move.

Zan handed the man and woman two cartons and two paper bags. "Anyone else like a hot meal?"

"There's a family living in that tent," the woman said, pointing. "I'll take the food over. And Buster..." She jutted her thumb at the man still sitting under the tree. "Is shy. I'll bring him food too."

Zan introduced Darcy and himself.

"They call me Peach." She smiled. Every other tooth in her mouth was missing.

"We're planning a protest to get this place cleaned up," Darcy said to Peach. "Considering staging it here."

"Cleaned up how? By throwing us out?" Peach asked, her voice filled with suspicion.

"No, the trash and debris. You'd have a healthier place to live."

A dog yelped and tugged from a stake in the ground, holding its leash.

Zan said, "Would your dog like some water?"

"Ain't mine," Peach said. "You bring people here and the police will roust us. Don't bring trouble."

Something or someone moved in the thicket left of the tree. Zan called out, "Are you hungry? We have more food."

Peach appeared anxious. "Thanks. Gotta bounce." Arms full and ready for distribution, she hurried away. Her male companion followed. Only Buster sat, shoveling food into his mouth, sauce dripping down his chin.

"What's wrong?" Darcy asked.

"Probably nothing." But Zan sensed danger. Peach's reaction added to his unease. "Let's go."

"I understood what Peach said, but I still think this is the right spot for our action."

The brush rustled again.

The hairs on Zander's neck rose. "We can talk in the car." He climbed into the passenger seat, closed, and locked the door. Maybe his anxiety came from the crap his mother talked about. Murder, people following her, and her car smashed. Or memories of his father, gone in seconds.

A sharp rap on the passenger window startled Zander. He hesitated.

Darcy pushed the button from her side of the car and Zan's window rolled down. She leaned across Zander. "We still have some food left. Are you hungry?"

The man ignored her. "You Zander Wright?" A keloid scar ran along the man's cheek.

What the hell? "Who's asking?"

"Tell your mother I'm not fucking around."

"My mom?"

"Yeah. She'll understand. Time is running out." He turned and walked away.

Darcy said, "Damn, was that the man your mother was afraid of, the man watching from across the diner?

"Drive." He fumbled for his phone.

Darcy swung the wheel and steered the car away from The Jungle. "It seems to me," she said. "We—"

Zan put his hand up to silence Darcy while he punched in his mother's cell number.

"Hey, Zan," Aria said through the phone speaker. "How are—"

"A guy just threatened us. Gave me a message."

CHAPTER FORTY-SIX
IGGY AND EMERSON

January 1987, South Bronx, NY

Iggy and SoSo drove around, checking on all their corners, lots, and stash houses. Business was great. Leaving the Commander was the right move. This part of the South Bronx was ripe. Now they had their own crew and steady income. Crack cocaine was their money ticket.

SoSo parked their Cadillac Seville on Vyse Avenue and 178th Street. A vast lot filled with trash, broken supermarket carts, cardboard boxes, and old mattresses defined one end of their territory. Ringed by burned-out buildings, the crack heads lived in abandoned, graffiti-covered structures that, decades earlier, were home to aspiring immigrants from the Caribbean, and transplants from the US south. The urban designer, Robert Moses, cut through the borough and installed The Cross Bronx Expressway. Construction spanned 1948 to 1977, devastating neighborhoods and displacing thousands. The Bronx had yet to recover.

The Lexington Line, Number 2 train, rattled by. Workers and homeowners traveling north ignored the devastation just outside their windows. Read their newspapers. Listened to music. Chatted with fellow commuters. Who cared about the Black and Brown folks living in one of the most blighted areas in the country? Why look at or think about so much misery?

But that wasn't what Iggy saw. He saw wealth.

Strapped with Glocks under their jackets, they started their day. It would be close to midnight before they returned home to the comfort of their shared house in Fieldcrest, just north of the Bronx.

"I'm thinking we take our trade to Westchester. Expand," Iggy said.

"Don't eat where you shit."

"We'd start in Southeast Fieldcrest. Lots of possibilities there. Far enough from home."

"You're the boss, but I vote no."

Iggy respected SoSo's instincts. They'd been working together now for two decades. More like brothers than business partners. Sometimes they ran into trouble between them. Iggy's girl of the month didn't like SoSo hanging around. Or SoSo brought home a ratty, flea-bitten dog he found on his travels and wanted to keep him. Minor shit. Overall, SoSo left strategy to Iggy and Iggy relied on SoSo's gut and intelligence gathering. They enjoyed the same television shows, so even though the house had three sets, they watched in the shared living room. Iggy liked women who had meat on their bones and loved to cook. SoSo was cool with that. When a female wasn't around, there was pizza and McDonalds.

The frigid January air slapped their faces. Iggy clutched his peacoat tighter against his throat. Heads ducked to avoid the full force of the wind, as they walked into a flop house, edging the lot. The acrid stink, like burning plastic, told them someone was cooking crack. Shade, one of their top dealers, approached.

"Lots of business today. Took care of everyone." He pulled out an envelope stuffed with $100 bills. "We can take the money over to the counting house if you want to check." He said this in a pleasant tone. No problem if you do. I'm here to please.

"Unnecessary," Iggy said, taking the money and passing the envelope to SoSo. "Have a lot of rounds to make."

Shade, a trusted, affable, and ruthless officer in Iggy's army, saluted Iggy and nodded at SoSo. Cross Iggy, and you get a beat-down from Shade. Cross Iggy twice and Shade took you out. Two bullets in the head and one in the heart, just to be sure. If you pissed off Shade, not managing the situation like a man, you got both a beating, often with a baseball bat, and shot. Other members of Shade's crew, soldiers, took care of users who didn't pay their bills. But Shade focused on the crew leaders, all working for Iggy and SoSo. He kept them in line for the general.

It was getting late, and both men were hungry. Snow drifted down. Windshield wipers going, they drove north to Fieldcrest and stopped at Mario's Pizza.

Iggy said, "I'm serious about expanding to Fieldcrest. Shade is the man to get us started. He has a few guys ready for promotion."

They'd moved to Fieldcrest from Harlem once their business took off. They liked the quiet neighborhood. Trees and grass dotted with wildflowers and dandelions rather than garbage and drug paraphernalia. They could see more stars at night since the light pollution was less. Iggy enjoyed bringing his ladies there. They respected him more. Gave more.

"Takes time to start up new. We'll need local help." SoSo pushed the restaurant's door open. Heated air smelling of onions and garlic greeted them.

Mario's was a dive, but also an institution. A place you ran into all kinds of folks.

Iggy and SoSo chose a booth and ordered two pepperoni medium pizzas and Cokes.

"Okay," Iggy said, biting into a slice. "So, we make new friends. Take our time. I'd like to work closer to home. You get what I'm saying?"

SoSo laughed. "Shorter commute? Like we're Wall Street guys who live in Bedford?" Bedford was a wealthy Westchester County town near the Connecticut border.

"I'm serious."

The door swung open. A square-built guy with mahogany brown skin entered. He pulled his ski cap off his head and unwound his scarf. Iggy was stunned. What were the chances? He kicked SoSo under the table.

Mouth full of food, SoSo, asked in an aggrieved tone, "What?"

"It's him again. The dude from Bangkok."

SoSo wiped his mouth with the napkin and peered over his shoulder. He nodded.

"Local talent? I think it's time I chatted with him. Since, evidently, we're neighbors."

•　　•　　•

September 1986, Fieldcrest, NY

The shelter stood on the corner of Fir and South 3rd on a despondent block. An abandoned church, its barred windows covered with wood, was the shelter's neighbor to the east. Check cashing and bail bondsmen establishments shared an office across the street. Emerson rang the shelter's bell.

"Yeah?" the scratchy voice from the intercom inquired.

"Cal Emerson. I spoke with someone—"

The door buzzed open before he finished. Emerson stepped inside. The place smelled like funky humans, disinfectant, musty bedding, and unidentifiable food lingering in the air.

"You got your paperwork?" the woman at the front desk asked without looking up.

An armed guard stood next to the desk. His eyes never left Emerson's.

"Yes, ma'am." He handed over the papers from his social worker.

"Twitch will show you around."

Emerson hadn't noticed the tall, thin man. A ponytail hung down his back and mutton chops covered his cheeks.

"You're in upper bunk twelve," the woman said.

Twitch put out his hand and Emerson shook it. "First time on the street?"

"Nah." Emerson held his belongings in a large garbage bag close to his chest. It was easy to get ripped off. Shelters weren't always safe, so Emerson moved around a lot.

By reputation, this was one of the better places. The dining room had microwaves, tables, and chairs for communal eating. Two overtaxed washing machines and dryers took quarters, and a vending machine offered boxes of Tide.

Twitch said, "You can put your things in that bucket, but I wouldn't unless you have a lock."

Emerson did.

"You should be okay. Though folks have carried footlockers out and busted them open."

A dingy sheet covered the thin mattress on the top bunk. Emerson brought his own.

"How long you been on the street?" Twitch asked.

"A while."

Nine months ago, he owned a house and a car, had a job and family. When Kiki walked out the day after Christmas and M.J. moved in with his best friend Freddie, Emerson went on a dark binge. It lasted a month or more. He found it hard to remember. Still, he'd recovered from them before. Cleaned up. Got his act together. Won Kiki back. Made amends with the boy. Not this time. How could his life fall apart so quickly?

He knew the answer. Iggy Smalls.

CHAPTER FORTY-SEVEN
ARIA

I let go of Jax's hand and almost dropped my phone. "What?" Sweat broke out on my forehead.

"Darcy and I were scoping out The Jungle, our next protest spot, and we just finished feeding some homeless folks."

I tried to keep up. Pictures from my online search of Ithaca's homeless encampment flashed.

"That's when this guy bangs on the car window. 'Tell your mother to stop her investigation.' He said you'd understand. Is this about the murder?"

We hadn't reached Jax's Jeep yet or called Errol. "Give me a second to think, son. Where are you now? Are you and Darcy safe?"

"From what? That man? He had a wicked scar on his cheek. Does that mean anything to you?"

Twitch's description of Emerson's killer matched, but was Twitch correct? Nor did I tell Errol or Jax. My legs sagged under me.

Jax grabbed me, took the phone, put his arm around me, and led me to his car. Crazy, but in the middle of all this drama, my child in danger, I focused on Jax's arm around me. He was so solid. And gentle. Shivers moved through me.

"Zan, you're on speaker. This is your mom's friend, Jax. We met—"

"I remember."

My son sounded offended. Another reason Jax and I... Focus. I took a steadying-breath. How would I get Zander to Pastor Joy? That was my top concern.

Multiple truths can coexist. Frightened and worried for my son while working on a solution. My nonprofit was in deep trouble. We're pulling in the police. A murderer roamed free. Together, we will track him down. Jax wasn't right for me. And the chills and sparks cruising through my body when he touched me made me feel alive and long for more.

•   •   •

Pastor Joy was an amazing woman and dear friend. She had her church, plus a full-time job at our local hospital, managing a team of nurses, and her twins were seniors in high school, playing sports and taking music lessons that required chauffeuring them around and showing up for games and concerts, and yet Joy's answer was, "I'll drive to Ithaca and bring him back with me. When I see him, I won't take no for an answer." One problem scratched off my mental to-do list.

Errol and his partner, Detective Yun, were on their way. Jax's admin planned to meet the detectives at the back door in case the crooks were watching. I suspected they'd want me to step aside and let them interrogate Wally and Tito, but I had to be there. Would the detectives want to take them both to the police station? We had no proof of fraud, just suspicion. I felt a headache building behind my eyes.

I stepped out of my heels and rubbed my feet. Jax stood next to me as I shrank three inches. He didn't appear to notice. We were standing in Jax's conference room at The Vault, waiting for Errol and Yun to arrive. Spotless off-white walls held framed prints of famous paintings. I recognized Monet, but not the others. The table was also off white, surrounded by twelve executive chairs. Against one wall, a long, narrow table held carafes of hot tea and coffee, cups, milk, and sugar. Cookies, sodas, and water added to the mix.

Jax looked down at me with eyes filled with caring and... Stop it.

"You okay?"

"Fine."

"Not fine."

A nervous laugh escaped. "Do you need to meet with your people about the hacker? I can wait for the detectives."

Instead of answering, he stepped closer. I moved back so I could more easily look up at him. That's when he leaned down and kissed me on the top of my head and cheek. My breath caught. His lips moved down to my neck. Chills and tremors surged through my body. His mouth touched mine. Stop, run, one part of my brain, the logical half, screamed, but my body didn't listen. I closed my eyes and let his lips press against mine. His thick hands slipped around my waist and lifted me onto the conference table. His mouth was warm and tasted so good. When his tongue slid into my mouth, I melted. Melted? Geez. So corny, but that's how I felt–all liquid-heat.

"Hey."

It was Errol's voice. I jerked away from Jax, slid off the table, and stumbled. Jax caught and righted me. How humiliating. We both faced Errol. He stood in the doorway with his dripping trench coat over his arm. It must have rained.

"What's going on?"

Did Errol mean Jax and me? Or the case or what?

Yun joined us. Flustered, I babbled. I told them about the potential fraud, Wally's predicament in the trailer, the four bad guys, and concluded with Twitch's declaration that Iggy Smalls killed Emerson, Iggy's description, and the man who warned Zander.

Errol pulled out his notebook. "Sit and start again from the top." He asked dozens of questions, especially about the suspected fraud. "I checked out Twitch. He's known Emerson for decades. They met in a shelter in the eighties."

"And?" Jax asked.

"Real name is Lloyd Bonds. Long rap sheet, but nothing violent. Theft, drugs, DUIs. We'll run Iggy Smalls through the system. See what comes up." He shifted his stance. Zeroed in on me. "How are you holding up?" The tone was his warm, caring one.

My face flushed hot. Perspiration soaked my forehead, cheeks, and armpits. "It's a lot."

"Yeah. I get that." He sounded as if he understood.

I forced my composure to return and kept my eyes away from Jax's face. "What do you recommend I ask Wally?"

Errol frowned and shook his head. "Let us do our job."

"He's my employee. And my name is on all the withdrawals."

"More reason to let us handle this."

"No police. He was quite specific. Look what happened to Wally. And they threatened my son." I squared my shoulders, but the high heels were steps away. When taller, in my mind, I came across as more credible, formidable. Nothing to do about that now. "I will question him. You can coach me, but I have lots of questions of my own."

Errol's frown deepened. "That's not happening. This is a murder investigation. You should be in a safe house with police protection. Your son, too."

I opened my mouth to protest, but he put his hands up, palms out, in a stop gesture.

I hadn't noticed Yun leave the room, but now she returned. "Iggy Smalls is a bad dude. I ran his name through our system. Drug lord. Used to be an enforcer for Commander, a long-ago Harlem kingpin who died in prison. Iggy broke away and took over the South Bronx. Then he expanded to Fieldcrest and other cities in Westchester. Lots of suspicions of murder, but nothing ever stuck. Don't know if his path crossed Emerson's."

Jax asked, "How old is he?"

"In his late seventies, just like the vic."

My mind went back to the murder. The muffled voice demanding I stop. The gun and blood covered knife. He ran up the stairs with vigor. I tried to picture him as an old man. "Does embezzlement show up in his history?"

"Not on the surface," Yun said. "We have to dig deeper."

"That's what we intend to do," Errol said. "And we're putting you..." He pointed his index finger at me. "In a motel out of town. I'll clear it with the ADA on the case."

He was talking about the Assistant District Attorney. The DA's office controlled the budget for the investigation, including police protection. "Don't point your finger at me." I was over the embarrassment of whatever Errol saw Jax and me doing. With my heels back on, I said, "I'm not going."

"You don't have a choice. This is a murder investigation. Mine."

"How will you protect my entire family? For how long? We've been down this road before."

Errol's tone softened. "Things have changed. A lot."

Yun said, "We could protect everyone for at least a day." She looked at Errol. "I'll call the assigned ADA."

Jax reached for my hand, but I didn't respond. "My brothers and I inherited a house in Bedford. We use it for out-of-town clients and other business related purposes. There are enough bedrooms for the entire family. Then you'd only need two protection details."

That sounded good. Would Jax stay too? Just the thought of spending the night with him... My parents and son in the same house made any carnal deeds off limits. I refocused.

Errol looked flummoxed.

I spoke to Jax. "I have a cat."

"I know. Princess. No problem."

Errol said, "Let me make a few calls."

"To clear it?" I asked. My phone rang. It was Lacy.

"They're both here. Tito is in his office and Wally is in yours."

Okay, this was it. Quiz them before Errol takes over. They'd both confess their roles or stumble enough to give me and the police clues. Once the detectives took over, lawyers would intervene and time escapes.

"Thanks." I turned to the detectives. "Jax will drive me to my house so I can pack my things, gather my parents, and get ready for the move. Lacy... You remember her from back-in-the-day?"

"Yeah," Errol said in a wary tone. "Of course, I remember."

"She says neither Tito nor Wally have returned yet. She'll call the second they do. I'll text her your number..." I pulled out my phone and thumbed in the digits. "You can interrogate them without the watchers seeing you. At least until we're all in Bedford." That ought to set Errol and Yun back on their heels and give me at least an hour to quiz my errant employees. Would Jax go along with my deception?

CHAPTER FORTY-EIGHT
ARIA

Ginger picked me up in the back lot of The Vault. I slid into her Kia. "Thanks for the ride. I'm pretending to go home."

Ginger side-eyed me. "And you are pretending why?"

"Errol, Detective Glover, doesn't want me to interrogate Wally and Tito, but they'll tell me more without Errol."

"Hubris is unbecoming."

I cracked a smile. "True. But I think I'm right." Wally would be the easier of the two. I'd already seen him terrified. He also seemed the most pliable, plus we had a relationship of sorts. Tito was going to be tough.

During the fifteen minute drive, I called Lacy to set up my clever sting. At least, that's how I thought about it. As agreed, I'd call Lacy on my personal cell phone. She was waiting for me in Wally's office. When her phone rang, she'd answer and pretend to be speaking with someone else. Instead of ending the call, she'd place it on mute, slide it into her pocket, and keep the line open. As soon as she reached her office, a minute away, she'd place the phone near a recorder so she'd both hear and save every word.

Ginger pulled up in front of The Way Station and dropped me off. I hustled past Gladys with a wave, dashed to my office, and made the clandestine call.

When I entered Wally's office after a sharp rap, Lacy and Wally sat on the couch sipping water. At first glance, they appeared in conversation, but I realized Lacy was doing all the talking.

"Does Claudia like the Catskills too?"

Wally's head snapped in my direction.

Lacy also turned. "Hi. Wally and I were talking about vacations." She rose. "I'll be in my office if you need me."

"Great. From here, I'm going to Tito's office. Let's meet there."

At this news, Wally blanched. His beet-red-in-distress coloring vanished.

My internal playlist banged out drumbeats. I walked to the couch but didn't sit. Instead, arms crossed, I stood over him and jumped in. "Why did those barbarians threaten you?"

Wally shook his head.

"Silence is not an option. The police are on the way." I pulled a chair over and sat in front of him, softened my tone, and quieted the drums. "Tell me what's going on. I can run interference for you. It will be too late once the police arrive.

"They'll beat you up." His voice squeaked and trembled. "No police."

"Too late. They'll be here in a few minutes, but I can send them away. Tell them you left for the Catskills. Is there still a place for you to stay until the police catch the criminals?"

His eyes met mine. "Can you do that?"

"Yes," I lied. "Detective Glover, he's in charge, and we're old friends." Color returned to Wally's unfortunate face. I tried to keep my eyes locked on his eyes, rather than stare at his large, shiny forehead. "Tell me how this started."

"I didn't mean to hurt The Way Station." Some of the squeaking subsided. "At first, I took the money as a loan."

A loan? What the hell? "What did you do with the money?"

Wally squirmed and grimaced. Then he cleared his throat. I waited.

"An acquaintance had a sure-fire deal. Needed investors."

Argh. "And?" I now understood why one might benefit from interrogation training. Drums started up again in my head. My lungs tightened.

"Okay. So, my contact was trading in crypto currency and using his substantial gains to invest in a casino in the Catskills. I buy in with

$100,000. Easy. He puts my money into the crypto trading and *boom*." Wally clapped his hands together. "Doubles my money, so I'm all in. With a $500,000 or even a $1,000,000 investment, working becomes unnecessary. For life.

I wanted to scream. We serve people who have nothing. Who are fighting to survive and this idiot, would be gangster, is robbing them. My breathing sped up, which was not okay. Not now. I reached for an opened bottle of water from my desk. With no idea how long it sat there collecting dust, I gulped down several mouthfuls. "What went wrong?"

"They're all crooks."

Ah, and you didn't see that coming? "How did you get the money?"

His head dropped forward, but I wasn't buying his shame-act.

"Padded the construction costs and used the excess for the investments. Then these thieves..." His head popped up. "Saw me as an ATM. They demanded more money and threatened to kill me and Claudia if I stopped. Lacy was raking in grants and donations for the project." His voice faltered. "I had no choice."

"Of course you didn't." I did nothing to camouflage my sarcasm and disdain. "Who followed me to Ithaca?"

"How would I—"

"Don't lie to me."

He looked caught. "They asked where you were going. Just to scare you. I had to give them *something*. The money was drying up fast."

For the briefest of seconds, I closed my eyes. Then I narrowed my gaze toward Wally. "Did Emerson discover the embezzlement, and they killed him?"

"No clue." He ran both hands through his slick black hair.

I took another deep breath. Lacy would record his full confession. "Did Emerson threaten to expose you, so you shot and stabbed him?"

"What? No. Is that what the police think?" He jumped to his feet. "I'm going to call my lawyer before they get here. Demand protective custody." Sweat poured down his face.

Was he telling the truth? "Who killed Emerson?"

"You better do the same. Get out of town. Hire a lawyer. These guys will hurt you."

"I plan to," I said without thinking. The Bedford house was a short-term solution. The minute the words came out of my mouth, I regretted them.

"Good for you."

I took another steadying breath. "Tell me their names."

"I can't..." He paused as if rethinking his answer. "Never saw the four men who tortured me before. I deal with Shade. He's not the boss-boss, but I'm confident he sent them."

Sirens wailed outside.

"I'm out of here. But your name is on all those transfers. You're in trouble too." He bolted out the door.

I slipped my hand into my pocket and extracted the phone. "Were you able to get all that?"

"Yes, but it wasn't much. He only gave us one name."

Lacy was right. Tito might have more. "I'm heading over to Tito's office. Ginger has him pinned down, signing a bunch of papers. I'll call as soon as I arrive."

CHAPTER FORTY-NINE

Tito Johnson was a big man with broad shoulders, a short neck, and dyed black hair and mustache. He served in the Army before joining the police force. Retired and took a job at The Way Station. Some of that military bearing remained. I placed the call to Lacy, slipped my phone in my pocket, and knocked on his door.

Ginger said, "Come in."

Tito growled. "I've been waiting for over an hour. What the hell."

"He's in a bad mood and not too talkative," Ginger said. She side-eyed Tito. "Acts and sounds guilty, if you ask me."

"Of what?"

"You tell us," I said.

Tito, his gaze on neither Ginger nor me, said, "You didn't keep me here. I could have left at any time. Out of courtesy to you..." He faced me. "I stayed. But not for long."

Neither Ginger nor I responded.

"My family is waiting for me," Tito said.

"I'll check on the detectives' ETA," Ginger said. With her back to Tito, she mouthed to me, "Be careful."

"Thank you." I nodded my understanding. In the past, Tito never concerned me. He had an old school manner, and didn't always treat me as a peer, much less his supervisor, but he did his job with competence, or so I thought. But now, something about his demeanor gave me pause.

Ginger, paperwork in hand, stepped into the hall and closed Tito's door behind her.

"Let's talk."

"About what?"

"How Emerson's murderer got past security with a knife and a gun. Start there."

He was better at this than Wally. "How would I know?" He crossed his arms and leaned against the high back of his executive chair.

Still standing, I said, "Bullshit."

"Whoa. Don't let any donors or Mr. Bannister hear your dirty mouth." The chair creaked as Tito shifted forward. "I'm not answering your questions. I did nothing wrong, and I have no information that I haven't told the police."

"What about your staff?"

He stared me down.

"Fine. Why wasn't the construction trailer guarded?"

"I fired both officers. Case closed." He returned to leaning against the chair-back with crossed arms and cold eyes.

"Tell me their names."

"No need. It's taken care of."

"Is Shade one of them?" He might realize Wally squealed, but so what? They were both complicit. The only sign Tito gave me was three successive eye blinks. But that was enough. "Who does Shade work for?"

"Who?" He recovered and returned to smirking.

"What if I fire you?"

"Don't think my union would allow that." His tone and expression were smug.

My heart rate sped up. Another asthma attack tried to surface.

"If I knew anything," Tito said, his eyes still in a flinty squint, "I'd warn you not to cross these men." He paused. "Whoever they are."

"Are you threatening me?" I heard the tremor in my voice and hoped he didn't.

"You think you're running this organization." He shook his head. "Whoever controls the money is in charge and that ain't you, *little* lady."

Everything about this conversation alarmed me. Breathing became more difficult. I wanted to grab my inhaler from my bag, but he'd already dissed and tried to scare me. Succeeded. Were he and Wally controlling our finances and connected to mobsters who killed Emerson and might kill me? For money? Ridiculous. My lungs screamed at me. Nostrils flared, not in anger but in desperation for more oxygen, I said in a hoarse voice, "This isn't over."

I dashed out and ran into Errol.

• • •

I sensed steam rising from Errol's head. But I couldn't stop and speak until I medicated my lungs. With the wall supporting my back, I pulled out my inhaler, closed my eyes, and sucked. Errol's glare bore into me. Puffs of angry breath hit my face, confirming he was only steps away. I opened my eyes and righted myself.

"Where's Wally Wallace? He's not in his office." His tone was icy. Almost professional except for the anger-spikes encapsulating each word.

"Went home." I felt like I was ten again and caught shoplifting the candy cigarettes my parents forbade me to eat. "I'm sorry."

"Go home and pack. Now." Each word pelted me.

I pointed my thumb towards the opened office door. Tito's threats seemed real and left me shaken. I worked hard to sound confident and in control. "He's a liar. Trust nothing he says."

Errol studied me. I knew he was battling his anger against what I might have learned.

"Do you want to know what he told me?"

Arms crossed Tito style, Errol said, "Okay. What?"

Verbatim, I told him what transpired, including Shade. "I have a financial forensic team investigating," I said, wrapping up my comments.

Errol continued to stare at me. In a lean-forward-still-angry whisper, he said, "You put yourself and our investigation at risk." He straightened. "Detective Yun, please escort Ms. Wright home. Don't leave her side. I'll meet you there."

Now, I didn't feel like a caught child. More like a thief being arrested.

•   •   •

Detective Yun and I walked towards the front door of the building. "I need a few things from my office. Computer and files for managing my operation remotely."

"You're supposed to go straight home. No stops."

"It will only take a few minutes." I pulled out my phone. The green connection light told me I still had Lacy on the line.

Lacy said, "Errol sounded upset. Will you tell him about the recording?"

"Yes. Soon." Why didn't I already? "Meet me at my office as quickly as you can." When I clicked off, I smiled at Yun. "Lacy can help me move much faster."

She glared at me for several beats. A copycat look Errol mastered, but Yun's heart wasn't in it. A curt nod gave me the permission I needed.

Lacy bounded down the hallway. I pulled her inside.

"Do we have everything on tape?"

"Yes. I played back a minute of each, and it came across clear and damning."

"So, you heard Wally and Tito say I'm in danger."

Lacy knew me better than anyone, even Joy. Maybe because Joy was also my pastor, I held back certain sides of myself. Although she'd say the Holy Spirit allowed her to see whatever I was trying to hide. Just thinking about her gifts made me smile. As grim as my situation was, imagining Joy's penetrating gaze gave me both comfort and a chuckle. As soon as she returned with Zander, I'd bring her up to speed. Lacy's voice brought me back to the urgency of the moment.

"We need to dig deeper into the finances. It must be even worse than we suspected," I said.

"This is getting dicier by the minute. I'm worried about you."

"Me too." A nervous laugh bubbled up.

Lacy squeezed my hand. "Ginger and I are on it. What about the forensic people? Weren't they supposed to start their investigation?"

"They'll uncover things faster than you and Ginger... but we're being watched."

"I'll go to them." Lacy gave me a determined look. "Do what Errol said. Go home. Be safe. We got you."

"Maybe you're in danger too."

"No one is stalking and threatening me."

"So far."

"What time are you going to Jax's place?"

For vastly different reasons, thinking about Jax comforted me just as thoughts of Joy did. "Zander should be home by six or seven, depending on how many stops Joy makes. We'll leave once he arrives."

"Okay, I'll meet you at your house and tell you what we uncovered."

I hugged Lacy–long and tight. We needed no words.

6:00 p.m.

Jax and Errol devised a complicated plan. Everyone assumed the killers were watching The Way Station and my house. My parents' home was also a possibility. So, getting my family to Bedford undetected would take a clever scheme and time. Part I required Joy to stop along the highway to purchase a burner phone and an undercover officer to meet Zander at a strip mall just outside of town. Zan called me upon arrival.

"Mom, are you okay?" His voice shook, reminding me of the boy he was just a few months earlier. "The cop gave me a burner, and they took my iPhone. My entire life is on it."

"Are you and Auntie Joy making good progress?"

"She says we'll be in Bedford in another hour."

"I love you, Zan. This will all be over soon."

"Darcy is with me."

I sucked in air. Crap.

"She's in danger too. I couldn't leave her, and Auntie Joy agreed."

One more element to go wrong in Errol and Jax's safe-house plan. Part II called for Jax to drive to Bedford with Yun, taking a circuitous route. She knew how to both detect and shake a tail.

Joy's role included handing off Zan to the undercover officer and continuing to Fieldcrest. Her husband took the twins out of town and Joy would join them.

Part III required my parents to make a show of going to the local movie theater. They'd already packed their luggage and filled the trunk while the car was in the garage. Their next-door neighbors, the Madisons, were joining them. Once inside the dark theater, an undercover police officer would slip my folks out through a side entrance and whisk them off to Bedford. We all believed the Madisons would keep our secret.

Part IV, the riskier leg of the diversion, included me packing an overnight bag, being driven to a motel just outside of town, and then, under the cover of night, slip out the back. Errol, who emptied my parents' trunk before the movie ended, would drive me to Bedford.

Now we had an extra factor. Darcy. Did she tell anyone? How would she fit in? Wouldn't someone notice her absence from Ithaca? "Of course, son. I understand." I did not. "Call me the minute you're in the safe house."

CHAPTER FIFTY
TITO

Tito paced his office, examining every angle of his situation. The only move left was calling Shade. No way around it.

"What?"

"The police are sniffing and getting close. They're on to the embezzlement and heading your way."

"Why? We're innocent."

It took Tito a second to understand Shade's meaning. Of course, they stole, but their fingerprints weren't on the theft or money laundering. Nowhere does any document have Iggy, SoSo, or Shade's name. A not-so-subtle reminder that Tito wasn't as fortunate. "Wally talked."

Tito heard Shade's breathing on the other end.

"I gave them nothing." Tito underscored his words. He understood what would happen if Iggy and SoSo lost confidence in him. He'd seen the beat downs. Listened to stories about ear-choppings and tongue mutilations. "But Wally shat himself. He's shaky." Best to lay the blame somewhere. With sweaty fingers, Tito wiped perspiration from his mustache and waited.

"Where's the woman?"

"Aria? Not sure. With the detective in charge or his partner, I'd guess." Despite the cold outside and frost on his window, the air in the office felt suffocating. Heat rose from Tito's torso.

"You've got nothing. Unacceptable."

How could Tito show his value? Ginger? Lacy? "I'll find out." Tito waited for additional instructions.

"Contact Barker at The Vault," Shade said. "Isn't the woman and that Jax guy together?"

"Might be," Tito said. Was Shade giving him information he expected Tito to use?

The phone clicked off. How might Tito approach Ginger or Lacy? His questions might tip them off. He smoothed his mustache. Try both. Send a security guard, one of his fake ones, to Ginger in the name of Aria's safety. And do as Shade ordered. Track down Barker. Not on the phone. In person. Scare Barker into helping.

•   •   •

Tito looked around The Vault's lobby. White and gold tiles gleamed. Three security guards manned a marble counter, with computers and cameras, shaped like eyeballs. The lobby resembled a Wall Street office, rather than a White Plains security firm.

He walked up to the pretty lady guard. She had a toothy smile and big eyes with fake lashes.

"Tito Johnson to see Jeff Barker," he said, with a warm smile and confident tone.

"Is he expecting you?"

"No, but he'll see me." Tito handed her his driver's license, held in the same pack as his ex-military ID and private detective badge. All quite impressive and official looking.

Rather than sending Tito up, Barker came down. He was a squirrelly man, thin, with a protruding belly and concave chest. "Let's grab some coffee," he said and walked toward the revolving front doors. Tito strode after him.

Once in Starbucks, they ordered, and found a corner table. The place was late-afternoon empty. Barker kept on his grey ski-cap and sunglasses. Tito found this amusing. From whom was the accountant hiding? We're on to you.

"What do you want?" Barker asked.

"First, thank you for your assistance. Your breach strategy worked well."

"My boss knows it was me."

What the fuck? "Since when?"

"What difference does that make?"

In the background, soft music played, and baristas chatted with each other and took orders from customers pondering their multiple choices.

Moisture gathered on Tito's upper lip, making his mustache itch. "What did he find out?" Before contacting Barker, Wally learned Emmanuel Castro, E-Man, was a trusted manager and close to Jax Oats. He shared the info with Tito, who told Shade. Barker's teenaged son was a fentanyl addict caught selling copper pipes stolen from a construction site. Shade via SoSo made the charges go away. A godfather move that required a future assist.

"I'm getting fired and prosecuted, so there's nothing else you can scare me with. I'm toast."

Things looked bad. He needed a fast exit. First, shove Shade off his back. "Tell me where Jax and his girlfriend are tonight."

"No clue. And if I did, why tell you?" Barker stood up.

"Wait. I can help you."

Barker didn't sit down, but he stopped moving.

"You tell me where they might be. And I protect you. You get fired, but I can keep you out of jail just like we helped your boy."

Barker stood still for several beats, then he lowered himself back into the chair. "That was drug related, your wheelhouse. Not like this."

Tito was winging it now, but he needed to sound convincing. Confident. Powerful. "My boss has money and pull in the courts, not just with drug enforcement. He's promised to cover for me, and I'm promising to cover you. But we have to stop Aria Wright from outing us. You laundered money. My... culpability differs from yours but equally damning and yet I'm not worried. I'm good. You can be too."

Tito watched Barker struggle. He wanted to believe, even though Tito's assertion was improbable. Desperate people grabbed at straws in the wind, as the saying goes. Cliché, but true.

"I might find out."

"Good enough." Tito grabbed a napkin and, pretending to wipe his mouth, dried his upper lip.

"Let me make a phone call."

Tito nodded and took a sip of his sugar and cream filled coffee. Once Shade learned Aria's location, Tito would exit. Grab his family and go. He stashed enough money over the years, mostly in cash hidden in his garage, basement, and bedroom, to get them gone for at least a couple of years. He took another swig and watched Barker place the phone between his ear and hiked shoulder while he wrote on a napkin. A good sign.

The finance hack returned. "Best I can do." He handed the napkin to Tito and sat.

Tito read three addresses. One in Bedford, a few towns north of White Plains and northeast of Fieldcrest, another on Long Island in the Hamptons, and the third an apartment on the Hudson River in Tarrytown.

"What are these places?"

He pointed to the first address. "A house the brothers own. They use it for clients and staff retreats. I've been there twice."

"On a main road or what?"

"Bedford has a minimum of four acres per house."

"What about the Hamptons? On the beach, I assume." The Oats brothers had money. They came from it. Tito had to fight for every dollar he made, saved, or stashed.

"Summer place closed up for the winter."

That could be a good safe house. "What makes you suspect they're in one of these places? He flapped the paper.

"These are possibilities. For all we know, they're hiding out in a motel somewhere or nowhere and she's home." Barker looked and sounded miserable. "I gave you the best intel I have. The third place is Jax's condo."

"Okay. You did good."

"So, you're going to fix things for me. With the cops?"

"One step at a time," Tito said. "But yeah." He was blowing smoke from multiple raging fires and Barker was toast.

•   •   •

The conversation with Shade went well. Tito sounded confident when he offered the three possibilities. No sense telling Shade these were guesses and their quarry could be anywhere. All Tito needed was enough time to grab his family and money.

Using Google's aerial views of the properties, each on his own computer and still on the phone, they eliminated the Tarrytown address. Unlikely, Jax would take Aria home. And how would the police protect her inside a seven story condominium with multiple apartments? The beach house was appealing. Since it was off season, there would be little traffic and therefore ease in spotting Shade's crew, especially because there was only one main road into the Hamptons. Tito's curser hovered over the street and driveway. A garage abutted the house, so undetected vehicles could park inside. The Bedford house was another reasonable choice. Tito zoomed in. A four-car garage stood at the top of the driveway. Both properties offered privacy.

"I'll send my guys to the beach house and Bedford."

"Good luck," Tito said with enthusiasm.

"You're going with crew two to the beach house."

Tito blanched.

"Ex-military, top security guy. You'll be an asset."

Now what? Sweat poured down Tito's face. Not only was Barker screwed. Tito was, too.

CHAPTER FIFTY-ONE

A police officer, one of the two guarding me, announced Lacy's arrival. Detective Yun dropped me off earlier and went to meet Jax. After escorting Lacy into the house, the officer returned to his vigil outside in the wet, chilly night.

Always pulled together, every hair in place and makeup expertly applied, Lacy looked a bit disheveled. It was that kind of day. We hugged. Princess pressed against Lacy's leg, looking for attention.

"Hey pretty girl." Lacy bent down and stroked the cat.

I hung Lacy's coat and left her open umbrella in the hall to dry out. "Want something to eat or drink?" It was dinner time, but I had no appetite. Shopping and cooking hadn't made my mental to-do list. I put a pot of coffee on. In the cupboard, a box of Walker's shortbread cookies had four left. Perfect.

Lacy jumped in. "The good news is I got everything recorded." She handed me her Garmay digital voice recorder. "It's all here."

"Thank you." Why wasn't I energized? Didn't I trap the evil doers? What useful info did I learn? I turned it on and together we listened to both conversations. "Not much there. Veiled threats."

"Overt."

I put the device in my purse. "Perhaps Errol would find something useful. He's coming to collect me in a few minutes. Any news from the forensic team?"

"They've just started their work. We might need a handwriting expert to prove you didn't sign the transfers. Ginger is researching."

Icy rain hit the roof and windows, making a tat-tat noise. Even though the house was toasty, a chill moved through me.

My personal cell phone vibrated. "It's Ginger," I said to Lacy. With my thumb, I pressed the speaker phone button. "What's up?"

"Trouble. Tito sent a security guard, one I didn't recognize, asking where you were. Claimed it was urgent and for your safety."

"Was he wearing one of our uniforms?"

"Yes, but something was off. I told him you were home. Thought that was safe enough."

Hmm. They might see Errol and me driving to Bedford and follow us.

"Did I say the wrong thing? Don't you have police protection there?"

"Yes. All good."

We hung up. Lacy hugged me goodbye, and I pondered what happened next.

•   •   •

I stood looking out the window, waiting for Errol to show up. A light precipitation fell, more rain than snow. Its pelting sound made music as the slush hit the glass. One of the two officers, their patrol car parked in front, walked the perimeter. I watched Errol drive up. I let him in.

"Better bundle up," he said. "As the temperature drops, this slush will turn to snow. We're in for a couple of inches." He shook icy bits off his hat. "You ready to go?"

"What happened with Tito?"

"Are you packed?"

"Did you learn anything important?"

Errol blew out a whoosh of air. "Were you always like this? Because I don't remember this stubborn streak."

"Yeah, well. Talk to my parents and my staff." I waited, but he didn't offer any information. "This is my life and livelihood. Please tell me what you learned."

"It's an ongoing investigation and I can't—"

"You and me. No one else is here."

Errol shrugged out of his wet overcoat. I hung it in the hall closet and put his fedora on the closet shelf. "I have a fresh pot of coffee. We may need it."

He followed me into the kitchen. Princess came over mewing. Errol bent down and stroked her fur. Such a hussy. After two pets, she rolled over on her back, inviting him to rub her belly. I guess I was wrong about Errol not being a cat-guy. We both sat down at the kitchen island, each with a mug of coffee.

"Whatever I share, it's conjecture," Errol said. "We have a lot of leads to run down."

"I understand."

"Here's my take. Iggy Smalls, a drug lord, and an un-convicted murderer, is also a money launderer. Wally got caught up and owed them, big time. He stole the money from The Way Station. Emerson found out and threatened to talk. Smalls or Wally paid Tito to smuggle in Iggy or one of his soldiers. Could be the man Wallace told you about–Shade. One of them killed Emerson." He shrugged. "Or something like that."

It made sense. Once again, I tried to imagine the killer as a man in his seventies. I played the voice in my head and saw him running up the steps. My dad was a vigorous seventy-three. Spent forty-five minutes most days on the elliptical and performed laps in the club pool. Golfed from spring until the first frost. My mother ran on the treadmill daily and played pickle ball with her friends. The killer could be like them.

"I have something for you. Don't get angry." I placed the digital voice recorder on the countertop.

"What's this?"

"Lacy and I recorded my conversations with Wally and Tito."

A deep frown brought his eyebrows together. "Why didn't you tell me?"

"Do you want to hear it?"

He nodded, and I pushed play.

Once finished, Errol pulled out a notebook. "Run it again."

We both listened to the end. The house was quiet and the recording clear. I turned it off and handed the device to Errol. "What happens now?"

"You get tucked away. My team is already running down Smalls and his crew, trying to find where they're holding up. With this," he lifted the recorder, "I'll work on securing a warrant to search his place once we locate it."

"Do you have enough to convince a judge? Is it legal when Wally and Tito were unaware?"

Errol gulped down the last of his coffee. "In New York, if one of the parties in the conversation consented to being recorded, it's legal. The problem is probable cause. Not sure there's enough, but we'll find a friendly judge."

My phone buzzed. "Mom. Darcy and I made it. When are you coming?"

"I'm leaving now. See you in an hour."

"Zander?" Errol asked.

I nodded.

He lifted his phone, letting me see a text from the officer assigned to my parents. "All clear. At the spot."

Tears of relief filled my eyes. "Oh, I almost forgot. Tito sent a man to intimidate Ginger, demanding my location. She said home."

"How long ago?"

"Thirty minutes."

"Okay." He grabbed his phone, but before punching in the number, gave me a look.

I understood the message. It was time to go.

"Let me grab my things. Give me a sec." I ran up the stairs, with Princess behind me.

CHAPTER FIFTY-TWO

Errol waited downstairs for Princess and me. I called, asking for a few extra minutes to gather myself. Fifteen minutes later, I still couldn't join him, but not sure why. Getting to the safe house was urgent.

Zander and my parents were safe. Errol believed his team was close to solving the case. The recordings would help secure a warrant. Everyone, including Jax, was waiting for me in Bedford. And so far, no sign of anyone hanging around waiting to follow us. Perhaps when they saw all the police protection... Or no one even tried. Lacy and Ginger reported progress from the forensic team, but nothing definitive to report yet. And Ginger, bless her, identified a handwriting expert in case I needed one.

All good things, and yet...

I sat on the bed I shared with Ben for the seventeen years of our marriage. The moment seemed pivotal. A tremendous shift in my life was imminent. I held Ben's photo, chatting with him. Princess curled up next to me as if she sensed my sadness, happiness, and confusion. Soft purrs rumbled through her.

Throughout my career, Ben was my chief consultant. We'd strategize over breakfast or dinner. I'd lay out my dilemma, and together, we worked it through. If Zander struggled, we did the same. Partners. He was also super protective. Men threatening me? Ben would help me fight back. I'd already explained to him, to his photo, what was happening at The Way Station, but I had other questions heavy on my mind. Jax was the one supporting me now. The one standing by me.

"What should I do? We promised to love each other forever, no matter what."

I didn't love Jax. Not yet. Not the deep, trusting love Ben and I shared. Chemistry wasn't love. Nor was lust or loneliness. Was that all I felt for Jax?

"Is caring about someone else betraying you?"

It sounds crazy, but I heard Ben's voice. "Baby. You're young, with thirty or more years ahead of you, God willing."

I touched my wet cheeks. Another unknown. For how long had I been crying?

"You and Zan are my everything. Be happy."

"Suppose Zan doesn't like him?" I tugged tissues from the square box on the nightstand and blew my nose.

"He will. You'd never be with someone who isn't good to our boy."

"Why do I feel like I'm breaking a precious promise to you?"

"You have the answer to your question."

That was another Ben technique. Ask me enough questions until I figure things out for myself. "Because I'm afraid."

"Of what?"

"Loving and losing again. In agony, being torn apart and buried in grief. I couldn't bear it." Chased by bad guys, deemed complicit in a felonious scheme, fired for malfeasance, none of these scared me as much as loving Jax Oats and being hurt again.

"God doesn't promise us anything. Each day is a gift. Live it. To the fullest."

"He's young. Suppose he wants children of his own, or I get old and wrinkled and he's still young and vigorous?"

Ben laughed. "You're being ridiculous."

Errol's voice boomed up the stairs. "It's time to roll."

"I'll be right down." I kissed Ben's photo.

Ben said, and I heard him as clearly as Errol's shouting from below, "Goodbye, baby. Be well. Be happy."

I scooped up Princess and eased her into her carrying case. Ben's photo watched me. Yes, he said goodbye, but... I slipped the photo into a pocket of my Tumi roller bag, and hefted Princess and the luggage down the stairs.

Engine running and warm inside, Errol's 2011 Crown Vic waited for me. I climbed in and tucked Princess' crate under my legs. "This is an oldie. Is the County police force still driving these?"

"Personal car."

With a sideward glance, I examined Errol's profile. I wondered if his two sisters weathered time as well as Errol had. "Are you still angry with me?"

"Yeah. But I'm getting over it."

"Hmm. I can tell."

"Can I ask you a few questions?"

Uh oh. His voice shifted from friend to his professional stance. "Sure."

"How much did the perps steal?"

Lacy and the forensic finance team made a preliminary judgment. Once Lacy explained the siphoning scheme we'd learned from Wally, the team understood where to look. "Three million or more."

Errol whistled. "I'm surprised you had that much."

"The contractors estimated the cost of the project at two million. New appliances and furniture for the apartments, daycare center, playground, community garden, and a maintenance endowment cost another million."

"How'd you bring in so much?"

"Lacy is super good at her job. She raised most of it from family foundations and local philanthropists."

"I've seen people get disappeared for less."

"Okay, but it seems like a lot of trouble for an amount that isn't breathtaking. Murder. Goon squad. Enforcers. It's not a billion. We're a small nonprofit, helping people who have nothing."

Errol stayed quiet for a few seconds. "Might be more to it."

My frustration bubbled up and out. "Like what? You said that guy Iggy Smalls is responsible, along with Wally and Tito."

"My gut says we're missing a piece."

That gave me pause. I assumed detectives based their intuition on experience. Plus, I agreed.

He turned and looked at me. "Is your board going to question your fitness?"

Ugh. "Could be."

I called Valentine from a burner phone Errol supplied. At first, no answer. Spam calls were super annoying. When I rang back the third time, he answered.

After brief niceties, I said, "The forensic team found fraud."

Valentine was a good man. Thoughtful. And an excellent lawyer. For the next fifteen minutes, he cross-examined me, not with an adversarial tone, but thoroughly. I answered his questions as honestly as possible.

"Are you safe?" he asked.

"Yes. I can't tell you where I am. We believe they're watching and perhaps listening."

"Now? To our conversation?" He sounded alarmed.

"Long shot, but possible."

"What happens next?"

"The police catch the bad guys, and our lives return to normal."

Valentine coughed—a nervous sound. "The board will demand a full briefing…" A long sigh came over the line. "Aria, how'd you let this happen?"

In the end, I was responsible. The crimes happened on my watch.

"Is the theft tied to the murder?"

"The police are operating on that assumption." But, if so, how? Emerson had no access to our funds, nor any connection to Hope House construction.

Once again, Valentine remained quiet. Me too. Depleted, I sank into the car seat.

"Be careful," Valentine said before hanging up.

Now, I turned to Errol. "I'm ready for a glass of wine. Is there some at the house?"

"Ask your boyfriend."

Ouch. "I appreciate all you're doing for us, for me."

His facial expression softened. Eyes hooded. "Are you and Jax…?" He let the unfinished sentence hang in the air. The last time he asked me, I responded with an emphatic no.

"Yes." Earlier, sitting on my bed speaking to Ben, I didn't know what I wanted, so my answer without explanation or qualification surprised me. Yes, Jax and I were becoming a couple.

He nodded. "I saw you, just confirming."

A crazy idea hit me. "You don't suspect Jax of anything, do you?"

"Covering all bases. That's how cases get solved."

I wrapped my arms tight around my torso.

"But no. I don't think you or Jax are complicit."

CHAPTER FIFTY-THREE
M.J. AND EMERSON

Fall 1986, Fieldcrest, NY

M.J.'s fight with his mom about staying in Fieldcrest and not moving to New Jersey with her was epic. But M.J. persuaded her. Emotional meetings with the school principal and Freddie's parents followed. They all agreed M.J. could stay with Freddie until M.J. graduated, provided he maintained excellent grades, stayed out of trouble, and kept Kiki informed. So far, so good.

M.J. sat on a rock in the park across the street from their used-to-be house on Washington Street. He played basketball here and skated. They'd only lived in number 14 for less than a year, but it was one of the best in his brief life. His parents... no, his mom and Emerson laughed all the time. Sometimes they danced in the kitchen while doing the dishes. Emerson took him to Yankee Stadium in the Bronx to watch the Yanks play the Kansas City Royals. Even though the home team lost, they had an amazing time cheering, booing, eating hot dogs and ice cream sandwiches, and drinking huge plastic cups of cola. M.J.'s eyes smarted at the memory. All gone to shit now.

Freddie told M.J. about the comings and goings at the house.

"Check it for yourself. I think there's drug running happening. They got women cooking and mixing. I'm telling you."

"Nah. My... Emerson wouldn't do something like that."

But now M.J. witnessed for himself. Men transferred boxes in and out of the house. On this unusually warm October day, women in two-piece bathing suits sat on the front porch, smoking cigarettes. According to Freddie, the suits prevented theft. No place to hide contraband or cash.

Someone tapped M.J.'s shoulder. He jumped and swung around.

"You're M.J., right? Emerson's step-kid?"

"Who says so?" He scrambled up.

"I'm Shade. A friend of your dad's." He thrust his hand toward M.J.'s, but he kept his hands in his pockets.

Shade let his hand drop. He pulled out a joint and lit it. Offered it to M.J. "I told you. I'm a friend."

The joint glowed from the tip, hanging in the air, inviting M.J. to take a drag.

He looked for police or watchful eyes. Marijuana was illegal and sometimes cops performed sting operations. No one seemed out of place. "Thanks." He sucked in the sweet smoke and let it go deep into his lungs.

"I've been keeping my eye on you," Shade said. "For your father. Seems like you're struggling a bit."

M.J. let the smoke haze around his face. He breathed in the cloud. "I'm okay, I guess." Freddie's hippie-throwback parents let Freddie and M.J. do whatever they wanted. No one asked about grades or helped him memorize lines for the big spring play. No one showed up for football games or urged him to eat more vegetables and fruit. He worked every day after school to buy pot and take Denise to nice places. Free parties, but also elegant restaurants like the places Emerson took Kiki. "Treat your lady right," Emerson instructed M.J. His shitty job made that difficult.

"Figured some easy cash might smooth things out. Interested?"

Shade appeared unstressed, easy talking. Life since M.J. moved in with Freddie had been just the opposite. What came natural for him when they all lived together now felt like climbing a jagged brick wall. The weed helped, but only a little. His after-school job at the gas station sucked. M.J. took another drag, then handed the joint back to Shade.

"Nah. Keep it. If you decide you want to make some real money, give up that dead-end job at the Mobil station, just knock on the front door."

"How do you know where I work? My dad told you?"

"Like I said."

Emerson called, but M.J. ignored each one. Even though he was also angry with his mom, he worried about her, but didn't want to speak with her. He lived with Freddie because Kiki ran away instead of working it out as a family. So, during the first couple of days after she left, he ignored her calls. On day three, she phoned every hour until he picked up. "Don't you dare ignore me," she said in her mad-mom voice. She'd found a job in New Jersey. Met some dude. Begged M.J. to join her. But he said no. For one thing, Denise lived in Fieldcrest. School stopped being fun, but it wouldn't be any better in Jersey. Besides, his mom and Emerson ripped M.J.'s life to shreds.

"I care about all my employees and their families," Shade said. "Your dad misses you and your mom."

M.J. wanted to believe him. But Emerson knew Freddie's address and failed to visit M.J. Okay, yeah. M.J. hung up on him each time he called. But if you love someone, you don't give up. You hunt family down, like his mother did.

Shade walked backwards for a few steps, his eyes leveled on M.J.'s. "If you change your mind, drop by. I pay $150 a week for a few hours after school. If you work hard, you'd pull in $1,000 a week." He stopped.

M.J. stared at him. $1,000. "Doing what?"

Shade reached his hand out, palm up, inviting M.J. to join him.

Illegal work? Drugs, like Freddie said. But straight-up Emerson, who preached integrity, wouldn't be a part of that. Maybe selling marijuana. Which was harmless. Why not listen to the proposition? Plenty of time to say no. Plus be with his father... Emerson. M.J. followed Shade into his family's former home.

•　　•　　•

Emerson rode his high. The second the crack filled his lungs and rushed into his bloodstream, he sailed above every trouble he ever had. Unconquerable. He could accomplish anything he set his mind to. He jumped up from the couch, looking around his kingdom. His subjects–lounging naked women, people carrying product in and out of the house–awaited his vision for their future. Call Kiki. She'd return. They'd reclaim the house. Tell Iggy to get the hell out. They'd all obey.

Then the crash came. Slammed him down. Knocked him out of his imaginings and onto the couch with a naked, sleeping woman. What the hell. Thirst and hunger gnawed at his gut. Rage took over. The craving for euphoria, for the exquisite high, rushed his senses.

Shade approached him. "Look who's here."

Emerson tried to focus, but only saw blurry images. He needed his pipe. "Dad?"

"What did you say?"

"It's me. M.J."

"Do you have my pipe?" He swayed on his feet. The craving ate at his belly. His heart raced at an alarming speed. Something banged on top of his head. His hand reached up to stop it.

The young man Emerson thought he recognized stood, transfixed.

"I'm here for you," the young man said. "Let's go." Sobs escaped.

Was Emerson supposed to say or do something? He thought he heard crying. "You got my pipe?"

A strangled sound escaped before the young man turned and ran.

Emerson's fog got thicker, cravings dominated his brain and every cell in his body. A question pierced his pain. M.J.? Yes. "Son, wait." Emerson stumbled and fell. Kiki? Unable to think or process the surrounding noise, he covered his ears. "Where's my pipe?"

The next time he came to, he remembered. M.J. came without Kiki. Did Emerson say the right things?

Iggy stood over him. "We need cash. You get more, and we leave your kid out of this." He slapped Emerson's face hard. "You hear me, junkie?"

He'd already turned over the deed for the house to Iggy. Paid the refinanced mortgage payment with money he borrowed from his parents. Depleted his savings account, including the one he'd set up for M.J.'s college tuition. "There's no more money." He wiped his dripping nose with the back of his hand. "Need my pipe."

"You're gonna work for your keep," Iggy said, his voice filled with disgust. "No productivity. No pipe."

Shade said, "He's harmless. Why torture him?"

Iggy swung on Shade. "Mind your fucking business. This is between him and me."

Emerson caught it all, but the words made no sense. He looked up. He was alone. Bereft.

CHAPTER FIFTY-FOUR
ARIA

Bedford New York, 8:30 p.m.

The house stood at the end of a twisty, dead end road, set back and high above its neighbors. Errol pulled in behind a dark gray Cadillac. We climbed out.

"Ready?" Errol asked.

A loaded question. Ready to deal with Darcy, wait for the danger to pass, accept my feelings for Jax?

"This is almost over," Errol said. He lugged my suitcase out of the trunk.

Princess complained, but she had to stay caged. Her meowing got louder. I looked around, trying to find the reason for her agitation. Perhaps she caught it from me, or danger lurked. Then I heard northern mockingbird males chattering as they got their territories marked and ready for spring mating. My dad birded. Taught Bella and me to recognize the calls of birds that lived in our backyard trees.

We walked up to tall double-sided wood doors with old-fashioned knockers gleaming in the moonlight. Jax opened the door.

Without regard to Zan, my parents, or Errol standing behind me, I placed the carry case on the floor and folded into Jax's arms. Tension eased out as he held me, my face somewhere between his stomach and chest. He was so damn tall.

"Mom."

Jax backed up. I rushed to Zander. "You're safe. Thank you, God."

My parents joined us for a family hug. Out of my peripheral vision, I saw Darcy's sour expression.

Errol cleared his throat. "Listen up, folks." He still wore his overcoat but held his damp hat in his hands. "Let's get everyone settled in their rooms and meet in the dining room in fifteen minutes so we can review the safety rules."

Arms still around Zander, I smiled back at Jax. "Please, lead the way."

It was a lovely old house. Three stories with nine-foot ceilings on the first floor, eight bedrooms and six full baths on the second and third. Zan, Darcy, Jax, and I trooped up the stairs. Jax carried my suitcase, and I toted Princess, still in her carryall.

When we reached the top of the staircase, Zan said, "We're unpacked." He looked sheepish. "At the end of the hall." He jutted his thumb to the right. "Grandma and Poppa are upstairs."

"Oh, so I'm holding everyone up." Of course, Zander and Darcy were sharing a room. Why wouldn't they, unless they cared what his grandparents and mother thought? Argh.

Darcy swept past me, took Zan's hand and sashayed, yes, swung her hips from side to side, and walked to their shared room. Double-argh.

I thought I detected an under-the-breath chuckle from Jax. Unhelpful and inappropriate.

"Zan," I called down the hall. So much danger. "Just need a word." I turned to Jax. "And I'm where?"

He pointed to the opposite end of the hall. "I'll wait for you down there."

Zander, his eyes cloudy, stood in front of me. "You're sure you're, okay?" He leaned in and hugged me. "Yeah. How about you?"

Just what I needed.

I joined Jax. He led me to a room with an ensuite bathroom, four-poster bed, vanity table and chair, walk-in closet, couch, armchair, and wide screen television on the wall opposite the sitting area. I almost expected a mini bar.

He put my suitcase on an unfolded luggage rack. I set Princess free. With caution, she inspected the spaces.

"How are you doing?" Jax asked.

I covered my mouth with both hands. A rush of jumbled emotions swamped me. Once again, he wrapped his arms around me, brushed my coils from my face, but of course, they bounced back. A soft piece of melodic jazz from Kenny G played on my internal playlist. Still holding me, he sat on the edge of the bed and pulled me onto his lap. Kissing like this was easier. A Lilliputian in the arms of a giant. I loved the sensation of his full lower lip pressed into mine, the taste of his tongue, the current zipping through me. He lowered himself onto the bed, legs hanging over the side, and me on top of him. He hardened and throbbed against me.

"I love you so much," he breathed into my hair. "For so long."

The rap on the doorjamb made me jump and roll off Jax. We both sat up.

Errol, standing in the doorway, said, "You're late. We're in the dining room, waiting for you." He sounded angry. Or some-kinda-way.

I sprang up and smoothed my clothes.

Errol left.

Jax said he loved me. Heat burned my neck and cheeks.

Still sitting on the bed, Jax put his hands around my waist and turned me toward him. "Are we real?"

"What do you mean?" I knew, but my family waited for us downstairs, and a killer lurked somewhere. I needed time to think and assess.

"Are we together? A couple? Ready for the next step?"

I closed my eyes and breathed. When I opened them, his steady gaze held mine. "Yes," I said, even though my head hollered, "Not yet."

•   •   •

Everyone stared at us as we entered the large, formal dining room. A cherry-wood table with seating for twelve centered the room. To the side, a matching China-closet filled with enough dishes, cups, saucers, and serving pieces to feed at least thirty graced one wall. Tall windows covered with heavy drapes provided privacy from any prying eyes.

My face flushed again. I took a seat next to Zander and Jax sat opposite me and to Yun's left. Errol sat at the head of the table.

"I appreciate this is a frightening moment," Errol began. "But you're in excellent hands." He looked at each one of us. "Four police officers are patrolling the area. Two locals and two from the county. You're safe." He paused. But no one else spoke. "Once we get the word, Detective Yun and I will head out."

"I'm armed," Jax said.

"What?" Errol swung his head in Jax's direction.

"I'm licensed and practice at the range."

I fought to stay quiet. Jax understood how much I hated firearms.

Darcy said, "Me too."

"Oh, no, no." My words bubbled out.

Errol jumped in. "Miss, it's one thing for a homeowner to protect his domain, but you're a guest here—"

Darcy stood up. "I'm licensed and an excellent shot. I've been teaching Zander too."

My father groaned and shook his head. Exactly.

Errol looked and sounded stern. "Not okay." He turned to Jax. "Do you have a gun safe for, I'm sorry, what's your name?"

"Darcy, and I'm not giving up my weapon."

Yun said, "Glover, we've got to roll. It's okay." She asked Darcy, "Let's have your license."

Darcy proffered a document in a plastic sleeve. "Never leave home without it."

I watched enough movies. Evil doers often breached the perimeter and left the people inside to defend themselves. The thought of Jax protecting us was one thing. But Darcy?

Errol said, "You cannot use lethal force unless you're threatened with lethal force. Is that clear to both of you?"

Jax nodded.

"Absolutely," Darcy said.

Throughout this exchange, my parents and Zan appeared numb. Violence, murder, and police protection didn't exist in their worlds. I reached for Zander, my hand landing on his thigh and rubbed. "Are you alright?"

"Yeah. I guess."

Jax's intense stare caused me to meet his gaze.

"What's your plan?" he asked Errol while still watching me.

"My team is trying to locate a judge who'll sign a search warrant. Then we move on Iggy Smalls and his top soldiers."

The meeting adjourned, and we each moved toward the staircase that led to the upper levels. Princess, finished exploring her surroundings, purred from a chair.

Jax said to me, "I'm going to stay down here. You get some rest."

With Princess following close behind, I climbed the stairs. At the top, I kissed my parents and Zander good night. My body felt heavy. It had been a crazy day, and bed called.

CHAPTER FIFTY-FIVE
MJ

Fall 1986

Unsure how it happened, M.J. found himself back at the house on Washington Street, sitting on a rock in the park across the street. The November wind, cold and damp, chilled his face, hands, and butt on the stone surface. Thanksgiving was less than a week away. Kiki begged him to celebrate with her in New Jersey. Of course, he'd go. No matter what, he loved his mom and didn't want her alone on a big family holiday. Would Emerson be well enough to join them? Not based on M.J.'s last visit. Hell no. But he'd seen Emerson clean up before. Get well. Even stay sober for several years.

For a long time, M.J. stared at the house, just like the first time he returned. Once again, Shade came out, crossed the street, and joined M.J. on the boulder. For a minute, M.J. thought to bolt. He never wanted to see Shade again. But he imprisoned Emerson, and M.J. wanted to save him. No clue how, but a powerful tug to try.

"How've you been?" Shade asked, pulling out a joint.

"Okay. How's my dad?" M.J. heard the hard edge in his voice. This man wasn't a friend.

Shade ignored M.J.'s attitude. "Real good. We got him working and attending meetings at a church a few streets over."

Amazed, M.J. turned to look at Shade. "For real?"

"Yeah. I remember how you reacted during your last visit. He's helped us a lot. Thought I'd do you both a solid." He passed the lit joint to M.J.

M.J. declined with a headshake.

"Want to come in and check for yourself?"

They walked across the street. Shade snuffed the joint before opening the door. The house looked neat. No sprawling naked women or spaced out junkies.

Shade said, "Been making some changes."

They found Emerson organizing papers at the long dining room table, the same one Kiki, Emerson, and M.J. used to eat their meals.

Afraid Emerson wouldn't recognize him, M.J. said, "Dad, it's me."

Bloodshot eyes met his. "Son." He hustled around the table and embraced M.J. They hugged for a long time. "I gotta get back to work," Emerson said, his voice raspy and dry.

"Mom sent me a round-trip Amtrack ticket to Jersey for Thanksgiving. Do want to come with me?"

Emerson looked at Shade, who nodded. "Sure."

After hugging Emerson goodbye, Shade and M.J. walked to the front door.

Standing side-by-side on the porch looking at the park, its trees bare and grass brown, M.J. said, "He's better but doesn't look good."

"Getting clean is an uphill, daily fight."

"Why are you helping us?"

Shade rubbed his chin. "You remind me of myself ten years back. Iggy and his partner SoSo rescued me, and before that someone helped them, so I'm paying it forward."

That sounded true to M.J. "You offered me a job."

"Interested?"

"What's the work?"

"Finish high school is job number one. You can run errands and help Emerson with the paperwork. Okay by you?"

"Yeah." He had work, a family Thanksgiving, a godfather to look out for him, and a potential future.

CHAPTER FIFTY-SIX
M.J. AND EMERSON

Summer, 2005

Thirty-four-year-old M.J. watched his bosses with feral eyes, but thanks to years of conditioning, a neutral expression stayed fixed on his face. Six men and two women sat around a conference table in Iggy and SoSo's office suite in downtown White Plains. Both still lived in Fieldcrest, but the more prestigious and convenient city better served their needs. Business in Harlem and the Bronx shrunk as gentrification took hold, another good reason to operate out of the suburbs.

Shade ran the meeting. Years ago, he gave up street work, except for those times Iggy required it. They had lots of muscle and enforcers on the payroll, but some jobs Iggy kept within a tight circle of three. Shade's primary domain included legal matters and government and police corruption, a challenging undertaking.

New York City Mayor Michael Bloomberg ran for his second term. New York City bustled with prosperity and real estate prices soared. Iggy pushed Shade hard. Find more revenue streams. Diversify.

Thanks to Shade, M.J. secured an undergraduate and law degree from N.Y.U. Shade befriended M.J., gave him a job, and promised to protect Emerson. Despite himself, M.J. still cared.

"Who's fixing our problem in the Bronx?" Shade asked.

New team member Corina, a stunning Latina with a law degree from Harvard, spoke up. "I am." Rumor had it she was Shade's latest lady.

"And?"

"We're good. Our friendly prosecutor is on the case. All will be well by Friday."

Most meetings went like this. No specifics allowed in the building in case security missed a bug. Unlikely, since they swept the place four times a day on a random schedule, but Iggy and SoSo believed in precautions.

Code-switching again, Shade asked, "What's the status of movement from the south?"

Street questions were more direct. "Where's the heroin and fentanyl from the Columbian cartel? How far out from arrival?"

Another member of the team spoke up. "Journey is half-completed. Arrival in a week."

The drugs came up from South America, through Central America and into Mexico. Hit the US border in Texas, Arizona, or California depending on who on the payroll could shepherd it through.

"Cousin Cali is expecting," Corina said.

That meant a San Diego drop-off. Then smugglers drove it cross-country, sometimes with another payload like illegal migrants or trafficked girls, women, and sometimes boys.

M.J. tried not to think about that part of his life–the ugly work Iggy, SoSo, and Shade mucked in. At first, Shade told him to focus on his schooling. Get good grades. Enjoy life. Denise, Freddie and M.J. received all the marijuana and beer they wanted. Ran errands for partying cash. A cleaned-up Emerson, Kiki, and Shade were at M.J.'s high school graduation. One of the best days of M.J.'s life.

He loved his college years as well. Senior year, M.J. worked for a respected member of the law school faculty, helping her with administrative work while she schooled him in different aspects of the law, prepared him for his LSATs, and introduced him to law firm partners. Kiki visited him at least once a month. Whenever Emerson achieved sobriety, he came around. They talked sports, and Emerson loved hearing stories about dorm parties and pranks. They never mentioned Shade.

Things changed after M.J. got his law degree. That's when he learned the price to pay for tuition, looking out for Emerson, and getting Freddie out of jail and his record expunged. For sending Kiki money on Mother's Day, Christmas, her birthday, all with cards from M.J. He became a member of the legal team. His mentor expressed disappointment when M.J. turned down a spot in a local firm where he interned.

"You're working for who?" she'd asked.

"Smalls Imports and Exports."

"As part of their legal team?" A deep frown underscored her aggrieved tone. "You're shunning incredible opportunities. I've never heard of this company."

"I appreciate all you've done for me," M.J. said. "But my parents encouraged this choice, and my godfather got me the job." The parents' part wasn't true, but Shade, M.J.'s godfather, ruled M.J.'s life.

•   •   •

Emerson paced the alley. He had to get M.J. out from under Shade. Emerson's own escape took years, sobriety, and luck. Shade stopped caring about what Emerson did. Freeing M.J. required more.

Reasoning might be dangerous. Suppose M.J. reported their conversation or someone overheard. Instead, Emerson devised shock-plan-A. He had B and C ready to tee up if necessary.

Two apartment buildings, one on each side, carved out the alley. They also provided shade from the August sun. The stench of urine and feces cooked in the heat.

"How much longer?" Tony, a ragged boy of fourteen, asked.

Emerson checked his watch. "Any minute now."

He'd been clean for three months. Twitch found him work at a local church serving the hungry and homeless. A band of staff and volunteers provided counseling for addicts and alcoholics, found safe shelters, and helped folks apply for food stamps. The work lifted Emerson. Gave him purpose, and helping others drove him to stay off drugs and drink. So did saving M.J. A grown man with a law degree lived alone and did Shade's white-collar dirty work instead of marriage, family, and an upscale house in Fieldcrest.

"Dad. What the hell?"

Emerson spun around and watched M.J. approach.

Ripples of fear came off in waves from Tony. Emerson steadied him with a gentle hand on his back.

When M.J. reached Emerson, the two men leaned in and gave each other's backs an affectionate pound. "What's going on? Why am I here?" M.J. asked.

"This is Tony. He's fourteen and needs your help."

That part of the plan was real. Skinny, with enormous eyes and curly lashes and hair, Tony's looks were a big part of the problem. "He's being sold. Passed around. Has no place to go."

M.J. squatted. "How'd this happen?"

"No folks. Illegal," Tony said in his soft accent.

"And what do you want for yourself?" M.J. asked.

"A house. School. Not to be hungry." He scrubbed his eyes with his clenched fists. "Not to be used."

"Where'd you find him?" M.J. asked, standing up.

"At the church where I work.... Son, he needs your help to get away."

"From who?" An edge tinged M.J.'s voice, as if he'd figured out Emerson's scheme.

"The people you work for."

M.J. nodded as if unsurprised.

"You have to leave also."

M.J.'s hands flew up. "No way." He shook his head. "I can't do that."

"Why not? This is what the people you work for do to children. Help Tony and yourself."

So much for his plan to keep the conversation about Tony and not M.J. If he learned Tony's story, and freed him, M.J. would realize his profession was devil-work.

"Shade paid for my college, supports Mom, and kept you alive all these years."

"What?"

"No overdoses, no jail, no beat-downs, or your stuff stolen. That's all Shade. He cares about me."

Tony looked about to bolt.

"Don't be afraid, Tony. I'll find you a placement. Somewhere safe." M.J. spoke to Emerson. "Plus, I'll watch out for him. I promise. But I can't leave."

CHAPTER FIFTY-SEVEN
ARIA

Pop, pop, pop. I sprang from the bed. Pop, pop. The sounds came from outside. Staying low, I dragged on jeans and a T-shirt and crept to the window. Careful not to stand in front of it, I rose, darted my head forward, peeked out, and pulled back. I saw only a dark sky, treetop shapes, and a moon-sliver, the rest hidden behind clouds. Barefoot, I slipped on a pair of sneakers and laced them. Placed my ear against the bedroom door. Listened. Pop, pop, pop. Still coming from outside. Gunfire? My parents and Zan. I had to get to them.

"Aria."

Jax. I opened the door.

He stepped into my room and eased the door shut.

"Who's out there?"

"Not sure, but the police are firing back. Where's your coat?"

"Zander and my parents?"

"They're next. Your coat?" he asked again.

"In the downstairs hall closet." Jax, dressed for the cold, wore boots and a jacket. "Are we making a run for it?"

"We need to be ready for whatever."

"Princess. Where are you, girl?" I pivoted in a circle, searching. "I can't leave her here."

A plaintive cry stopped me. I scooped her up, grabbed her travel cage, and together we stepped into the unlit hallway.

Jax held his gun shoulder high. Swung left and then right. "Stay against the wall."

We inched toward Zander and Darcy's room.

From the top of the staircase on the third floor, Dad called down. "What's that noise?" Mom stood behind him, both in their flannel pajamas.

Jax said, "Get them ready to go. I'll find Zan and Darcy."

I ran up the stairs, still holding Princess, and hustled my parents into their room. "Get dressed. Fast." I had to reach Zan. In less than three minutes, we returned to the third-floor hallway. To my relief, Zander was already there and running up the stairs to assist his grandparents and take Princess and the carrycase from me. Darcy and Jax waited for us on the second floor, guns out and their backs to us as they guarded the stairwell that led to the first. I hated guns, but now felt grateful.

We dashed down the steps.

Jax said, "Darcy, you lead everyone to the kitchen. Stay vigilant and quiet. The shots came from the front. We can reach the garage from the kitchen."

"What are you going to do?" I asked.

"Reconnaissance. Figure out what we're up against. Then, I'll join you."

"Be careful." I wanted to hug and kiss him. Beg him not to take chances.

Zander stood next to Darcy as she led us to the kitchen on the first floor. I followed, shielding my parents as best I could. Which was ridiculous since my dad stood ten inches taller than me and towered over us all. He stood out, even doubled over, as we each made ourselves as small a target as possible.

We reached the kitchen without incident.

The kitchen back door burst open. A man in a black ski mask, gun high, stepped in and fired.

"Get down," I screamed loud enough to alert an army.

Darcy got off a shot before falling backwards. The masked man yelped. Blood blossomed on Darcy's shoulder. Her gun clattered to the floor. I scrambled for it, saw the wounded gunman stumbling toward me. I raised the gun and fired. Then fired again. And again.

"Shit." The gunman, one hand covering his chest, and the other still holding his weapon, looked down. Blood seeped from his wounds. He raised his gun with a trembling arm. Zander tackled him from behind, and they both landed on the tile floor, the gunman face down and Zan on his back. Jax burst into the kitchen. He placed a booted foot on the shooter's arm, kicked away the gun with the other and helped Zander up.

"Is anyone but this piece of crap hurt?" Jax asked.

"Darcy," I said.

Trembling, Princess mewed from her carrycase.

An officer I didn't recognize walked into the kitchen, gun out, blood dripping from his side and down his thigh. "Everyone okay?"

Blood rushed from my head, my knees collapsed, and I crashed to the floor.

CHAPTER FIFTY-EIGHT
EMERSON

December 2023

Christmas was always bittersweet for Emerson. He lost his family on Christmas Eve, too many years ago to count, but not so many that it still didn't hurt. Kiki stayed in touch. He kept her informed about his whereabouts. She told him how M.J. was doing, but since she was unaware of how M.J. made a living, or the type of people he worked for, her updates rang hollow.

Emerson tracked M.J.'s whereabouts and true wellbeing via a few friendly members of Shade's crew. While no one gave Emerson specifics, they let him know Kiki's son was fine. Not using and staying out of jail. Girlfriends, but no one special. It all grieved Emerson. He'd wanted so much more for M.J. but failed to rescue him. Guilt added to the bitter parts of Christmas.

The holiday also lifted him. The new CEO of The Way Station, Aria Wright, had a big heart. She lived the organization's mission. Every member of the staff and volunteer teams "adopted" a child, or family, for the holidays. Children wrote their Christmas, Hannukah, Kwanzaa or winter solstice lists. The Way Station teams shopped and then all came together for a wrapping party. Paper, bows, tags, tape, and cards lay scattered across worktables. Aria provided punch, eggnog, and munchies and wrapped alongside them. No alcohol, of course. The older children and adults received gift cards to discount places like Target and Walmart, thanks to the generosity of Jax Oats' company, The Vault. Jax and his kitchen volunteers, instead of being with their own families, provided Christmas Eve and Christmas Day special dinners, including turkey, stuffing, gravy, cranberry sauce, cornbread, veggies, and three different pies.

Emerson's mobile phone rang. He glanced down at the number. It was M.J.

"Hello, son."

"Hey, Dad. Wanted to wish you Merry Christmas."

The two men hadn't spoken for a long time. Tears filled Emerson's eyes. "How are you?"

"Good. I was wondering if you wanted to join Mom and me for Christmas dinner?"

Wow. Emerson prayed for this. "I'm clean, son." He wanted to reassure M.J., just in case. Put it out there. "Hit year five and then had a bump, but back on."

"That's great. Mom told me."

"I'd love to join you both. In Jersey?" Kiki still lived there, next door to her sister. He had no way to get to her house, except Uber and trains. Emerson hadn't owned a car since his days addicted to crack.

"No. In Fieldcrest."

That was surprising. "Where?"

"My godfather's place," M.J. said, a wariness in his voice. "I hope that's okay." His next words came out in a rush. "He loves me like a son. I know you don't... trust Shade, but he's invited us, and I thought, since we'd be so close to you... Please, Dad. I miss you. Let's make things right and have a good Christmas."

Loves him like a son. Emerson had no counter. "Sure. Text me the address and time. Everyone dressing fancy?"

M.J. laughed. "Mom will be, for sure. But come comfortable."

"I'll be there."

•   •   •

The Uber driver pulled into Shade's driveway in upscale-Westwood. Even though Emerson lived in Fieldcrest for decades, he had few opportunities to visit this part of town. The brick house was lit up with Christmas lights. A huge wreath with a red bow hung on the door. Everyone hoped for snow. At least the reporters on the local TV station claimed. But Emerson was happy with crisp, moisture-free air.

He climbed out but didn't move towards the steps leading to the front door. His list of worries was long. First, he always had trouble during the holidays, watching others drink. The tug for a glass of wine or celebratory bourbon or rum pulled hard. He hadn't seen Kiki in years but thought about her often. Not a sucking-him-in way like booze did, but a wistful ache. Regrets.

Being around Shade was another problem. Their lives, thanks to M.J., remained entwined. Fine on one level since Shade looked out for M.J., but awful on the other, since Shade was a crook doing evil. Emerson rang the bell.

When the door opened, a big guy who looked like a mob soldier asked for Emerson's name. After checking a list, he invited Emerson in. The party was in full swing, packed with men, women, couples, and children. Booze flowed. Emerson smelled it. Hit him hard. He wouldn't stay long. Wish M.J. and Kiki a merry Christmas, give them the small presents he'd brought with him, and leave.

"Dad." M.J. hugged his father. "Sorry about all the alcohol." He had a glass of wine in his hand. "Will you be okay?"

"Sure," he said, hoping it was true. "Can't stay long. I have another invitation but wanted to see you..." He stopped mid-sentence.

Mouth agape, Emerson stared. Surrounded in the living room, in the middle of the throng, drink in hand, stood Iggy Smalls.

CHAPTER FIFTY-NINE
ARIA

Jax held me. Images from the gunfight flashed. A sickly sweet metallic odor mingled with an acrid, smoky smell. Sirens wailed outside. A cop, his side bandaged, told us help was on the way. Smears and splatters of blood covered the floor and wall. I looked down and saw bits of flesh on my clothes. I touched my face. Sticky stuff stuck to my fingers. Oh God, what had I done? I couldn't think straight. My lungs cried for air. With effort, I slowed my breathing. Fought to calm my mind. I killed a man. Took a life.

The dead gunman on the tile floor lay on his back, his ski mask still in place. Did he murder Emerson? Why try to kill my entire family? A wave of dizziness swam over me again. My stomach grumbled. "I'm going to throw up."

Jax grabbed a garbage can. I upchucked. Coughed.

My mother handed me a damp paper towel. "I'll take care of her," she said to Jax. She sat down on the floor next to me.

Jax eased his hands from around me and stood. He said to the bandaged cop, "Is Glover coming?"

"Yeah."

Mom held my forehead while I threw up again.

When it stopped, I asked. "How is Darcy?" I didn't see where the bullet hit her. "Will she be okay?"

The bandaged officer said, "I'm not a doctor, but it didn't look life-threatening to me. She lost a lot of blood, so maybe more dangerous than it appeared."

Jax said, "Ambulance is coming from Northern Westchester. Those sirens might mean it's here."

"Zan?"

"He's with Darcy. They might not let Zan accompany her. Often, it's family only."

I tried to sit up.

My mother said, "Stay still. Rest."

"I'm fine. So embarrassed." Fainting, throwing up. Killing a man. No, not fine.

"You're a hero," Mom said.

"What?" A hero? A killer. Sweat broke out on my forehead. I put my head between my legs.

"When you shot the horrible man, you saved our lives." Her voice quaked.

Errol and Yun entered the room with two other detectives, a medical examiner, and three uniformed officers. "We have to secure the scene." He turned to a patrolman. "Collect shell casing and weapons." Then he faced Jax. "Yours too."

"I didn't fire."

"I believe you, but we have to test the gun, anyway." He held out his gloved hand. Jax pulled the Glock from his waist band and gave it to Errol, who looked at me. "You keep surprising me."

Jax frowned at Glover. "She needs to go to the hospital to make sure all is well."

"What about my parents and son? We can't leave them here."

Glover said, "Everyone's going to Northern Westchester to be checked out first and then questioned." He reached a hand down to help me up. "Let's go."

Jax appeared upset. "How did this happen? Street thugs overwhelmed your officers? They could have killed everyone in this room."

Glover's eyes swept over me. "I'm sorry." His gaze returned to Jax. "We'll figure it out."

Jax ratcheted down his tone. "Are your officers okay? Did they catch anyone?"

"One's in serious condition. The others are fine, and yes, we arrested two shooters. The third you caught, but the fourth escaped."

"Are they the same men who roughed up Wallace?"

"Could be," Errol said. "One is already turning on the other."

Jax appeared unsatisfied with Errol's answer. "Are Iggy Smalls and the man they call Shade, still free?"

"They weren't here," Errol said. Impatience colored his words. "All we have on them are Aria and Lacy's recordings. Not enough. Not yet."

I listened, but my head swam with emotional pain. My throat ached from retching. The body blows from the car accident still hurt. I reached for Jax's hand. He looked at me and appeared to understand. He slipped his arms around me. Together, Jax, Mom, Dad, Errol, Princess, and I left the kitchen and all its gore.

CHAPTER SIXTY
EMERSON AND IGGY

Christmas Eve 2023

M.J. asked Emerson, "What's wrong?"

They stood in the entranceway of Shade's home in Fieldcrest. Emerson, still dressed in his coat and hat, faced his son. "Why is he here?" With a trembling finger, Emerson pointed to Iggy, still standing in the center of a crowd of celebrating men and women. Children, in a spirited game of tag, dodged between the adults' legs, giggling and screeching. A decorated Christmas tree shook as they zipped by. In the background, a carol played, but the mingling of so many voices made it difficult to distinguish the words or melody.

"He's the big boss." M.J. put his drink down on a nearby table. "Don't make a scene. It's my godfather's party. Mom is coming."

Without meaning to, Emerson said, "He killed your father. Iggy murdered Mo. Stole our home. Turned me into a junky. I can't be here." Shade worked for Iggy, but Emerson seldom saw Iggy after the day they ripped off Emerson's house on Washington Street. That's how he remembered the events. Not willingly turning his home over to them, but Iggy taking it by force.

M.J. looked thunderstruck. "What did you say?"

Emerson recognized his mistake. He spun around. "I gotta go. Sorry. Forget—"

M.J. grabbed Emerson by the shoulder and yanked him back. "Forget what? That for all these years, you kept this from me? Iggy killed my father? Did you tell Mom?"

"I..." Emerson couldn't explain his omission. Like his slide into alcohol and drugs, he hadn't processed the impact of M.J. being part of Shade's life. "I never told her."

M.J. lowered his pain-racked voice. "Does my godfather know?"

Lie again? "Not sure." He paused, trying to think. "Please don't ask him." Bringing up the murder to Shade would hurt everyone, especially M.J. Emerson turned, opened the door, and stepped out into the cold evening.

"Wait." M.J. joined Emerson on the top step. "What happened? Why did Iggy kill him?"

"It's history. I'm sorry."

"You're always sorry. And leaving. That's what you do. Abandon us." He balled his fists. "Tell me how my father died."

Emerson's body and determination sagged. It was too late to stop this train heading for no good. "In a bar fight in Bangkok." He gave M.J. an abbreviated version and left out Mo's cheating.

Tears streamed down M.J.'s face. "Mom and I visited the Vietnam Memorial in DC, searched the wall for his name and it wasn't there." He snuffled and wiped mucus from his nose. "Did you help him?"

"I tried."

"Oh yeah. I forgot. You try, lie, apologize, and leave." He paused. Emerson waited.

In a faint voice and not looking at Emerson, M.J. said, "Shade wasn't even born back then. He doesn't know." M.J. walked back into the party.

Emerson shuffled down the steps. He'd used his last few dollars for the presents and Uber. Fieldcrest ran free busses Christmas Eve night, Christmas Day, and the same for New Year's Eve. There was a sheltered stop several blocks away. Head down, he slogged his way there to wait.

• • •

With his peripheral vision, Iggy watched the exchange between Emerson and M.J. Saw the darted looks his way and the pain playing across Shade's protégé's face. They left together and only M.J. returned. Good. Let it all come out.

Iggy gulped down the last of his rum and signaled the circulating waitstaff for another. What Shade saw in M.J. was hard for Iggy to fathom.

Not a customer or dealer. Not connected to anyone useful. A decent lawyer, but they had dozens of good ones on the payroll. And he was the make-believe son of Emerson. Yet Shade kept M.J. on the payroll, protected him and his useless drug-addled father.

SoSo volunteered to take them both out since M.J. and Emerson agitated Iggy. But Iggy needed Shade. He was an excellent manager and enforcer. Loyal. Smart. Clean. If keeping M.J. was important to Shade, so be it. For now.

Most of the people at the party met Iggy, but very few were close. They spoke to him only if he invited conversation. Iggy needed a quiet moment to think. He headed upstairs to Shade's bedroom and a private bath, pulled out a joint, cracked open the window, and lit up.

Sweet smoke filled his lungs. Just enough to think creatively, but not enough to get high. A new line of inquiry emerged. What role could Emerson play in Iggy's side hustle–embezzling and laundering money via The Vault and Way Station? The guy practically lived there. Trusted, according to Tito. Iggy needed insurance in case the scheme hit a snag. Tito, Barker from The Vault, and Wally-limp-dick all claimed the money was drying up. Not surprising. Skimming wasn't a steady cash cow like drugs and prostitution, and riskier than Iggy liked. Easy money, but too many ways to go sideways. They'd been successful with a number of other nonprofits, but their luck was running out. He had to prevent any blowback on him. How could Iggy use, to his advantage, Emerson's concern for M.J. and fear of Iggy?

CHAPTER SIXTY-ONE
ARIA

I sat propped up in the hospital bed, IV pumping fluids into me. I'd thrown up so much, including in Jax's Jeep, that my electrolytes were too low. The ache behind my eyes and throbbing at my temples reminded me how close I came to dying. Once again, a police officer stood guard.

Darcy was in surgery, her prognosis positive. She's the actual hero who saved us. Despite not liking or trusting the woman, I felt grateful. My family was alive and wouldn't be if Darcy hadn't acted as fast as she did.

Zander slouched, napping in the recliner in my room. Jax, Yun, and Errol conferred in the hallway. So much happened, so quickly, I'd forgotten to ask if Errol secured a search warrant for Tito and Wally's homes, and if they located Iggy Smalls and the man called Shade.

My cell vibrated. It was Joy.

"I heard what happened. How are you?"

"I'm..." Fine, great, how are you, sat on the tip of my tongue. "I killed a man." Saying this aloud sent spasms through me.

"In self-defense. Your mom told me."

"Yes... but..." Once again, my voice faltered.

"I'm on my way. We'll pray together. Talk. How's Zander?"

I looked at my sleeping boy, his face lined with fatigue. "In need of prayer as well."

·   ·   ·

Jax knocked on the open door to my room. "We have to stop meeting like this," he said with an almost laugh. "How are you?"

"Better." I was super glad to see him. Lines spidered out from his weary eyes and etched commas on each side of his mouth. "You look beat."

"Because I am." He nodded toward Zander. "How's he doing?"

"It's been a lot for all of us."

Jax sat on the edge of the bed. "I spoke with your parents. Exhausted too. They're napping at home. Glover sent a patrol car to monitor them."

"He told me."

"Of course he did." Jax sounded jealous, but I ignored it.

"Is the case over? Almost?"

"With your tapes, Glover convinced a judge to issue a search warrant. It might not stand up during a trial, but they have workarounds. At least that's what Glover said."

"So, these cretins–Iggy and Shade, they're behind the murder, storming your Bedford house, as well as stealing money from The Way Station?"

"That's the working theory, but Glover isn't sure."

"Where does The Vault fit in?"

Jax rubbed his face with both hands. "Part of the money laundering scheme or blackmail. This is a messy case. Detectives are questioning our finance guy, Barker."

"Does Errol know why they killed Emerson?"

"Not really." His eyes were red and dark smudges lined them.

I reached for his hands. "When last did you eat or sleep?"

Jax grinned. "I like your concern."

"Concerned is a mild description of what I feel."

He leaned forward and kissed me. I sank into his arms. "Ouch." I pulled back. "Sorry. I'm still sore from the accident."

With tender light kisses, his lips traveled over my banged-up sternum and down my chest to my breasts. My nipples turned hard and pressed against the flimsy hospital gown. I sank back and closed my eyes while he traveled back up to my neck and then found my mouth. He tasted hot and wet as he held my face and kissed me again.

He eased back. "When all this is over, let's go on a proper date. Movie or a play, dinner, and dancing."

"Yes, perfect, I love the theater, and I especially enjoy... Wait, *you* can dance?" White boys, in my limited experience, often lacked rhythm and moves.

He laughed. "Your bias is showing. But yeah. My brother Charlie wouldn't let us hang with him until Stephen and I learned. Like the movie Footloose."

"This, I must see. I hope you have videos." We kissed again. "Can I ask you something?" I took a quick look at Zander, making sure he was still asleep.

"Anything."

"Have you ever been with... someone like me?"

"Smart, beautiful, brave as all get out, stubborn, and carrying a heavy chip on her shoulder?"

"I'm serious. Short?"

"*What*?"

"Stop laughing. You're a giant."

"And how is that a problem?"

I gave him an annoyed look. "Don't make me spell it out."

It must have dawned on him. His face flushed pink, but he also grinned from ear to ear.

"My concerns are legitimate. Laugh all you want."

"First, I'm liking the direction of this conversation." He touched the tip of my nose with his finger. "We'll figure it out together and have fun experimenting."

Now it was my face that flushed.

CHAPTER SIXTY-TWO
M.J., EMERSON, IGGY

January 2024

"Did you know?" M.J. confronted Shade.

They'd not spoken since the Christmas Eve party. Emerson's revelation gnawed at M.J. The two men sat in Shade's Fieldcrest home in the breakfast nook, drinking expresso. The pale winter sun streamed through the windows and bounced off bright, colored wall tiles.

"Ancient history."

"That's not an answer." Even though M.J. never met his father, the betrayal weighed heavily. M.J.'s whole life was a lie. Emerson wasn't the man who took them in. He failed to save Mo and lied about how Mo died. M.J.'s real father wasn't a war hero, a soldier fighting in a dishonest war, doing the best he could. Iggy killed him in a Bangkok bar fight.

"I never met him." Shade dug all ten fingers into his scalp and rubbed. "This isn't productive."

True enough. Why would Iggy confess murder to Shade for no reason? "Sorry. Emerson's revelations rattled me."

"I get it."

"He gave no reason for Iggy killing my father."

Shade slammed his miniature cup down on the round table. Expresso puddled. "You got to let this go."

"What if it happened to your father?"

"I don't have one. Grew up in foster care, bouncing around. No mother either. At least no one claimed me. Iggy pulled me out and up. Shepherded me the way I've been doing for you. He's a good guy until he isn't. See what I'm saying?"

M.J. understood Shade's message. Let it go because you owe me. Let it go because I owe Iggy. Back away because Iggy's dangerous. But M.J. couldn't. "I need to ask him why."

Shade reached across the table and grabbed M.J. by his sweater collar. "Drop it." Bright, dark eyes bore into M.J.'s.

· · ·

Twitch and Emerson, like others in the group, eyed the newcomer. Petite, shapely, glossy black hair, and Mediterranean coloring. Of course, they all stared. At their weekly meeting held in the Fieldcrest Community Center, she introduced herself as Sonia, an alcoholic and user. Everything about her said polish, education, and money. Booze and drugs didn't discriminate. With fentanyl rampant, no one was safe.

Twitch said, "Isn't that one of Shade's soldiers talking to the new woman?"

"Yeah." Emerson noticed the two arrived together and now whispered over coffee and doughnuts. The exchange appeared heated.

"You cover the woman, and I'll take the man," Twitch said, already on the move.

"No," Emerson hissed, but too late.

Twitch poured coffee into a Styrofoam cup to the right of Shade's soldier. Concerned for M.J., Emerson approached the woman with caution, and stood just far enough away to listen, but not spook her.

"We're screwed. Need to get out," Sonia said.

"Iggy's all in."

A jolt shook Emerson. Twitch grabbed a cruller and eased away. Emerson stayed put, sipping his now cold brew.

"Five nonprofits. No problems. But Hope House is a mess. Incompetents running the game," Sonia said. "You guys need a smart, fast exit."

She must have sensed Emerson's scrutiny because she looked over her shoulder at him, turned back to her partner, and said, "Talk later."

Heart thudding, Emerson selected a doughnut and refilled his coffee cup, careful not to confirm her suspicion that he eavesdropped. He'd warn M.J. first, and then go to Tito Johnson.

. . .

Emerson's shift manning the showers ended. Before the cleaners arrived, he wanted his own hot shower. The open space included seven stalls lined on one side, sinks and urinals facing them from the other, and privacy stalls catty-corner to both. He stripped, turned on the spray and stepped in. Under normal circumstances, he luxuriated in the soap-scented steam and streams of water cascading from the top of his head to his toes. For so many unhoused folks like him, a shower was a luxury. But he showered every morning.

Today, instead of standing under the hot water for ten minutes or more, he hurried. He had to save The Way Station, his beloved home. Once dressed in clean clothes, hair combed and wild eyebrows smoothed down, he tucked his soiled pants, shirt, socks, and underwear into a laundry bag, took a last look at the mirror over the sink, and satisfied, headed to his meeting with Tito Johnson.

With the bag at his feet, Emerson sat on the edge of the uncomfortable chair, facing Tito.

"What can I do for you?" Tito asked.

"I can't tell you how I learned this," Emerson began. He chose Tito because, over the years, they'd worked together to solve problems. Once, Emerson reported thefts occurring while men cleaned up. On another occasion, someone stole the basement portable heater. Each time, Emerson spoke with Tito, and he uncovered and stopped the thieves.

Now, Tito raised both hands palms up, inviting Emerson to continue.

"I think you're being ripped off."

Tito's body shot forward. "Me?"

"No. The Way Station. They're skimming money from Hope House construction funds."

Tito's eyes narrowed. "That's crazy. Who's 'they' and how'd you come by this?"

Emerson tugged on his lower lip. How to get Tito to believe him without revealing the source of his information? "Let's just say I overheard a privileged conversation." Everything said at meetings was confidential, and part of an honor code. "And they've scammed other nonprofits, too."

Tito sat back and eyed Emerson. "If what you're saying is true..." He paused, as if reluctant to finish or to underscore his words. "Sharing this info might be dangerous."

Emerson thought about that. But The Way Station and M.J. were worth the risk. "Look into it. That's all I'm asking. Check your books."

•　　•　　•

Iggy and SoSo ate pizza at their favorite Fieldcrest dive. Bambino's, tucked away in a strip mall, Christmas lights still up even though January arrived days ago, smelled like garlic, roasted tomatoes, and fresh dough. Heat from the ovens kept the establishment toasty. Outside, the temperature dropped, heading to freezing. Mugs of hot chocolate accompanied their meals.

"It's time to do something about Emerson," Iggy said before taking his next bite.

"What's up?"

"Shade has a leak, idiots are managing the current target, and Emerson told Tito." Iggy, always careful about speaking in public places, felt safe in Bambino's. He and SoSo owned a piece, ate in the last booth by the back door for easy escape, and no one sat within earshot.

"Hope House?"

"Yeah." Iggy sipped his drink. They'd gotten greedy. The first three nonprofits they hit proved easy. Investigations yielded nothing. They moved on to the next two. No problems. Then Hope House. That idiot, careless, shitter Wally Wallace. Iggy shook his head. No sense wallowing in the past. Time to wrap things up. Tight. "Take care of it for me."

"Make Shade. It's his mess."

Iggy thought about it for a few seconds. Maybe do it himself.

CHAPTER SIXTY-THREE
M.J. AND ARIA

Wednesday, 6:00 p.m., March 20, 2024

Clouds covered the sky, and a light drizzle fell. M.J. drove his BMW, a gift from Shade, to The Way Station. Iggy Smalls murdered both of M.J.'s fathers. Even though M.J. had no proof, he also had no doubt. Kiki professed shock and ignorance when M.J. questioned her and he believed her. Guilt swept over him. He should have left her clueless. At peace with the past.

He parked in the back lot. When he called to set up the appointment, Ms. Wright's assistant said she'd meet him in the lobby at 6:00. He hurried around the building to the front entrance. A neat redhead waved to him.

After introducing herself as Ginger Ryan, she explained, "The offices are closed for the day, but Ms. Wright is expecting you." Ginger escorted him to Aria Wright's office, knocked, and entered.

"Mr. Alexander, your 6:00," Ginger said to Aria. "I'll wait for you."

M.J. remembered Aria from the funeral but didn't appreciate her beauty.

Aria said, "No. Go home to your family. Officer Applegate has guard duty and Jax is on his way. I'm fine."

"You're sure?" Ginger side-eyed M.J.

"Yes. Thanks. Just inform Applegate." She turned to M.J. "How can I help you?"

"Do you remember me?" M.J. asked. "We met at—"

"Of course, I do. How's your mother?"

"Fine, thanks." Aria was easy to speak with. His confidence lifted.

"I only have a few minutes."

M.J. jumped in. "Have the police solved Emerson's murder?"

Her head jerked back, and she studied him. "Lots of clues." Something painful rippled across her face, taking her gaze from his.

"Are you okay?"

Her lovely smile reappeared. "Yes. It's been a challenging time. For you too, I'm sure." She extended her hand toward a chair facing a sofa off to the side of a large desk. "Please, have a seat."

They both sat.

M.J. said, "I know who killed him."

Aria sat up straighter and leaned in but said nothing.

"His name is Iggy Smalls. He murdered my biological father, and Emerson, too."

She took several beats before responding. "Go to the police." She pulled a card from a stack. "Here's the officer who is investigating."

M.J. read the name Detective Errol Glover. "Has Iggy's name come up?"

• • •

"Yes," I said with confidence. "They're rounding his crew up as well." Wally caved, but Tito proved craftier. "How did you find out about Iggy and why did he kill Emerson?"

"Iggy's been robbing this place and Emerson discovered it. He called to warn me."

"They sent men to kill me."

"What? When? How?"

I brought M.J. up to date. "It's almost over. Detective Glover will be happy to hear from you." I glanced at my watch. Jax would arrive any second. He'd invited me to dinner, our first proper date. I'd dressed for the occasion. After shedding my business suit in my private bathroom, I donned a short leather skirt over black tights, matching belt, and off one shoulder top, but I forgot to put on lipstick and wanted to up sweep my coils into a French twist. School girl behavior, but so what? The police were wrapping up the case as life returned to normal. Darcy, recovering in the hospital, and Zan, ensconced in my home, seemed chastened by the shooting. Even my asthma behaved.

"Give me two minutes," I said to M.J. "I have a dinner... appointment. Will be back in a flash, and I'll tell you what else I learned about the investigation's progress, which isn't much. Detective Glover can fill in the gaps."

"Thanks. I'm glad they're onto Iggy."

With my index finger, I pressed the decorative button. The discrete panel to my ensuite bath slid open. I grabbed my purse, stepped in, and slid the door shut.

Lipstick in hand, squinting into the mirror, I stopped. Voices.

"You're too late," M.J. said.

As silently as possible, I turned the lock. Listened.

Someone with a rough and commanding voice said, "Where is she?

Another man said, "Put the gun down. We won't hurt her. Just talk."

Gun down? M.J. came armed? Where was Officer Applegate?

M.J. said, "You killed them both. Shade, let me take Iggy to the police. They're already on to him."

I dug out my cell phone and dialed the security office. No answer. I tried Jax.

"Hey, babe. Just pulling into the parking lot."

I couldn't answer for fear the intruders might hear.

Crash. Bang. It sounded like a scuffle.

I panted into the phone like some nut case in a scary movie, hoping he'd sense the danger.

"I'm coming. I'll phone Glover. Hang in."

CHAPTER SIXTY-FOUR
JAX, M.J. AND ARIA

Jax slammed the Jeep into park, flung the door open, and hopped out. His feet hit wet asphalt. First problem, how to get inside. He ran to the side entrance, hoping to find a security guard. Banged on the door. No one was on duty. A bad sign. He punched in Aria's number.

"Are you okay? I'm here, trying to get in. Text me."

Within seconds, her message arrived. "I'm locked in my bathroom. Two armed men are in the office with M.J., Emerson's stepson. Iggy Smalls and Shade, I think. Armed. Find Applegate."

Jax texted back. "Stay put and quiet." He dialed Errol Glover's number.

"Detective Glover."

With as few words as possible, Jax explained the situation. "I'm at the side door." He wanted to say, bring my Glock, the one you took for ballistic testing, but recognized a yes was unlikely.

Another text arrived from Aria. "Ginger and Lacy both have keys to the front and side doors." She included their cell numbers and addresses.

Jax called Lacy, who lived the closest. He explained.

Lacy said, "Five to ten minutes out."

Jax hung up and walked the perimeter, looking for any way in.

"Help." A female voice came from the bushes close to the emergency back door. Jax hurried over. Her face, bloodied and bruised, looked painful, and her left arm hung at an unnatural angle.

Jax called Glover back and described the scene. "She's bad and needs immediate help, but I didn't call 9-1-1. Sirens wailing might tip off the killers."

"I got it." Glover ended the call.

"What's your name?"

Through swollen lips she said, "Applegate. Security. Two perps took my Sig and keys." Her body shuddered. "Tito Johnson let them in."

"Help is on the way." Jax pulled off his jacket. The sky drizzled rain, and the temperature continued dropping. He wrapped her up and carried her to his Jeep. Laid her on the backseat. "Hang in."

"Wait."

Jax turned. With her good hand, she slid out an ankle-holstered Walther and handed it to him.

. . .

M.J., legs apart for balance, left hand bracing his right to steady his aim, and his TaurusG2 pointed at Iggy's head, said, "On your knees."

Shade watched.

"This is a big mistake," Iggy said, still standing.

"Down."

"What do you think I've done?" Iggy asked, lowering himself to the floor.

"You murdered my father and killed Emerson."

Shade said, "Don't be stupid. Put the gun down." One hand behind his back, he took a step towards M.J.

M.J. swung the Taurus towards Shade. "This isn't about you." He pivoted to Iggy. "It's him."

Iggy said, "You're wrong. I neither shot nor stabbed the man. Your cheating low life father, yeah, I did that, but not drug-addled Emerson."

"You're just saying that, so I won't kill you."

"It's true. Tell him, Shade. Explain how *you* killed Emerson."

•   •   •

I listened from inside the bathroom. Jax and Errol were on their way. If M.J. killed the two crooks, he'd destroy his life. Plus, another murder at The Way Station. I had to stop him. But someone might shoot me. My hand hovered as my mind spun.

"You're lying," M.J. said. "Protecting yourself."

With caution, I cracked the door open and peeked out.

M.J. looked at Shade. "Right?"

Shade tucked his lips under, one hand still behind his back. "Things happen in the heat of a drug war. You've seen it. A soldier does his duty."

"War? Dealing drugs is not a war. Emerson served in a real one. It messed him up and you promised to look after him." M.J.'s gun-clasped hand shook. "Iggy forced you." M.J. steadied his right hand with his left, narrowed his eyes, and looked ready to shoot.

A new fear whipped through me. If M.J. pulled the trigger, jail would be the least of it. Shade, Iggy, or the police might kill him. I stepped out. "M.J., don't do it."

Startled, M.J. swung his head toward me.

Iggy pulled a gun from the small of his back, aimed, and fired at M.J.

Shade dove sideways, pistol gripped, in front of the speeding bullet. It hit his shoulder; the force spun him around. Blood splattering and still flying sideways, he shot Iggy twice and landed with a thud.

Errol, Yun, and Jax burst into the room, guns drawn. Shade, now on the rug covered floor, looked up at M.J.

"Drop your weapons," Errol ordered. "Drop them now."

Blood spooled out around Iggy's head. Yun eased closer and kicked Iggy's gun away.

M.J. lowered his gun but kept it in his hand. So did Shade.

Shade said to M.J., "I follow orders."

Tears, mingling with mucus from his nose, streamed down M.J.'s cheeks.

Yun covered Shade. Jax stared at me.

"Drop. Your. Weapons," Errol said again, his gun leveled at M.J.'s head.

"Don't shoot him." I dashed in front of M.J.

Jax yelled, "Aria. Stop."

I pleaded with M.J. "Put down your gun. No more killing. No more dying."

M.J. looked at me, then back to Shade, blood pouring from his wound.

"I'm sorry," Shade said, brought the pistol up in a swift motion and shot himself.

M.J. dropped the gun and fell to his knees. He gathered Shade in his arms.

Glover retrieved the weapon.

Jax hustled to my side. "That was crazy. And brave." He pulled me close.

My knees sagged as I sank against his chest.

CHAPTER SIXTY-FIVE
JAX AND ARIA

Tuesday, March 26, 2024, Jax's Tarrytown Condo

Jax strove for perfection. He'd followed his mother's recipes with care, double checking via phone several times during the preparation and cooking. Baked chicken, roasted vegetables, and baby potatoes. "One pan cooking. Easy and special. The secret is in the seasonings," Mom said.

This would be Aria's first visit to his home. Jax looked around with a critical eye. Bathroom scrubbed, fluffed towels, newly purchased decorative pillows on the couch, fresh flowers in the living room and bedroom. Of course, he changed the sheets. Just in case.

The birthday cake he ordered from "Susan Lawrence Catering" in Chappaqua. Baking, beyond his skills, also required equipment he didn't own. The shop provided a fresh baguette. Infused olive oil and butter, not knowing which Aria preferred, purchased to accompany the bread.

Jax, still buzzed from their date the previous Saturday, tried to tamp down his excitement. They saw the latest play by Fieldcrest's own Roxy, a friend of Aria's, as well as her hair stylist. The People's Theater, a nonprofit, staged Roxy's debut murder mystery a few years back. Now, a second project hit the circuit. Despite the snow, freezing rain, and high velocity wind gusts, friends, family, and fans packed the theater. He and Aria went backstage and met the actors and celebrated Roxy's success. But the best part was running into Laura Garrison, the philanthropist on the theater's board. Although Aria and Laura only exchanged a few words, Jax felt confident of Laura's future investment in Hope House now that the murder investigation was behind them, Tito and Wally arrested, Shade and Iggy dead, and SoSo in the wind.

Jax also had a surprise for Aria. The Vault, Jax's brothers, and Jax, planned to invest in the project.

•   •   •

Nerves tried to get the best of me. What a whirlwind seven days. Earlier, Errol called. The courts will fine M.J. for carrying a gun without a license, but nothing more than that. Even though he worked for Shade, they had no proof of M.J.'s illegal actions. Poor M.J. So much loss. I urged him to stay in touch, but I didn't expect him to. Put Fieldcrest and the killings in the rearview mirror, as they say.

Spring arrived with a crazy storm. My best winter coat, boots, gloves, hat, and scarf helped me get from my house to the car, and from the car to Jax's lobby. Zander and Darcy, now out of the hospital, remained at my home since the storm made travelling north dicey. Zan agreed to return to Cornell. For now. While Darcy continued to mend, she agreed to no protests until next semester. Not everything I wanted, but grateful.

I stood in the lobby but didn't ring the bell. Every year, Bella and I celebrated our birthdays together. My parents, Zan, and Bella offered, but a party seemed out of place, considering all the deaths. Jax invited me over. I said yes too quickly. Maybe. Now, I stood in his entranceway, afraid, excited, nervous. My engagement ring and wedding band left behind in a velvet box. I rang the bell.

His enormous feet thundered down the steps of his duplex condo. The door swung open. Jax, grinning, pulled off my hat, grabbed and kissed me. Deeply. For a long time. Oh my. No song played in my head. Instead, a passage from one of my favorite authors reverberated. "Wanna fly, you got to give up the shit that weighs you down." Toni Morrison (Song of Solomon). I was ready to fly.

THE END

"Not everything that is faced can be changed; but nothing can be changed until it is faced." -James Baldwin (As Much Truth As One Can Bear, New York Times)

According to the U.S. Department of Housing and Urban Development (HUD), 653,104 people experienced homelessness in the United States on a single night in January 2023.

Over forty-four million Americans face hunger each day, including 1 in 5 children.

ABOUT THE AUTHOR

Karen E. Osborne is an award-winning and best-selling author of four suspense novels, including historical fiction, murder mysteries, and family sagas.

Karen believes in generosity and giving back. She hosts a weekly video podcast *What Are You Reading? What Are You Writing?* supporting fellow authors. She serves on the board of directors of Easterseals Florida, helping the differently abled, is an Elder in her church, volunteers for several professional organizations supporting nonprofits, and feeds the hungry and unhoused weekly.

Native New Yorkers living in Florida, Karen and her husband, Robert, have two grown children and three grandsons.

OTHER TITLES BY KAREN E. OSBORNE

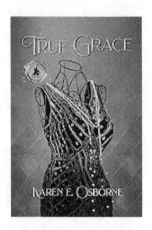

NOTE FROM KAREN E. OSBORNE

Word-of-mouth is crucial for any author to succeed. If you enjoyed *Justice for Emerson*, please leave a review online—anywhere you are able. Even if it's just a sentence or two. It would make all the difference and would be very much appreciated.

Thanks!
Karen E. Osborne

We hope you enjoyed reading this title from:

BLACK ROSE
writing™

www.blackrosewriting.com

Subscribe to our mailing list – *The Rosevine* – and receive **FREE** books, daily deals, and stay current with news about upcoming releases and our hottest authors.
Scan the QR code below to sign up.

Already a subscriber? Please accept a sincere thank you for being a fan of Black Rose Writing authors.

View other Black Rose Writing titles at
www.blackrosewriting.com/books and use promo code
PRINT to receive a **20% discount** when purchasing.

www.ingramcontent.com/pod-product-compliance
Lightning Source LLC
Jackson TN
JSHW020040080125
76750JS00001B/2